tree
house
down

sean
patrick
brennan

tree house down

*

For Andy, who encouraged me to
write something crazy,
for the crazy
world we
live in.

* *

tree house dawn:
plotting and pantsing my way to bloody murder

Conventional wisdom has it there are two ways to write a book: plotting or pantsing. You can either *plot* out a story with copious notes, or you can cozy up tight to your keyboard and just start typing the damn thing out by the seat of your *pants*.

As an active participant in NaNoWriMo (National Novel Writing Month), I've heard plenty of good arguments made for one or the other approach, and the authors I've spoken to directly most often favor pantsing, despite all their very best plotting intentions at the start.

In the summer of 2016, months before I wrote the very first word of *tree house down*, I'd already laid out some rudimentary ideas for what I hoped to accomplish with this book. I sketched out notes for some of my characters, ways in which these complex creatures could move my plot forward as they interacted with one another over the course of a summer, as well as some cool side plots I thought would work well too.

Looking at all those notes now, however, you'd think I was planning an entirely different book. Names changed, personalities evolved, and whole plots transformed completely over the past three years. So much of what I *knew for sure* totally disappeared in every conceivable way.

To put it more succinctly, I plotted this motherfucker out day after day with increasing excitement, then pantsed my way through hundreds of changes over the next 34 months of my life.

The pantsing process is by no means a *bad* thing though, and it actually opens you up to some super cool possibilities all the time, possibilities you'll never discover if you're too reliant on notes. In my case, for instance, my plotting led to my pantsing, which soon led me right back to plotting again in the midst of my pantsing.

By keeping detailed notes on each character's birthday, personality profile, and all their important life dates, I was able to write about them like they were already old friends—which I'm happy to say they now are.

A character map came next, where an Excel file showed me with just a glance who shows up in which chapters, helping me keep my main characters involved in the novel as much as possible. If I hadn't mentioned a character in three chapters, for instance, I made sure to find time and space for them in the ensuing copy.

Calendar pages from the years and months involved in the story (2000 and 2017 respectively) painted a perfect picture of how the timeline moved along, and by filling in notes about which chapters and events occurred on which specific dates, I had a priceless tracking system for the entire book. This kind of behind-the-scenes work is extremely important, because it allows me to do the kind of thinking you the reader should never have to do.

While I take no joy in the death at the heart of this story, it was a fascinating journey to start the book well after the event in question. By jumping into this family's story seventeen years after a murder changed their lives, I was able to focus on the ramifications and reverberations it had for them much more closely, something that's rarely explored in a traditional murder mystery.

A few years ago, I was a guest speaker at a college on Long Island, and I quickly surprised the students and teacher alike when I announced to the room that I never have any idea how a given book will end until I write it. They were shocked that an author wouldn't know this going in, but the truth is, why would I *want* to know how it ends? What's the fun in that?

Not knowing *who* killed Kerry Ann Jefferson seventeen years earlier was an absolute gift to my creative writing process throughout, especially in the first draft. I needed to honor these people and the lives they're living now, so that if one of them turned out to be the poor girl's killer, you'd see how easy it is for a murderer to blend back in with the rest of society.

So without any further delay, I offer you *tree house down,* a murder mystery set in Ludlow, Vermont in the year 2017. Have a great trip! We'll chat some more when you get back.

*

A dysfunctional family is any family
with more than one person in it.

Mary Karr
* *

Chapter 1

June, 2017

Sam Newhaus is no murderer. If you take a moment to ask him, and if he cares to talk to you at all, that's what he'll tell you anyway. The truth about how and why Kerry Ann Jefferson died though, well, that's a bit more complicated. One thing to be absolutely sure of at the start: no matter what Sam ever told his family and friends, he's no innocent.

But that all happened some seventeen years ago now, and while certainly none of it is forgettable, everyone connected to both Kerry Ann and Sam have tried their best to put it behind them.

Kerry Ann's family celebrates her birthday each year with posts on Facebook and Instagram, and though her cause of death is never mentioned anymore, you can easily read between the lines.

"You were ripped away from us far too soon," her sister wrote last year, and the replies to her post ran the gamut between sympathetic wishes and angry-face emojis. None of them ever mention Sam by name, at least publicly, but some of her friends forever refer to him as either 'that sick man' or 'the animal'.

The Jefferson family isn't perfect, but they sure as hell didn't deserve any of the heartache and pain caused by the sudden, horrifying loss of sweet Kerry Ann.

Most of them still live nearby in central Vermont, although Kerry Ann's brother Eddie moved to Denver a few years back, just after a fallout with his parents over some nonsense regarding their will, as the story goes.

Yeah, the Jeffersons have their fair share of issues, as any family does, but no family has nearly as many quirks as the Abrams clan does, which may be at least part of the reason why Sam Newhaus ran away from them when he did.

The Abrams family, past and presently residing in three homes in Ludlow, Vermont, is comprised of only eight people—well, nine if you include accused murderer Sam Newhaus, but they'd prefer you not.

Alan Abrams, grandfather extraordinaire—*his words*—is now 75 years old, and comfortably if not always happily married to his wife Phyllis, three years his junior. Originally from Brooklyn and briefly Port Jefferson, New York, Alan and Phyllis long dreamed of a life in Vermont when they were younger, but they didn't end up moving to Ludlow with their two kids, Olivia and Lenny, until they were both finished with grade school.

This proved itself a particularly sore spot for Olivia, as she had to transfer to Black River High School in Ludlow the summer before her junior year, only after Lenny finished the eighth grade back on Long Island.

Alan Abrams is rugged and handsome for his age, but he doesn't move around as well as he used to, and spends most of his time complaining about a great many things. Doctors just out to make money, cashiers who spend too much time chatting with one another, not *nearly* enough time tending to his groceries, and music—*if you can even call it that*—a far cry from the classics he grew up with in Brooklyn.

Phyllis just smiles at Alan's complaining, and laughs him off when he dares air his grievances out loud. 'Don't mind him', she jokes with the clerks at the pharmacy. 'He hasn't been happy since I married him.'

Her hair is always well coifed, clipped back tightly on both sides like she hopes to never introduce it to her face, and she likes keeping her nails painted silver to match her jewelry.

Alan and Phyllis live on the southeast side of Ludlow, not far from the entrance to town off Route 103, and their now adult children, Olivia and Lenny, each live within the village proper.

Lenny, now 43 years old, is very happily married to Caroline, 42, while his big sister Olivia, now 45, is very happily *divorced* from one Sam Newhaus, 43, suspected murderer, residing somewhere in Las Vegas, Nevada.

Lenny and Caroline are themselves parents to two girls—Erika, 17 years old, and Peaches, 16 years old—while Olivia lives alone with her only daughter Haley, now 22, who against all her mother's pleading over the years to change it, has still held on tightly to the Newhaus name regardless of what anyone says about her father.

Unlike the Jeffersons, you'll never catch anyone in the Abrams family even mentioning either Kerry Ann *or* Sam on their social media feeds. Instead, most choose not to discuss her at all anymore, lest the past haunt them even further than it already does.

Sam did try friend-requesting Haley on Facebook two years ago, but she denied it right away, and sent him a short, private message back.

"Maybe we can follow each other instead, Dad," she suggested. "But," she quickly added, "please don't comment on any of my posts, or, you know, *like* any of them."

Haley decided this was for the best, but neither did she mention any of it to her mother, Olivia. She felt sure no one would fault her for simply allowing her dad to follow her posts online, and as long as Sam didn't like or comment on any of them, no one would even notice they were connected anyway.

Sam rarely posted anything on his own wall, and Haley ended up unfollowing him less than a year later, opting to only rarely check his page for updates instead, so when he recently posted about selling his place in Vegas, and his plans after sixteen long years to 'finally move back east', Haley had no idea.

Chapter 2

Alan Abrams, *grandfather extraordinaire,* couldn't care less about woodwork, or learning to build anything with his own two hands. He'd forfeited enough blood, sweat, and tears pursuing his own dreams over the decades to waste any time learning a skill he knew he'd never have.

His father though, a strong man and proudly observant Jew, was obsessed with wood. *Crazy* obsessed, Alan thought. Wood and nails, he taught Alan, could be thrown together to create all sorts of things: barns, benches, bridges—even crosses.

"It doesn't take more than two hands to slap something together, Allie," his dad always said, "but any true artisan worth his salt will tell you the more time you spend getting it right the first time, the less likely you'll have to go through the whole process all over again."

It was a phrase Alan thought about often after watching his father divorce his mother, and then divorce his second wife only two years later.

Still, Alan knew a good build when he saw one. As a little boy, his father once brought him out to Amish Country, Pennsylvania— that was what he called it anyway, as if there were no towns or roads, just Amish countryside as far as the eye could see. He'd stopped the car suddenly one crisp October morning, and ordered Alan to get out and look around.

"Look over there, Allie. You see that? That's gonna stand taller and longer than half the shit those guidos put up back in Brooklyn. You see, these people out here do it all themselves, and they get much better results because of it."

Alan stared out across the field, watching as a team of men pushed a wall of wood up from the ground. It looked like they might be building a huge barn for the house, but he was afraid to ask. Instead, he just nodded obediently until his dad ordered him back in the car.

Driving through Ludlow, Vermont that morning some 64 years later, Alan couldn't help but notice the paint chipping off front porches, their posts bent slightly with age. *Nothing is built like it used to be,* he thought, *not even these old homes, and no one cares about wear and tear anyway, as long as things hold up enough to not fall down.*

Through his windshield, he spotted Haley up ahead, one hand typing away on her phone, the other tipping back a large cup of coffee. He beeped his horn far too loudly with a wave as he passed.

"Hi, Grandpa!" Haley waved back with a happy smile that faded right away.

She pushed open the door and walked in, making eye contact briefly with Doctor Finny to let him know she was back. He was still inside with a patient, the same older man Haley brought in earlier after he'd filled out all his paperwork.

No missed calls. Good.

A missed call meant she had to dial the number back and apologize for missing the call in the first place. It also meant Doctor Finny had *heard* the phone ring while she was out, and probably cleared his throat in that angry way of his. She'd only been gone seven minutes this time, but Haley knew how much he hated it whenever she left the front desk unoccupied.

The doctor was a friendly man for the most part, dotty and a little weird, but self-aware enough to smile through his eccentricity. He was easily in his 60s, but still quite healthy and sharp.

Putting her phone away and lifting her coffee for another sip, Haley glanced down at her magazine again, trying to find the place where she'd left off before she'd run out.

"Your blood pressure's a bit high, John, but if you're on that medicine, you should be fine. Do you want a full physical too, or should I just top off the fluids and change your oil?"

"What? What does that mean?"

"Sorry. Just a little joke. How 'bout I check your eyes and ears quick. Hang on."

Doctor Finny walked out into the hallway and opened a drawer to grab something. He made eye contact briefly with Haley, who smiled. She'd heard his 'top off the fluids' line enough times now already, so it'd become an inside joke between them to see how new patients would react. Some laughed or grinned right away, but others were too confused to understand.

She leaned back in her chair and took another sip of coffee, looking out at Main Street and life outside.

Haley never wanted this job, but knew she had to earn money doing something until she figured things out. With very few positions available for journalists in her part of central Vermont, let alone photojournalists, her degree seemed destined to collect dust for a while.

Glancing back toward the examination rooms to make sure Doctor Finny was still occupied, she stood up and walked over to the window.

Ludlow was quiet this time of year—*too quiet*—but the summer crowds would be in soon. The number of cars in their one-traffic-light town would more than quadruple most days come late spring, especially weekends, and everyone and their mother would hijack all the best parking spaces in town.

Across the street, she spotted a couple in their thirties walking past DJ's restaurant holding a tourist map of the area, and it made her sigh. The flatlanders were already beginning their invasion.

The phone rang from behind her, and she darted back to her desk to pick it up. One ring only, Doctor Finny told her. One ring only, or they'll hang up and try a different doctor's office instead. Haley knew this was ridiculous, of course, as no one was *that* impatient, not even the loud tourists from New York, but she kept to his rule nonetheless.

"Hello, Doctor Finny's office," she said.

She turned and looked back toward the examination rooms again, where she wasn't surprised to see Doctor Finny staring back at her over the patient's left ear.

"Yes, Mrs. Dougan. Next Tuesday should be fine. Do you want— Okay. Yeah, ten o'clock should be perfect, actually. Let me just check to make sure. Annnd, yep. That works for us too. Ten is open. Okay, great. We'll see you then. Thank you. You too."

Haley tossed the pen and pad aside, then pulled her chair in tightly to the desk to type the information into Excel. She could sense the doctor's eyes were on her still, so she moved quickly. When she finished logging the info, she crosschecked the notepad with the screen, and then threw the small piece of paper away.

Doctor Finny had scolded her on her very first day of work for not checking the note one last time before throwing it away, so now she always did. Even though she'd been working there for over a month already, he still watched her every single time, just to make sure she didn't forget.

A few minutes went by, and as she slowly turned the pages of her magazine, she could tell Doctor Finny was beginning to finish up with his patient.

"Just get plenty of rest, and drink lots of water. You won't do yourself any favors getting too upset over this. I'm sure things will work themselves out. Haley will get you squared away, and if there's anything else you need, call me anytime."

Haley went into autopilot mode, triple-checking Mr. Caraway's paperwork in case Dr. Finny glanced back one more time on the way to his office, which she was pretty sure he always did. She stapled the man's paperwork together—another of Dr. Finny's instructions for this period of time when a patient left the office, so as to come across as extra efficient—and then smiled and asked him for his $30 copay.

"Gosh, is it really that much now?"

"Yeah, it actually just went up," Haley said, offering him her most sympathetic smile.

He took out his wallet, and handed her a twenty and a ten. Haley thanked him, opened her lock box to deposit the money, then updated his part of the Excel file as paid.

"Okay, looks like you're all set, Mr. Caraway. Is there anything else you need?"

"No, I don't think so, unless you know of any wedding photographers?"

He smiled at her kindly, as Haley's own smile wilted.

"My daughter's getting married next Saturday, and the man we hired is—well, he's suddenly unavailable."

Haley just kept staring at him without saying anything, so he smiled politely one more time, then turned to leave. She watched him leaving as if in slow motion, unsure if she should say something, then turned and looked toward the back, to see if Doctor Finny's office door was shut. It was.

"Sir, wait," she called out.

Haley didn't know what to say, or how to even do this. She knew she'd stumble over her words too, but needed to make the pitch anyway. Mr. Caraway paused at the door, his eyebrows furrowed with concern.

"It's just that, well, I have my degree in photojournalism? Well, it's in journalism. But my specialty is photojournalism? From Middlebury? And, anyway, well, I think that maybe, if you'd like, I could probably do it? I mean, if you don't want to trust me, I understand, but maybe? I don't know. I'm sorry. I just thought that maybe I should ask in case you wanted to hire me?"

John Caraway stared at her sympathetically, and she could tell he was about to decline her offer as sweetly as he could muster. He was already thinking he could do it better than she could, and save some money at the same time.

"I think I may just do it all myself," he said, and Haley wasn't surprised at all to hear it.

"I've been known to capture the occasional great shot on my wife's iPhone. Thank you, though."

He opened the door to leave again, and Haley just nodded with disappointment, looking down at her feet.

Her whole life had been this way. She'd tried too hard, come on too strong, and just learned that no matter how pushy she was, nothing and no one ever came her way. But as the door closed slowly behind him, something deep and loud bellowed out from the very depths of her soul.

"Wait!" she screamed out, jumping up from her chair.

Doctor Finny ran out into the hallway right away.

"Haley, what's wrong?" he asked.

She looked back at him briefly, but then at the door again, where Mr. Caraway was standing in the entrance looking surprised.

"Sir, I'm sorry, but can I just show you something quickly on the computer here?"

As she sat down again and started typing, the two men glanced at each other with confused shrugs and approached her desk. In a few seconds, Haley had called up her website, which she'd pieced together on her own throughout her final semester at Middlebury.

Clicking the "Portfolio" link as they watched, the screen soon filled with all the beautiful photos she'd taken. She scrolled through them slowly as they both watched.

Finally, as she reached the bottom of the screen, she pushed back from her desk and looked up at Mr. Caraway, who seemed to be thinking.

"I'm sorry, sir. I know I don't have any real experience, but—"

"Is next Saturday morning at 10 good for you?"

Her eyebrows went up as she smiled.

"Yes! Absolutely!"

Mr. Caraway smiled and pointed to the paperwork waiting on her desk.

"My phone number's in there somewhere. Call me tomorrow, and I'll give you all the details."

He turned and walked out, and as Haley beamed up at the doctor, she soon noticed the ashen look on his face.

Doctor Finny walked around her desk and sat down in one of the waiting room chairs, taking a moment to scratch the back of his head with his pen.

Haley was supposed to be there at the office next Saturday until two in the afternoon, and he was about to remind her of this. He was about to scold her, in fact. He was about to grow very upset, very quickly, because Doctor Finny did *not* handle stressful situations well at all, despite all his good advice to patients.

"Sir, I promise you I'll get a replacement for that morning," Haley said before he could start in on her. "My cousin Peaches will be here at 8 AM next Saturday, and she'll be great, I promise."

Doctor Finny leaned back in the chair, doubtful of her plan. Without a second's hesitation, Haley grabbed her cell phone and dialed Peaches, who picked up right away.

"Peaches, it's Haley. Hi. Listen, I need a fav—yes, yeah, right, I know. Peaches, listen. I need you to do something for me. Could you— Peaches, listen to me! I need a favor. Can you work my shift at Doctor Finny's office next Saturday from eight to two? What? No, 8 AM to 2 PM. Why would it be at night? Yeah. It'll be easy, I promise. Okay, great. Yeah, we'll talk tonight. Thank you so much. Gotta run. Bye."

Doctor Finny had made all sorts of faces as she spoke into her phone, but he could tell it was all a done deal now, so he didn't even try. He just shook his head and went back to his office.

"Just make sure she knows what to do," he called back to her. "Give her the binder. And tell her to pack her food. I don't want her disappearing on me for lunch."

Haley smiled back at him and nodded. She was so excited to have finally landed her first real job as a photographer. As she closed her website and tucked herself in at the desk, she watched as Doctor Finny flashed her a sweet smile as he walked back into his office and closed the door.

Too many disappointments had crowded her life. Too many boys who said no, or who had ignored her from the start. Too many friends who moved away. One too many *fathers* who'd moved away. Too many wrong turns, U-turns, and one-way streets of frustration. But this new adventure felt different. She'd finally prove herself in life, and everyone would see it. Everyone would see that Haley Newhaus was a changed woman.

Twenty-two years old and inspired by just the idea of a new career, she felt completely recharged to take on the world. Nothing would stop her now, and she was confident the wedding job would lead to many more after that. Everyone would see her photos, and hire her for their own weddings, graduations, and grand openings. She'd be the talk of the town, and maybe even the county.

As she walked in the door that evening at a quarter past five, Haley was still on a high from the good news of the day.

"Mom, I'm home!" she called up the stairs.

She began looking through the stack of mail on the table by the door, not surprised to see only advertisements and bills. A moment later, Olivia blew the smoke from her cigarette across the coffee table, and Haley jumped back in surprise.

"Jesus, Mom. You scared the shit out of me. Why didn't you say hello when I walked in the door?"

Olivia made a face and then shrugged, like she didn't know why she hadn't.

Haley noticed the empty glass of melting ice cubes next to her on the end table. She'd forgotten to use a coaster again. Haley marched over and added one for her, quickly wiping up the condensation with a tissue.

They stared at each other with equal measures bittersweet disgust and disappointed love, until Haley returned to the other side of the couch to grab her mail and head up to her bedroom.

Olivia watched her daughter carefully, and noticed something different about her. Something was off, she was sure, odd even. Unless she was just imagining it, Haley seemed strangely *happy?*

"What's up with *you?*" Olivia asked.

Haley couldn't help but smile, still giddy with the exciting job offer ahead of her. Though she hadn't called Mr. Caraway yet for the exact details, any wedding shoot meant good money, she was sure of that.

"Well, I got offered a photography job today. One of the patients at Dr. Finny's office said he needed a photographer for next weekend, and when I told him I could do it, and showed him my portfolio, he hired me right away. I'll be shooting his daughter's wedding next Saturday."

She watched her mother's face change as a sly smile appeared. Haley thought she was about to congratulate her, but then—

"And does this idiot know you have absolutely *no* experience doing that kind of thing? That you've *never* photographed a wedding in your entire life? That you've barely accumulated enough experience for assignments at school? Did you tell him any of that? Did you even *bother* to tell him who he was dealing with?"

Haley quickly turned her back on her, and punished the stairs with a furious glare. She debated whether or not to even try to argue with her mother, but decided not to.

"I'll be in my room," she announced to the wall, retreating up the stairs with only half the energy she had when she came in.

Olivia shook her head at her, then took another long puff of her cigarette. *Haley should know better than to lie to some stranger about that kind of thing,* she thought. She had half a mind to warn the man too, if she ever found out who he was.

"Don't forget we have cake for Erika's birthday tonight at seven!" Olivia screamed up the stairs. "And there's some leftover pasta salad in the fridge, by the way!"

Haley didn't respond, and Olivia heard her door slam shut a second later. Relaxing deeper into the couch, Olivia stared at her cigarette for a while. The ash was long now, about to fall off.

She wiggled it in her hand a bit to see if she could get it to fall, but it didn't. As she took another puff a moment later, the ash dropped onto her blouse, and Olivia once again stared at it like it was a beautiful treasure worthy of adoration and respect. She watched it as if it would move on by itself, then flicked it off onto the couch with a grunt.

Chapter 3

Lenny strode down the hallway toward his front door with relief. His one saving grace had arrived at last. As he opened the door, Olivia and Haley smiled in at him from the stoop.

"Hi Uncle Lenny," Haley said, leaning in quickly to kiss him on the cheek.

She moved past him on her way to the kitchen in the back of the house, happy to get away from her mother.

"Your cousins are in the backyard hanging out with their friends," Lenny called after her, then turned back to his sister Olivia, who seemed firmly against entering the house at all.

"Mom and Dad are inside," he said, then laughed as she turned around and pretended to leave.

"But there's a bottle of wine open in the kitchen," he added.

Olivia turned back around and leaned forward, offering Lenny her cheek for a kiss. Then they exchanged a glance that said, '*here we go again*'.

Lenny was two years younger than Olivia, who he knew had a rough life in many ways, so perhaps because of that, and due to her overall sullen personality, he never tormented her the way many other younger brothers would have. He was instead her very best friend, and always would be.

They seemed to have made an unspoken pact as children not to criticize the other too much, mostly because they each knew their parents offered them quite enough of that already.

As Olivia made her way into the kitchen, she spotted the wine before she saw her parents' faces, and was grateful for that, certain the merlot would provide a much friendlier welcome than her mother would.

She poured herself a full glass, then started gulping right away, finally making eye contact with Caroline as she did.

Caroline, Lenny's wife, was drinking already too, but she always seemed to tolerate her in-laws just fine.

"Hey, Car?" Lenny called over to her. "Can you help me with the garbage? Mom? Dad? Livi's here."

As her parents turned around, Olivia shot Lenny a glare, mouthing a sarcastic 'thank you' his way.

Olivia walked over and kissed her parents hello, watching as Phyllis sized her up like she was dressed in garbage bags. None of it surprised Olivia anymore, but neither did she find it amusing.

'That's just her way,' Caroline once told her. *'Playing the judge and expecting perfection from everyone is just who she's always been, and who she'll always be, so there's no point trying to change her at this point.'*

"Olivia, darling. I was wondering if you'd be coming too," Phyllis said. "You know the party started over twenty minutes ago. Haley came through here earlier."

"Yeah, we came together. I'm sorry Haley reached you a full thirty seconds before I did, but she's 22, and moves faster than 45-year-olds do."

"Your father and I are both in our 70s," Phyllis said. "By your logic, we should still be struggling to put our seat belts on."

Olivia shook her head and walked away from them again, back to the kitchen island and the wine.

"I can help you with that seat belt any day, Ma," she muttered under her breath, so only Caroline could hear.

"Hey, Phyllis? Alan?" Caroline said. "You guys want some wine? We have red and white."

Caroline looked across at their faces after she said this, and she already knew how they'd both react. It was all practically a script at this point.

"You got any Jack?" Alan asked.

Phyllis walked into the kitchen then, grabbing the wine bottle out of Olivia's hand just as she was pouring herself a second glass.

"Oh," she said with a frown. "The red's not refrigerated? I like it refrigerated. It's much better that way."

Olivia pretended to vomit, and flashed Caroline a look of dark judgment from behind her mother as Caroline stifled a smile.

"No, we keep the red at room temperature, but I'll get you some ice."

"Oh, okay. I guess that will be fine, dear, as long as the ice doesn't melt too quickly. Oh Olivia, darling, did you hear? I saw *Sam* in town this morning. He was coming out of the hardware store while I was on my walk with Nancy Hensley. He came over and gave us both big hugs and kisses, of course. I hadn't seen him in so long, you know."

Olivia just stared at her mother for a moment in shock, half at her mother's ignorance, and half at the fact of the matter. No one had heard from Sam in years, as far as she knew. Then she turned back to Caroline.

'Does she know she's being such a bitch?' her face said. *'Or is she really just this fucking obtuse?'*

It was a question she could never figure out, and as much as Caroline and Lenny both swore to her that Phyllis really didn't know any better most of the time, Olivia wasn't so sure.

She hadn't spoken to her mother at all that day, so how could she have known she saw Sam? And why would she care how sweet her ex-husband was to her mother?

"Yeah, well, I haven't seen him in quite a while either, Mom."

"Well, he looked fantastic."

Phyllis moved past her with her wine glass, and sat down on the couch, soon poking her ice cubes with her nails to make sure they were solid.

Alan stared up at Olivia with his brow furrowed in thought for a while, then raised a finger as he remembered something he wanted to tell her.

"Oh! And I saw Haley in town today. She was walking with a cup of coffee toward that doctor's office. That *what's-his-name* guy she works for."

"Doctor Finny?"

"Yeah, that's the one. Funny Finny. I don't go to him, you know. I go to my doctor in Rutland. He's much better. Best ratings on Zillow too."

"No, Dad. Zillow is—"

"Prices are ridiculous either way, of course. Goddamn copays are astronomical too. Although it would've been much worse if Crooked Hillary had won."

"Dad, stop."

"I mean it. She would have tripled all our bills. But of course the goddamn liberals wanted her anyway. They had no idea. Totally clueless, as always. Thank God for President Trump, that's all I've got to say."

Alan couldn't help himself around Olivia sometimes. He knew she'd let him say whatever he thought about anything, and he liked that. He liked having kids who tolerated their parents, even when they disagreed with him.

"You know, Dad, I'm a goddamn liberal who voted for Hillary."

"Yeah, I know," he said with a nod, then flashed a grin her way a few seconds later.

In the backyard, Haley found Erika with two of her friends, and had just finished telling them about her photography job. All three of them said it sounded 'super cool', but Haley was pretty sure they didn't really care.

Erika and her friends were seniors in high school, and for the first time in her life, Haley noticed how much younger they all seemed. They were each drinking bottles of beer Erika had snatched from the fridge inside, and though Haley was pretty sure they'd had less than one beer each, they were acting much more drunk than they could have possibly been.

"Wait. You're 22, right?" Erika asked.

"Yeah," Haley said with a sigh. "The big 2-2."

Jenn and Isobel both laughed really hard at this, and Erika nearly spit out her beer as she was guzzling it. Haley sighed. Part of her wanted to mock them for being so dumb, but she knew she wouldn't have enjoyed a buzz kill if she was in their shoes.

"So listen," Erika went on, "you should totally hang with us tonight. We're going up to the woods on Okemo to get wasted.

Jenn's brother's driving. And if you want, maybe you could bring some beer too?"

She'd made it sound like an afterthought, but Haley quickly realized they wouldn't be able to get more beer on their own. She was only asking her to come so she could buy some for them.

"No, I don't think so, sorry. I have too much to do tonight," she lied.

"Eh, it's alright," Erika said. "I can probably just steal some more beer from my dad. He'd probably offer to come drink with us if he knew."

"Oh, that's cool," Haley said, thinking how much cooler her Uncle Lenny was than her mom.

"No way, Haley. Don't get me wrong. I mean, I love my dad? But he's always freakin' staring at Jenn's tits. He can be a real perv. *Not* a party we're inviting him to."

The three girls all laughed at this, and Haley did a little too, but only nervously.

In the silence that followed, Haley looked at Jenn, and thought about how to ask the question now on her mind.

"Hey," she finally said, "so you're Jonathan's little sister, right?"

"Mm-hm, he's driving us tonight, but his license is suspended, so he can't get us beer. Wait, so do you know him?"

"Yeah, he was in my class at school. Just tell him I said hi."

Haley immediately felt foolish. Jonathan was the source of one of her biggest embarrassments senior year of high school. She'd been watching him walk one day, because she liked his ass, and suddenly he was staring her down with his hand out to stop her. Before she realized what she'd done, she had apparently followed him right into the boys' bathroom.

Deciding she'd had enough of their company, Haley looked around for her other cousin.

"Hey Erika, where's Peaches? Is she here tonight?"

Erika was gulping down the last of her beer, making sure to get every last drop from the bottle before she responded.

"Yeah. I think she's on the hammock back past the tree."

"Okay, thanks," Haley said, squinting toward the hammock as she stood up. "Oh, yeah. I see her."

As she walked toward the back of the property, Haley relived the moment in her head: the bathroom incident with Jonathan Fisher. The joke was mercifully over three days later when Bobby Tinson flipped off the principal, but for three weekdays straight, the whole school teased her about it. All she could do was laugh with embarrassment, as her face found new and brighter ways to shine red. But if Bobby Tinson hadn't given Principal Montgomery the finger that Friday afternoon, the whole school would've been talking about her for weeks more instead.

"Hey, Peaches," she said, sitting down on the woodpile nearby. "Thanks for subbing for me at work next week. It'll be really easy, I promise. I can walk you through everything."

Haley examined her shoelaces, wondering if she had enough money for a new pair of shoes. The wedding money would come in handy, at least. Even if it wasn't too much, it had to be enough for a nice new pair.

Looking back up at Peaches, she wondered why she hadn't answered her. She leaned forward and waved her hand, and Peaches turned over on the hammock and took her ear buds out.

"Oh hey, how are you?" Peaches asked.

"I'm good, thanks. I didn't realize you had ear buds in, sorry. I was just saying I appreciate you helping me out by subbing for me next weekend."

"Sure, no problem. I'm looking forward to it."

"Well, it's honestly pretty boring, but it's really easy. I'll walk you through the binder and show you what to do and stuff. I'll bring it over one day next week."

"Yeah, it should be fun."

Peaches was a year and a half younger than Erika, and by all accounts, she was the strangest 16-year-old anyone knew. Before that, she had held the title of strangest 15-year-old anyone knew, the strangest 14-year-old anyone knew, and so on. Ever since she was a toddler, Peaches was *different*. Her personality was charming to some, strange but acceptable to others, and just plain weird to everyone else.

Behind her back, even their grandfather called her a weirdo, though Peaches would have never known.

"Trust me, Peaches, the job's not fun."

"Well then I'll make it fun. It must be cool to meet the patients and see what's wrong with them, at least."

Haley shrugged and nodded.

"Yeah, I guess."

The door to the back deck slid open, and Caroline's face poked out into the cool night air. She tried to see what Erika and her friends were up to, but part of her really didn't want to know anyway. Caroline believed that ignorance may not always be bliss, but it's still most often the best path to family harmony.

"Alright guys, it's time for cake!" she yelled out to anyone who would listen.

She watched and waited until faces started appearing from the dark, walking toward her. First Haley and Peaches, and then a moment later Erika and her friends. Caroline tried to ignore the familiar clink of beer bottles in the distance.

Once inside, a new dance began.

Haley loved her family, but she wondered how much they were all just going through the motions sometimes, pretending to like each other out of some sort of centuries-old tradition. She knew they loved her, and she knew her Uncle Lenny and Aunt Caroline were happy together, but there was so much unspoken animosity between certain people too, especially between her mother and grandmother.

Worst of all, Haley worried that she and her mom were already repeating all the same patterns in reverse, that the two of them would always be at each other's throats for the rest of their lives, just like Olivia and Phyllis were.

"So Haley," Lenny said. "A little birdie told me you were hired to photograph a wedding next Saturday?"

"Hey, Uncle Lenny. Yeah. I just got the job today. I'm really excited. I don't know all the details yet, but I think I'm gonna do well with it."

"That's great, kid. Good for you. My boss's nephew is getting married next Saturday too though, so if you see a tall bald guy with a bright white beard, that's probably him. His name is RJ Tarisi, and he can be a real dick, so best steer clear of him."

Haley laughed.

"Okay, will do. The man who hired me is the father of the bride. Mr. Caraway. Does that name sound familiar?"

"No, I don't think so."

Olivia approached the two of them from behind, already more than halfway through a piece of birthday cake. She licked the fork, then poked Haley in the back to make her presence known.

"Ow."

"Did you tell your Uncle Lenny that you have *zero* experience photographing weddings, and that you might just fuck the whole thing up? I doubt you'll ever have more work in the field if all your pictures come out blurry. You can't be right up in their faces, either. Does your lens even reach that far if you're taking pictures from a distance?"

"Mom, please. Of course it will. Everything will be fine."

"Now, now, Livi. Leave her alone. I'm sure she'll do great."

"Thank you, Uncle Lenny."

"Whatever. Your funeral," Olivia said, then dropped her plate and fork a little too loudly on the countertop as she went back for more wine.

"Don't listen to her," Lenny said. "She's probably just jealous. I bet shooting a wedding is a lot more fun than whatever she does at the bank. And it sure as hell beats my job in accounts payable."

He smiled at her again, but quickly excused himself when he spotted Caroline looking annoyed over by the kitchen sink.

"What's wrong? Erika drinking again?"

Caroline smiled fakely.

"Probably, but no, that's not it. Did you see her birthday cake?"

"Yeah, it looks beautiful. Why, what's wrong? Do we not have enough candles to stick in?"

"Your sister already helped herself to a slice."

"Are you fucking kidding me?"

"Don't. It's not even worth it when she gets like this. We'll only make it worse if we raise a stink. I'll spread in some whipped cream, and it'll be fine. Don't say anything to her."

"Fine," Lenny said, "but you know I'd be happy to give her hell if she deserves it. I don't care how fucked up she is. She shouldn't have helped herself to cake until we were ready."

"It's fine. Never mind. I'll fix it. I just want the rest of the night to go as calmly and peacefully as possible."

A huge crash came echoing in from the dining room just then, and as everyone ran over to see what it was, they found Olivia staring down at a rack of DVDs she'd accidentally pulled away from the wall, now barely leaning on one of the dining room chairs. DVDs were strewn everywhere below the table and across the shiny wood floor.

They all stared at Olivia then for an explanation, but she just stared back at them blankly, as if she had walked in on the mess herself only a moment before they had.

She took a long sip of wine as she took note of each of them, pausing to nod toward Erika's friends in the back. Then she looked back down at the floor, and finally leaned down to pick a DVD up, scanning the front and back of it with a smile.

"Oh. Here it is."

Chapter 4

"Another super fun night with your family," Caroline said, her back up against the closed front door and a twisted smile on her face.

The last of the guests had finally left, and Lenny looked at her like a sad puppy who knew he was guilty—of being related to his own family.

"Sorry."

"No you're not."

He walked over and kissed her on the lips, then wrapped his arms around her back and squeezed her warmly.

"But it's okay," she said. "I knew what I was getting myself into when I married you. I'd be nuts if I expected anything different."

She moved past him, letting her hand slide across his belly as she did, and walked back toward the kitchen to give the counters and tables a final wipe down.

Lenny turned around in place and watched her with a silly grin. She was a saint, he decided, if he wasn't sure of it already, and she should honestly be declared one for real if there was any justice left in the universe.

Caroline was an only child, and her parents had long since gone on to their eternal reward: a large, lakeside assisted living condo in Boca Raton.

Her penance, for whatever sins she *did* have, was to put up with Lenny's family alongside him for the remainder of her days.

"At least the girls turned out alright," she said, reading his mind as he walked back into the kitchen a moment later.

"My mom might agree with you," he said, "but I'm not so sure about Livi or my dad. They nitpick all three of them mercilessly."

Caroline and Lenny moved around the house in silence for the next few minutes, each throwing out garbage and pushing in chairs. Though there wasn't too much mess to clean up, it was more than they wanted to deal with the following day.

At one point, Caroline smiled at something, and once Lenny noticed, he had to know what she was thinking.

"What?" he asked with a smile.

Caroline shrugged.

"Oh, nothing. It's just I have a theory about your mom."

Lenny stopped what he was doing and raised his eyebrows.

"Oh? Do tell."

"Well, I think she goes extra easy on Haley because it pisses off your sister. The old doting grandmother routine. She probably agrees with Livi about the whole photography business, but supports Haley and disagrees with Livi for fun. It's like a game for her, a sport. She's like some crazy old lady at the racetrack, setting firecrackers off by the horses to see which ones startle the most."

Lenny laughed and nodded his head.

"Wow. Yeah. That sounds frighteningly accurate, actually. You are wise beyond your years, my dear."

"Oh? All 21 of them?"

"Yes. All 21 of them."

They kissed each other again briefly in passing, then Caroline announced she was done for the night, and ready for bed. She walked away from him toward the stairs with a yawn.

"Okay, I'll be up in a few minutes," he called after her. "I just gotta call Sam back first."

Caroline stopped near the top of the stairs when she heard Sam's name. She turned her head back in surprise, but continued on without asking.

Lenny wandered out onto the backyard deck, closing the sliding door softly behind him. Half collapsing into a lounge chair, he opened a can of beer and took a few long gulps, then set it down beside him.

He found Sam's number in his cell, but before he called, he took a moment to look up at the stars. There were hundreds of them out, all of them shining brightly in the crystal-clear moonless night sky.

As his eyes followed a satellite passing overhead, his gaze soon landed on the silhouette of the tree house in the distance. He allowed himself to look at it just a few seconds longer, then shook his head and returned to his phone as he pushed the button.

"Hey, what's up? I'm sorry I couldn't talk before, but everyone was over when you called. I didn't want to— No, nothing bad. It's Erika's birthday today, so we just had people over for coffee and cake. Yeah. No, totally not a problem. I just figured you didn't want Livi or my mom—yes! Yeah, I know, I know. You're right. It was more like wine and cake anyway. It was a mess, actually, but I'll spare you the details. So what's up with you, man?"

The crickets sang, the breeze blew, and the lounge chair squeaked softly below him as Lenny listened to Sam speak on the other end. He gave him a few uh-huhs and okays at first, but soon he was completely silent as he listened. His eyes rolled back up to the stars for a while, back and forth as a cloud passed between him and the rest of the universe, and then before he knew it, he was looking out at the tree house again.

Dark. Empty. Looming.

"Yeah, I'm still here. I'm just uh, well you know, I thought everything was working out with what's her name. Right. Okay, no, that's cool man, you should, you totally should. Yes, I did hear that piece of news already. You don't think my mother would see you and not be sure to tell *everyone* you were in town, did you?"

Lenny laughed and sat up, reaching down for his beer. He took a sip and walked out into the yard a bit.

His head drooped down toward the grass, making sure he wasn't stepping on any piles of shit out in the yard. They didn't have a dog the past two years since Rusty died, but wild animals nearby occasionally roamed through. That was one of the downsides of living on such a large property, he realized soon after he bought it. Their yard overlooked a beautiful hill in the distance, but the lot across the street was completely empty, so deer, moose, and porcupines had their run of the area.

As he paused again and looked up, Lenny could just make out the inside shell of the tree house. He thought he saw the outline of the old pillows still inside, but it could've also been other garbage they'd thrown in at some point later. He saw the outline of where the ladder had been before they took it off, but only barely.

Then, for a brief second as he began to turn away, he thought he saw someone moving inside, and it scared him enough that he backed away toward the house again, reminding himself as he did that it was probably just his imagination.

"That's great, man, totally," he said to Sam. "I'd love to see you. I'm sure everyone would. Or, you know, almost everyone. And you should totally check out the new condos they just built over there near the mall. Nice places, supposedly. Two of my coworkers live over there. Yeah. Yeah, totally. It'd be sweet."

Lenny glanced back anxiously one more time toward the tree house, then stepped through the open sliding door, put his beer can down, and locked the door behind him. He closed the curtain then too, giving one last glance into the yard, and flicked off the switch for the patio light.

"Yeah, Monday at 6 should be perfect. Uh-huh. Yeah, of course I know where that is. Sure. You want me to call Haley for you too, or? Oh, right, cool. Yeah, just text her then. That'd work. She might be at work that day, but— Yeah, she started working at a doctor's office in town. Place across the street from DJs? Yeah."

He listened for a second, then interrupted.

"No, not AJs. DJs. The big restaurant in town. You know it. Yeah, yeah the one with the nice salad bar. Right. Yeah, she started there a few weeks ago, I think. I forget what she said. She works every day except Sunday, but Saturdays the guy is only open till midday sometime. Yeah. Oh, really? Yeah, you might have walked right by her then."

Lenny was pacing nervously around the room now, grateful when Sam started ending the call.

"Totally. Okay. It'll be great to see you. Yeah. Alright, buddy. Yeah, I'll see you then. Okay. Alright. Bye."

He ended the call, then looked around to make sure everything was set. Gulping down the last of his beer, he rinsed out the can and threw it in the bin. Grabbing two bottles of water from the

25

fridge, he turned off all the lights except the one by the stairs, so Erika could find her way up whenever she came home.

Inside their bedroom, Caroline was under the covers and deep into her latest book purchase, something dark and smutty she'd found in town at The Book Nook. Lenny eyed the cover briefly with a smile, then made his way around the bed to his side.

They didn't speak at first, but once Caroline turned the page and closed her book, the atmosphere shifted. She put it down on her bedside table, thanked him for the water, and then waited patiently until he locked eyes with her.

Lenny knew what she wanted, and he knew he had to give it to her. Their marriage had always been based on 100% honesty, even when the truth hurt. He smiled and turned to face her.

"He's moving back. He's gonna check out the inn first, and then maybe those condos over in Rutland. Says he wants to find something manageable, nothing too big or crazy, so he can take off again if he wants."

Caroline just stared at him without saying anything, trying to read his face. Some things didn't need to be said, some were already spoken about enough times in the past, and others still were never to be spoken of at all. If anything, she just wanted Lenny to say what was on *his* mind now, after he'd talked with Sam again. She wanted to know if Sam said anything new, or sounded any different than before.

"He sounded good, a little stressed, but I think that's more about moving back up here again. He said he didn't miss the snow, but at least he has another five months before he has to worry about that again. He and Kim broke up. I think that was probably a couple months ago by the way he was talking. She moved back to Utah. Apparently always hated living in Vegas anyway."

Lenny tried his best to read her face, to figure out if she was pissed, or scared, or what.

"Car, you're just staring at me, and I have no clue what you're thinking," he finally said, allowing himself another smile.

26

Her eyebrows went up as she smirked and turned away, and he watched her carefully as she rolled down onto her back.

"No wonder he was in town and didn't tell anyone," she finally said. "He must have known your mom would spread word quickly enough, though. Seeing her must have been like lighting the fuse. He knew it was only a matter of time before he'd have to get back in touch with you."

Lenny didn't respond this time, because he knew he didn't have to. She'd said it all, perfectly succinct as always. And for Lenny's part, his silence *was* his answer.

Caroline had always seen Sam as Lenny's best friend more than Olivia's ex-husband. Lenny and Sam went to high school together, and even though they weren't very close until after Sam and Olivia started dating, the two had forged a great bond over the years. It was the kind of friendship that transcended any attachments to anyone else, and Caroline knew that.

They spoke each other's language, followed all the same sports teams, and even seemed to like many of the same foods. If they were related, it would make sense, but looking at the two of them side by side, you'd never even mistake them for cousins.

Lenny was shorter than Sam and stocky, balding at the top, and looked more haggard than his 43 years would suggest. He was a nervous kind of a guy at times, but fiercely loyal to Caroline and the kids. He even insisted on a family vacation every year so they could all be together, and family dinners were an absolute must.

Sam on the other hand was tall, thin, and boyish looking, and he still had a full head of thick, blond hair. *The blonde Rob Lowe*, as Caroline often called him. He seemed like a family man himself for a while there, but in the last two years of his marriage, he'd changed on a dime

It was obvious that despite his huge falling out with Olivia, he still loved Haley, and had done his best to keep in touch with her through FaceTime and texts, but he'd only been back twice to visit her since moving to Vegas when she was only seven.

He came up for a weekend when she was 10, and then surprised everyone when he showed up at her Sweet 16, but except for the checks he sent Olivia for Haley, no one else but Haley ever heard from him.

"I'm meeting him Monday after work," Lenny finally announced to the ceiling, in case it cared.

Caroline nodded once in her pillow, then leaned over and turned off the lamp on her side, facing away from him.

"Good night," was all she said.

"Night," he said a few seconds later, then cozied down and turned off his light as well.

It was another forty-nine minutes before either one of them could fall asleep.

Chapter 5

On Monday evening around six, the door from the sidewalk to Doctor Finny's office squeaked open a few inches, and there was Peaches—*sort of.*

Only the very top of her head peaked in between the door and the wall, followed shortly afterward by her forehead, and finally her eyes and nose. Haley smiled nervously, but nothing else happened.

Peaches stared in at Haley with a strange look, and Haley immediately sensed Doctor Finny's eyes on both of them.

"Peaches, just come in."

The door closed again, with Peaches still outside, and another long moment passed where nothing happened at all.

Haley saw Doctor Finny out of the corner of her eye somewhere behind her, and knew this had gone from odd but cute to just plain absurd.

The door cracked open slightly again, and this time Peaches looked in at both Haley and Doctor Finny. She smiled warmly at Doctor Finny, and then her head swung back toward Haley.

"Um, Haley? Can Roger come in too?"

Haley turned to look at Doctor Finny, who to her surprise had come all the way out from the back, and was now standing right beside her.

"Roger who?" Haley asked.

Peaches opened her mouth to answer, but Haley cut her off.

"Never mind. Yes, he can come in too."

As if some magic word had finally been recited, the door swung all the way open as Peaches walked in, followed by a tall black boy who looked like he might be around 16 or 17 as well. He closed the door behind them, and followed Peaches to Haley's desk.

Without realizing it at first, all three of them quickly found themselves caught in a tractor beam of judgment from Doctor Finny, and Peaches looked to Haley for help.

"Doctor Finny," Haley said, "this is my cousin Peaches. She's the one sitting in for me this Saturday."

"Oh," he said. "Well, nice to meet you, Peaches." He approached her and shook her hand, before offering the same to Roger. "And who are you, young man? Pears?"

Both Roger and Peaches cracked up at this, but Haley just scratched her cheek nervously with a smile.

"I'm Roger. Nice to meet you."

"Guessing Peaches isn't your real name then, young lady?"

Peaches shook her head with a smile, but didn't answer.

"Jessica. Her name is Jessica," Haley blurted out, "but we've called her Peaches forever. If you don't want to call her that—"

"No, no, no. Peaches is fine. I like Peaches. They're good for you too."

Peaches smiled at Dr. Finny like this was the nicest thing anyone had ever said to her.

"Uh, Haley," he went on, "I'm almost done inside. You can leave soon. Just give me another few minutes."

He smiled at them all, then turned around and disappeared back into his office, closing his door most of the way.

Haley sighed with relief once he was gone, then looked back at Peaches and Roger, wondering why they were even there.

"Was there something you needed help with?" she asked them.

She looked at Roger again, quickly sizing him up. He was cute, she decided, even if he was only 16. He seemed more mature than Peaches though, and she began to wonder if they were dating or just friends.

Peaches dating a black guy would almost certainly kill their grandfather, and she doubted it would go over too well with her mom or grandmother either, but Aunt Caroline and Uncle Lenny probably wouldn't care. They always seemed to support Peaches in everything she did.

"Your dad and my dad are meeting right now over at the lake."

Peaches had just said something to Haley, but the words weren't computing.

The lake? Meeting? My dad? Here?

She made a strange face at Peaches while her brain put itself back together again. Then she shook her head.

"Wait. What? Did you just say my dad is here? Like in Ludlow? Right now? With Uncle Lenny?"

Now Peaches looked confused.

"Yeah. How'd you not know that? Grandma was telling everyone on Saturday that she saw him in town. I figured you spoke to him already. He didn't tell you he was moving back?"

"What?! He's *moving* back here? Peaches, who told you that?!"

Peaches looked at Roger with some concern, like she'd just opened a can of worms that were now crawling all over the doctor's office. Then her mind went off of Haley completely, and she wondered why that was even a phrase. Whenever she'd seen anyone with worms to fish with, they were in a plastic container, not a can, and it would take hours for the worms to spread out that much anyway. Even if they were in a can, she was sure they could get them back in without too much effort.

She blinked back to reality a few seconds later, and saw Haley texting furiously on her phone. Roger pulled Peaches gently by the arm then, and Haley didn't even notice them leaving.

##

Four miles away on the north end of Ludlow, Sam looked down at his phone with a grimace.

"Everything alright?" Lenny asked him.

Sam shook his head.

"Well," he said, "from what I gather, Haley just found out from Peaches that I'm in town, and she told her you and I were meeting over here right now. She's pretty pissed at me for not telling her I was back."

The two men stood next to each other on Red Bridge Road, both leaning over the railing and looking out at Lake Rescue.

Lenny nodded in case Sam was looking, not sure what he should say. He sympathized with Sam's dilemma, and wasn't sure if he would've done things any differently if he was in his place.

Erika and Peaches would've been pretty damn pissed at him too though, he was sure.

"She'll get over it," Lenny finally offered, more to the lake than to Sam, and Sam's concentration was still fixed firmly on his phone anyway as he texted Haley back.

A cool breeze blew past them from Lake Rescue across the road to Lake Pauline, the smaller lake on the other side of the one-lane bridge. Beneath them, a concrete enclosure caught the overflow from Rescue, feeding Pauline whenever Rescue flooded.

The whole area became a wild river when Hurricane Irene hit in August of 2011, when the water level on Pauline rose over seven feet high in some places. Seven people in the area lost their lives because of Irene too, one right there on Lake Rescue. It was a damn miracle Red Bridge Road survived at all, especially considering so many other nearby roads and bridges were completely demolished and washed away.

Lenny remembered driving over to the area the next day to help people clean up. Even with all the downed trees, mudslides, and infrastructure upheavals, he and so many others like him who didn't have any extreme damage of their own back in town pitched in to help their neighbors. He'd never forget hugging one woman who lost her entire deck, Jacuzzi, and refrigerator in the floodwaters that day.

Behind him, Lenny looked at the upward arch of the trees. The water had nowhere to go but down in the little lakes and valleys between the mountains, so any poor souls living at or renting homes on the lakes that day were quickly surrounded by rising water. He had the strangest sensation just then that something similar was coming back again this summer, although not in the form of a hurricane.

A car with Maryland plates drove slowly behind them across the bridge, and Lenny returned a little wave from the family inside.

Tourists looking at any of it now would never be able to tell what had happened there that year, but like so many other permanent residents, Lenny couldn't see any of it now *without* remembering.

"God, she's so pissed," Sam said, finally putting his phone away. "I don't blame her either. I'm such an asshole. I should've at least texted her before I came back."

He paused, taking a deep breath and shaking his head, only continuing once he saw Lenny remaining silent.

"I offered to come by the doctor's office or whatever, or even the house later on, but she didn't think either was a good idea. She's leaving work now, so she's gonna meet me over here in a few minutes. Neighbors are gonna get a bug up their ass with three cars lined up over—"

"No, I'll get going," Lenny said, cutting him off. "If you'll be living up here again, we can talk anytime. We don't have to deal with everything right now anyway."

The word *everything* fell like a lead balloon on the gravel between them, and Lenny turned away from Sam before he had to look at it.

Lenny crossed back over the bridge toward his car, but stopped when he spied a large rock on the street. He picked it up and hurled it into Lake Pauline, waiting till he heard it hit the water.

Sam turned around to face him as Lenny pulled his car keys out of his pocket then and opened his door.

"Look, Lenny," he said, standing up straight, his hands quickly buried in his jeans pockets. "I'm not gonna let the past keep chasing me anymore. That's one of the reasons I'm moving back. I'm sick and tired of everyone treating me like a goddamn dog with its tail between its legs. I'm over it all, even if no one else is yet. And I liked living up here too. Hell, it was all I knew until I moved away, and you just don't find anyplace like this anywhere else in the country. Vermont is in my bones. I can't shake it."

He paused and looked around, taking a deep breath of the fresh mountain air.

"Haley's asked me a few times to move back, and now that I don't owe Livi any more legal favors for Haley's school costs or clothes or any of that crap, I can just be her dad again, and maybe even her friend. Hell, a friend and uncle for Erika and Peaches too. They're great kids, and I want to be their uncle again if you'll all let me. Maybe I can start over with you and Caroline too? I'd like to at least try to be friends with you guys again, you know. And your mom and dad, well—maybe them not so much."

Lenny laughed at this, and Sam was grateful for it, breathing out a nervous laugh of his own. He watched as Lenny tossed his keys back and forth in his hands for a few seconds before crossing back over and offering Sam his hand to shake.

"To leaving the past behind us," Lenny said.

Sam smiled and shook his hand.

"To leaving the past behind us."

##

Lenny was long gone when Haley finally pulled up in her car. Sam recognized it from the pictures she'd posted online, and he was happy to see it looked like a solid automobile too, something he hoped would keep his baby safe.

He braced himself for whatever would happen next, and behind the wheel of her Corolla, Haley was busy doing the same.

They made eye contact for just a second while she turned off the car and undid her seat belt, but as she walked toward him a few moments later, her eyes were anywhere but on his face. Haley had been on blind dates much less stressful than this.

For the first time in his life, Sam worried there was a chance she might even hit him.

Her walk from the car, parked right where Lenny's had been 15 minutes earlier, seemed to take minutes. Time slowed down for both of them, and try as he could, Sam couldn't shake the feeling that Haley was about to have it out with him.

Instead, to his great relief, Haley finally offered him a half smile as she approached, and then a long hug once she reached him.

Sam felt his whole body relax, and as Haley leaned back from him again, he smiled at her, and took note of how she looked.

"God, you're so beautiful. Even prettier in person than you are on Instagram."

She laughed before she could take it back, then thanked him. He looked older, she thought, but still mostly the same. There were shadows under his eyes, and little wrinkles here and there she didn't remember from the last time they'd seen each other, but life does that, she figured.

Haley wondered if they'd still text as much now that he was back. She'd enjoyed that, and his frequent auto-correct errors always made her smile too. Even so, this was strange. The man looking down at her was more like a long-term internet friend now than he was her father, and Sam knew it just as much as she did.

"So when did you get here?" she asked, trying her best to keep things casual.

"About a week ago."

Her face dropped immediately, and she couldn't help herself.

"What?! Jesus Christ, Dad, and you didn't tell me?"

"Honey, listen. I'm not gonna stand here and make any excuses. I wouldn't do that to you, but please just understand, I'm *scared* of you all, you know? I was scared to come back, to go through all this, to get called out for every last thing I ever did all over again. For every last thing I *never* did all over again. Your mother practically screamed me out of the state last time I came to visit."

Haley rolled her eyes and shook her head, looking away.

"But Dad, how is *anything* supposed to change if the first thing you do when you come back is sneak around like this?"

"How am I sneaking around?"

"Are you serious? We're *literally* standing on a bridge outside town. And you just met Uncle Lenny here first, right? Not to mention the fact that you've apparently been back for a week already, and I didn't even know you were here until twenty minutes ago. How is that *not* sneaking around?"

"I'm staying in Killington."

"What?"

"I'm staying in Killington. You know, at least until I make my way to something around here."

Haley shook her head. She wasn't saying what really bothered her, and dancing around the truth wasn't getting them anywhere.

"Why didn't you at least tell me you were gonna be in town? We talk like once a month, and you're always liking my pictures on Facebook and Instagram with that stupid fake account lately. You could've at least mentioned somewhere in there that you were moving back here again. I could have totally kept it a secret too, you know."

"I know you could have," he said, looking away, "but I *did* post about it on Facebook. Sorta. I didn't tell you by text, because I wasn't sure how you'd react, and I guess—I guess I thought just coming here would be easier than telling everyone I was coming, you know?"

"No. No, Dad. That makes no sense."

"Jesus, Haley, it makes sense to me, alright?!"

He turned his back on her, gripping the railing of the bridge like he was trying to rip it off. A man walking his dog came by just then, and stared them both down like he was making sure everything was okay.

Sam looked at them as they passed, then stared back out across Lake Pauline. Once they were gone again, he looked at Haley.

"Dog kinda looked like Rusty, right?"

Haley nodded, brushing past him a bit as she joined him over at the railing.

"I want this to work out, Dad. I don't want the fact that you're living here again to make things worse. I want it to be better."

"Well, that's what I want too."

She nodded again, but neither knew what else to say about that. They both stared out across the part of the lake they could see from there, each admiring the evening glow in the sky above.

A family of ducks flew overhead from Lake Rescue behind them, landing somewhere in the distance around the bend, and

Sam thought back on his many happy memories of the area. Lake life beat Las Vegas life any day of the year.

Two minutes more passed in silence, as if they were both worried fate could rip them apart again at any moment.

"You know," Sam finally said in a near whisper, "being up here again reminds me of all the times we used to go fishing back in the day. You ever come over here to fish anymore?"

Haley shook her head.

"I don't even *eat* fish anymore," she said. "Except for shrimp and scallops, and maybe the occasional clam dip. Not like fish-fish, though. I usually eat pizza."

"Anchovies?" he asked.

"No way," she said, a big smile surprising them both.

"Well, on my first visit back here after I moved to Vegas, me and your Uncle Lenny took you and the girls over to the Sugar House. We parked the car on the end, and though you and Erika pleaded for us to take you in for a treat, we made you do some fishing first. We said you could have your dessert once you helped us catch dinner. Peaches was too small to care either way, and Erika was still using a toy rod, but I set you up with one of my lines. You caught a nice one that day too."

She remembered the Sugar House stops and some of the time with her dad, but the fishing not as much. Even before their divorce, Sam and Olivia had grown apart, and they never spent much time together as a family.

Haley could recall plenty of times she'd spent driving around with her dad, or shopping at the mall with her mother, but hardly any dinners together with both of them. She wondered when that had stopped, and if she'd even noticed it at the time. There were lots of nights she'd hear them yelling, but there wasn't one moment when things were ever at their worst.

Even the day Sam moved out of the house was a blur now. At first she thought it was only temporary, but when the postcards from Vegas stopped coming, and the school year started up again that August, Haley realized something fundamental had changed in all their lives.

"Where are you gonna move, Dad? I'm sure there are some apartments in town you could rent. I could ask Doctor Finny if he knows any—"

"There's no way I'm living in Ludlow, honey, I'm sorry."

"But why not? You'd be so close. And I'd see you every day."

"No, Haley, listen to me. First of all, we don't even know if *you'll* be staying around here much longer. It's a big world out there. You shouldn't stay cooped up in Ludlow the rest of your life anyway. As for me, well, I don't want to be cooped up in there either. Too many eyes on me all the time in town. I couldn't even go to the goddamn hardware store without running into your grandmother. I'm happy to be back—honest, I am—but the one thing I'm sure of is, small town life isn't for me."

"Well, where are you gonna be? Rutland? I doubt it's anything like Vegas, but it's a much bigger city, at least. Easier to get lost in."

Sam laughed.

"Rutland ain't nothin' like Vegas, baby girl, believe you me. Not sayin' I'm not craving a poker table or even a frickin' slot machine parlor 'round here—at least one of them up this way wouldn't suck, trust me—but no, I don't think I'll buy in Rutland, either. I just wouldn't feel at home there."

Haley shook her head, and Sam felt he'd lost her again. She was off in her own universe, deep in thought or bad memories or worse, and he wasn't sure what else to say. He'd been away so long, he'd forgotten how to be a parent, and even when he was still living there, Haley was a child. Being a dad to a 22-year-old college graduate was a new ballgame.

She sensed him looking at her now as she turned around, but maintained her gaze out at the dimming light over Rescue.

"Hey, walk with me for a minute," he said. "The cars aren't going anywhere."

They walked slowly for a few minutes around the bend, where Red Bridge Road twisted up to meet the much larger Route 100 and the way back to Ludlow. Sam asked Haley as they walked about her new job, and her hopes of launching a photography career, as well as her first real gig coming up later that week. He was proud of her, and hoped she'd figure out all the answers to life he still hadn't arrived at yet himself.

Not too far into their stroll, he turned into a private driveway that led down to the shore of Lake Pauline.

"Oh Dad, this is someone's house. We shouldn't walk this way."

"It's alright, I know the owner. He doesn't care."

They walked down the grassy lawn to the lake, and onto a wooden dock with a rowboat on either side. Out in front of them, the mountain rose high and proud above the water, where the sun's light still shone warmly across the tops of the trees.

Another family of ducks swam past them, as if to take a look at the two newest humans to arrive, and three other ducks were already walking up the lawn to their left, poking around for bird seed beneath a feeder. A fearless chipmunk ran up and took his own piece of the leftover bird food on the grass, all as another duck watched him suspiciously from a few feet away.

"God, it's so perfect over here," Haley said, and Sam just nodded his agreement.

After another minute though, Haley turned to Sam, a new kind of determination written on her face.

"Dad, I don't want you living up here again if you're just gonna make me drive three hours to see you. You've gotta find something in town, or Rutland, or somewhere else close by. Please don't be an idiot about this. Mom can handle seeing you now and then, and I don't care what she says anyway. I'm an adult now, and I can see you anytime I want."

He smiled, then gently turned her around to face the house.

"It's got four bedrooms and two full bathrooms. Really nice layout too. Good bones. And from what I'm told, it's easy to rent out in the summer and winter. You're welcome here anytime."

"What?" She blinked in silence for a moment in shock. "You— you *bought* this? You live here?"

"Well, I will soon," he said with a smile. "Haven't closed yet. But it should go through pretty quickly. I'm gonna flip her over the next few weeks, remodel a bit, put the Sam Newhaus style on the place, and then probably rent her out like the last owners did. Oh, and the deal came with the smaller house next door there too. That one's got three bedrooms and a bath. I'm thinking I'll live there, at least while I renovate the big one, but it wouldn't suck to be so close to my renters. Sure as hell would save me some money to clean the place up myself instead of hiring a service."

Haley almost looked angry at first, and Sam wondered if she was pissed at him for keeping yet another big secret from her, but when she grabbed him into a tight hug a second later, he knew she was okay.

"I guess that means I did something right?" he asked.

"Yes, you idiot," she said. "I'm really happy for you."

She let go of him again, looking around at the lake and property with new eyes. Everything about the view and the area was so incredibly peaceful. She could see why he'd bought it, and even without seeing the inside of either house, Haley knew it would make a great rental too, if that's what he wanted.

"Just promise me one thing," she said. "That you'll let me help you. You may have experience working with your hands, but I know you well enough to be sure you're gonna need a woman's help making this place look extra pretty inside."

"I do need your help with that kinda thing, and I promise," he said. "You'll be my go-to for all the color choices and decorations. Let's go back and get the cars, and then I'll show you the inside."

Chapter 6

By Wednesday afternoon, Olivia had seized all new opportunities and methods available to verbally destroy Sam to anyone who would stand still long enough to listen to her do so.

Though she hadn't seen or spoken to him yet, just knowing he was back was like a brand new challenge for her, an occasion for which she must proudly rise again.

Sam was a public menace, and as far as Olivia was concerned, the community needed to know he was a clear and present danger. It was her civic responsibility to warn everyone she could about him, and to remind all who knew Sam what he was charged with doing to "poor Kerry Ann".

Most of the stories people knew already, and Olivia kept them holstered like a pack of Tic Tacs— *Need a mint? Or some dirt on that scumbag beast I used to call my husband?* —but for this new crusade, she dug up every last memory of hair in the kitchen sink, spilt coffee on the carpet, or money carelessly squandered away at casinos from Montreal to the Long Island Sound.

To anyone she spoke to at work or over the phone, Olivia's purpose was clear and thorough. She didn't want to simply sway them from speaking to Sam. No. A mere smear was far too easy. Instead, Olivia made certain they understood that Sam Newhaus was the kind of vicious creature they must avoid even making eye contact with at all costs. He was a wild animal incapable of any sound moral decisions, and far too dangerous to approach out in the wilderness.

The front door of the bank opened with an extended vacuum whoosh of air, and Olivia glanced up from her nail file as her father came limping in with his cane. Alan had used *the goddamn thing* plenty of times in the past, but not as much recently, so it stirred something deep in her bones to see him out with it again.

She locked eyes with him briefly as he began to offer his friendly but thoroughly fake hellos to all the girls behind the glass, speaking to each one like he truly cared about their lives and families, and then stood up by her desk as he finally approached.

She kissed him on the cheek, then crossed her arms and stared down at the cane, as if waiting for the thing to explain itself. 'What the hell are *you* doing here?' she seemed to ask it.

"My knee is acting up again. It's nothing. I fell last night—*I'm fine, I'm fine*—so your mother insisted I bring the goddamn thing with me today."

He sat down in one of the two matching leatherette chairs across from Olivia's desk, resting his cane on the end by her lamp. She sat back down as well, returning the nail file to her drawer and looking around to make sure everything else looked tidy.

"So what's up, Dad? Everything else okay?"

He looked at her with a frown, then leaned forward a bit across her desk to retrieve the Rubik's Cube she kept there as a decoration, forever disarranged. Alan owned neither the intention nor the desire to do much at all with the thing, but he liked the feel of it in his hands just the same. The hard corners were themselves a kind of challenge, he felt, even if he didn't care to understand the mechanics of the toy at all.

"Remember that guy who sold Haley her car?" he asked. "The one with the weird neck?"

Olivia scrunched up her nose with a crooked nod.

"Yeah?"

"I saw him over in Queechee yesterday. Your mother wanted to do some shopping, and while *she* was off buying God knows what that she doesn't need, weird neck guy walks by me and says hello. We get to talking, mostly nonsense about the weather, but then he says he heard Sam was back. He didn't remember Sam's name, but he did know my daughter's ex-husband was back in town, 'cause he heard you were trash-talking Sam to anyone who would listen."

"Dad, I haven't even seen that salesman guy in two years, and I certainly haven't talked to him about Sam."

"I know that," he said. "That's my goddamn point. Weird neck guy heard it from his wife, who works in Shaw's in the produce

42

department. Or maybe dairy? Anyway, she heard it from *her* friend, who's friends with one of Haley's old teachers or something. I can't remember now, and I don't *care* to remember, either."

"Dad, look."

"Why the hell are you doing this, Livi? To Sam and to yourself? What's the point? What's your end game? To have Sam leave right away, and leave Haley without her father all over again?"

Olivia opened her mouth in anger, ready to pounce.

"I'm sorry. Look," he said. "All I'm saying is, there's no point stirring something up. If Sam stirs the pot himself, everyone will know, right? So just leave him be, and see how it all plays out."

"I agree with your father, Olivia," a woman's voice came from behind Alan. "You should listen to him. That's *very* good advice."

They both glanced up and saw Mary, Olivia's coworker, poking her head above the cubicle wall. She looked down at them over reading glasses she wore on a beaded chain around her neck, and offered Alan a warm, friendly smile.

Mary was twelve years older than Olivia, and with her arms resting comfortably atop the wall of the cubicle divider, she looked back and forth between them like they'd invited her to join them for a chat, desperate to get *her* take on everything.

"Mary?" Olivia asked.

"Yes?"

"This is a private conversation. Could you please mind your own fucking business?"

"Not private enough," one of the tellers said from across the way, but Olivia didn't seem to hear her.

Alan grinned sideways at his daughter's quick temper, then placed the Rubik's Cube back on her desk. He'd actually managed to line up a single row of blue squares on one side, and was extremely proud of himself. In fact, he was sure he'd broken some sort of a world record, and wondered if the security cameras had managed to capture it.

Olivia leaned back in her chair, and quickly pulled out her cigarettes and lighter from her purse. She stood up and stepped away to tuck her seat in then, to show Alan she wanted to take the conversation outside, and after a brief but quiet burp, he reluctantly stood up to join her as well.

He nudged the cane across her desk a bit before grabbing it, then followed her out the front door of the bank, waving goodbye to a few of the ladies as he did.

Outside, it was starting to rain, and though neither of them had brought along an umbrella, an overhang nearby was easy enough to reach from the front door of the bank, not too far from Alan's car. He'd parked in the handicapped spot, and though he didn't have an active decal to hang from his rear-view mirror, he'd hung an expired one there just the same, along with a scribbled note on the dashboard daring anyone to ticket him.

Olivia lit up, making sure to keep the smoke away from Alan, and as she blew it out and waved it away, she looked at him again for a long time, deciding on her approach. She didn't want to fight him over this. She just wanted him to understand.

"Dad, listen. If Mom put you through half the shit Sam put me through, don't you think you'd have a few things to say too? Don't you think you'd be telling everyone who'd listen what it was like?"

Alan raised his eyebrows and looked away toward the street.

"I'm just really on edge now that he's back here, and it makes me crazy to think I'm gonna have to see him and deal with all this again at some point soon. And even if I *can* keep him away from my house, Lenny's bound to invite him over there, so sooner or later, Sam and I are destined to have it out."

Alan shook his head then with a sigh. He'd partaken in more than his fair share of arguments with family over the years, and once even witnessed his Uncle Ira punch his Aunt Milly square in the face, so he was no stranger to domestic violence. But Sam? Sam had never laid a hand on Olivia as far as he knew, and he'd done a good job for years now of just staying away from them all.

No, Sam's faults, Alan always felt, were emotional. Scarring of another sort, perhaps, but for some reason Alan never understood, Olivia refused to heal from any of it, even after years of heartache.

44

What bothered him most though was his daughter's sincere and total *expectation* of a fight. She was shuffling through emotions like she was picking out a new dress to buy, shouting out keywords to anyone who would listen, as if that kind of target practice would somehow make her stronger for the battle to come.

Alan had seen too many real battles fought in his lifetime to get himself worked up over an emotional one, even though deep down, deeper than he usually preferred to dive, he was a sincerely emotional guy himself. He wanted love and attention just as much as the next guy, only Alan survived by imagining the spotlight was already his, that he was the rightful center of attention in every room he walked through. It was his drug of choice, and brought him a strange kind of peace at the same time, a sustenance he'd built up by nature as a way of sheltering his ego from attack.

Maybe, he thought, as he looked back at her again, Olivia's approach was just her honest way of defending her castle. Where Alan went to a place of forced confidence and sheer willpower, shielding himself against the opinions of others, Olivia took control of her situation by wielding her sword, and building up an army all around her.

It seemed to him that this was her way of controlling her life, that if Olivia just told enough people about Sam's weaknesses, he'd be forced to skulk away on his own, defeated by all the soldiers of judgment she'd lined up to stop him from ever crossing the moat to begin with.

"I ever tell you about your Great Aunt Mildred?" Alan finally asked her.

Olivia squinted her eyes at him, taking another drag on her cigarette, and then she shook her head.

"No? I don't think you ever mentioned her?"

Alan smiled.

"She was a good woman, but very quiet. A lot like you."

"Me? Quiet?" she laughed, blowing away more smoke.

"You're a lot quieter than the rest of us. You only pounce when you have to. Like when your mother snatched that damn raincoat from you so she wouldn't get her blouse wet. You let her have it as I recall, but you also *let her have it*. And then some. Honey, you used words I'd never heard before, and I grew up in Brooklyn for crying out loud."

Olivia stifled a grin.

"And your Great Aunt Mildred was the same way. She'd sit in her rocking chair, knitting some new blanket or scarf or whatever goddamn thing she'd been working on for weeks, but if you looked at her from across the way, you'd notice she still had her eyes on everything and everyone else around her. She listened. She absorbed it all. She was like a super computer, grabbing up all this data from her surroundings, and then coming up with a list of her own conclusions.

"You'd think she was sitting apart from people because she didn't care to partake in their conversation, but it was often the complete opposite. She'd actually position herself just close enough to hear, but not so close she had to participate, like she was some kind of a sponge, a secret agent working only for herself."

He paused and laughed to himself as he remembered.

"But she was good, Aunt Mildred. Good woman. Like you."

"Dad, is there a point to all this? What the hell does your Aunt Mildred have to do with me and Sam?"

Alan turned and faced her now with a keen smile. He'd watched Olivia grow up, seen her fall in love with Sam, seen it fall apart too, and through all of it, he'd gotten to know how Olivia ticked better than she did.

"You *know* Sam, Livi. You know all his flaws and issues. You know them all too well, I know, I know. But he isn't *hurting* you anymore. He hasn't done anything to cause more hurt in your life. He paid all the expenses for Haley over the years, all the court-ordered ones and a shitload of gifts besides. And when he surprised us all by showing up to Haley's Sweet 16 a few years ago, he was a changed man. He looked better. He sounded better. He'd wrestled his demons down, and there was nothing left of the guy who the whole town thought was—"

Alan trailed off, not wanting to say the words.

"My point is, what the hell are you doing still judging him, Livi? Why are you trying to make things worse all over again? People know. Enough people remember what happened back then. They aren't stupid. They remember. But history is history, and you're not doing either Haley or yourself any special favors by digging up that particular grave."

He leaned back and stood upright, proud of himself, prouder than the Rubik's Cube even, and wished someone had been there to record him just then. It was the perfect thing to say to her, he felt, and now she would melt before him and tell him how wise he was, how much she needed to hear those words. Instead—

"I gotta get back to work, Dad. Be careful walking in the rain."

She leaned in and kissed him quickly on the cheek, then threw her cigarette out into the street and walked away.

##

Twenty-three minutes later at his job across town, Lenny stared at the Excel document on his screen, trying to make some sense of an expense report that literally wasn't adding up. He'd already switched from one of their long-time vendors to save costs, but the reports still showed much bigger losses for the quarter than they ought to have incurred.

He looked over at his manager's office to see if he was free, but saw he was still on the phone.

Something's not right here.

When his manager finally hung up a few minutes later, Lenny walked over and knocked on his door.

"Hey, what's up?"

"Hey Joe, you got a second?"

"For you, Lenny, I've got two."

Lenny smiled and rubbed his temple, trying to stay calm. Joe was a nice guy, but he was still his manager, so Lenny always proceeded with caution.

"Well, I was just looking at the latest expense report, and I think I'm missing something. It isn't adding up. Tarisi's trip to Shanghai is all accounted for: his airfare, hotel, meals, and incidentals, but there's another four grand or so missing from the total."

Joe smiled and nodded.

"Close the door," he said.

Lenny shut the door behind him, then looked back at Joe with his eyebrows up.

"What is it?"

"Tarisi lost four grand on the Sox while he was over there. He doesn't want anyone to know."

Lenny tried to stop himself from asking, but it was too late. The words left his mouth strangely, like he was having a stroke.

"Why...is it...on...the...firm's...account...though?"

Joe smirked at him and then looked away for a few seconds before responding.

"Your guess is as good as mine. Listen, Len. He runs the place. He can do whatever the hell he wants. I couldn't give a damn how he spends the company's money, and I sure as hell don't want to lose my job trying to make trouble for him. It's just four grand. I'd say let it go. In fact, I meant to fix that one before you saw it, but you beat me to it. Look, you're cool with that, right? If not, you can give it to me to fix it."

Lenny waved him off.

"No, I'll do it. I only needed to make sure all the zeros lined up. I'm good, don't worry. Four grand on a random game in the spring, though? I'm jealous he's got that kind of money to play with."

Joe laughed.

"You and me both. Look, I don't want to get into it, but this isn't anything new, either. He'll send me a cryptic text or an email reminding me to double check the books. And look, the firm's making a fortune lately, and there haven't been any layoffs for the past three years, so I don't think it's that big a deal, you know?"

Lenny smiled and nodded.

"It's all good. Like I said, I just wanted to make sure everything added up. I'll put the other 4K in incidentals. It's no problem."

"Perfect. Thanks, Len."

Lenny walked back to his desk and sat down. In a few quick clicks, he'd moved the money over and closed the Excel.

A Gmail Hangouts window was still open on the screen behind it, and he took a moment to re-read Caroline's last message.

Just a reminder, I've got that meeting with Mrs. Tate tonight. Be home a little late.

Caroline's absolute worst client, an annoying, somewhat elderly drug addict who lived across the Connecticut River in Claremont, New Hampshire, needed constant handholding. They usually worked together over the phone, and Mrs. Tate was often able to handle things herself, but once every two months or so, she'd call Caroline up, and beg her for an appointment, an in-person meeting.

"Have fun!" Lenny typed back, adding a smiley face beside it. He saw that Caroline had read it, but she didn't respond.

\##

By 5:30, Caroline was almost there. She passed the airport, then took a quick look in the mirror at a red light a moment later, checking her makeup one last time. A quick flick of an AWOL eyelash, and she was content enough with what she saw.

Five minutes later, she pulled into the motel parking lot and looked around. Glancing at a note in her hand to double check the number, she found the door and knocked.

At first she heard nothing, and looked around her to make sure no one was nearby, but then she heard footsteps from inside. The door swung open, and there he was, smiling at her.

"Hi," she said, biting her lips. "It's good to see you again."

"You too. C'mon in."

He scanned the parking lot too, and then closed the door behind him.

Chapter 7

"Who told you that?"

"No one," Peaches answered honestly, flashing Roger her trademark mischievous grin. "I just know."

"You just *know* my dead grandmother is watching over me?"

Peaches reached out and grabbed his hands, holding his fingers warmly in her own. She knew Roger still didn't believe in these things, even though he'd already come a long way since he started attending their circle.

"I can sense her aura around you. She's there."

She looked past him briefly, and then back into his eyes, and corrected herself.

"She's *here*."

A few of the others giggled, and Roger rolled his eyes and smirked. He and Peaches were by far the youngest members of the Stir Call Circle. Most were in their 40s and 50s, with a few others in their 60s and 70s.

They met just once a month on a Friday night in the basement of a shop in Ludlow called Chaos Casbah, a new-age spirituality center that opened there in 2012. The shop's signature tagline is "Special Gifts for Unique People", but the circle often advertises themselves as sharing the special gifts *of* unique people.

"Look, I'm not saying you're wrong," Roger said, "but if she's watching out for me, or protecting me or whatever, how come I don't feel it? How come I don't feel any more *protected*? Know what I mean?"

"Because your ability to sense her," a new voice said from the back of the room, "has nothing to do with the spirit's ability to provide it."

Roger turned around, and everyone welcomed Shaman Gloria, arriving later than the rest after her long drive north. Gloria lived an hour and a half south of them in Amherst, Massachusetts, where she ran another circle out of her home, but she happily made the drive to Ludlow once a month to run this circle as well.

"I am sorry I am late," she added with a warm smile.

Gloria was a dark-skinned Haitian woman in her mid-50s, with a smile so wide and bright, it could light up a room. As she slipped off her sandals at the door beside everyone else's shoes and sneakers, Gloria took a brief moment to close her eyes and feel the spirit in the room, as well as inhale the remnants of burnt sage still floating through the air.

Roger liked Gloria, the only other person of color in the circle, but he still hadn't decided what he thought of some of the things they did there in the room. Prayer and meditation were one thing, but seeing energy around a person? Communicating with dead people? Journeying to outer space or underground in a Shamanic Journey? It all sounded too crazy to him.

Gloria hugged Krystal and Corinne as they stood up to welcome her, then took her place in her chair at the center, putting her bag down.

"Is Roger still our doubting Thomas?" she asked the room, but smiled at Roger sweetly as she said it.

Roger had attended the circle with Peaches since the two first met at a poetry reading in February.

"I'm not a doubting Thomas," he came back at her with a sly smile. "I just don't think it's right to believe everything you hear. It seems too easy to make stuff up, you know?"

"I do know, yes," she agreed, pulling out her drum and laying it across her lap. "And it's good, because you add something to the circle when you do that. You help us all by your challenges and questions. If we simply sat here and believed every last thing anyone said, we would never learn. We would never grow. If Peaches came here and told us she heard from her guardian angel that we should start worshiping cookies, I would certainly hope you and the others would see through her little trick."

Everyone laughed, especially Peaches.

"I already *do* worship cookies," she announced proudly.

Again they laughed, but once they were quiet, Gloria asked them all if they were ready to start.

"Yes," they told her.

"Good," she said, and then they stood up to set the circle.

At the center of the room, the others had laid out a beautiful prayer cloth and candles, along with a small collection of special items that meant something to each of them.

Turning to face the eastern wall, they watched and listened as Gloria began her chanting, some shaking their rattles or beating their drums softly in rhythm with her words.

"We look to the east," she said, "the place of enlightenment, the source of all inspiration and clarity..."

Gloria continued calling in each of the four directions one after the other like this, and each time she invited helping spirits to join them all in their circle.

With each new direction—east, south, west, and north—everyone turned ninety degrees to their right, to face the corresponding wall of the large room.

"We look to the south, the place of limitless emotional strength and healing...we look to the west, the place of fire and rebirth...we look to the north, the place of knowledge and wisdom..."

With every direction, the Circle members beat their drums and shook their rattles together before Gloria called in their spirit guides and teachers with very specific names and meanings, and very intentional messages of hope attached to each one.

After she had called in the four cardinal directions, all nine of them formed a circle around their prayer cloth and candles in the center of the room, and they looked up together toward the dark ceiling, lit only by dancing candlelight.

"We call on Father Sky..." Gloria continued, offering a special blessing with prayers to the heavens for their journeys ahead.

A moment later, they genuflected to the ground, some with a hand or two on the carpeted floor.

"And we call on Earth Mother..." she said, once again with special prayers for hope and healing, and a promise to return all their blessings back to Mother Earth after they returned from their shamanic journeys.

Rising again to finish the call-in, and still standing in a wide circle around the makeshift altar below them, they looked at one another, some with a hand or two on their chests, as Gloria spoke the last of the special words to set the circle.

"And finally, we look to each other. We feel the spirit that has already grown in this room, around us and through us and in us, and we pray that each of us knowingly returns some of our own spirit to the circle tonight, so that we may all grow and be strengthened together. Aho."

"Aho," they repeated as one, offering her in return the Native American word meaning both *thank you* and *amen*.

They took their seats again, Gloria in her chair at the front, and the others seated around her on the floor on yoga mats and cushions. Once they were settled in again and comfortable, she looked at each of them smiling back at her, and told them what was on her mind.

"We journeyed last time, and we did some Reiki healing the month before, so tonight I was thinking we could spend our time together doing something I have only tried one other time."

Several of them exchanged smiles of happy anticipation. Gloria was an experienced Shaman and Reiki 3 practitioner, having taught both for over twenty years up and down New England. Though she didn't share Dennis's gift as a medium, or Krystal's ability to read tea leaves, she was a master at helping others tap into their own gifts, and they looked to her as a wise leader and spirit guide.

"Tonight," she announced, "I would like our four Reiki 2 practitioners to work with the four others in the room as they journey. Since we have four of you here tonight who can do this, and four of you who do not yet possess the skills, it should be a good opportunity to try it out. If you can, I don't want you to touch them, but try to work your magic by holding your hands over them as they journey. We'll see how the two souls working together affect the journey, or perhaps also the one performing the Reiki, and we'll discuss afterward. How does that sound to everyone?"

"Awesome," Peaches said, and everyone else seemed to agree.

"Wait," Roger asked. "So whoever is doing the journey is supposed to think about the Reiki healing, or we shouldn't even focus on that?"

"The Reiki practitioner who works with you will keep their focus on sending you energy as you journey, and you should only focus yourself on the journey as much as possible. It isn't wrong for you to think about the Reiki, but try not to."

"So what are we supposed to journey on?" Peaches asked.

"Nothing specific this time. No instructions. I'd like you to simply journey on whatever it is your heart leads you to journey on. Maybe you have a new job, or something in school you need to focus on, or an argument or issue with a family member or friend, or maybe it's just a fear that's been nagging at you for too long. Open yourself up to whatever it is the spirit is calling you to deal with, and as you do, the Reiki team will help you out. Does that sound okay, Reiki team? I know it means you can't journey with the others this time, but is that alright?"

Everyone sounded enthusiastic, so Gloria helped match them up. Corinne positioned herself near Roger, Krystal did the same near Peaches, Dennis teamed up with Marty, and Jane with Ellen.

Once they were all ready, the four journeyers lying down on their yoga mats with their arms at their sides and a blindfold or small towel over their eyes, and the four Reiki practitioners sitting on the floor near each of their heads, their hands ready to hover over them, Gloria turned the lights out and began to drum.

She beat the drum softly at two hundred beats per minute, taking note occasionally of the small clock on the opposite wall.

For twenty minutes, they stayed in position like this, sitting and lying by candlelight, as Gloria kept the beat going. Finally, after about twenty minutes had passed, she changed the beat of the drum slightly, and slowed it down to bring them back. Then she rested her drum on the floor and switched the lights back on.

One by one, they all sat up or went back to their seats, and they began writing down what they saw or experienced in their journeys. As Gloria always taught them, this step was extremely important.

Just as you'd wake from a dream and think it would stay with you while you got up to use the bathroom, a journey 'might escape before you can catch it', so it's important to always write it down right away before you forget what you saw and felt.

A few minutes went by like this, with each one writing their impressions down, or typing them out on their iPads, and finally they went around the room sharing what they each experienced.

The Reiki healers reported feeling strong vibrations from those who journeyed, which they said made a lot of sense considering how much each of them were probably moving in their individual journeys, but to *almost* everyone's surprise, Roger corrected Corinne on the matter. He swore he didn't do anything, and stayed conscious of the drumbeat the whole time as the others journeyed.

He looked proud of himself, as if trying to prove his point, that it was all bullshit, no matter how much they tried to convince themselves otherwise, but Corinne smiled and shook her head.

"What?" he asked her.

She picked up her iPad and showed him, as the others all leaned in to read it as well:

Roger fought me tooth and nail. I couldn't even focus my own energy because he was fighting me so much. I doubt he even journeyed.

Some laughed, while others smiled at him sweetly, but he wasn't having it. He stood up right away and went for the door, slipping on his sneakers as fast as he could.

"Roger, don't leave. Come back," Gloria tried, but he was gone very quickly, and the upstairs door slammed shut behind him.

After a few minutes passed in which everyone tried to postmortem their feelings about what had happened, Gloria finally asked if someone would like to share their journey, and Peaches raised her hand timidly.

"Go ahead, Peaches," Gloria said.

"Well, I had a really good experience. It definitely felt much different than it has in the past, but I honestly totally forgot about Krystal doing Reiki on me, so I think what she did really helped. I journeyed to my spirit animal, and asked him to take me to my

Uncle Sam. He just moved back to town, and though I haven't seen him yet, I know it's going to cause some issues in my family."

"Isn't he the one who—" Dennis started.

"Yes," Peaches said, cutting him off quickly with a firm smile. "He's had some, well, some *issues* in the past? And I thought if I could journey to him, I could help him get past them, and help my family get past it all too, somehow. So I thought of his face, or whatever I could remember of his face, and I felt myself go to the place he's living. I don't know where he is, but it kinda looked small, like there was just a bed and a TV, maybe a small microwave and refrigerator, like a hotel room? But I really don't know.

"He was there by himself eating a slice of pizza, and he just seemed really, really sad. So I held out my hands and tried to bring light to the room. Like, first I saw light by my hands, and then I saw light around him, so I don't know if I did it, or if it was just there, but I felt good about it.

"Then something *really* weird happened. I had the feeling someone else was there with me, also watching him, only it wasn't Krystal or any of you. It was like some other spirit. It wasn't my spirit animal either. We looked at one another, but I couldn't see the person's face, just their hands. They were helping me bring light too, I realized, so I just smiled and kept doing it. A minute later, you changed the drumbeat, and I was back again."

"I think you succeeded in bringing your uncle some much needed light, then," Gloria said. "Is his name really Uncle Sam?"

A few of the others chuckled at this, but Peaches nodded with a smile.

"Yeah. He is for me and my sister, at least."

Gloria smiled and nodded.

##

Twenty-two miles away from them in a small hotel room in Killington, Vermont, Sam tossed his pizza crust into the box and closed it up. He put his finger into his ear for a moment, rubbing it quickly, then stood up and walked across the room to the bathroom on the other side, and washed his hands. He looked at himself in the mirror, generally pleased with the face he saw there, then grabbed the towel and dried his hands.

Lying down on the bed again, he turned on the TV and stared mindlessly at the screen, the plot of some sitcom already in progress totally lost on him.

A few seconds later, he picked up the papers off his bed and stared at them some more. He'd already read through them from start to finish at least three times, but he wanted to go through all the details again.

What he was about to do was the soundest judgment he'd ever made, he decided, even if everyone else in the world would think he was insane.

Chapter 8

Haley took a deep breath and collected her thoughts. She'd arrived at the church a full half hour early, but already felt the flop sweat creeping ever so unattractively down her back, threatening at any moment to break forth into a full river dance of pure liquid stress.

She stared down into the trunk of her car, deciding which pieces of camera equipment she needed to bring inside. Grabbing her small point-and-shoot, she took a few photos of the church from across the street before tossing it back in the bag she'd grabbed it from. The photos looked decent enough, but she decided it'd be better to just stick with her DSLR on the tripod, and leave the little one behind. That would make her look much more professional too.

Twenty minutes later, she was all set up at the front of the church by the steps to the large altar when she noticed people finally starting to come in. From the back.

Wait, what?

She watched the proceedings with a blank stare for about 15 seconds, soon realizing with great horror that her responsibilities this day would be far from stationary.

Grabbing the tripod with the camera attached, she quickly made a beeline for the back of the church, capturing as many random shots of people entering as she could. Once it looked like the wedding party and announced family members were arriving too, she began asking two young women nearby who was who, relieved to spot Mr. Caraway walking up the front stairs of the church outside a moment later.

She smiled nervously in between shots, waiting until he got in, and once his eyes adjusted to the dark inside the church vestibule, he saw her there. Haley smiled with a wave as he walked over.

"Haley, hi. You all set up?"

"Yes, I think so. I went through a few websites studying best camera angles for weddings? And I have backup batteries and a backup camera ready in case I have any issues? But I think this one should be good, right? Oh, and I typed up all the notes you gave me over the phone, but I just realized I don't know who anyone is. Like, you said to make sure to get you and your wife, and the groom's parents and his grandmother, and your Aunt Gertrude, and the whole wedding party, but I really don't know who's who, you know?"

She'd been speaking extremely fast, and was clearly quite nervous, so much so that nearby guests had taken note as well.

"Haley, don't worry. The program has all the most important people processing in on schedule. Look at the aisle there. It's wide enough for you to plant yourself near the middle somewhere and take a bunch of shots as we all process in, and then as I walk my daughter up the aisle—you know who she'll be, right?"

"Umm—"

"I'll give you a hint. She'll be wearing a really big white dress."

Haley blushed with a smile and nodded.

"Right, right, sorry. Got it."

"You'll be fine. Don't worry."

Haley did as she was told, taking many more pictures than necessary, just so she'd have a lot to choose from later on. Except for a minute or so while she turned around to take shots of the groom and best man near the front of the church, everything was going perfectly.

By the time Mr. Caraway and his daughter began processing up the aisle to Pachelbel's Canon in D, Haley had already taken well over 200 shots. All the preview images she saw in her camera's screen made her smile, and by the time she saw the bride, it took everything she had to keep back her own tears enough to focus on the job.

She'd always dreamed of having a huge wedding of her own one day, so seeing the young woman's face beneath the bridal veil, a big smile blessing her from cheek to cheek, Haley was awed by the miracle of it all. Some lucky girl had found the man of her dreams, and some lucky man had found the woman of his dreams. The two of them were about to be married in front of all their friends and family members, and everyone in attendance looked so incredibly happy to be there.

Visions of her own wedding began to appear. Her dad would walk her down the aisle, tears of joy streaming down his face, and by the time they reached the altar, Sam would shake her fiancé's hand, and bring the two of them together. It would be the happiest moment of her life. It *was* the happiest moment of her life. *How did I ever get so lucky?!*

"Haley?" Mr. Caraway seemed to whisper as he came back into focus. "Haley? We need to get to the front of the church now."

She stared at Mr. Caraway's face for a moment in confusion, before she realized they were already on top of her, and she and her tripod were fully blocking their way. The other members of the wedding party had found their way past her easily enough, but the bride's gown and trail just made the aisle that much more narrow.

"Sorry," Haley said, flustered by her foolishness, before she ran around the pews to the front again, just in time to capture the moment when the bride and groom were brought together.

She snapped pictures of the handshake that turned into a hug, and got a few good shots of Mr. Caraway kissing his daughter softly on the cheek, clearly beaming with pride as he did so.

To Haley's relief, the rest of the ceremony went off without a hitch. Because she was able to move about from a respectful distance on and off the altar, she managed to get tons of great pictures, many of which she knew the bride would love.

At the close of the ceremony, she was back with her camera and tripod in the aisle, snapping dozens more photos of first the bride and groom walking down past their family and friends, and then the rest of the bridal party and parents following afterward.

Once she was finished taking photos of everyone outside, including staged shots on the church steps, pictures of the bride and groom inside their limousine, and other random captures of guests meandering outside, Haley looked around for Mr. Caraway. When she spotted him, she walked over to thank him again for hiring her.

"Sir, I just wanted to thank you for this opportunity. This was a lot of fun, and I promise you, you'll love all the photos I took. So I guess you'll just pay me at some point in the future? Like send me a check at the doctor's office or something?"

"Haley," he said, looking alarmed. "You're not done yet. We haven't even gotten to the reception hall. There are another four hours of photos we need from you still."

For the second time that day, Haley's vision wavered, and she thought she might faint then too, not just at the shock, but at her stupidity as well.

As his words fully grabbed hold of the part of her brain that most needed to hear them, Haley nodded and apologized, assuring him that she knew all this of course, but just wasn't thinking clearly in the moment.

He reminded her of the address for the catering hall, then told her he'd see her over there in a little while.

Back in her car two minutes later, Haley was furious with herself for not realizing the job meant much more than just photographing the ceremony. Rummaging through her bags, she made sure her spare batteries and SD cards were there, then looked up and over her steering wheel as the cars around her in the parking lot started leaving for the reception.

A panic attack threatened to blow up the entire planet, but she didn't have time for that now. She had to get to the reception hall as soon as humanly possible, and then find someplace nice to take some staged pictures of the bride, groom, family members, and wedding party.

No wonder her notes mentioned shots of the bride and groom with their immediate families, and as many other "cutesy" shots as she could manage. She had wondered how she was going to do all of that in the church, and cursed herself again for being so foolish.

Twenty-five minutes later as she arrived to the reception, happy to see she was still—*miraculously*—well ahead of the bridal party, she checked in with the catering hall staff to make sure she was in the right place.

They laughed at first, thinking she was just kidding, but then the manager, a kind woman with bright blonde hair, stylish red glasses and matching red lipstick, pulled her aside with a smile.

"So uh, lemme ask you something," she asked Haley. "Is this by any chance your first time shooting a wedding?"

"Yeah, I'm sorry. I'm still figuring this all out as I go."

"Well don't you worry, honey. I'm gonna get you through this. My name is Meredith, and I'll be here all afternoon to help you anytime I can, as long as I'm not already busy somewhere else.

"Now we have some beautiful gardens right over there around the side that you can stage photos in front of, and I even have a list of suggested photos you can take if you want to use any of those. Some of our guests don't have any photographers at all, so we do that too when they hire us. I'll be happy to share all our info with you, so don't you worry."

Haley felt her entire body relax, and thanked Meredith "*so much*" for all her help and kindness.

She got all her equipment set up in the gardens a few minutes later, then flagged down the bridal party once they arrived.

Meredith had the wait staff bring out trays of champagne to welcome them too, and positioned them halfway between the entrance and the photography staging area, so they'd walk forward in the right direction.

The whole day was filled with these kinds of half-step-ahead moments, so by and large, Haley wasn't just surviving, but thriving too, and she felt a huge sense of pride when the bride and groom approached her halfway through the photos and thanked her for doing such a wonderful job.

Humility was Haley's greatest virtue, and pride forever her downfall, but today, in this moment, she decided she was *allowed* to feel good, and her heart swelled with a healthy kind of grateful pride. For all the threatened hiccups she'd stumbled through along the way, she was still doing well, and was so glad they seemed to appreciate her work.

Once the bridal party was introduced at the reception hall, the workload got much easier, and felt significantly more relaxed. The DJ team showed Haley their schedule of special dances and toasts, as well as when they planned to do the cake-cutting ceremony, so Haley was thrilled to have the head's up before everyone else.

Somewhere late in the day though, long after the cake was served and guests were up jumping around on the dance floor again, Haley took a step backward to catch a shot of the groom's father dancing with the bride, when she collided into a man walking behind her with his drink.

"Watch where you're fucking going, bitch," the man snapped, flashing her a glare so foul and mean, Haley felt all the air go out of her at once.

She started to apologize, but he was gone again quickly.

Haley recognized him from one of the photos she'd been asked to take earlier, but something else about him seemed familiar too. By the time the evening ended, and it seemed as if her job was finally done, Mr. Caraway approached her with an envelope and a soft smile on his face.

"You were fantastic, Haley. Honestly. Thank you for everything you did today. We can't wait to see all the pictures."

He kissed Haley on the cheek, and as Haley made her way to the parking lot later on, she saw the same man again from before, this time yelling at one of the valet parking boys.

"Alright, shithead. You better not have fucked anything up inside my Porsche, or you can kiss this job goodbye."

He held out a dollar bill for the boy, then got in his car and closed the door hard before driving away.

While she waited for her own car to be brought up, Haley texted Lenny.

Hey Uncle Lenny, I think it was your boss's nephew's wedding. Bumped into a tall bald guy with a white beard. Does he have really angry eyes, and yells at like everyone?

She sent it and looked around, watching as the valet boy started backing her car out in the distance. A chime from her phone caught her attention a few seconds later.

That's def him…all ok?

Yeah, all fine and wedding went great…car here, have to go

Okay, ttyl

She handed the valet a ten-dollar bill, and thanked him with a smile. He was the same boy her Uncle Lenny's boss had yelled at, so she felt bad.

As she drove home, Haley couldn't stop thinking about the day. Stumbling blocks and learning curves aside, everything had gone great, and she was thrilled to have done so well on her first real job as a photographer.

By the time she got home, she'd completely forgotten about her payment, so when she saw the envelope sticking out of her purse as she grabbed it from the passenger seat, it was like getting paid all over again.

Inside the house as she opened it up, Haley was shocked at the amount. She'd already looked up a few websites to see what the family might pay her, but the amount of the check was so much more than she'd guessed. A short, handwritten note on letterhead from the catering hall was wrapped around the check.

Dear Haley, we all appreciate everything you did today. While most of the time my attention was understandably on other things, I marveled at how swiftly you moved around the room and got up close to people to take their pictures. You were a master! I have every confidence the photos will turn out beautifully. Please accept this check as the best way I can say thank you for everything you've done. Warmest wishes, John Caraway.

Haley wanted to just jump up and down with joy, but then she saw her mother in the kitchen, staring her down like she'd done something wrong.

"Where the hell were *you* all day?" Olivia asked her.

"Mom, I had the wedding. I reminded you last night that I'd be up and out early today. And it went really well, by the way. I mean,

I made a few little mistakes, but nothing big, and you've gotta see Mr. Caraway's check! Oh, and look at this sweet note he—"

Olivia had pulled her cigarettes from her pocket and walked out the back door before Haley could continue. As the door shut behind her, Haley wanted to scream out at her. Instead, she just sighed and went up the stairs to her room.

Out on their back patio, Olivia sat down in an old plastic chair she kept near the door. Her crystal ashtray, filled to the top with the stubs of old cigarettes, welcomed her back like an old friend.

She blew out the smoke from her first puff, and listened to Haley turn the music up loudly inside her room upstairs. Then she laid her cigarette down in the ashtray, half in and half on top of an old stub, and leaned forward with her head in her hands.

Olivia had spent her day crying, throwing things around and cursing up a storm, but now she was too tired for any more of the same. Sam was back in town, Haley was still siding with him despite all the facts, and no one seemed to care what *she* thought.

The night air was warm, and the crickets loud. In the otherwise dark, silent night of her worsening depression, the ring from her cell phone gave her a new glimmer of life. She grabbed it quickly from her pocket, smiling when she saw who it was.

"Hey," she said, standing up. "What? Oh, thank God. I'm so glad it worked out. Yeah, I know. Okay. Alright, I will. No, I understand completely. We'll talk about it more next time I see you. Thank you again for doing this. Yeah. You too."

She pressed the end-call button with a flourish, then pumped her fist in triumph.

Looking up at the light coming from Haley's room, she had to stifle a new smile. While Haley wouldn't approve of these tactics, she didn't have to know her mother was behind it all anyway.

There were so many people who remembered what happened that summer, so it could have been anyone who did this. For now, it was time for Sam to face the music he'd been running from for so very long.

Chapter 9

By a quarter after 10 Sunday morning, Haley was out the door and off to the bank in Rutland. Somewhere around halfway there, Peaches finally returned her texts from the night before.

Where are you? Haley had texted her. *How did everything go at Dr. Finny's? All ok? Peaches?*

Haley didn't look at her phone while driving, but heard a whole bunch of chimes going off as she made her drive over to Rutland. Once she pulled into the parking lot at the bank a little while later, she was finally able to check the texts from Peaches, all sent in separate short phrases.

Hey! ... It went great ... I helped him examine one of his patients ... He said I wasn't sposed to, but he didnt stop me either ... LOL ... How was your wedding? ... Who did you marry again? ... LOL ... ;) ... LOL

Haley smiled and shook her head.

Wedding was great, she typed. *Have to tell you about it. You home today? Can I stop by soon?*

This time Peaches responded right away.

Sure, we're all here...come anytime

An hour later, Haley sat at the head of her Uncle Lenny's dining room table and reached out for a leftover piece of bacon he'd cooked. On a spare chair to her right, three piles of DVDs still waited to be sorted out, with another four piles stacked below them on the floor.

"So all went well at the wedding?" Lenny asked.

He looked really tired, like he hadn't slept at all, but since he was wrapped up tightly in his bathrobe and sipping a huge cup of coffee, Haley guessed that maybe they all just slept in late.

"Well, yeah, I think so," she said, "only I had a problem just now with the check I got. I went to Mom's bank in Rutland where my account is, and tried depositing the man's check, but the machine wouldn't accept it, so now I'm a little worried."

Lenny shook his head.

"I'm sure it's nothing. It's Sunday. Just go and deposit it in person with your mom tomorrow. She'll sort it out for you. May just be the machine too. New security feature or some crap like that. Did you have fun, though? Get some good free food at least?"

"Eh, it was pretty hectic. The food was okay, but I didn't eat too much. I mean, I guess I could have taken more breaks than I did, but I really wanted to do a good job, so I kept taking pictures most of the time."

"Hard work pays off," Caroline offered with a smile from her seat at the other end. She took a sip of her coffee and looked past Lenny to her right. "Even Erika knows that now. Right, honey?"

Erika rolled her eyes and offered Haley a weird smile as she walked through the room.

"She's babysitting now," Caroline went on. "She finally realized that to live the life she wants to with all her fancy gadgets, she's gotta earn the money for herself."

"The Andersons don't pay me enough for a new iPhone, Mom!" Erika yelled in from the other room.

Haley felt happier and more relaxed just spending time with them all. They were like the perfect family she never had, or at least the kind she couldn't remember ever having.

Her Uncle Lenny and Aunt Caroline were super cute together, Erika and Peaches always seemed relaxed and happy too, and everything about their house was perfect. The woodwork shined brighter, the house was always neat and clean, and everywhere she looked, things were much nicer and prettier than at her house.

If any of them came over and saw how messy her house had gotten the past few months, she would have been extremely embarrassed.

It was perhaps the *only* thing she appreciated about Olivia anymore: her mother's ability to maintain what was left of her dignity by keeping the rest of the family far, far away from their filthy domicile of despair.

"Hey," Lenny said, putting his mug down on the table as he retightened his robe. "My boss give you any trouble yesterday?"

"Oh no, it was fine, Uncle Lenny. He was a jerk, but I hardly spoke to him. He mostly left me alone."

Peaches walked back into the room from the kitchen just then, and put a plate filled with pancakes in front of Haley.

"Here you go. I heated them up. They're probably a little too soft, but Mom's reheated pancakes are still better than anyone else's, I promise."

Caroline couldn't help but look up and blush briefly, but mostly kept her sight on the crossword puzzle in front of her.

"Oh, you didn't have to do that," Haley said. "Besides, I should take you out to breakfast or lunch for covering for me at the office yesterday. In fact, we still can if you want?"

Peaches made a face. She looked too comfortable in her pajamas to want to go anywhere.

"Nah, I'm good. Rain check, though?"

Haley nodded and ate some of the pancakes, watching as her aunt and uncle soon went back into the kitchen with their coffee. Peaches was on her phone now, and Erika had disappeared already.

Haley enjoyed being treated like one of the family so much that she was ignored as if she already lived there. It actually made her smile to feel so comfortable in someone else's house like that.

Even so, she couldn't escape the loneliness that soon sank back in. Being treated like a member of the household was great if she was included, but she'd only been there 10 minutes, and already she was being ignored. She could get the same treatment at home anytime, and dish it right back at her mother anytime too.

Peaches was still there, but Haley saw she had her ear buds in as she mindlessly caught up on all her Instagram stories.

At some point in the middle of this newest mood swing, and her seventh forkful of pancakes, the phone rang in the kitchen, and Haley listened as her Uncle Lenny picked up.

"Hello? Yes, it is. Okay, but—who is this? Yes, I'm his brother-in-law. What?! Jesus Christ, are you kidding me? Okay. Yeah, I'll be right there. Do I need anything, or—right. Okay. Yeah. Okay, bye."

He slammed the phone down and reappeared in the doorway to the dining room a moment later, looking back and forth between Caroline in the kitchen and Haley at the dining room table.

"Haley, your dad was apparently arrested last night. I've got to go down to the police station and bail him out."

She just stared back at her uncle like he was joking.

"Lenny, who *was* that?" Caroline asked. "What did Sam do?"

Caroline was in the entrance to the dining room now too, and looking at Haley with a frown.

"It was some cop at the place in Woodstock. They picked Sam up last night and brought him over to the Sheriff's office for questioning. I don't think he did anything, but the guy said he was 'extremely uncooperative and belligerent', so they kept him there at the jail overnight. He still wasn't saying anything to them this morning, so they asked him for a number they could call. I gotta get dressed."

Haley just sat there in stunned silence as Lenny left the room and ran up the stairs, with Caroline following right after him. She turned to Peaches for sympathy, but saw she was just smiling to herself and bobbing her head to some kind of music.

An hour and a half later, Lenny, Caroline, and Haley sat together in silence outside the sheriff's office, still waiting for Sam to be brought out from wherever he was being held.

Lenny's near-violent leg shaking made the whole hallway seem to vibrate nervously beneath them, while Haley chewed her fingernails close to bleeding and Caroline just stared at the wall in front of them, waiting for it to do something.

An officer was supposed to have retrieved Sam for them by now, but at least another fifteen minutes had gone by without anything happening.

Finally, the officer they'd seen earlier came back out from behind a closed door and was followed right afterward by Sam, who looked both exhausted and—*unsurprisingly*—guilty as all hell.

"He's all yours," the officer said to them.

Sam avoided eye contact with all three of them, signing a sheet of paper and waiting for them to lead the way out.

Their long walk to Lenny's car was even more silent than their wait for him inside had been.

These three souls, for Sam, were his whole world at the moment, and he knew he'd just let them down all over again.

Lenny was Sam's best friend on Earth, whether or not Lenny thought the same about him. When Sam gave the officer Lenny's number, he understood Caroline might come with him too, but he hoped she wouldn't. And Haley, well, Haley was an unexpected surprise of the very worst kind.

Haley was his offspring, and as such, Sam knew he'd set a horrible example for her as a parent. There was no way he'd ever forget the look in her eyes when they first saw each other by the lake, but he knew by the slouch of her shoulders now that this was yet another disaster in a long string of disappointing daddy-daughter moments between them.

And Caroline's face, as always, spoke of a special kind of brainless compassion. She was falling in love with him all over again, he guessed, and he wasn't sure yet what he thought about that. It sure was a recipe for disaster, but what else was new?

It wasn't until they were halfway home to Ludlow that Lenny finally looked at Sam in the rear-view mirror and coughed.

"So uh, any chance you'll enlighten us about what the hell happened, and why I just shelled out 500 bucks to get you outta there? Or will we once again be left confused as to what's going on in that tiny brain of yours?"

Sam's vision remained fixed out the back passenger-side window, and Lenny noticed Haley look sideways at him from the back for an answer. Sam deserved Lenny's dig, he knew, but he needed an extra minute to process it all, especially with Haley sitting right there next to him.

Still, there was no point keeping them in suspense any longer, so Sam prepared to give them the answer they were all so desperate for. The sin he'd been trying to avoid for so many years, to keep as far away from Haley as he could, was once again coming back to haunt him. No matter how many times he tried to walk away from it, to *run* away from it, Sam knew it was all pointless.

Taking a deep breath and clearing his throat briefly, Sam watched the scenery pass by one moment longer, then gave them the words he knew he'd have to surrender at last.

"They asked me to tell them what I knew about Kerry Ann Jefferson's death."

Just the sound of the girl's name filled the car like a stench. It was a name they never discussed, a name they never dared even speak out loud at all, lest it somehow summon her ghost back from the grave.

Hearing Sam had been arrested again, brought back in for a new round of questioning about the case, was like knowing the darkest part of all their lives had returned to haunt them once more, no matter how much they'd all hoped it was gone forever.

Though Sam was always the center of the investigation in the past, the weight of that girl's name on *all* their lives was impossible to shake loose. It was destined to turn their stomachs each and every time it was spoken.

When they got back to Lenny's house, Sam was the last to come inside. They all waited for him in the living room, as if the conversation to follow was mandatory now, and he should know it.

Peaches was gone, and breakfast cleaned up by the time they returned, but Caroline put on a fresh pot of coffee while they waited for Sam.

She and Lenny had already poured their cups when they heard the front door open and close, and they exchanged a nervous glance as Sam finally appeared in the living room a moment later.

He sat down in a chair by himself, and finally looked up at each of them with a dark smile.

"I'm not surprised this happened," he said. "The case was closed, but never cold, and though I stayed up here for a year, and gave them my address in Vegas after that, they never told me it was over, so I had no reason to believe it ever was."

He paused and shook his head.

"None of this is normal. I hope you can at least recognize that. The case should have changed course years ago, and I've already told everyone who matters exactly what happened that night. The fact that some asshole out there still has a bone to pick with me, still trying to make something out of all this? It's just ridiculous."

Though each of them in turn locked eyes with him briefly as he spoke, no one responded, and their eyes soon found various spots of the living room floor more worthy of their thoughtful analysis.

For the first time in his life, Sam realized they doubted his version of the story, and seemed to believe there was more he'd never told them.

"Look, I don't know what else I can say here. If you guys don't even believe me, I should have never come back."

He stood up and began to walk out, but Lenny stopped him.

"Sam, wait! Hold on now. We didn't say we don't believe you. This is just as crazy for us as it is for you, okay? I thought this was over too. But listen, man, if you won't even cooperate with the police, well, I mean, what does *that* say? What message are you giving them? Or us for that matter?"

Sam kept his back to them, and after a moment, he sunk his hands in his jeans pockets with a shrug to no one in particular.

"I don't know what you want me to say, Len."

He waited at first, then turned around finally and looked at them all again.

"I told them my story years ago. What the fuck are they expecting me to say now? Bringing me in last night was dumb. They even seemed to think so. No one there was anyone I dealt with years ago anyway. It's not like I have any enemies among the new recruits. Sergeant *Fender Benders* is retired, and Captain Kipps moved up to Maine. This is a joke."

"Then why did they call you in?" Caroline asked, speaking for the first time since they picked him up.

He looked at her briefly, another wide valley of history between them, history that would have to stay between them for now, and then he averted his eyes again quickly.

"Apparently they got an anonymous tip from someone," he told the wood floor a foot in front of him. "Maybe someone who heard I was back and wanted to make my life miserable all over again? But they wouldn't say who it was. Know anyone like that?"

He looked wide-eyed over at Haley as he asked this, and Lenny jumped in quickly.

"Now hang on a second. You don't think Livi did this, do you?"

"Bingo! Give the man his prize behind curtain number two!"

"Jesus, Sam. That's crazy, and I'll tell you why."

"Oh yeah? Please do. Please tell me why it's crazy, Len."

"Well for one thing, Livi would have used her own name. She has no reason to hide *anything* from you. She hates you, and you know it. We all know it. No reason to make an anonymous tip then, right?"

A moment of silence followed this, but once Sam broke into a big smile, they all smiled too, even Haley.

"Okay, fair point," he acknowledged.

A longer silence followed this, with nothing but a slight gurgle from the coffee pot letting out steam in the kitchen, reminding Sam that healthier sanity was just a cup of coffee away.

"You want some coffee?" Caroline offered. She walked toward the kitchen right away. "I just made a fresh pot."

"No, actually, no, thank you. I should just head home and go to sleep. Didn't really sleep well in the cell last night. Would one of you mind driving me back?"

He said it to the room, but had locked eyes with Caroline more than anyone else.

Lenny nodded and grabbed his keys off the kitchen island.

"If I knew you wanted to go right back to your place again, I wouldn't have driven you all the way over here," he said.

"I'm still moving stuff over, but I live in Ludlow now," he told him, offering Haley a soft smile. "I'll show you. It's not far."

A minute later, they were both gone.

Caroline walked back over and sat down next to Haley on the couch. They didn't speak at all, just sat and moped in their separate space, in their separate way. Each had their own long history with Sam, yet both still loved him in their own stupid way.

In her head, Caroline went back 25 years. She remembered the day she first met Sam, years before she met Lenny, and she thought about all the many things he'd done to her over the years, as well as everything she'd ever done to him.

"Aunt Caroline, I think I'm gonna go now too, actually. Could you tell Peaches I'll text her later?"

"Yeah, sure thing," Caroline said.

She offered Haley a big fake smile as she left, and watched her as she disappeared out the kitchen and down the hall, the front door opening and closing a few seconds later.

Once she was gone, Caroline stood up again and walked into the kitchen with her mug, topping it off with more coffee, and then cream and sugar. She took a long sip, and looked over at the living room where Sam had just been, thinking once more on all he'd said. And all he hadn't.

A moment later, she turned her attention to the sliding glass door to the yard, and approached it slowly.

Staring out through the glass, Caroline looked past the deck and her potted plants toward the tree near the back of the yard. More precisely to the small tree house built between its two large trunks, and she allowed herself a moment to remember, to recall what she'd seen out there that night almost seventeen years earlier.

Chapter 10

On her short drive home that afternoon, Haley wasn't sure if she'd even ask her mother about Sam's arrest. Bringing him up at all was always risky, and if she *had* been the one to get him arrested, nothing good would come from them arguing about it anyway.

As she pulled up to the house a minute later though, she was surprised to see her grandmother's car in the driveway, and knew it would be an even worse idea to bring it up now.

Phyllis had stopped by unannounced, Haley was sure of it, and she was just as sure Olivia was pissed by the surprise visit. For all the tension that existed between Haley and Olivia, Haley still sympathized with her mother's ongoing issues with her grandmother.

The two were already shouting loud enough for Haley to hear them from the driveway when she first got out of her car.

"Listen to *me,* Olivia. You don't get to tell me what I can or cannot say about my granddaughter *or* her future. I just don't want you to fuck this up for her any more than you already have."

"You have no idea what you're talking about, Mom. As a matter of fact, Haley does fine without me as it is, and she's been doing just fine without Sam too, for the record. You're clueless as usual, so just butt out of business you have no place snooping around in!"

Haley opened the door just then and stared at them both, then shut the door quietly and put her purse down on the table as they watched her.

She walked around them into the kitchen without saying hello, pulling a bottle of water out from the open pack on the floor.

"Hello dear," Phyllis tried warmly, but Haley didn't respond.

Olivia and Phyllis exchanged an uncertain glance, then watched as Haley walked back past them again and sat down in their little living room at the front of the house.

She twisted the cap off her bottle and took a few gulps, then resealed the bottle and put it down on a coaster next to her. Looking at her mom and grandmother at last, and carefully sizing them up, she decided she didn't want to get caught up in their screaming match.

"You know," she said, "I'm 22 years old now, and while that may not make me an adult yet in either of your small minds, I am one regardless. I think for myself, I feel for myself, I generally have to feed myself more often than not too, and I—"

"Haley, listen—" Olivia started.

"No. You listen," she barked back. "Both of you."

The two women exchanged another glance, this time more seriously, then came around and sat on the couch across from Haley to listen.

"My father is not a perfect man. I can see that very clearly all on my own. But you know what? No one in this family is even close to perfect, short of *maybe* Peaches, but give her enough time, and I'm sure you'll all find a way to corrupt her too."

Haley watched as Olivia rolled her eyes and Phyllis made a face as she looked away.

"I appreciate that maybe one or both of you actually cares enough about me to try to protect me from whatever happened years ago, but I have this thing called the internet? And I can look up news stories without waiting around for either of you to fill in all the details for me."

"Haley—" Olivia tried again.

"Look, all I'm saying is, you don't know him like I do, okay? He's always feeling super guilty about the past, but he's not a bad guy, no matter what you all think of him. Don't ask me how I know this, but I do, okay?"

Olivia opened her mouth to speak, but Phyllis put her hand out and interrupted instead.

"Haley, your mother and I agree with you…mostly."

"No, Mom, I *don't*," Olivia said.

"Well, I certainly do," Phyllis went on, "but there are some things you just don't understand about what happened, Haley, nor should you. You may not be a child anymore, but that has nothing to do with it. No news story you read could possibly capture all the nonsense of that situation, or the bullshit your father put your mom through back then."

Olivia was caught completely off-guard by the statement, no less shocking when coupled with her mother's hand squeezing her own as she said it, and she turned her head halfway at her in surprise, a look of deep confusion written all over her face.

Phyllis didn't ration out affection very often at all, and Olivia wondered if she should grab her phone quickly to record it.

"I am happy to be your father's biggest fan in this family," Phyllis went on, "short of you perhaps, but your mom has every right to be pissed at him just the same. And *you* don't get to tell her she shouldn't be, understand me? All moms are entitled to their feelings, even the fucked up, bat-shit crazy ones. It's what we're made of. It's who we are and who we'll always be. It's the only reason we stay sane, to be honest with you, because we're more used to our emotional rollercoasters than men can ever hope to be. That's our *privilege* as women, and as mothers, so don't you dare let anyone ever take that away from you. And I sure as hell won't let you take it away from your mother right now either."

Haley couldn't help but smirk at this, and saw Olivia holding back a raw smile of her own. She'd never heard her grandmother talk like this before.

"So don't pay any attention to your mother and me when we're bickering, just as I try my best to turn a deaf ear when you two go at it. It's part of our relationship. It's just our way."

She paused and thought to herself for a moment.

"Sometimes fighting with our children is our way of protecting them, you understand? Mothers were put on this Earth to mother, and goddamnit, that's what we're gonna do, so you may as well get used to it!"

Olivia stood up a moment later with a growing smile, and turned from them both on her way to the kitchen.

"You're so full of shit," she muttered as she walked away.

Phyllis made a face to Haley, and after a few seconds, they both started laughing. It was the first time in years Haley could remember any of them getting along so well, even though even now they were fighting over their right to argue.

She smiled at her grandmother, then watched as she leaned back into the couch and rested her head on the cushion like she needed a nap.

Haley felt the strangest desire to walk over and sit down next to her grandmother, and cuddle up close to her like she hadn't done in years, only she didn't want to upset her mom at all if she did.

Over in the kitchen, Olivia opened the refrigerator and peered inside, soon finding exactly what she needed to survive the moment. To the surprise of the others, she promptly brought not one but three new bottles of beer out into the living room, handing Haley the first, then holding the second one out in front of her mother until Phyllis opened her eyes and took it from her with a twisted smile.

"I haven't had a beer in years," Phyllis said, looking at Haley in shock as if the idea itself was completely ludicrous.

Olivia took the caps off all their bottles with a quick flourish each time, each cap rolling away this way and that, and then she held her own bottle out high over the coffee table for a toast.

"To mothers and daughters," she said, "even if we'd rather just kill each other and be done with it."

They clinked their bottles together, and each one took a sip, though Olivia quickly showed herself a master by gulping down half her bottle in one shot.

In the long silence that followed, each woman stewed inside her own little pot, and no one wanted to be the first to speak next.

Phyllis thought about the week ahead of her, and her plans for Mahjong with friends on Wednesday. She remembered the lamb stew she promised to make for Alan, and their plans to drive down to Long Island the following weekend for a Bar Mitzvah.

Haley thought about the wedding, and the new lens she decided she'd treat herself with using Mr. Caraway's big check. Thoughts of the lens soon brought her to Sam and his new house, where she hoped to photograph the lake and surrounding scenery one day too. She still worried about whether or not things could ever be normal for the two of them again, but for her part, she was certainly willing to try.

Olivia thought about Sam too, and about the call she'd received the night before, and the texts Lenny had sent her.

"Hey Mom?" Haley said, looking across at her sympathetically, hoping she wouldn't flip out. "Do you know anything about Dad being arrested last night?"

Olivia didn't look at her, and took another long swig before answering with her attention.

Phyllis, who had closed her eyes to think, opened them briefly before shutting them again. She didn't seem all that surprised by the news though.

"Uncle Lenny said they wanted to ask your dad some questions," Olivia said, looking at Haley intently.

She purposely said no more than this, and in the long stare the two of them exchanged, it was clear Haley wasn't satisfied yet.

"No. I know that. I mean, do you know anything about how his arrest came about? Apparently there was an anonymous tip or something like that?"

Olivia blinked once, and then lied.

"No? I don't know anything about that."

Phyllis said nothing, having no desire to make the situation any worse, and Haley reluctantly let it go as well. She guessed her father probably had more than one enemy left in Ludlow anyway.

"I need to stop by the bank tomorrow morning before work," Haley announced then, happy to change the subject. "I was there this morning, but the machine didn't take my check. Uncle Lenny said that sometimes happens, that I should just deposit it through you tomorrow."

"Yeah," Olivia said, looking away. "That sometimes happens."

She finished her beer and put it down, glancing over to see if Phyllis was drinking any of her own.

Olivia and Phyllis looked at each other, and then Olivia looked down at the full bottle of beer in Phyllis's hands to make her intentions known. Phyllis was more than happy to get it out of her hands a moment later.

As Haley took another long chug from her own bottle, and Olivia made a healthy start on her second, Phyllis stood up and walked around to the hallway by the door. She put on her windbreaker and picked up her purse, then paused, staring at the closed door. By the time she was ready to speak, her daughter and granddaughter were both watching her.

"Olivia? Be careful," she said, still looking at the doorknob ahead of her. "Some sleeping dogs should not be roused from their evening slumber."

Olivia looked away and raised her eyebrows, taking another long sip from the beer.

"I'll see you ladies soon. Have a nice evening."

"Bye, Grandma," Haley said, grateful to spot half a smile on her grandmother's face before she was gone.

When she looked back toward her mother, familiar disgust had reappeared on her face.

"The woman puts ice in her red wine but turns her nose up at a bottle of beer? Seriously?"

Haley just smirked, then glanced over at the cable box and saw it was almost 3:30 already. Her Sunday hadn't gone as she'd wanted it to at all. She looked at her mother again, hoping she'd make eye contact, but when she didn't, she decided to leave it alone.

On her way to the stairs though, Haley noticed the phone said there were four missed calls, all from the same number.

"Mom, what's this? Someone called four times, and you didn't pick up?"

Haley grabbed the receiver and started dialing, but Olivia turned around quickly to stop her.

"No, wait. Hang up."

Haley hung up again, and looked at her mother with a frown.

"Why? Who is it?"

"That was the sheriff's office. They called here first looking for you, because he wasn't giving them anyone's number. I finally picked up and told them you were out. Gave them Uncle Lenny's number instead."

Haley looked at her a moment, annoyed and frustrated, but not at all shocked. Nor was it even slightly surprising to hear her mother knew the sheriff's number by heart.

Not wanting to start any new trouble, Haley was up the stairs to her room, beer and water bottles in hand, before Olivia could say any more.

In the newfound silence and solitude of the living room, Olivia listened as Haley shut the door to her bedroom upstairs. There was too much going on to let her get caught up in matters too. She needed to keep her out of this, and would do all she had to, even to the point of lying to her face, to protect her. If she found out more, so be it, but she was determined to keep this brew bottled as long as she had to.

Resting her bottle down on the table, Olivia pulled her phone out and started swiping rapidly. She paused a few swipes in, staring at the screen, then reluctantly continued.

She pressed the call button and waited. It rang twice and was on the third ring before it stopped.

"Hi," she said. "You free to meet now? Yeah. Okay. Yeah, I know where that is. I'll be right there. Okay, I will. Bye."

She got up and walked around to the front door, grabbing her keys and purse. Looking up the stairs, she thought about calling up, but could hear the music already on loudly in Haley's room. *She wouldn't hear me anyway.*

##

Lying on her bed upstairs, Haley texted Peaches back.
So all went well at Dr. Finny's???

Yep...and he even said I could sub for you again anytime....so watch your back! Hahahaha

Lol ok. Was it busy? I know there were only 2 or 3 scheduled appointments, but sometimes people walk in.

No, not busy at all…two people n a third canselled
Ok cool. I'm glad.

Haley stared at the phone, wondering if she should ask Peaches what *she* thought about her dad. They'd never really talked about anything like that before, or at least not much. Haley needed a sounding board though, so even if Peaches had nothing to offer, she wanted to ask.

Can I call you quick?
Sure.

Haley turned off the music and called Peaches. It rang four times before she answered.

"Sorry," Peaches said. "I was just talking to Roger online. He says hi."

"No problem. How is he?"

"He's just being annoying, acting weird. I don't know why."

"Boys are weird," Haley said with a sigh. "Trust me. Just give him space. Guys like that. Messes with their heads sometimes too."

Peaches laughed on the other end, and Haley smiled.

"So what's up?"

"Well, it's just this thing with my dad. I hardly know him, you know? But I don't know what to do. Like, everyone either hates him or talks about him like he's really messed up, so I'm scared to get too close. I never talk to Erika anymore, but I was wondering what *you* think. Like, what have your mom and dad told you about my dad?"

"Eh, I don't really hear them talk about him much," Peaches said, "and I haven't seen him in a long time, so I don't really remember him too well."

"Oh, okay."

"But my mom and dad seem to like him. They talk about him like he's their friend, and Mom once said your dad may have been framed back then, so I dunno. Maybe he's just had bad luck."

"Yeah, Grandpa said the same thing to me once too. It's just so messed up, though. He seems like a really sweet guy, and he doesn't say bad stuff about my mom at all, like ever. No matter how much she goes off on him, he's always been quiet about it. I think he might feel guilty though, like, for whatever went down with that girl. You know about what happened, though, right?"

"Yeah, Erika told me once. Weird."

"Yeah."

Haley realized as they both sat in silence that there really wasn't much more to say, and she wasn't feeling any better for the conversation anyway. That's when Peaches surprised her.

"I'm pretty sure he's completely innocent, though."

"What? I mean, I hope you're right, but why do you say that?"

"I'd tell you, but I don't want you to laugh at me."

"No, no, of course not. I won't. Just tell me."

"Well, I think I met the girl in one of our classes at the shop."

"Who? What girl?"

"Kerry Ann."

Haley shook her head at her, as if she could see her doing it. Just hearing the name unsettled Haley, but it was that much worse knowing Peaches seemed to be inferring something else.

"No, Peaches. That all happened a long time ago. You hadn't even been born yet. There's no way you could have met her."

Haley had gone from sad to annoyed, and she was beginning to understand why some people didn't like Peaches and her weirdness.

"I didn't like *meet her*, meet her. I mean, I met her in one of my journeys. In my Shamanism class. We connected spiritually, and I think she told me in a way that your dad was innocent."

Haley shook her head again.

"Peaches, I'm sorry. I know I promised I wouldn't laugh, and trust me, I'm not laughing at all, but that's just crazy. Like, I dunno, nuts, you know? You couldn't have seen her. She's dead."

She listened on the other end for Peaches to say something, and when she didn't, she spoke again, but nicer.

"Look, I'm sorry. I shouldn't have said that. It's just, as much as I like what you say this girl said or did or whatever, that's still pretty freaky, you have to admit. Right? Know what I mean?"

"Okay," Peaches offered. "I know what I saw and heard, but it's cool. I didn't expect you to believe it."

Ten seconds of silence filled the air between them then.

"Hey Peaches, I gotta go. I'll talk to you later, though, okay?"

Haley ended the call before Peaches could reply, then tossed her phone across the bed and shook her head again.

If the phone call was supposed to make her feel better, it had only made things worse. Peaches was always like that, though: unpredictable. Fun and flighty one second, but serious and strange the next.

Even so, after a while, Haley began to regret some of what she said, and grabbed her phone quickly to apologize by text.

I'm sorry. I just don't know what to think anymore, and your spiritual stuff wasn't what I wanted to hear right now. Sorry for snapping at you.

Thirty seconds later, her phone chimed back with a response.

No problem! I understand! :)

Chapter 11

The coffee machine beeped three times, and Caroline rolled into the kitchen like a robot reporting for duty. The first cup would help pry at least one of her eyes open wide enough to pack lunches and drinks for Lenny and the girls.

She poured the coffee into her mug, then opened the sugar bowl and practically threw the first spoonful across the top, most of it landing on the countertop and some on the floor.

"Shit," her mouth managed to say.

After she cleaned it up and finished stirring in her cream a couple minutes later, she heard Lenny walking down the stairs by the front of the house. As if fulfilling some strange court order, she fell into her usual position, her back to the counter and her mug to her face, ready to receive his kiss on her right cheek as normal.

"G'mornin'," he mumbled, leaning in just enough to allow his lips to form a kiss halfway between her ear and her lips.

"Morn—" she offered back in a grunt.

Cavemen and women exchanged more thoughtful morning greetings than either of them usually did.

Lenny's pure hatred for mornings was matched only by Caroline's, and she took pride in the fact that the girls seemed similarly in tune with the family's elemental programming. It certainly worked out well when the girls were babies, and Caroline's parents often told her she was the luckiest woman on Earth to have two kids who both slept so soundly.

It mattered just as much now whenever they went on vacation together as a family. There was no need to wake up early, not even for Walt Disney World. What was the point of losing quality sleep when the parks would be open all day anyway?

"Do you have any idea where I put my tie clip on Friday?" Lenny asked, some nervous adrenaline temporarily superseding his need for caffeine.

Lenny began searching the kitchen for it as Caroline's gaze fell on the shiny item sitting right beside the toaster. She thought about saying the words, 'oh there it is, over there by the toaster,' but her mouth didn't seem willing to open up for anything other than coffee. Instead, she just stared at it for a while until Lenny walked by again, and she managed to point with her head in the direction of the toaster.

"Oh! Thank you."

He clipped it on, then grabbed a mug from the cabinet and poured himself a cup of coffee. Once he'd taken a few sips, he positioned himself right next to her against the counter, and the two of them stared out at nothing in particular for the next three minutes in silence.

Erika was down the stairs after that, also looking sleepy, but she gagged at the thought of coffee. Instead, she made a beeline for the fridge and pulled out a yogurt and the container of orange juice.

Lenny and Caroline soon found themselves watching her eat and drink, and in between swipes and types on her phone, Erika finally noticed them, looking up at her zombie parents like they were crazy.

"Mom?" she asked, noticing her mother still in her bathrobe.

"Huh?" Caroline responded.

"Did you make me a lunch today? And don't you have work?"

Lenny glanced sideways at Caroline now too, soon wondering the same thing. He couldn't remember her saying she was off.

"There might be some leftover vegetable quiche in the fridge," she said, walking over and opening it up. "Or maybe not."

She turned around and smiled at them both, then crossed the room and sat down on one of the couches with her coffee. Lenny and Erika exchanged the same confused, bemused look, similar thoughts running through both their heads.

"Hon? You okay?" Lenny asked.

Caroline looked up from the magazine she'd opened, took note of their curious stares, then went back to the magazine again.

"Yeah, I'm fine. Just thought I'd go in late last night."

Lenny looked at Erika quickly, then back to Caroline.

"You mean late *this morning?*"

"What? Yeah. I got in late today, so I'm going in this morning."

"Oookay," he said, piecing it together. "Okay. So you had a meeting last night after work? I don't remember you mentioning anything about—"

"Mrs. Tate. She asked me to come by again. I didn't want to say no. She kept me out later than expected, so I left a voicemail with Debbie. Said I'd be in a little late this morning. And honey, there may not be quiche, but there's plenty of cold cuts still in the meat drawer. If you're running late, I can make you guys sandwiches in a minute. Just lemme read this first."

It was like her coffee had suddenly kicked in, finally reached the deep recesses of her brain that needed it most, and she was present and conscious in the room for the very first time that morning.

"No, no, I'm running late anyway," Lenny said, looking as Erika picked up her yogurt and dumped the empty container in the garbage. She rinsed off her cup and spoon, leaving them both in the dish rack.

"Dad, can you drive me?" she asked. "I'm low on gas. I can get a ride home later."

"Yeah, sure," Lenny said, computing it all. "Where's your sister? Weren't you gonna drive her to school today?"

"She left early. Said she had a breakfast meeting."

While not too much surprised Lenny about Peaches anymore, the concept of his 16-year-old daughter having a breakfast *meeting* before school still took him a moment to process, and in the quick glances he shared with Erika and Caroline, it was clear they were thinking the same.

The two of them said their quick goodbyes to Caroline, and were out the door a moment later. Once she heard the car start and then pull out of the driveway, Caroline looked up finally, and allowed herself to think.

Sam had said he'd call her in the morning, but he didn't mention whether he'd call the house phone or her cell, so she was scared to go off to work. After she took a few more sips of her coffee though, she decided he must not have meant the house line. He wasn't that careless.

She pulled her cell out and looked it over again. It was on and working fine, but he still hadn't called, so she decided she'd just hop in the shower and keep the cell phone close by in case he called her while she was still in the bathroom.

##

Over at The Hatchery down in town, Peaches sat with Roger having breakfast. She looked across the table at him with a smile, but he didn't seem to notice it. He was too preoccupied with what she'd just said to him.

Peaches was much smarter than most kids her age, but she *was* still a kid in many ways, and often stumbled over herself trying to make people happy. Today, Roger wasn't having it. In fact, he wasn't sure why he even agreed to meet her there at all.

"Why don't you at least come again next time, and if you think something is crazy or weird, just tell us, and we'll talk about it. When you storm out like that, there's nothing else we can say."

"Peaches, there already is nothing else you can say. Your friends—they're really nice and all, but I'm just not into it. I don't believe in God anymore, and I don't think it's right that you're trying to force this crap on me. It's not cool, and it's starting to piss me off. Can't we just chill and eat breakfast or whatever, without you constantly bringing this shit up?"

He was immediately annoyed with himself for raising his voice. His mother always taught him not to, especially in this 'little white town', as she called it. Strangers will look across the room when anyone raises their voice, but when your skin is dark, they fear you too, and rumors start to spread. None of it is right, she said, but it is a fact, and facts matter.

Roger offered a fake smile to the woman across the way, who he could tell was staring him down from behind her napkin. *God forgive me for raising my voice, lady. Geez.*

Peaches looked hurt now, and Roger was sorry to have made her feel that way, but he was also very *not* sorry. He hated being pushed around at home, and he didn't want to feel that way from his friends either. Why couldn't she realize that? Why did she always have to be so pushy?

She looked up at him with a soft, sad smile, then picked up a piece of bacon and took a bite without taking her eyes off him.

"Look. Can I *ushay* one more *ting*?" she asked through chews.

"Yeah, sure. What?" he asked, trying to relax.

Peaches finished chewing, then took a conscious breath to focus as she looked at him.

"We could all learn stuff from you too, you know. I'm not saying we'll all become atheists, but who knows? You might teach us all to be better people just by being there and arguing with us about stuff."

He smiled a moment later and shook his head with a sigh of defeat. Why did she have to be so incredibly sweet all the time?

"I'll *think* about it," he finally offered.

Peaches smiled, happy with his answer, and then bobbed up and down in her seat a little. Roger would come back to the circle. She just knew it.

As she looked out the window a few seconds later in between bites of her toast, she spotted her grandfather walking toward them. She knocked briefly on the window, but he was too far away, so she just watched him get closer instead.

He was moving much slower than he usually did, and was using a cane. *Why don't old people just move around more so they don't ever get that old and crusty*, she thought to herself. And then her mind drifted to what she herself would be like as an old woman. She pictured herself dancing down the street, everyone stopping to applaud her, and marvel at how nimble she was, and the thought made her smile with a giggle.

A moment later, she realized her grandfather was very close now, so she knocked on the window again and waved. This time he looked over at The Hatchery and saw who it was. He offered her a half smile, took note of Roger, then kept on walking without waving back.

Up ahead, Alan spotted Phyllis's friend Nancy Hensley walking toward him from further up the block. He forced a big smile onto his face as they approached each other, and he started rehearsing what he should say to her. Nancy always smelled much better than she looked, but she was pretty enough just the same. She also had a knack for coming on very strongly, so Alan often felt at odds about how he should talk to her.

This was the first time he'd seen her by herself in quite a while too, as he usually only saw her with Phyllis. By the time they met on the sidewalk, his rehearsed greeting meant nothing, as she launched quickly into a speech once he was close enough to hear her begin it.

"Here he is," she said, "the man at the top of Ludlow's most intriguing family tree."

"Oh, stop it."

He said it with a little laugh, but he was already cringing at what she might say, and why she'd said it that way to begin with—though Sam's recent reappearance certainly must have had something to do with it.

"I'm just teasing, honey, don't worry. To be honest, I don't know how you do it, keeping track of all those women. Your wife, your daughter, and your three granddaughters—they all look up to you, you know."

Alan *sincerely* doubted that. Olivia may have been something of a daddy's girl growing up, owing mostly to Phyllis being such a colossal bitch, but everyone in his family kept him at arm's length, and he'd gotten used to that a long time ago.

Their loss, he felt. Besides, he couldn't really fault them for doing what he himself had always done right back to each of them. His distancing tactics had been faithfully taught to him as a boy, and he was long used to getting treated like that in return.

"Your granddaughter is gorgeous, by the way. Why is she not dating anyone, do you know?"

"Which one are you talking about, Nancy?"

"Well Haley, of course. Erika's still in high school, isn't she? And she wears far too much makeup, as I'm sure you've noticed, and the other one, the little girl with the strange name, she's still in grammar school, right? I don't know, I don't keep track of all the kids, but Haley, she's a woman now. She should be with some nice boy. Or is she a lesbian? Is she? I hadn't heard if so."

"What?!"

"So many of them are now, you know. It's like the internet is tricking them into it or something. I mean, I like Ellen, but sometimes I just don't know what to think, you know? There was a program on brainwashing on recently. Maybe there really is something going on. Have you ever—"

"Haley's not a lesbian," he interrupted her with his hand out. "I've heard her complain enough about not having a boyfriend, so I assure you, she does *not* prefer the companionship of women. She doesn't even like her own mother, for crying out loud."

Mrs. Hensley thought this was just about the funniest thing she'd heard all day, and she laughed and laughed after he said it. Her perfume hit Alan hard just then too, so it was unfortunate timing that she'd also taken the moment to touch him gently on the arm as she collected herself.

He couldn't deny it. He just wanted to lean in and kiss her full on the lips right there and then. He imagined he'd be giving the town something *else* to talk about if he ever did something so outrageous. *If I manage to outlive Phyllis,* he thought to himself, quickly dismissing the thought.

"Well, she'll find some nice young man soon then, I'm sure," Nancy said. "She's too cute not to, you know? And there's a good man out there who'd be lucky to find a good woman like her as well. Good women are hard to find though, you know, and whoever that lucky man is will realize it when he meets her."

"You don't need to tell me that, Nancy. I'm married to a nurse. You don't think that worked out well for me?"

She gave him another hearty laugh at this, and then, sizing him up quietly, she said, "Well, you two *both* did okay. That's true."

Alan nodded at her with a nervous grin, not sure what else to say, but as Nancy was an expert at these kinds of chats, she jumped in first before he needed to.

"Okay, Alan. It was good to see you. I better get going. Have to get my steps in, or Doctor Finny will have my hide. You have a nice day now, okay? Bye."

She turned away quickly and continued on in the direction she'd been heading, back up toward the supermarket.

"Okay, you too. Bye," he called after her.

I'd like to have your hide.

He shrugged off the encounter, then went on his way up the block. Who Haley did or did not date was not only completely off his radar, but completely off his list of things he ever chose to care about too. As he glanced back to get one more look at Nancy Hensley though, he was both glad she was gone and sorry to be rid of her at the same time.

##

Forty-five minutes away in downtown Rutland, Haley spotted her mother's car parked off to the side of the bank as she got out of her own car near the front. She eyed it carefully, like it was an extension of her mother herself, and in many ways it was.

Olivia's 1993 Ford Aerostar was the last of its kind in the region, making replacement parts almost impossible to come by whenever she needed something, which was fast becoming a twice-yearly occurrence. A machine boasting significant wear and tear, the Aerostar, much like its current owner, had survived countless attacks to its frame *and* interior, yet still managed to get from point a to point b without blowing up.

As soon as Haley walked in through the front doors of the bank, check proudly in hand, her mother took note of her, and looked at the time on her monitor with a scowl.

"Don't you have to be at Dr. Finny's office? I thought you'd be in by now. I was waiting for you."

"I stopped by the office first, opened up and got the coffee machine set up for him. As soon as he came in, I told him I had to come over here and deposit the check. He was annoyed at first, but when I reminded him that once I cashed the check, I could afford to have my lunch delivered all week, he let me go."

Olivia smirked. *The Almighty Dollar wins yet again.*

"Give me the check, and I'll run it through myself quick so you can get back to work. I'm sure it's fine. The bank probably just blocked the deposit because it was a Sunday. You know how Mish is with ID."

Mish was Michelle, Olivia's boss. She'd been the bank manager for the past 11 years since their previous manager, Stewart Rollins, had retired.

Haley spotted Mish on the phone in her large office in the back, and offered her a quick wave as they walked by on their way to the tellers. Mish waved back briefly as she kept talking to the person on the phone.

Once she was on the other side of the Plexiglas wall, Olivia typed something into the computer, and deposited the check from Mr. Caraway into the machine. Haley watched casually, barely able to focus, as her mind was now stuck on her father. She wondered what Sam was doing for work now, and whether he'd be staying in town after all. He'd seemed so positive when they'd spoken by the lake, but after the police thing, she wondered if he'd even bother sticking around.

"Ugh. It's not working, Haley. Hold on. I'll ask Mish."

Haley nodded and stared out at the parking lot and her mother's car. She knew she'd gotten it soon after Sam left town the first time, and how bruised it had been even back then. Had she bought it with all that damage, though? She couldn't remember.

"Excuse me, Haley?" Mish called from her office.

"Yeah?"

Olivia was standing in the doorway of Mish's office, and they were both looking her way.

"Could you come here for a minute, please?"

Haley walked over with a smile. They both looked concerned though, and Mish was holding the check like it was a term paper with a bad grade.

"Oh, no. Is there a problem?"

"Honey, your mother says you just got this check as payment for a wedding?"

"Yeah. On Saturday. Why, what's wrong?"

"Well, the man who wrote you this check? John Caraway? He died. The home office in Burlington locked his account right away yesterday morning when they got word he'd passed."

"Oh my God," Haley said, swatting a hand to her mouth. "When did it happen?" she asked a few seconds later through parted fingers. "I don't understand. I just saw him Saturday night. The reception was over early, by like 6 o'clock. I know there was an after party somewhere, though."

"All it says here is that he's deceased as of June 10th."

"But that was this past Saturday. How is that even possible?"

Olivia put a hand on Haley's shoulder and shook her head.

"Honey, something must have happened to him. He may have had an accident or a heart attack that night. You said he was an older man, right?"

"Yeah, but he seemed so healthy."

"Well, things happen. Listen, I'm sure the family will take care of your payment for the wedding soon enough. Don't worry."

"I'm not—I don't care about the check, Mom. *God.* This is crazy. He was so sweet. I can't believe this."

The next hour was a blur, and by the time she got back to Dr. Finny's office, Haley had stopped crying and taken the time to wipe her eyes well before walking in.

She told him what happened, her voice breaking as she did. He didn't seem to care about the specifics, which was at least some comfort to Haley after what her mother had said, and before she knew it, he was offering her a hug. It wasn't the warmest hug she'd ever felt, just a short one, but Haley was grateful for it nonetheless.

"His blood pressure *was* high," Doctor Finny said, "but that's not enough to kill a man. Of course, I didn't do a full physical on him either, so anything's possible, but—"

Doctor Finny didn't want to come across as only caring about himself, especially as Haley seemed so sad, so he just walked away to his office then, not finishing the thought.

He spent the next few minutes rereading John Caraway's file with Haley for anything he may have missed, but by the time he was done, he was satisfied there was nothing.

"It may have been an accident or something completely different anyway," he said.

Try as they did, neither Haley nor Doctor Finny could find any local news or obituaries online yet about Mr. Caraway. They would just have to wait until they heard more.

Chapter 12

On Tuesday evening that week, Haley attended the wake for Mr. Caraway. She'd finally found the information posted online about it on Monday night after work.

At the wake, she spoke to the bride and groom from the wedding, who both remarked how sweet it was that she came. It took her a while before she brought up the check—as casually as she could—but they assured her she'd get paid as soon as possible, and they apologized for the awful timing, as if they'd somehow done something to cause it all by getting married.

"No, don't worry," Haley said. "I shouldn't have even brought it up tonight. I'm sorry."

She promised them over and over again that the check wasn't at all why she came, that she really was so genuinely sad about their loss, and the young woman hugged Haley tightly when she saw her begin to cry.

"We put off our honeymoon," she said. "We were already on our way to the airport when I got the call. My sister wouldn't tell me what it was over the phone, but said we should come back right away. I was so upset."

"God, I can't even imagine," Haley said. "And it's awful that you had to cancel your honeymoon too."

"Postpone, not cancel," the groom quickly clarified with a smile.

"Right, I'm sorry," Haley said to him, shaking her head and feeling stupid.

"No, it's okay," he said. "But under the circumstances, with everything going on now with Stephanie's family, my family wants to pay you for your services. I already asked my dad, and he's on it. We had a call from the DJ as well, but I think everyone else was paid in advance, so it's okay."

Haley thanked him, then locked eyes with Stephanie, who she could see was teetering on the edge of more tears.

"I'm so glad he was able to make it through my wedding and reception. Oh Daddy—"

She broke down crying then as soon as she got the words out, and it took all of Haley's strength not to burst out crying as well. As the groom pulled his new bride in for a hug, Haley excused herself and found a chair at the back of the room.

She watched as people came in and knelt by the coffin, or hugged each other, or shook hands. While there were *some* smiles around the room, especially as people pointed to photos of Mr. Caraway on various bulletin boards, the room was very quiet for the most part.

The man she knew was her Uncle Lenny's boss entered a minute later and grabbed Kevin, the groom, for a half hug and a big handshake before he approached the coffin and shook his head.

Haley didn't want to stare, but not knowing anyone else, her attention returned to Stephanie and Kevin by the door, and she watched as they both welcomed new mourners entering the room, or said their thanks to others who were leaving already after paying their respects.

Every now and then, she looked up toward the front of the room at the coffin and Mr. Caraway's body. He looked so real and alive in there, she thought, like he might open his eyes at any moment, but she knew that wouldn't be good if it happened. She'd seen enough television shows and horror movies over the years to cause such silly daydreams, and put the thought out of her head as quickly as it arrived.

An old woman walked past her just then and smiled, and the strangest idea came over Haley, that the woman was actually a ghost. Why she thought this she didn't know, but she guessed it might be because the woman was all by herself and walking alone without talking to anyone else. When the woman reached Stephanie and Kevin by the door and they each bent down to hug her though, Haley shook her head and thought how stupid she was for ever thinking it.

It was Peaches' fault, she decided a moment later, remembering her story about interacting with the spirit of Kerry Ann Jefferson. Why did she have to tell her stuff like that?

She shook it off as another bad daydream, allowing the freshly vacuumed carpet of the funeral parlor to calm her nerves. This new plan only lasted a few seconds though, as she was soon interrupted when a pair of shiny black shoes stopped right in front of her. Looking up, she saw the stern face of her Uncle Lenny's boss staring down at her from high above, and he very quickly extended his large hand to shake hers.

"Haley? I'm RJ Tarisi. How are you?"

"I'm good, thank you," she said, shaking his hand and wondering if he even remembered cursing her out at the reception just three nights earlier.

"My brother mentioned he's offered to pay you for your services, but as I owed him a bit of money anyway, he suggested I could just take care of you, and we'd call it even. Would that be okay with you?"

Haley froze, unsure what to say. The plan was presented so neatly, so simply, and she watched in a kind of daze as this large, angry-looking man was already pulling a checkbook from his jacket and clicking open a pen.

"What was the amount we owe you?"

"Um, well, I think it was—"

"I'm pretty sure he said it was close to two thousand dollars. Does that sound about right? Tell you what. I'll just round it up to 2K for you, no problem."

"No sir, it was much higher than that, 4500 I believe, but I'd have to double check. I really don't remember offhand, but I think if I just—"

"You know what, Haley. You're very kind to have come down here tonight, but I think you should leave now. Here's two thousand dollars."

He ripped the check from his checkbook, and thrust it at her hands, practically forcing her to grab it.

"As I'm sure you know, this is quite a lot of money. You have a good night now," he said, pointing her toward the door.

He left for the front of the room again before Haley even realized what had happened. In her confusion, she found her way to the door without saying anything to anyone, not even stopping to say goodbye to the bride and groom, and she was out before they realized she'd left.

All the way home, Haley felt like she'd been railroaded by a swindler, but there was nothing she could do about it. Could she? How? The only one in their family she had any contact info for was Mr. Caraway, but calling the dead man's cell phone was certainly its own dead end.

"I can't believe he did this to me," she said out loud to the car, the truth of what he'd done finally becoming clear. "What kind of a fucking asshole would do that?"

By the time she got home, Haley decided to deposit the check right away, in case something happened with the new one too. This time, she wasn't risking any bank issues, and instead just deposited it into her savings account instead, which she could do right from her cell phone. A few clicks and a photograph of the check later, and she was done. From what she could tell from the new balance, it went in without any problem.

She took a deep breath, letting out a brief scream of exasperation inside the car. Then she crumpled up the check and shoved it between some old tissues and receipts on her car door.

Once inside, she saw Olivia in the living room, and thought about telling her what had happened, before quickly deciding against it. Her mother would only mock her for her stupidity, and this time she'd be right.

"So how was the wake?" Olivia asked, muting the television.

"It was fine. Sad. The bride and groom had to cancel their honeymoon, but they said they'd reschedule it."

Olivia looked over at her, trying to read her face. Something else was up, but she couldn't pinpoint it.

"Well, they're lucky they didn't get all the way to wherever they were going when they found out. That would have been much worse, trust me."

"Yeah," Haley said, looking on as the television silently danced through inane images that meant nothing to her.

"So how did he die?"

Haley looked at her mother first with shock and second with even more self-loathing than she'd already carried.

"I totally forgot to ask."

Now Olivia looked annoyed.

"The obituary just said he died suddenly. He looked good though in the coffin, so I guess it wasn't anything too horrible."

Olivia made a face.

"What?"

"Honey, 'horrible' doesn't necessarily *look like* anything at all. His head could have been chopped off, and they still would have found a way to make his face look pretty."

"Mom!"

"Hey, I'm just saying."

Despite her feelings, Haley couldn't help but smile then, and Olivia was glad to see it. She unmuted the television, then looked over one more time as Haley walked up the stairs to her room.

##

Four hours later, Lenny and Caroline were jarred awake by the sound of their phone ringing. Lenny turned on the light and looked at the clock. 1:33 AM. A deep fear overtook him as he sat up and answered. Caroline, too, had shot up straight in bed, and was watching him in a panic.

"Hello?"

"What? Yeah. Oh my God, okay, yeah. You scared the shit outta me."

Looking at Caroline, he shook his head and rolled his eyes, and she relaxed a little more.

"Yeah, yeah, I know it. Okay, I'll be there as soon as I can. No, stop it. You did the right thing. I'll see you soon."

He hung up and turned to Caroline.

"Erika's drunk. She and her friends lost track of time. Isobel took off with her boyfriend, and now Erika and Jenn are stranded up on Okemo."

Caroline sighed with relief, and quickly put her head back on the pillow. By the time Lenny had his jeans and sneakers on, she was snoring again, grateful the call was nothing serious. He looked at her sleeping peacefully with more than a little jealousy, then grabbed his wallet, cell phone, and keys, and went downstairs as quietly as he could.

As he drove, Lenny remembered the last time this had happened a year earlier, and the conversation he'd had with Erika back then too, when she'd walked for an hour and a half before finally calling him for a ride.

"Just call me anytime you need me to pick you up. I won't get mad, I promise. I don't want you driving or even being driven by anyone who's been drinking."

Lenny was glad she'd listened, and reminded himself not to yell at her this time either. He didn't envy the headache she'd have at school that morning, but decided on the spot that he wouldn't let her stay home sick.

By the time he reached them, it had begun to rain lightly, so Erika and Jenn had snuck back a bit under a large tree. Erika used the flashlight on her phone to signal him after she saw his headlights growing near, then remembered at the last minute to snuff out the joint she was still pinching between two fingers. She also hoped the rain might take away some of the smell before they got inside the car.

They climbed in, Erika into the front seat and Jenn into the back, and no one said anything at first. Lenny smelled the pot right away, but decided not to mention it, at least not until the next day.

As he drove down the mountain carefully, keeping an eye out for deer, foxes, and bears, he realized he had no idea where Jenn even lived. He asked her, but Erika answered first.

"Brook Road. It's in Cavendish up past High Street off—"

"Yeah, I know where that is," Lenny mumbled.

He made no attempt to mask his annoyance, pissed to learn he still had another half-hour round trip ahead of him.

"Okay. I'll drop you off first, and then bring Jenn over there."

"Thank you, Mr. Abrams," Jenn said from the back seat.

He meant to say *you're welcome*, but was so tired, he never got around to uttering the words out loud.

A few minutes later, he pulled up to their house, as close to the front door as he could, so Erika wouldn't get too drenched on her way inside.

"Thank you, Daddy," she said, then jumped out of the car and ran in.

Lenny was soon caught completely by surprise when Jenn slid into the passenger seat a moment later, and smiled at him as she put on her seat belt. He had guessed she would have just stayed in the back seat.

Seeing her next to him all of a sudden though—wet hair, clothes, and face—instantly woke him up.

She smiled at him one more time, then glanced back at the house as Lenny pulled out of the driveway. Except for their front light, the house was completely dark.

"I'm so sorry we woke you up for this," she said once they were driving a bit.

"No, it's fine. I'm happy to help."

He decided against lecturing her, not just because it was so late and he didn't know what exactly Jenn may have done, but also because her skirt was extremely short, and her legs had looked dangerously attractive when she first sat down next to him when the light was still on. He was sure he'd never forget the little beads of rainwater he'd seen atop her left thigh.

As they drove on for a while, Lenny's mind wandered helplessly to fantasies of what he wanted to do with her. It would start simple with kissing, he decided. They'd make out first, before his hands started up the inside of her t-shirt for her breasts, those tight, perky tits he'd been aching to rub since the moment he first laid eyes on her.

Very soon after that, his hand would be on her leg, feeling her smooth skin and wondering what her pussy looked like. He imagined it was shaved and beautiful, pink and small. He imagined her taking her shorts off and climbing on top of him as he let the seat down to give them more room.

When he turned onto Main Street, he could feel himself growing hard as he thought of her. It was too late to stop it now, but he was grateful that in the darkness of the car, she'd never be able to notice it.

Ridiculous, he realized, *a girl like her wanting someone like me.*

But that's when he felt it. Her hand on his thigh. For real.

He stole a quick, terrified glance at her in the glow of a passing streetlight, and saw she was staring at him, horny herself, her eyes wild with her own dark thoughts of a secret affair.

"You shouldn't do that," he whispered, but Jenn could tell he didn't really mean it.

He wanted her to touch him even more, and she knew it. Her eyes made it clear she knew her power over him too, and as she moved her hand back and forth on his leg, she began massaging him closer and closer to his crotch. When she found his hard dick at last, she let out a joyful, silly kind of purr, and Lenny couldn't help but smile.

"I mean it, Jenn. You shouldn't. We shouldn't."

He was reciting the words like he had to, like someone had a gun to his head from the backseat, and not at all because he really wanted them ever said out loud. Inside Lenny's mind, a different man had awoken.

This new, braver Lenny wanted to find a place to take her just then, to kiss her and touch her and fuck her till he came. Even so, the more she rubbed him, the more tortured he was by the conflict growing within.

"No, this really is wrong. You need to stop. I mean it."

"I'm legal," she said, trying to calm him.

"But you're still my daughter's best friend, Jenn. You're 17. This is insane."

"That's what makes it so hot, Daddy."

"I said no!"

He grabbed her hand and flung it off him as she gasped, clearly ashamed by the unexpected physical and verbal rebuke. He'd done it almost mechanically, like yanking his own hand from a fire, and his dick still screamed for him to reconsider.

They drove on in silence the rest of the way there, except for a few times when she pointed and whispered the directions to her house. Lenny's hard-on was mostly gone, but he still needed the conversation to end naturally. He needed Jenn to know he *wanted* to do more, but just couldn't, and that it had nothing to do with her.

"Look, Jenn," he finally said. "You're beautiful, and to be honest with you, I really want you bad right now, but I just, I just don't think we should. I don't want to take advantage of you, and I don't want Erika or my wife to find out. If they ever did—"

"I wouldn't tell anyone. I promise. I wouldn't want you to get into any trouble with them, or with my family either."

He looked at her strangely then, and shook his head as he turned back to the road. He hadn't even *thought* of her parents.

If Caroline or Erika found out, it would be a disaster, but if Jenn's father found out, he'd literally kill him. As in for real. Game over. Death. The guy was built like a linebacker, and had graduated from Black River three years ahead of Lenny.

"Shit," he said, less to Jenn than to the world.

He pulled the car over quickly and turned off his headlights. They were on a stretch of road without any houses, and the nearest one was up ahead still with all the lights out. Jenn turned and looked at him, wondering if he'd suddenly changed his mind.

"I just want to say something to you," he said, still facing forward. "I'm flattered. I'm, well, actually beyond flattered. The fact that a girl as pretty as you would want someone like me is extremely flattering. And honestly, yes, I do want you to keep touching me and for us to do much more, but we can't. We just can't. I need you to understand that if this were some little bubble of reality that could never be popped, I would take you in my arms

104

in a heartbeat, but I sadly know all too well how quickly and violently bubbles get popped, and dreams are destroyed."

His mind flashed back sixteen years earlier to Sam sitting in a courtroom, cuffs around his wrists and ankles. His *not guilty* verdict meant nothing to the grieving family, to her mother who couldn't stop crying, or to her father who officers had to watch to make sure he didn't lunge across the room toward Sam.

Sam's actual guilt or innocence regarding Kerry Ann's death meant nothing. His DNA on her underwear was all they needed in those first few weeks after they found her to launch the case and turn public opinion against him.

Lenny shook his head and allowed himself to stare at Jenn now. She was so pretty, but so fragile. He was sorry he'd yelled at her, and though he was confident he could do anything he wanted to her, with her permission too, things would never be the same with Caroline again if he did.

Jenn looked shell-shocked, and Lenny didn't want that either, so he leaned over and kissed her softly on the cheek.

"Let's talk again soon, okay? Please don't be mad at me, though? I don't want you to be mad at me."

She shook her head.

"No, no, of course not. Thank you. I'm sorry. It was stupid."

He went to turn the lights back on, but stopped then and looked back at her again.

"No, it wasn't. It wasn't stupid at all, Jenn. You wanted to, I wanted to. That's not stupid. It's normal. It's just, we could get caught here, and I don't want to tempt fate anymore by—"

"No, you're right. It's cool. We'll talk another time."

"Okay."

He turned the lights back on, and pulled into the street. When he dropped her off, he waited to make sure she got in the front door okay, and then drove home.

It was 2:52 AM when he slid back under the covers at home, where Caroline was still fast asleep.

Chapter 13

Sam and Haley exchanged nervous pleasantries as she came in. She put her purse down on top of an old couch, then Sam began showing her around the new house some more.

Haley was so impressed with all of it, especially the incredible view of the lake and deck from the downstairs living room.

"I'm apparently losing a shitload of rental income over the summer by not waiting until the fall to start flipping it, but I didn't want to wait too long to get started."

Sam had already emptied out most of the furniture and torn up the downstairs carpet, but even with all that, it didn't take much for Haley to see the potential of turning a profit.

"I thought about moving the kitchen down here, but I read a bunch of reviews people left of the place online, and there was no way I was gonna mess with a proven formula. People really like having the living room on this level. I'll upgrade it, though."

"That's good," Haley said, but she didn't sound convinced.

"You don't think I can do it?" he asked.

"No, it's not that. It's just—"

She looked at him sadly, wondering if he was simply in denial or if he really was too stupid to realize what he was up against.

"Look, Dad, the past isn't staying in the past. Someone's obviously still trying to get you, and I feel like, I dunno, maybe you shouldn't have even come back here. No one was raising a stink about that girl until you showed up again, but now it's like you woke a sleeping monster, and things could get a lot worse before they get better."

She paused, trying to read his face.

"Mom says—"

"Oh? What does your mom say? I'd like to know," he asked, folding his arms quickly in defense.

"She says you have a really bad habit of *looking* for trouble."

Sam just shook his head in reply, too pissed to argue. He walked away from her toward the deck, sliding open the screen door and trying to exit before the door got jammed.

Despite his anger and impatience, he didn't force it though, just looked up and down at the track trying to figure out what the problem was. When he moved it next, it rolled open perfectly.

Haley followed him out onto the deck, but got caught trying to close the screen door once she was out.

"Look, honey, down there. See how it's lifting up a bit? Just slide it slowly, and don't let that happen."

She did as he told her, and it worked.

"Okay, good. So as long as you just stand there all the time whenever people need your help to open or close it, everything will be fine.

"It's on my list. I'll fix it, you'll see."

Haley sat down in one of the outdoor chairs, and put her feet up on another one after kicking off her sandals. Putting her hands to her forehead to block the sun, she tried to see who was rowing slowly across the lake. Sam waved to the person, unsure who it was himself, and then sat down in a chair next to her.

Noticing the sun was in her eyes, he got up right away again and opened the large umbrella on the table next to them. As he did, a bee flew out quickly, off toward the lake.

Sam smiled, happy to see he had freed the little bug, given it a new chance at life in Ludlow or beyond. Then he sat down next to her, and thoughtfully rubbed the stubble on the side of his face.

"Haley, I didn't wake up a monster, and I'm certainly not looking for any trouble. I was getting calls from investigators and lawyers the whole time I lived in Vegas. That case has never, *ever* left my life, alright? Someone is always trying to ask me another question a different way hoping to trip me up, or checking in to make sure I still lived where I did.

"I didn't come back here to cause anyone any trouble either, least of all myself. I came back here to end it actually, once and for all. There's nothing I can do to change what happened between me and Kerry Ann, and I can't ever bring her back. Her family knows that. Our family knows that too. Well, most of 'em do, anyway. Your mom won't let some things go, as you may have noticed."

"Dad, if it was just an accident or something, why don't you just tell them that? Why not just explain to them that you don't know exactly what happened, but that it wasn't your fault?"

Sam didn't look at her now, which unnerved Haley. Whenever she came close to getting a real, honest-to-God answer out of him, he did this. He shut down on her, and he shut her out completely.

"Dad, please. Just tell me what happened. It'll be okay."

"Jesus Christ, Haley, I said leave it! How many times have I asked you to stay out of it? I've said all I need to say to the police, and I've said all I need to say to your mom. There's nothing else to be said or done at this point, except for me to clear my name once and for all. Now, I'm sorry to raise my voice, but that's just how I feel, and I need you to just leave it be, okay? Can you do that?"

She nodded, assuring him she would, but after enough silence passed between them, she needed to at least *try* to say more.

"Dad, I don't think this will ever go away, though. At least not until whoever's harassing you about it dies or enough time passes. What is that called again? A statue of limitations?"

Sam laughed, despite himself.

"A *statute* of limitations. There's not an actual statue."

He paused, then shrugged as he thought about it some more.

"At least I don't think there is."

They sat there for a while longer and watched the clouds pass by, their shapes changing with the wind, and their shadows changing the look and color of the lake below them as well. Another person rowed past in the distance, too far out for them to see their face, but close enough for both of them to imagine being in the little canoe along with them. There was peace out there in the world, and other people had been lucky enough to find it.

After another minute or so passed, Sam asked Haley how everyone was doing. He still hadn't really caught up with anyone since he was back.

"Good. Mom is Mom. Uncle Lenny and Aunt Caroline are fine, Peaches is fine, Erika's fine. Grandma and Grandpa are fine too, the same as usual, I guess. Mom said they'll be missing Erika's graduation and party because of something on Long Island."

"Erika's graduating high school already?"

"Dad, really? Yes. You knew that, didn't you?"

"I don't remember you mentioning it. So what is she, 18 now?"

"Yeah, she just turned 18 a couple weeks ago. We had cake."

She turned away, following a butterfly flap its wings across the front of the deck, and then she smiled to herself.

"You should have come."

He looked at her sideways, and saw her concealing a big smile, knowing he wasn't about to show up to something like that. He shook his head with a grin and closed his eyes, thinking once again of Caroline. He'd seen her three times since he came back, and had only seen Lenny twice. He decided he owed him another call.

"Well, maybe I'll surprise you all and show up to her graduation. When is it? Sometime this month?"

Haley looked over at him suspiciously, wondering if he was serious, and not sure she should even tell him the details.

"It's this coming Saturday. The 17th?"

"Well okay then. We shall see what we shall see."

Sam was pleased with himself, proud of his unexpected flair for the mysterious, and Haley just shook her head at him. His likeability was infuriating, she decided, but beyond all his smiles and secrets, there was still something dark there she didn't understand.

Either he *was* a murderer, accidental or not, or someone else responsible for that girl's death was still out there somewhere. If so, they were probably trying to frame it on her father.

He seemed far too relaxed, though. How do you get like that, she wondered. How do you smile and laugh, and act like life is good, even when you're the lead suspect of a horrible murder?

Haley's phone chimed, and when she went to check it, she saw she had a missed call from a number she didn't recognize. Sam watched her click through and then put the phone to her ear to listen to the voicemail. She looked concerned as she began to listen, then a little more relaxed a few seconds in.

"Hi, Haley. This is Stephanie. Thank you again for coming last night. It was so sweet of you. I heard Kevin's uncle paid you. Sorry again about the mix-up. But listen, I totally forgot to ask you about the pictures. Is there any way you could just give me the memory card so I can start to go through them? After everything with my dad, we could really use some happy moments, and I was even thinking I could share a few pictures of him from Saturday at his funeral tomorrow morning. I know that's probably like totally ridiculous, but it would seriously mean so much to me if you could help me out. God, even just a few pictures of him? Anyway, I'll text you my information, so please just call me back at this number as soon as you get this. Thank you."

Haley sighed as she clicked out of her voicemail, then told Sam she had to go. There was no way she was handing over her memory card filled with pictures, many of them personal photos too. She'd also taken several shots of the hot waiters that night. Even so, she totally understood Stephanie's request, and was happy to do everything she could to help her.

She got back home a little while later, and told Olivia about the call. Olivia made a face Haley couldn't interpret, so she decided not to even get into to it with her.

"Don't forget to find out what killed her father," Olivia called out, watching as Haley ran up the stairs to her computer.

"Oh, right. Okay, I won't forget!"

Haley replied to the text and told Stephanie she'd get her what she needed on a thumb drive ASAP that evening, then went to work looking through her photos. It was a task she'd already begun, but had only barely gotten through color correcting the first few photos so far. Specifically looking for photos featuring Mr. Caraway was much easier, but would still take her some time.

The first thing she did was click through every single picture, even if it didn't seem to be one with Mr. Caraway in it, in case he was just off to the side. In her head, she imagined she might stumble upon a shot of the bride and groom dancing, with him smiling at them from a distance. She knew she could put a spotlight on him if a picture like that existed somewhere.

About thirty pictures in though, she saw Lenny's boss, Mr. Tarisi, standing in the back of the church. His massive frame wasn't hard to miss, but Haley had only been capturing random shots of guests entering the church at that point.

He and the man he was talking with weren't in the shots really, just off to the side and easily cropped out, but a few photos later, she saw it was Mr. Caraway he was talking to. Haley nodded with her tongue between her teeth, happy to have located him now, and she began checking the next few pictures carefully to see if there were any clear shots of him that she could use. Mr. Tarisi was tall and bulky, so he was mostly blocking Mr. Caraway's slender frame, but she knew they wouldn't have stayed there forever, so she kept clicking through, waiting for the best open shots of him to appear.

Once he did show up in the aisle though, away from Mr. Tarisi and a few others, he looked very ill. She wondered if maybe he was sick, or hadn't told Dr. Finny about something. He was a new patient though, and hadn't wanted a full physical, just a quick checkup, so that didn't make sense for someone dealing with a serious illness.

She kept clicking through until she had a clear shot again, but the next time his face was in view, he looked extremely upset about something. Haley shook it off quickly, convinced she was just reading into it too much.

His daughter was about to get married, and he was probably just stressed out, she figured. But something about the way Mr. Tarisi was looking at him a few photos later concerned her. He had his hands in his pockets and his head turned slightly as he watched Mr. Caraway walk away.

Haley flipped backwards then through the photos to see if there was anything else she'd missed, but didn't see them together any earlier.

She went forward again, clicking through all the photos she'd already seen, but she still couldn't find any clear shots of Mr. Caraway until later when he walked his daughter up the aisle. By then, he was smiling and looking much better, which made Haley smile too.

She was actually thrilled with how great some of the shots came out, in fact, and knew Stephanie would be happy with them too, especially those of Mr. Caraway giving her away up at the front by the altar. One shot in particular made Haley start to cry when she saw it. It was a beautiful image of Mr. Caraway half smiling, half crying as he shook the groom's hand.

She'd snapped the shot by luck just as she arrived at the front again after Mr. Caraway told her she was blocking their path. Haley was certain the photo would be one of the shots Stephanie would end up using for the funeral the next day.

With each new photo she found of Mr. Caraway, Haley saved the file separately into a new folder, then kept searching for more. She was only up to the very beginning of the reception photos when Stephanie started texting her again to check in.

Hey, any luck? Don't spend too much time on this if it's too much trouble. I really don't want to be up late tonight anyway...funeral's at 10 tomorrow Need to print them tonight

Haley was shocked to see it was already close to 8:30 PM. She was nowhere near done yet, and still hadn't eaten, so her stomach was aching for food. She replied right away.

Sorry! I'm still going through the photos. I found a few nice ones from the wedding, but haven't gone through the reception photos yet. When is the latest I can meet you with a thumb drive?

She sent the text, then ran down the stairs and asked her mother if they had anything to eat, on her way to the fridge to investigate for herself.

"I was thinking of ordering pizza, actually. You interested?"

"Oh my God, yes! Totally. Mushrooms or regular cheese."

"Okay, I'll do half cheese, half mushrooms."

"Thank you. Gotta run. Still going through the pictures."

Haley was upstairs at her desk again quickly, and picked up her phone right away to see if Stephanie had responded. Two new messages had already come in.

OMG…thank you, Haley…those will be great!

Don't worry about the others for now…can you just drop the thumb drive off to me now, or if you can't, I can head over to you and pick it up if you give me your address? Thank you so much!

Haley's stomach rumbled, and she thought about how long the pizza would take to be delivered. Stephanie sent her address, and Haley once again responded quickly.

Okay, I'll bring it over to you now. You're not too far. Should be there in 15 minutes.

After copying the photos onto a thumb drive, including four shots of the bride and groom together so Stephanie would get a sneak peek at the album, she grabbed her phone and purse, and went down the stairs.

Halfway between the door and telling Olivia where she was going and why, her phone chimed with a new text, and Haley opened it up as she closed the front door behind her.

OMG perfect! Thank you! C u soon!

The handoff went quickly, and Stephanie gave her a big hug when she got there. Haley was already waving goodbye and walking back to her car when she remembered to ask Stephanie about what happened to her father.

"Oh, Stephanie, I'm so sorry to ask, but I never heard. How did your father die?"

"Oh," she said, her face quickly drooping into a frown. "He slipped and fell in the bathroom at the catering hall. He hit his head and, yeah. He died in the ambulance on the way to the hospital."

"Oh, okay. I'm so sorry to hear that."

"Yeah, thanks. It sucks. Thank you again for these pictures, though. I'm sure they're great. I really appreciate you rushing this for me."

"No problem. Happy to help. I'll talk to you soon."

So he just slipped and fell. Nothing suspicious there.

The thought occurred to her just then that she'd only been thinking the worst because of what happened with her father. She decided her mind probably went to such dark places quicker than most people, and made a mental note to stop doing that.

She pulled into the driveway just as the pizza guy pulled up behind her, and was psyched by the timing, as she was now extremely hungry. When he got out of his car though, Haley realized she knew him.

"Oh, hi. I forget your name, but I'm Peaches' cousin, Haley. You came into my job with her recently."

"Hey, yeah. I'm Roger. Nice to see you again."

He held out his hand beneath the pizza box, and shook her hand with a smile. They looked at each other awkwardly for a moment before Haley realized she needed to take the pizza in and pay him. She shook her head with a new smile as she realized, then went for the front door and nodded for him to follow her in.

"I'm back," she called, not seeing her mother there. "And the pizza's here."

She paid Roger with a nice tip, but he just stood there for a moment smiling at her. Just then, Olivia came down the stairs behind her and asked if she needed money to pay him.

"No, it's fine. I got it. Thank you, Roger. I'll see you around town, I guess."

She closed the door as Roger waved and left, then carried the pizza box into their small dining room and put it on the table.

"You know him?" Olivia asked, walking into the kitchen for paper plates.

"Yeah, he's friends with Peaches."

Olivia walked back in and smiled at her.

"He's cute," she said.

Haley blushed slightly with a smile, and quickly grabbed a slice of mushroom pizza.

"He's also 16," she said with a laugh.

"Oh," Olivia said, thinking about it. "But if he's driving, he may be 17."

Haley threw a look at her like, *that'd still be too young for me*, so Olivia decided not to push it further.

##

An hour and a half later, Roger finally got home after finishing his shift at Village Pizza. He was counting his money with a smile as he thought about Haley. *So what if she's Peaches' cousin? She'd be cool with it.*

He walked over to the kitchen island in their huge kitchen, and laid down his money on the marble countertop. Fishing out the coins along with his cell phone, he thought about texting Peaches just then, but wasn't sure if he should.

The front door opened a few seconds later, and he heard the voices of his mother and her boyfriend as they came in.

"Hi hon," his mom said, kissing him on her way into the den.

A moment later, her boyfriend walked in too, already untucking his shirt on his way to the refrigerator. He pulled out a beer, flipped off the cap, and bounced it across the kitchen counter before turning around to stare at Roger as he took a drink.

"What's up, fag?" RJ Tarisi said, passing Roger on the way to the den.

He stopped then and came back briefly, grabbing a $20 bill from the top of Roger's pile of money.

"Thanks for the rent money, buddy."

Roger watched him disappear into the den, then shook his head and collected his things.

Chapter 14

"Lenny, listen to me. We have more than enough food, but I'm still worried about soda. Can you pick more up on your way back? Yeah, two more of each is good. Okay, thanks."

Caroline hung up the phone and got halfway to the backyard for a cigarette when the doorbell rang. She was already losing her mind trying to get ready for Erika's graduation party, and Lenny off picking up Peaches from some art festival in Springfield wasn't helping her at all. She knew she should've told Peaches she couldn't go, but it was too late for that now.

As she swung open the front door in a sweat, ready to yell at whoever was trying to sell her something, Caroline was shocked to see her mother-in-law staring back at her.

"Phyllis. Hi. I thought you guys were out of town. The party's not until after the graduation, and I still have a ton to do here. Lenny's not here either. He's picking Peaches up from—"

Phyllis was in the door before Caroline could stop her.

"This will just take a minute, dear."

Caroline closed the door and turned around as Phyllis disappeared into the kitchen. When she joined her there a moment later, she found Phyllis sizing up the room, surely looking for things to complain about or mock later on at the party.

Caroline stood patiently in the kitchen and wiped her forehead with the hand towel she'd tucked in her apron earlier. There was no point interrupting Phyllis and her mental card catalogue now.

When Phyllis finally turned around again though, she faced Caroline with an odd sort of smile.

"What is it?" Caroline asked.

"Is it possible, dear, that in some alternate version of this shitstorm reality we're all suffering through here," she began, pausing for dramatic effect, and watching Caroline's face change, "that you've been *fucking* Sam behind Lenny's back?"

It took everything in Caroline's power not to look shocked, but try as she did to look surprised *in the right way*, Phyllis wasn't having any of it.

"Let's not play games, dear. I know it's true. You were *spotted.*"

She said it like she'd hired an army of little old ladies to stand watch from rooftops all around the area, something that wouldn't have come as much of a shock to Caroline if it was true.

"The *real* question is," Phyllis went on, "just how stupid are you? Don't you realize someone would have caught you sooner or later? Doesn't *Sam* realize someone would have caught you two in the act? I mean, really. How completely brainless are you both?"

Caroline looked ready to vomit. She walked past Phyllis and fumbled for her cigarettes on the way out to the deck.

Phyllis's eyes narrowed, and she followed her closely, watching her every movement. Once it was clear Caroline was taking her time responding, Phyllis finally looked for a place to sit down.

Everything looked filthy, so she whipped the towel out from Caroline's apron, hurting Caroline a bit as she did, then laid it down carefully on a deck chair before sitting.

"Phyllis, listen. I don't know what to do. Sam and I—we broke this off years ago, and I never meant for it to start up again."

"Stop."

"Things just got—what?"

"You didn't *mean* to meet him at a private motel room in New Hampshire? You didn't *mean* to drive all the way over there to meet him when you could have talked just as easily right here in town?"

"Well, we didn't think—"

"Caroline, cut the bullshit. I may be old, but I'm no fool. I just wonder how foolish you think Lenny is. Don't you think he'll find out sooner or later? Because I think he will. I think he will absolutely find out very soon."

Caroline turned to face her quickly, her cheeks flush with fear. She took the cigarette from her mouth then in a nervous flourish, waving it as she thought through her words.

"Phyllis, please. Please don't tell him. Let me do it. Please."

"What?!" Phyllis asked, her face contorted with confusion. "God, you're even dumber than I thought you were!"

"What?"

Phyllis stood and grabbed the cigarette from Caroline's hand.

"These things will kill you, you know."

She inhaled it briefly, then threw it on the ground and stomped it out.

"Stick to pot instead. It's much better for you. Listen, Caroline. I'm not going to tell Lenny, and you shouldn't either."

Caroline stared at her like she'd gone mad. She'd cheated on the woman's only son, multiple times, with Lenny's best friend no less, yet his own mother was encouraging her not to tell him? Was this a trick?

No, she quickly surmised, Phyllis was genuinely serious. Before she could speak again though, Phyllis went on.

"Lenny is a good man. He's not perfect, God knows that, and whether or not he's ever cheated on you has nothing to do with it either. He's wanted to, you better believe that much, but if he found out about you and Sam? He'd lose it. He'd crumble. Lenny's a weak man in a dead-end job, and I don't want to see him unravel any more than he already has under your watch. He loves you, I'm sure of that, but if he found out about this? Well, I don't want to even *think* what would happen. You can't tell him."

Caroline looked into the house to make sure Erika hadn't come back from her breakfast plans at Jenn's house yet, then looked at Phyllis again. She shook her head and looked away, then put her hands through her hair.

"You think I should—"

"Call things off with Sam. Tell him it needs to stop now once and for all. And that'll be the end of it. Lenny won't find out, and you and Sam can just agree it's for the best. Sam will understand. He's put this family through enough goddamn shit over the years as it is. He ought to respect the fact that he shouldn't fuck things up any further."

Caroline nodded, then smiled darkly as she looked at Phyllis.

"What?"

"I've just never seen this side of you before, Phyllis. I mean, I knew you could be a bitch, but you're a hell of a lot tougher than I would have ever guessed you were."

"I'm a nurse, dear. I've had to put up with an awful lot of shit in my time. *Literally.*"

Caroline smiled once more before hiding it as Phyllis turned back again.

"I just do what I have to for my family, Caroline. Which reminds me. Your oldest was making out with some *boy* in our garage last night. She probably thought we'd gone to bed already, but I'd fallen asleep while reading with only a small light on, and Alan was knocked out on the couch after his game ended. I heard Erika giggling from our sitting room, and when I looked out the back window, I saw her out there with some jock.

"Varsity jacket and the whole nine yards. Not that I care what she does, mind you, but I don't want them doing it on *my* property, you understand. So I turned a few more lights on around the house, and that's when they skulked away to some other den of iniquity somewhere else."

"Okay, I'll talk to her. I'm sorry."

"No, don't. I don't want her to dislike me. I just wanted to let *you* know it happened in case she's been acting up or anything. I imagine it's just to do with graduation and going away to college. You do need to make sure she doesn't get knocked up, though."

"Jesus, Phyllis. She's only a kid."

"Oh God," Phyllis said, looking at Caroline with pity. "She's 18 years old, Caroline. She's not 12. She could have had three abortions by now, and *you'd* never know. You need to keep a closer eye on her."

"Oh my God. Jesus. Okay," Caroline said, running her hands through her hair again.

As they walked back in the house, Caroline couldn't believe Phyllis had found out about her and Sam. They'd been so careful, she was sure of it. Still, she was more worried now that Phyllis may have heard it from one of her gossipy friends, someone like Mrs. Hensley who'd be telling the whole town about it.

"Phyllis, wait. Before you go, I was just wondering who you heard this from, I mean about Sam and me. I don't want anyone in town talking."

Phyllis shook her head.

"It's still a secret. The person I heard it from is not the type to gossip, I promise you. Just let it go. And break it off a-sap."

She turned around to leave again, then stopped and looked back at her.

"Just break it to him gently," she said more quietly now. "Sam's strong, but I don't want you to hurt him, either."

Caroline nodded and offered a smile again before she left. As Phyllis closed the front door behind her, Caroline turned back into the kitchen and put both hands on the kitchen counter with a very long sigh.

##

Back at her house a little while later, Phyllis rested her purse on the table and began checking the mail before finding Alan inside watching TV.

"How'd it go?" he asked.

"Fine. She's got her head on ass backwards over this party for Erika, but she seemed to appreciate my *wise* counsel and advice."

Alan smiled.

"You mentioned the thing with Erika and that sack of meat foggin' up our garage?"

"Yes, although I decided at the last minute to omit the part where the boy had his entire arm up her skirt. I didn't think Caroline needed to know about that particular assault against gravity, let alone decorum."

Alan snickered at first, then laughed out loud, and the two enjoyed the glance of mischief they exchanged, though his attention turned back soon enough to the television screen.

Phyllis picked up her reading glasses from the table as she sat down across from him, and strained to see her cell phone. She seemed to be taking several minutes to compose a short text message to someone. Once she finished it and hit send, she put the phone and her glasses down, just as Alan muted the television.

"What did she say about Sam?"

Phyllis put her head back thoughtfully, then looked over at him without saying anything at first.

"Not much. It'll work itself out now."

"You mean you hope it will."

"Hope is all I have, Alan. We made the right decision to cancel the trip to New York, though. This family needs watching right now. If Sam can't keep his dick in his pants, and Caroline can't keep herself *or* her daughter from whoring their way through the Green Mountains, then there's nothing more we can do but hope it all works out."

Alan smiled, then winced suddenly as his knee pounded with a horrible new ache. It was the worst one yet, but he wasn't about to tell Phyllis that. Painkillers would help more than another lecture from Nurse Ratched.

She watched him just the same, waiting for him to answer, or to tell her something, and the shake of his head was all she needed to leave him alone.

"We're expected at the school in an hour," she finally said, standing up again. "Make sure you're ready in time. And don't wear that ugly goddamn tie. It looks terrible on you."

She left the room then with a sigh, and went up the stairs near the front of the house.

Once he heard the bathroom door close in the distance, Alan grabbed his knee again and let out a long, quiet moan, his eyes already welling up with fresh tears.

Chapter 15

Outside the high school two hours later, the graduating seniors had just tossed their caps up into the air at the close of the ceremony, and were laughing and embracing each other all around the open outdoor area.

Behind them, friends and family members finished clapping, and many already began leaving their seats to go and find their graduate of choice to congratulate them up close and take pictures.

"I'm glad you two were able to make it after all," Lenny said, leaning in to kiss Phyllis on the cheek.

She smiled, and looked over at Caroline.

"Well, we just decided this was where we should be this weekend. The Kleins and their bratty grandson will survive without us. We'll just send him a check. Or a Transformer or something."

Caroline laughed nervously, then grabbed Lenny and moved away quickly in Erika's direction. Phyllis beamed with pride, and gave Alan a sideways glance that seemed to say, *you see that? I've got her scared of me now.*

As everyone hustled and bustled around them, Phyllis and Alan just closed up their fold-up chairs on the lawn, and lumbered up the hill to their car as quickly as Alan's knee would allow them.

Erika looked up from her phone, her friends gathered around her after a selfie, and saw her parents approaching fast. She and her mom were in a tight hug before she knew it.

"I am so proud of you," Caroline said, reluctantly leaning away to let Lenny in to hug her as well.

As he did, he smiled nervously at Erika's friends, especially Jenn, who he was grateful to see so thoroughly covered up by her loose graduation gown. The way it sat on top of her, her breasts were barely evident, but he dared not even glance.

"Oh my God," Erika said, turning back to her friends, "did you see Mr. Allenby's face when I kissed him on the cheek? He turned beat red! Imagine if I had kissed him on the lips like I was planning to? Holy shit, I wanted to laugh so hard when I saw the look he gave me!"

Erika was back in her circle of friends very quickly, and Caroline and Lenny just stood there for another 20 seconds feeling dumb before they finally realized their brief moment with her had long since ended, and there wouldn't be a part two. Caroline snapped a few candids with her phone first, and then looked at Lenny, who shrugged.

"Okay honey," Caroline called out. "We'll see you at the house," but Erika just gave her a half nod of acknowledgment as she and Lenny went back up the hill toward the car.

About halfway there though, Lenny stopped short, looking off to the side.

"Holy shit."

"What is it?" Caroline said, afraid at what he must have seen.

She turned and followed Lenny's gaze across the lawn and up the driveway next to the school, as Sam's pickup truck pulled out and drove away from them in the opposite direction. They were both sure it was him.

"Hey!" Olivia yelled over to them on her way to her car, making them both jump. "Your house open for food yet or what? I'm starving! And I believe this kid belongs to you?"

They met up with her as they walked toward their cars, and saw she had Peaches with her. Peaches mentioned she'd meet them at the ceremony, but they couldn't save any more room in their row other than for Phyllis and Alan, so they lost track of where the others might be.

"We're heading back now," Caroline said. "The front door's unlocked if you beat us there, but it looks like your mom and dad might get there first."

She pointed past Olivia to the lot, and everyone looked over together, where Alan and Phyllis were already driving out toward the street. They watched as Alan pulled his car out far too quickly onto the road, making a car on the street stop short with a beep as he cut him off. Lenny shook his head, but Peaches just giggled.

"Old people are funny," she said.

"I just gotta wait up for Haley," Olivia said. "She wants to get some shots of Erika with her friends first."

"Oh good," Caroline said, squinting back down to see if she could spot them, to no avail.

Once they were all in their car, Lenny asked Peaches where she'd been.

"I walked over, and by the time I got here, the only spots left were in the way back by Aunt Livi and Haley, so I just sat down with them."

Lenny seemed satisfied, but by the time they were out on the road, Caroline turned around to look at her strangely.

"Honey, why did you walk? Why were you even awake early enough to get out that early?"

Lenny and Peaches exchanged a glance in the rear-view mirror.

"Daddy picked me up at the Renaissance Faire at eight this morning. I slept there last night, remember?"

"Oh. Right. Okay."

Caroline turned around again in her seat, and looked out the passenger-side window at the passing scenery, as Lenny and Peaches glanced at each other again in the mirror.

"I dropped her off at Chaos Casbah on the way home. I mentioned that to you earlier when I got back to the house." She didn't respond, so he went on. "You okay? You seem really on edge all of a sudden."

"What? Oh, no, I'm fine. I was just—don't worry. I think I'm just stressed out about Erika finishing high school. She doesn't seem old enough to be going away to college this fall."

"*Is* she going away to college this fall?" Lenny asked, but Caroline just bit her lip, electing not to respond.

When they turned left onto Depot Street and passed The Hatchery, Peaches lit up when she spotted Roger having breakfast with his mother and her boyfriend. She tried waving, but he didn't see her. Neither Caroline or Lenny seemed to notice, nor did RJ Tarisi see them.

124

"Her friends just seem so much more ready than she does," Caroline went on, "especially Jenn. That girl looks much more like a college freshman than Erika, don't you think?"

"Does she?" Lenny asked, trying to sound aloof.

"Totally. She reminds me a lot of myself back then."

Lenny smiled, but hid it quickly. *You never had half the tits Jenn has, and sure, you were cuter back then, but Jenn is sizzling.*

As he turned onto their road, he imagined Jenn sitting next to him again in the passenger seat. He could almost feel her hand still rubbing his leg.

"So who's coming today?" he asked.

"Too many people," Caroline answered, already counting them out in her head. "It's us, your parents, your sister and Haley—that's eight—six of Erika's classmates, their parents, grandparents, and a few other people. I think the total is somewhere close to 40."

"Holy shit."

"I told you that," she snapped back, getting pissed.

"Well, I don't remember it being that many," he said. "Jesus."

"He's not invited," Caroline said with a smile, hoping to relax him and her both, but she knew it wouldn't be enough.

"That's not funny, Mommy," Peaches said from the backseat.

"Oh, stop it. I was just being silly. You and your Jesus friends can invite him to your parties anytime you want, but that doesn't mean I have to invite him to mine."

Lenny pulled in the driveway and popped the trunk.

"I forgot the soda's still back there. I'll bring it in."

Caroline just rolled her eyes at him. She wasn't planning to help him anyway.

As she got out and headed for the front door, she noticed there were already two cars there, and one of them was Alan's Buick. The other one had New York plates, but she had no idea whose that one might be.

When she walked inside, Caroline immediately heard Alan in the back of the house saying something about his knee, and how "goddamn canes aren't made like they used to be".

She walked through the dining room into the living room and saw Phyllis and Alan there facing forward, with another man standing with his back to her.

"Hello dear, welcome to your home," Phyllis said with a chuckle, raising a glass filled with red wine and ice her way.

The man turned around, and Caroline realized it was Phyllis's younger brother, Ben. Caroline had only met him a few times, but she knew he was one of her biggest fans, a feeling that was most decidedly not mutual.

"Caroline, my love! Where have you been all my life?"

He cozied up close and gave her a big squeeze, and Caroline thought it reminded her so much of the exact same thing he'd said and done the last two times she'd seen him.

"Benjie, what a nice surprise," she said with a big smile, squirming to escape, as he didn't let go of her as quickly as he should have.

Lenny came in behind them, resting two bags of soda bottles on the kitchen counter, and Ben rushed over to offer Lenny a big handshake hello.

"Hey, Uncle Benjie! Good to see you. I'd chat, but I still have some more soda and groceries to get from the trunk."

"Oh, let me help you."

Lenny tried assuring him he was fine, but Ben was already heading out the door with him to help.

Alan took the opportunity to sit down on one of the couches in the living room, and as Caroline began lighting the Sternos under each of the food trays, Phyllis put her glass of wine down on the countertop and smiled at her coyly.

"Did you invite him to this just to torture me even further?" Caroline asked.

Phyllis shook her head with a quiet laugh.

"No, Alan mentioned it to him weeks ago, but we both completely forgot about it. It's just a very happy coincidence."

"Oh yeah, great."

126

"Hey listen, sweet cheeks. We were supposed to go to a party on Long Island. Imagine if we had? Benjie would be staying here with you all instead."

"Well, thank God for that," she said, her voice growing louder. "I've never been *so* happy to see you both."

Alan raised a Solo cup of whiskey her way, the TV already commanding his attention.

Guests began arriving pretty quickly after that. First there was Erika, Jenn, and Isobel, who Lenny watched run up the stairs by the front door. Then Olivia came in soon after that, saying that Haley had to stop back at Doctor Finny's office to make sure he was okay, and finally more of the other graduates and their family members and friends arrived.

In her head, Caroline counted more than 50 people, and could see the cars already lined up on the lawn and out on the street.

"Honey, you need any help?" Lenny asked, approaching her calmly with a beer. He was smiling and looking as relaxed as ever.

"Do I need any help? Is that what you're asking me?"

"Yeah, if there's anything I can do, just let me know."

He smiled again and kissed her on the cheek, but before she could say anything, he was already walking away from her toward the deck.

Her only saving grace, Caroline felt, was that the sun was shining and there was no rain at all in the forecast, so at least most of the guests would stay put between the living room and the backyard, saving her some embarrassment from the mess piled up in the dining room. And perhaps, she hoped—*if she was lucky*—the crowds would keep Lenny's Uncle Benjie far away from her too.

Two hours later, everyone was outside enjoying the nice weather. The yard was huge, easily twice as big as their house, and between the extra tables and chairs they'd rented, plus the extra chairs some of the guests brought with them by request, everyone seemed happy and comfortable.

Caroline sat beside Lenny as they chatted with some of the other parents, an empty plate and plastic fork balanced delicately on her knee. She was just beginning to feel comfortable too, laughing and enjoying her third cocktail, when two little boys, maybe 11 or 12 years old, started climbing on the tree just below the tree house.

She stood up at her seat, the paper plate and fork falling quickly to the grass, and all around the yard, the other members of their small family were likewise staring over in the same direction.

Olivia seemed frozen in time as she exhaled a cloud of smoke sideways toward the fence, her back against the house and an empty plastic cup clinched tightly in her other hand.

Phyllis and Alan, at first pretending to listen to Ben go on about his business prospects in New York, were likewise transfixed on the little boys playing beneath the tree house, who looked like they might be preparing to climb up soon to explore it. They'd already yanked an Adirondack chair up close to the tree so they could get a foothold and climb into the opening, which started almost six feet up off the ground.

"No!" Caroline called over the music and conversation, walking toward them as calmly and quickly as she could. She knew a few of the guests were watching her now too. "You can't climb on that, guys! It's not sturdy!"

She smiled then, urging everyone back to their conversations, and silently congratulated herself on an award-worthy performance as the boys ran off in the other direction.

On her way back to her chair though, Caroline stopped suddenly, staring across the crowd to the inside of the house.

Lenny, Phyllis, Alan, Haley, Erika, and Peaches *all* noticed her abrupt stop, and one by one, each of them followed her gaze to see what she was looking at. Olivia was the last to look, and only did so after she saw all the others doing the same, but just as she did, Sam appeared in the doorway.

For 90% of the guests, nothing had changed, and conversations didn't stop or even pause much at all, but for the Abrams family, something crazy was playing out before them.

As everyone looked on, their mouths hung open in a mix of fear and bemusement as Olivia and Sam were now just three feet from each other for the first time in at least six years.

The music continued playing, the conversations rambled on, and nothing but a light, warm breeze passed through the yard, but for the second time in only thirty seconds, the flimsy force field surrounding their family received an unexpected, violent shake.

As Caroline sat back down and retrieved her garbage from the grass below her seat, Lenny stood up and smiled fakely as he walked over to greet Sam by the door.

Sam stepped out onto the deck and shook Lenny's hand, then Lenny put his hand on his back and intentionally turned him away from Olivia, bringing him over toward the coolers filled with beer.

Olivia made eye contact with Haley first and then with Phyllis, who both looked at her like she was an uncaged animal about to attack. Instead, Olivia simply dropped her cigarette to the deck and stomped it out, then retreated into the house to pour herself another cup of something strong.

"Sam looks good," Alan said to Phyllis.

"You haven't seen him yet?"

"No, I haven't seen him yet. When would I have seen him?"

"I thought maybe you'd caught him while out on one of your walks through town. Nancy and I saw him outside the hardware store two weeks ago, and he said he'd been back and forth there quite a lot."

"Well good for you and Nancy. You think Livi's okay?"

"*She'll* be fine," Phyllis replied confidently, turning back around. "Sam's the one who should be afraid."

Alan thought about it for a moment, and then decided to go inside and check on her anyway. He reached for his cane, stood up slowly, partially with Ben's help, then limped off toward the house, his eyes filled with deep thoughts and a strong urge for some much-needed mirth.

Once he got inside, Olivia glanced at him from the entrance to the dining room. She was already propped up there against the doorway, holding a red Solo cup filled to the top with liquor, and quickly returned her gaze toward Sam out in the backyard.

"Who are you watching?" Alan asked, pretending not to know. "Haley? Erika? Her weirdo little sister?"

He looked at Olivia sideways, hoping he'd see a little smile, but got nothing.

Alan prided himself as a man of considerable good advice, whether or not anyone ever took it, and most of them never did. Still, he knew that as Olivia's father, it was his duty to at least *try* to shake her out of this.

He dropped a few ice cubes from the freezer into his cup, then poured himself another helping of Jim Beam. Walking back over to Olivia a moment later, he held out his cup to toast her. She stared at it for a moment like it was a joke, then tapped her cup against his and they each took a drink.

"What are we drinking to?" she asked him, after the fact.

"Do we need a reason?" he said, eyebrows raised.

"No. Guess not. Although I have a few ideas."

"Oh, cut the crap," he said, walking over to the couch. "Don't be such a whiny little bitch."

"Excuse me?"

She watched him move, much slower than he should have, in the direction of the couch, and noted how he struggled to sit down once he got there. When had her father gotten so old, she wondered. He was only 75, but he moved around lately like he was closer to 90.

Alan sighed once he was comfortable in the couch, his back to the yard and his face to Olivia. He looked up at her as he decided what to say and how to say it. She was a tough cookie, and he liked that about her, but he didn't want her to be so pissed off all the time either.

He knew getting so worked up over this wasn't doing anything for her, or her looks for that matter. He sized her up as she stared out the window and the sliding glass door, depending, Alan guessed, on where Sam was at the moment.

"Are you still in love with him?" he finally asked.

Olivia looked right at him now with her mouth wide open, shocked at the question—no, the *accusation*.

"Are you kidding me, Dad? Am I in— No, I am not in *love* with him. Holy shit. Why would you even ask me that?"

"I'm just asking, geez. Leave me alone, I'm old."

"Yeah, I've noticed."

Alan smiled at this, then bobbed his head in agreement. He took a sip of his bourbon, then shook the cup around a bit, watching as the ice cubes glistened in the light from the overhead high hats.

"You know, Livi. My dad used to take me out on little trips to teach me things. It wasn't often, but I always knew it was meant to be a life lesson he'd thought about in advance. This one time, he brought me over to the New York Aquarium on Coney Island. This was in 1957, right when it opened. I was only 15 years old.

"He brought me all around the place, pointing out different fish in the tanks, telling me their names like he was a goddamn expert, even though I could see all he was doing was reading the signs and repeating back to me what he'd just learned seconds earlier. I listened to it all just the same though, of course. But do you know what we did *after* the aquarium?"

Olivia glanced at him briefly, then back to the yard.

"I don't know, Dad. He bought you a hotdog at Nathan's?"

"No. The hotdog would come later. I *wanted* the hotdog, but no, he said he wanted to show me something else first. He brought me over to the boardwalk, and he made me sit down on a bench. Then he took off his coat. It was June, like now, but he always wore this long overcoat, I'll never forget it. He took off his coat, he folded it in half, and then he tossed it down on the bench right next to me.

"Then he untucked his shirt, messed up his hair a bit, and ran over to the other side, lying down on the boardwalk like he'd just been shot, or kicked in the balls or something. He held up a finger at me to just wait and watch. Well, not five minutes later, a couple of guys came by, young guys too, and as soon as they saw him there, they went right over to help him up.

"He stood up and thanked them, assured them he was okay, and then he came back over to me. 'Did you see that?' he asked me. 'Those fellas didn't know me from Adam, but they came over to help me anyway.'"

Alan took another sip, and shook his head with a smile.

"Jesus, that was 60 years ago, but I can still remember it like it was yesterday. I can't remember *yesterday* like it was yesterday, but I can remember that day pretty damn well."

"Dad, was there—*I dunno*—a *point* of some kind to your story?"

"Of course there was a goddamn point. The point is, when someone's in trouble, there will always be good people who'll stop to help them."

Olivia shook her head and took a drink.

"You watch too many superhero movies."

Alan watched her sadly as she moved toward the kitchen to get more ice for her drink, her gaze still fixed out the windows above Alan's head.

"Livi, listen to me. Sam's in trouble. He's been in trouble for a long, long time now. There are some people out there who are trying to help him, I imagine, but it seems many more just want him dead."

Olivia stopped what she was doing and stared at him, eyes wide open as she waited for more, but soon realizing he was done.

"Dad, I don't know what to say to you right now. Are you *trying* to make me angry with that little fairytale?"

"Well I thought that—"

"Seriously, what the fuck? And where's the story about the little girl who grew up to marry a cheating asshole and accused murderer? Got any little stories like *that* in your memory bank too, or was the one about how I should help the poor little killer your only one?"

She slammed the freezer door closed, then disappeared down the hallway. He heard the bathroom door slam shut a moment later too, and shrugged it off quickly as he took another sip of his drink.

"What *did* I do yesterday?"

Outside in the yard a few minutes later, Sam was chatting with Haley and Erika about the property he'd bought on Lake Pauline. Erika seemed really interested, and told him he should throw a huge party there soon.

"Uncle Sam, you are *so* cool," Erika said. "I totally need to introduce you to my friends. Oh, and we're partying over in Manchester tonight too if you wanna come."

Erika grabbed his arm and led him over to a large group of her friends, and Haley just watched and smiled. A moment later, Olivia came up behind her, now watching Sam and the girls from a distance as well.

"Haley, I swear to God, your father should know better."

Haley opened her mouth to argue, but Olivia shook her head and stopped her right away.

"No. *Listen* to me. This has nothing to do with me, so don't even start. This has to do with him being the suspected murderer of a 16-year-old girl, and being so completely brainless as to show up here and casually wander into a group of giggling young girls with all their parents watching."

"Oh."

"Yeah. '*Oh*.'"

Olivia walked away from her and over to Lenny and Caroline, where she quickly complained to them about the same thing. Before Lenny heard the end of it, he watched as Haley began leading Sam inside.

"Well, it looks like Haley took care of it," he said, but as Olivia sat down, Lenny decided to go in and check on things for himself. He passed Alan leaving the house as he went in.

"Dad."

"Leonard."

When he got inside, Lenny saw Haley and Sam already heading

out the front door, so he put his beer down on the counter, planning to follow them out.

As he watched the door close in front of him though, Jenn's face suddenly appeared in the hallway between him and the door. She'd just left the bathroom, and was as surprised to see Lenny as he was to see her.

He turned around instinctively to make sure Caroline was still outside, and by the time he turned back, Jenn had moved up even closer to him. She turned her head and looked at his lips, but as she leaned in to kiss him, he stopped her gently with his hand.

"Why don't we meet soon to talk about this some more. But not now, okay?"

She looked like she might argue with him at first, but then she nodded with a quick smile.

"Okay, when?"

He looked behind him again, and then back at her, still thinking it out.

"Uh, how about Monday? Peaches has a thing after school, and Erika will be away at a concert—unless you're going too?"

"No."

"And my wife will be working. I'll leave work early, at say, three o'clock? And I'll be back here by 3:45. You can come by then. Does that work?"

Jenn nodded with a smile, then passed him as close as she could on her way back to the party. He felt her left breast graze his chest as she did.

Alone again with a slight erection growing in his pants, Lenny wondered what he'd just done. Had he just invited her to come over to fool around, or to break her heart all over again?

He had the strangest feeling just then too, like some part of his brain was working on auto-pilot, detached from all common sense and good reasoning, yet he felt helpless to find her again to cancel.

Why should I? I haven't done anything wrong. I just scheduled a meeting. To discuss. That's all.

134

Lenny's mind filled quickly with every dark thought he'd ever had about the girl, every fantasy and daydream, every inch of her he ached to explore and taste and enter.

Before he got any more *excited* than he already was though, he went back into the kitchen and retrieved his beer to go outside, the cold bottle helping to chill the inner burning of his idiot male brain.

Halfway out the door, he realized he'd already forgotten about Sam and Haley. Just as well, he figured, looking back. Haley took care of it. The crisis had been averted, and that's all that mattered.

Chapter 16

Olivia was getting very drunk very fast, and Haley could tell, even while still avoiding her from across the yard.

Haley sat beside Peaches on the hammock, the two of them chatting with Roger across from them in a chair.

Twenty-five minutes earlier, she'd told Sam he should probably leave the party, that it wasn't a good idea after all for him to be there with so many young girls around, and he thankfully agreed. She'd hoped he wasn't hurt by the rebuke, but his face was once again hard to read.

"So how do you two know each other?" Haley asked Roger.

"We met at a poetry thing a few months ago. Peaches told me about the circle she goes to, and I went the last two times."

"Oh, okay. So you're not in the same class at school then?"

Roger and Peaches looked at her with their mouths wide open, and after glancing at each other, they both broke into hysterics.

"Oh my God, Haley. Roger is 21. I'm only 16."

"What? You're 21? No way. You look so much younger."

"You thought I was only 16?"

"No, no. I mean, well, yes, at first I did, but when I realized you could drive, I figured you might be 17 or maybe 18."

Roger shook his head, picking up a stick off the ground to play with it.

##

"Who is that colored boy talking to our girls over there?" Alan asked. He straightened up in the chair, his cup paused midair just an inch from his mouth. "I saw him with Peaches in The Hatchery this past Monday too."

"Colored boy?" Caroline asked him, her whole face contorted with shock. "And what *color* would that be?"

Alan looked at her for a moment with some confusion, then back over at Roger again as he shrugged.

136

"The hell if I know. Dark chocolate, I suppose."

"We used to call them Negroes," Benjie said. "You know, back in Brooklyn."

He nodded confidently with a smile, like he was happy to teach the younger generation a new lesson.

"They call themselves niggers," Alan said. "But we're not *allowed* to say that. At least not to their faces."

Caroline looked back and forth between them, unable to speak.

"What?" Alan asked her.

"Alan, I don't even know where to begin—and did you call them 'our girls' before, like Roger was some kind of a danger to the two of them?"

"His name is Roger?"

"Yes, his name is Roger, and I promise you, there isn't a dangerous bone in that boy's body. He's very sweet, and I really don't like you implying anything otherwise."

"Whoa, whoa, whoa," Lenny leaned in with a hand out, only half paying attention to their conversation. "I don't think that's what my dad meant."

"Yes it was," Alan said.

"What?"

"I said yes, it *was* what I meant, Leonard. But I was simply making sure the girls were okay. Never mind," he said, taking another drink.

Caroline sighed, looking away from him with her hand over her mouth, deciding to let it go for the moment. There were too many people around, and she didn't want to spoil Erika's party.

##

Back on the hammock, Haley was busy asking Roger far too many questions, and she knew it. She'd never been with a black boy, but couldn't escape the intense attraction growing within her, especially knowing his real age was actually so close to her own.

All the boys she ever dated were pasty white boys, the only crop she had to choose from up there, even at college. Outside of heavy petting, and a blowjob Brad Colley pressured her into giving him, Haley wasn't very experienced with boys anyway, no matter what they looked like. While some girls proudly *got around*, Haley barely got nearby.

"So do you like delivering pizzas?"

What? Why are you asking him that? What a dumb question.

"Yeah, it's okay. The money's not great, but you get to see the inside of a lot of people's houses, and that can be cool. Plus some people order every week, and you get to know them pretty well."

In her brain, Haley leapt between crazy thoughts.

Is Roger a good kisser? switched to *Why does Roger want to know what people's houses look like? Is it so he can rob them later?* to *Oh my God, what a crazy racist thing to think!* and then back to a thought about Roger fucking her after delivering pizza one night.

As she smiled at him and nodded, Haley made a mental note to order pizza more often.

##

"Someone should take Olivia home," Phyllis finally said.

It wasn't that she minded Olivia drinking or smoking, or even making a complete fool out of herself. It was that she minded her giving up, and giving in. For the past 16 years of her life, Olivia had *decided* to be angry.

She woke up each day and reaffirmed her rage, finding new reasons to be pissed, and she went to bed pissed as well. Anger was her drug of choice, and Phyllis knew it wasn't the kind of substance Olivia would be able to quit cold turkey.

Phyllis understood her daughter's anger too. She was just as pissed at Sam as Olivia was, right from the beginning, only she'd lived longer and seen enough heartache over the years in all the hospitals and nursing homes she worked at to let it affect her the same way.

For Phyllis, anger was something you wielded like a sword, something that protected you from all the heartache the world threw at you. Anger, she believed, could be an asset, and certainly not a hindrance to finding happiness. It wasn't an emotion you should allow to master you.

Even so, she knew Olivia couldn't hold her anger as well as most people could. She couldn't let it help her. Instead, she seemed to let it control her life, and even blind her to the truth.

Lenny laughed, halfway through a story.

"And did you see how they looked at each other before? It was like a cat and a dog staring each other down for a fight."

Everyone laughed at this, and Caroline and Phyllis locked eyes briefly as Phyllis tuned back in.

"Yeah, but which one's the cat and which one's the dog?" Uncle Benjie asked, slapping his leg hard with laughter.

They all laughed again. Everyone but Phyllis.

"Oh, hush now, all of you," she said, collecting her thoughts and looking at them with a sly smile. "Besides, the answer to that is quite clear to me at least, and should be to all of you too."

"*Mom,*" Lenny tried to stop her.

"My daughter's had her claws out for a fight since the day Sam left town. As for him, well, I think he's just a poor little pussycat."

"Well," Benjie said, "I'll bet Sam will never have it half as good as he did with Olivia. He's probably going from one piece of trash to another, a slut in every town."

It took everything in Phyllis's power not to look at Caroline just then, but she burst out laughing just the same, and by the time she finished laughing, and did steal a glance Caroline's way, she was happy to see how angry she looked.

Serves her right, Phyllis thought.

"Come now, Alan, Ben," she said, standing up. "We should go. Ben, can you drive Olivia home? I'll drive her car, and you can follow along in yours. Alan, you go home and rest. I don't want to risk you crashing the Buick."

Alan stood up gingerly, then dropped his empty cup down on the table, watching it carefully as it rolled over off the edge and onto the grass.

"Should you be driving, Dad?" Lenny asked him.

"You mean because of my knee or because of the liquor?"

"Um, I don't know. Both?"

"I'm fine, don't worry. I've only had a few drinks. And besides, at my age, people *expect* me to go 20 miles an hour while swerving."

"It's only a couple miles," Phyllis said. "He'll be fine."

##

Across the yard, Haley was smiling, happy to have finally gotten a chance to chat with Roger some more, when the mood shifted.

"So what's the deal with your dad?" Roger asked her. "Peaches said he got mixed up in something really big years ago?"

Haley's face sagged, and she looked away at nothing in particular with a very long *"Umm,"* as Peaches shot Roger a look.

"Oh, God. I'm sorry. Never mind. My bad. I shouldn't have—"

"No, it's fine. I just—I don't know what to say. It's all been kept a mystery from us," she said, looking at Peaches. "It happened when I was little, and even though my Uncle Lenny says my dad was innocent, it was enough to really mess things up between my mom and dad. They don't even talk anymore."

"Things are weird between my mom and dad too," Roger said. "She doesn't talk to him too much, and I hardly ever see him."

"The thing is," Haley went on. "There's something really strange about—"

She stopped mid-sentence when she saw her grandparents approaching them. It looked like they were leaving, and she'd have to say goodbye, but she also wanted to talk more about her father. The past was one of her favorite things to think about, especially since she was always told not to.

"There was this girl," Haley said, locking eyes with Peaches as she spoke.

Peaches knew the topic was taboo, and she gave Haley a guilty smile as she began, encouraging her to say more.

"My dad was seeing her behind my mom's back, and the girl was still in high school, so it was its own kind of creepy crazy—"

She shook her head, not wanting to go down that road, as the cheating itself was something she couldn't forgive her father for.

"And, anyway," she finished, "the girl was found dead, and the police thought my dad did it, or they still do, or whatever."

Peaches laughed a little when she saw Roger's face, a look of great shock arriving as he struggled to close his mouth, but Haley was already jumping up from the hammock with a big smile as Phyllis, Alan, and Benjie approached them to say goodbye.

"Bye Grandma, bye Grandpa, bye Uncle Benjie," Haley said, kissing each of them on the cheek.

Peaches got up and did the same, and Roger just stood up and grinned oddly, noting their faces when they looked at him. He could sense they felt at least as awkward as he did, and for the moment, that would have to be alright. He wanted to hear more from Haley, and he wasn't really interested in whether or not her grandparents liked him anyway.

"I'm sorry. I shouldn't have even mentioned it," Haley said once she turned around again, looking at Roger now just two feet away. "It's just, I'm not supposed to talk about it, so if you could please just forget I said anything, and definitely don't tell my mom or anyone else in our family that I told you?"

He was smiling at her though, and Haley didn't know why.

"What?" she asked.

"Nothing. I was just thinking how much closer I feel to you all of a sudden, because you trusted me enough to tell me all that."

"Oh, okay. Good," she said with a quick smile back.

"But I was also thinking," he said, pausing to look at Peaches, "that you need to tell me the rest of the story now too."

"Yes!" Peaches said, giggling.

Peaches, who knew very little about the situation, sensed Haley knew much more than she was letting on.

"Oh my God, no. I really shouldn't have even said anything. I could get into a lot of trouble, you guys. And Peaches, your mom and dad would be really mad at me if I told you. Everyone in our family keeps these things low-key for a reason, and I don't want it to get out of hand."

Peaches, who had already fallen back into the hammock, stood up again quickly and pulled Roger and Haley into a tight huddle.

"No. We need to hear *everything*, Haley. And we'll both keep it a secret, I promise. Roger and I don't have any friends anyway, except for the people in the circle, but they're the sweetest people ever. You *have* to tell us."

Peaches pulled her arms off them, and Haley looked over toward the house. She saw her mother walking inside with her grandparents, Uncle Lenny, and Uncle Ben. Despite all her attempts at keeping things silent, she really *did* want to tell them what she knew, if only to compare notes.

She and Erika were never very close, but now that Peaches was old enough, it felt like maybe she *should* talk to her, and talking with Roger about anything wouldn't suck either. With her father back in town, Haley was aching to talk to somebody about it all, and Peaches and Roger did seem to be the perfect people.

"Fine. Okay, I'll tell you what I know. But you can't tell anyone, okay? Like, no one. It's extremely important that you don't talk to anyone about *any* of this. Promise me?"

They both promised, swearing up and down to keep quiet.

"Okay, but I can't say more here anyway. What time is it now?"

She went for her phone, but Peaches beat her to it.

"3:07," Peaches said.

"Okay," Haley said, thinking out possible places they could talk privately. There would be people just about everywhere though on a nice Saturday afternoon like that. "Meet me over by—no, that won't work. I don't want us to meet anywhere where my dad might see us talking, or anyone else really. How about—no, that wouldn't work either."

"I know a place," Peaches said, a huge smile on her face, "and it's someplace I *guarantee* you none of them would ever visit."

She beamed at them, so proud of herself for the brilliant idea.

"Where?" Haley asked.

"The Weston Priory. Drive over to Weston, but make a right instead of a left on 155, then make the very first left turn where the sign is for the Priory. There'll only be monks and tourists up there, and either way, there are lots of little spots we can sit and talk for a while without anyone hearing us, or anyone in our family even seeing us together."

Haley was impressed, and nodded at her with a smile.

"Okay, yeah, I know where that is. I was there once years ago, and I pass the sign all the time."

"I know exactly where that is," Roger said.

"Okay, cool. Roger, can you drive Peaches, then? I just want to check on my mom first, and then I'll meet you guys over there at like 4, okay?"

"Yep, no problem. See you then."

##

Roger and Peaches pulled into the parking lot at 3:57, and saw Haley was already there. She was leaning on her car looking at her phone when they pulled up, and offered them a wave when she saw it was them.

Peaches got out first, and after looking around and taking a deep breath, she encouraged Roger and Haley to follow her over to a few chairs off by themselves on the far side of the pond. It was so quiet and peaceful up there too, only the occasional sound of birds chirping in the distance.

As they sat down and got comfortable, Peaches could hardly contain her excitement, realizing Haley was finally going to tell her more of what happened all those years ago.

"Okay, listen," Haley started. "First of all, you both need to swear to me again you won't tell anyone in the family I told you this, and you can't tell anyone else anything I say either, okay? My dad has been through so much, and the last thing I want to do is hurt him in any way, okay?"

They both nodded seriously, and Haley was glad to see Peaches wasn't smiling anymore.

"Okay. So basically, this all happened back in 2000. I was only like five or six years old, Erika was, what? One? And Peaches, you weren't even born yet. Everything back then was different. My mom and dad were super close, or at least they always seemed like it, so it all came as a shock to me when my dad moved out.

"My mom didn't tell me too much at the time because I was little, only that she and my dad needed to get a divorce. I didn't even know what that meant. He moved to Vegas not long after. Now, I had no idea what was happening or why, but I do remember that girl's death, because everyone in town was talking about it. Back then, I had no idea the two things were connected. I knew my mom and dad were getting a divorce, and I knew the police were around, asking my mom a lot of questions, but I had no idea my dad was involved. I didn't think in a million years my dad would be caught up in something like that, you know?"

"Yeah," Roger said, nodding seriously.

"Anyway, as I got older, I started to figure it out. It was hard not to, actually. But no one, not even my mom, would ever talk to me about it, and they always made it clear I wasn't even supposed to ask questions or say anything to anyone."

"Yeah, same with me," Peaches said, glancing at Roger.

"But once I got to college, I realized I just needed to know, you know? So I went through old newspaper clippings, local stuff mostly that was on file in my school's library. The internet had helped a little too, but since it all happened like 13 years earlier, and was just a local story there in Ludlow, I couldn't find a whole lot."

"But you found something?" Peaches asked.

Haley took a deep breath and nodded. Peaches pulled her chair in a little closer then, and Roger followed suit.

"So my dad and this girl, Kerry Ann Jefferson, had apparently been having an affair. She was like 16 when they first met, and he was in his 20s. They hooked up a few times apparently, but on the night of their last date, someone killed her, and she was found dead the next morning, like out in a field or whatever."

Haley paused, and took a moment to look away from them before she continued.

"Two witnesses said they saw my dad with her earlier that night, and she and my dad had spoken on the phone just before it happened too, so that's why he was arrested. The girl's friends said it *had* to have been my dad, because he'd been seeing her secretly, and like, buying her stuff.

"The case went to trial, but the police couldn't prove he killed her. He said he wasn't with her that night, or out in that field, but the police reports all said he seemed like he was lying to them. At least that's what the newspapers said *about* the police reports.

"They said something didn't seem right, but because they had no hard evidence—well, except for his semen on her underwear, which he swore was from the night before—there was nothing else they could do. Like, I think the jury appreciated he was telling the truth about weird things like that, but they still didn't know what to do. And the family of the girl was split too. Some were sure my dad was guilty, but then Kerry Ann's family wanted it all to just go away after a while. They didn't even want to press charges in a civil suit after the criminal trial ended with a hung jury."

Peaches and Roger just looked at her then, waiting for her to go on, but Haley seemed to be finished.

"That's it?" Peaches asked.

"Yeah," Haley said, looking back at them. "Why? What else would there be besides that?"

"Well, do you think he's telling the truth? And how'd she die?"

"Oh. Well, she had bruises on her body, and internal bleeding too, but they said she died of asphyxiation, so like, strangled or something. The reports were really crazy, and no one knew why she was out in that field there anyway. There was no sign of anything suspicious nearby, but it rained that night, so they said some evidence may have been lost."

Peaches leaned back in her chair and shook her head.

"What?" Haley asked, suddenly looking scared. "You think my dad really killed her?"

"No. *Well,* I mean, maybe? But what worries me the most about everything you just said is something you *didn't* say."

Haley made a face.

"What didn't I say? That's seriously all I know, Peaches."

Peaches looked at Roger, and then back to Haley.

"You didn't mention my tree house."

"What? What does your tree house have to do with anything?"

"Don't you think it's weird that we're not allowed to go near it? Ever since I was little, I was told to stay away from that thing. They even took off the ladder that went up the tree."

"So?"

"Haley, they only built the tree house months before that girl was killed. It isn't in any pictures from before Erika was born. She and I were never allowed inside. Doesn't that seem odd to you?"

Peaches looked away for a while as she collected her thoughts, and then turned back to stare at Haley before she spoke next.

"I think the tree house has something to do with all this, and what scares me even more is, I'm pretty sure everyone in our family except you, me, and Erika knows something about it."

Chapter 17

Erika slowly raised her eyelids to look around, unsure of where she was or how she got there. Her vision was fuzzy, but she heard laughter coming from people nearby, and after another minute or so, she realized she must still be at the house party she'd traveled to five hours earlier.

"I think she's waking up," a boy's voice said nearby, and two girls laughed.

There's nothing funny about this, the boy wanted to say to them, annoyed by their laughter, but he also knew it wasn't worth the trouble. *You should care that your friend passed out like that.*

"She's done this before," one of them said, noting the look on his face.

"And that doesn't concern you? She's blacking out *often,* and you find that amusing?"

This time he'd said it out loud, and his sudden anger seemed to sober the girls up more than they wanted.

"Seriously dude, she's fine. It's cool."

"No, *dude.* It's not cool, actually. Drinking so much your body collapses like that is not at all cool *or* normal."

He watched as the girls just shook their heads and walked away, one with her middle finger out to her side. As Erika finally came to, too slowly realizing what had happened to her, the boy spoke again.

"I'm Chris. We met a couple hours ago. There were a lot more people here then."

As her vision cleared, she saw the boy's face appear in front of her like a friendly apparition through the late-night mist of the mountainside, the rising fog of her drunken headspace. Erika couldn't remember him from earlier, but was just sober enough to appreciate how cute he was.

"Where am I? What time is it?" she asked him, forgetting there was a contraption tucked inside her pocket that had all the answers and more.

"It's after 3 now," he said, having just checked his phone. "And we're at a house party in Manchester."

"Wait, 3 AM?"

He looked up at the stars in the sky with some confusion at first, and then back at her.

"Uh, yeah?"

"Fuck. Where is Nicole? She's my ride home."

"Which one is she?"

"Short brown hair, always looks surprised?"

"Oh, yeah. She left like an hour ago."

"What? Fuck!"

"There were two other girls here a minute ago, but they walked down the hill, and I think one of them mentioned something about an Uber."

Erika looked around her now, realizing no one else was there. She'd been left alone in a stranger's yard with a boy she didn't know, even though anything could have happened to her. *Why is he still here?*

"Why didn't you leave too?" she asked him.

"Foxes, bears, moose, mosquitos—I figured someone oughtta make sure you weren't eaten alive out here. And it didn't seem like your friends cared too much."

"They're not my—thank you."

She looked into his eyes, sober enough now to wonder if he was attracted to her, or simply kind enough to prove himself a decent human being. The soft brown swirls of his eyes, hiding just beyond his delicate eyelids, captured her in a trance she didn't want to shake.

"Why are you staring at me like that?" he asked.

Fuck.

"I'm sorry," she said, immediately looking away, the mountain spinning around her as she did. She raised her hands to her head and tried to focus. "I can't believe it's already after three."

"You miss your curfew or something?" the boy asked.

"No. I mean, yeah, but they don't care. Well, I mean, they *care*, but they don't usually make a big deal about it. They're not, like, waiting up for me or anything."

She looked at him cautiously then, unsure if she should have told him this. Her eyes narrowed briefly as he turned away and smiled, and she figured he would have tried something by now if he was an asshole.

"I'm Erika," she said, getting him to look at her again, getting him to point his beautiful brown eyes in her direction once more.

"I know."

Huh?

"I mean, that's what your friends were calling you before."

"Oh, right."

"I'm Chris."

"Hi, Chris. This isn't your house, is it?"

"No, I live up in Vershire."

"What? Where is that? That doesn't even sound real."

"Ha. Yeah, it's real. Vershire. It's a combination of Vermont and New Hampshire. Vershire."

"Wait, are you just kidding, or—"

"No, it's totally real. It's about two hours north of here."

"Oh, okay."

"How 'bout you? You live here?"

"No, Ludlow. By Okemo."

"Okay, so not too far."

"Yeah, a lot better than your drive home," she said, collecting her things.

"Yeah, but I'm not going yet anyway. I'll wait till the sunrise, and then head out. I don't want to run into any moose or bear on the way home."

"You get them by you?"

"Oh, they're all over. Not *too* many, but they're a hell of a lot easier to crash into when it's still dark out. At this point, I'd rather watch the sunrise here, and then start up."

Erika nodded, unsure what to say, and wondered how much longer it'd be for the sun to come up. She'd only graduated from high school hours earlier, but the whole world already felt different.

"So you're just gonna sit here till like 6 AM?"

Chris smiled, sizing her up more than he had before, and taking a moment to appreciate her more sober self. He liked how cool and relaxed she was, and could tell she wasn't nearly as obnoxious as her friends were, although if she had friends like them, well, maybe he wasn't so sure yet.

He looked up at the stars again and tried to catch a satellite. Once he spotted one, he watched it move slowly across the horizon, amazed that men had built the thing so many years ago on Earth before releasing it into the heavens.

"Around 4:30," he said after another minute had passed.

Erika looked up from her cell phone confused. She stared at the back of his head then, begging it to speak more.

"What?" she decided to ask.

"Around 4:30," he repeated, sure now he had her attention. "The darkness will begin to lighten up a bit as the Earth spins closer to the dawning sunlight. First light of the sunrise comes just after 5 AM. I'll drive home then."

Erika looked back down at her phone. 3:28 AM. If she was gonna shell out fifty bucks for an Uber, she'd have to do it now, but if Chris could drive her home instead—*she'd already looked up where Vershire was*—she'd have to wait another hour and a half.

He peeked back at her, sensing the computer hard at work in her brain, and decided to save her by making the offer first.

"I can drive you back to Ludlow if you don't mind waiting a little while longer."

He held back a big smile then, knowing his idea of *a little while* was not at all the same as hers. She didn't answer right away, still thinking it out, and choosing to look away from him as she did.

"There are some chips stuffed in the red cooler over there."

She looked back at him quickly with a wry smile, like he had just read her mind without her permission. Standing up, and shaking off the chill in the air, she surprised herself as much as Chris with her balance and control, soon stomping confidently in the direction of the cooler.

A bag of Cool Ranch Doritos floated sadly on its side next to three unopened Coronas and a can of soda. Erika felt ill just at the sight of the beer, but she yanked the Doritos and soda out, and shoved a few chips in her mouth as she faced the house. The back door was shut, but she was pretty sure it would still be unlocked.

Now that she was standing, and having just shoved her hand into ice-cold water, the urge to pee came fast.

Glancing back toward Chris out on the lawn, she was amused to see him still staring up at the stars, as if they alone were worth spending hours looking at. She glanced up briefly, then back at him, sure she must be missing something. Then she went in the house to use the bathroom.

By the time she came back out again, after taking some time to fix her face and hair, she watched him first from the window.

Chris was a lot thinner than most guys she knew, and clean-shaven too.

Don't be gay, don't be gay, don't be gay. She repeated it over and over again like a mantra, first out loud in a whisper, and then in her head, all while marching back down the grassy hill to where she found him still lying down and looking up at the stars.

"You missed the Space Station," he said.

Erika made a face.

"You can see that from the ground?"

He looked at her with a new kind of smile.

"So, don't take this the wrong way or anything," he said, "but how do you not know that?"

He'd just called her stupid, and they both knew it, but Chris hoped some combination of him being her only ride home and the general sweetness with which he spoke his harsh words had helped soften the blow.

Erika didn't really mind, as she'd long since given up trying to reach whatever intellectual milestones others had found for themselves. She'd gotten her high school diploma at last, and was content to just glide through the waters of life for a while, both oars firmly inside the boat.

She narrowed her eyes at him with a smile though just the same, as if warning him to tread carefully. The look said *strike one,* and if Chris was straight after all, he'd just received his first pushback of the night.

"You're really cute," he said with a smile, surprising them both.

She had only just gotten comfortable on the grass, a bag of Doritos in one hand and four or five chips already halfway through her mouth with the other when he said it, so there was no elegant way for her to thank him for the sweet compliment while still appearing worthy.

"Sorry," he said, looking away again with a sheepish grin. "I'd normally wait till I know a girl a while longer before coming on to her, but what the fuck. It's almost 4 AM, I'm tired, and you're hot, so whatever."

He said all this while still looking up at the stars, so as Erika chewed her chips and looked at him, she felt like she'd just met him again for the very first time. He caught her staring a half a minute later, and she allowed exactly four seconds of eye contact before turning away.

"I thought you were gay," she said to the bag of Doritos, and then, in case he thought it a slur, she quickly clarified. "You know, because you were being so polite and kind to me, and hadn't hit on me yet."

Oh God, she thought, *now I sound obnoxious.* She shook her head with a smile, and he couldn't help but laugh.

"Well, I *wanted* to hit on you right away, but you didn't seem to be ready for much conversation earlier." He could tell she was blushing. "I'm sorry if I broke protocol by not informing you earlier about how hot you looked."

Their eyes locked once more, for much longer this time. He'd managed to erase the strike against him, and she was now two strikes down instead.

"How often does the Space Station pass over?" she asked, abruptly changing the subject. "Like once every few days, or what?"

"Twice tonight, but most nights only once."

He'd been waiting for her to ask, as he'd already pulled the information up on his phone while she was in the bathroom, hoping to impress her.

"Wow," I had no idea. "Cool. So do they like, still use it? Or is it just a bunch of old computers up there now?"

"There are a few astronauts up there right now. Some of them just do a few months, but others stay a year or more."

This part Chris knew without checking, as he watched a lot of programs on space travel on cable TV.

"Jesus," Erika said.

"I don't think *he* ever went to space, but I'm also not a Mormon, so I dunno about that."

"No, I mean, there are people up there *right now*?"

He smiled, more amused that she didn't get the joke than he would have been if she had.

"Yep. Astronauts from several different countries have been up there consistently since it launched in 2000."

"Wow!"

She took three more Doritos, then closed the bag again. She thought to put it down, then tossed it halfway to Chris as an afterthought.

"Sorry," she said with half a laugh. "Thought I threw it further."

He sat up and pointed.

"Twilight".

She looked where he was pointing, and noticed the darkness was a tick lighter than it'd been before. Had an hour passed that fast? She looked at her phone. 3.47.

"I don't think that's the sun yet," she said. "I mean, I'm no scientist? But based on what you told me before, it's still too early."

Chris sat up straight and reached into his pocket for his phone. He looked at it with some confusion, and then across at the horizon again.

"You're right. What the hell is that?"

Erika shook her head, unsure herself, then watched as he stood up and looked around, trying to figure out which direction was which, and after a few seconds, he gave up and opened an app. Spinning around, he muttered something under his breath, then pointed behind them.

"Yeah, the sun would rise over that way. So what the fuck *is* that?" He turned back around, half looking at his phone and half at the sky. "Holy shit. I think it might be a fire."

"What?!"

Erika stood up now too to take a look.

"No," he said. "No, I'm sorry. Not a fire. A fire wouldn't look like that." He looked at his phone again. "I think that's Okemo in the distance, though. They must be checking their lights or something."

"Oh, well the country music festival is tomorrow night, or tonight or whatever. They must be preparing for that."

He stared at the light in the distance for a long while, then shook his head a little, but she didn't notice. He was sure she was wrong, that they wouldn't have put lights on at that hour, but decided against arguing, figuring he'd just investigate after dropping her home.

"You ready for that ride home now actually?"

"Yeah, totally."

Erika grabbed her purse and the soda, dropping the chips off on the deck before following him out to the road.

##

On the east side of Okemo Mountain, over two dozen people began spreading out once the lights were on, and all of them were calling out the same name: 'Skip'. It may have sounded like they were looking for a lost dog, but instead it was eight-year-old Skip Spieth, a boy from Danbury, Connecticut who'd wandered off on his bike earlier in the evening and presumably gotten lost.

Skip had been missing for hours from another part of the mountain, but when his bike was finally found on the east side of the mountain, a new search began, and the power grid switched on for the nighttime ski slopes on Okemo.

If his bike chain had broken off or his tire had gone flat, everyone would have understood why he'd left his bicycle behind, but it was still in perfectly good shape, which concerned them all that much more.

"Skiiiip!" his father Henry yelled out, nearly breathless with fear.

His wife Heather squeezed his hand tightly as they walked up the slope a bit more, then she called out as well, her voice breaking off as she choked back tears by the end.

"Skip, honey! It's Mommy and Daddy. Where are—"

A police officer across from them shook his head. If the boy was lost, the lights and their calling would have brought him out for sure, but still they heard nothing. He already feared the worst.

##

After driving for a few minutes in silence, Erika finally realized she'd never told Chris what she thought of him, and wondered if she needed to.

"It's really sweet of you to bring me home. Thank you," she said softly, looking at him as he drove.

He kept his eyes on the road, but smiled.

"My pleasure."

She glanced down at his legs, and thought about whether or not to do it, then just reached over quickly before overthinking it, rubbing his knee slightly as she spoke.

"Seriously, I really appreciate it," she said, pulling her hand back into her lap again.

He looked at her quickly and smiled.

"Does that mean you're into me, or do you still think I'm gay?"

Erika blushed and shook her head, turning away from him to look out her window before responding.

"No, I do *not* think you're gay."

He looked at her again, still facing away from him, and in between his careful watch of the road, he stole a glance at her legs now too. Her thighs, turned slightly away from him, looked tan and silky smooth, even in the darkness of night, with just flashes of street lights briefly illuminating them. They practically beckoned for him to touch them, and if he wasn't such a goddamn gentleman, he would have already made a move.

Erika's hand on his knee was a good start, but Chris had made this kind of stupid mistake before. The only thing girls hated more than aggressive confidence was *unwanted* aggressive confidence. He wished girls were more transparent, less cloudy when it came to this kind of thing, especially since he didn't want to *only* feel her thigh. He wanted to feel her pussy too.

She looked at him again, watching him as he drove, watching as he looked all ways in case an animal came out. His right leg still beckoned. *Should I put my hand on him again? Leave it there longer this time?* She didn't want him thinking she was a slut, but she also didn't want him to think she was disinterested. *So what if he's straight and thinks I'm cute. He might have a girlfriend. He might be purposely behaving himself because of her. I shouldn't push him if he doesn't want more.*

The problem was, she didn't just want to put her hand on his knee. She wanted to put her mouth on his cock, to give him road head right there and then. But instead, she had to wait. Maybe he didn't want anything. *Why are boys so hard to read?*

##

"Over here!" someone yelled, and everyone came running at once, including Henry and Heather Spieth, desperate for news, still frantic it wouldn't be good. They reached the crowd last, and everyone parted as they ran through them from the back.

"We didn't find him yet," the Sherriff called out before they got too close. "But is this that green jacket you said he was wearing?"

156

"Oh my God. Yes, that's it. Why would he take that off, though? It's chilly out tonight."

"Ma'am, I don't know, and I don't want to make any promises, but it's certainly very possible he left us a pretty good clue right here. The nearest road is a twenty-minute walk back in that direction near where we found his bike, so he may have forgotten which way to go, and left this here as a kind of arrow. I think we should all move ahead that way through the trees. The arm of his jacket seemed to be pointing that way."

The little boy's parents nodded without speaking, both of them still fearing the absolute worst, especially if he'd wandered off into the woods between major trails and ski slopes. As they followed behind the others, Heather let go of her husband's hand and held herself tightly, feeling the chill in the night air much more than she had before.

She wished she could keep her baby warm, and hated that they still hadn't found him. She was afraid he'd fallen asleep somewhere too, unable to hear their shouts, and unaware of any bears or foxes nearby that might attack him.

##

When they got to the other side of Weston and reached the road back to Ludlow, Chris quickly pulled over and turned off his car, leaving them in the dark except for a street light in the distance.

"What are you doing?" Erika asked, uncomfortably surprised by the sudden maneuver.

"I just want to ask, in case you'd prefer I be straightforward about this," he said.

"Ask what?"

"If I can kiss you."

She smiled with an eager nod, and Chris leaned forward right away to lock lips with her. Her mouth tasted like Doritos, not unpleasant to Chris, while his lips tasted to her like pure sex and testosterone, with just a hint of Southern Comfort. He was by far the best kisser she'd ever known, and though Chris couldn't say the same about her, she was easily the most beautiful girl he'd ever met.

After another ten minutes of making out, they finally slowed down, and let each other's mouths go reluctantly as they each leaned back. Despite the boner now fully grown in his shorts, Chris didn't feel he needed any more from her for the time being, and for the first time all night, he felt nervous even looking at her.

Erika looked away as well, and Chris wasn't sure if she was happy. Did she want him to start the car again and drive her home? Was she just being polite to have kissed him back at all?

"Say something," he finally said, staring at the back of her head.

She kept her gaze out the side window. At the road. At nothing. Finally, after a long while, she exhaled and turned around to face him again.

"I'm sorry," she said. "Being serious isn't really my thing, so I'm sorry if this freaks you out, but that was just a really awesome make-out session, and I like you a lot, so I'm trying my best not to acknowledge the fact that you may just be horny and looking for a little tip for the ride home."

He was shocked, but not unhappily. Her assumption was completely valid, he decided with a nod, if also totally untrue.

"Well, for the record?" he said. "I don't usually like to get too serious either, but you're turning me on so much, and not just physically. I totally get why you'd think I'm just horny, but I'm very sober right now, and I want you to know I would kiss you like that every day if I could."

Erika blushed, amazed at the mutual feelings.

"Same," she said, smiling.

"Do you mind giving me your number?" he asked.

"No, not at all."

They both took out their phones and typed each other's numbers in, and Chris sent her a 'Hey' right away. The chime on her phone made him smirk, and she looked up at him.

"Thought it was a fake number?"

"Eh, I dunno. Better safe than sorry."

They both looked out the windshield again and said nothing for a full two minutes until Chris finally looked at the time and started the car.

"Okay, I should get you home."

Erika didn't argue, and the two seemed to agree it was best to leave it there for the night. Once they were a few minutes from her house, Chris mentioned in passing that he was going to investigate the lights on Okemo quickly after dropping her off.

"Oh, can I come?" she asked, more wide awake now than she'd been under the stars earlier.

"Uh, sure, if you'd like. I've gotta drive back down the mountain again anyway."

When he reached Ludlow, he turned left on 103, then drove up Okemo Mountain Road. As they got closer to the lights, they started seeing ambulances and police cars parked around two dozen or so cars. They got out pretty quickly, and an officer spotted them approaching.

"You two family members?"

"Family members of who?" Chris asked. "What happened?"

The officer sized them up, realized they were just teens out too late, but decided to tell them anyway.

"A boy was reported missing since a little after eight tonight, but they found him now."

He said no more, so Erika and Chris looked at each other and then asked in unison if the boy was okay.

"Oh yeah, he's getting checked out. A bit scared understandably, but he seems okay."

"Oh, thank God," Erika said.

"You two should get on home, though. Everything's under control up here now."

"Sure," Chris said, and they returned to the car.

"Jesus, that's scary. I'm glad they finally found him," Erika said, looking back at the scene as they drove away.

"Yeah," Chris said, but he was very quiet as they started down the mountain road again. By the time they pulled onto her street and parked outside her house, Erika decided to ask.

"You seem a bit rattled about that kid on the mountain."

"Yeah," he said, looking away from her toward her house.

"What is it?"

"Eh, it's nothing," he said, shaking it off with a smile as she grabbed her house key. "My dad's little sister was murdered when I was still a baby. They found her body in a field near Okemo, and so this thing with the kid just spooked me a bit. Can I have a good night kiss?"

Erika froze when she heard the words, but smiled awkwardly with a nod and leaned in as he kissed her. She got out with a quick *thank you,* and held her phone up, as if inferring they'd talk more soon, and that was it.

He drove away, none the wiser, and Erika was left alone.

"Holy shit," she whispered, her hands trembling with her phone and house key. "Fuck. Fuck. Fuuuuuuck."

Chapter 18

All throughout the workday Monday, Lenny had trouble concentrating. He kept glancing at the clock on his computer, wondering why time was passing by so slowly. His mind was already on Jenn's ass and tits, and the secret meeting he had planned with all three of them that afternoon.

No matter what he tried to get done at his desk that day, he couldn't shake the many thoughts he had about her, and what he wanted to do with her body. While his brain still screamed out to explain to Jenn once and for all that they couldn't do anything, his dick turned the pages of an entirely different kind of book.

The day started off early as it was, because Lenny forgot he'd scheduled a car inspection for 7:30. The rental car was ready much sooner than he expected too, but that meant he'd gotten into work around 8 AM.

By 2:30, he was busy finishing up the billing for the previous week when he spotted yet another anomaly in his numbers, this one much larger than the last one he'd found.

No less than $6,583.41 had been transferred from accounts received to the same private account as last time, labeled rtarisi, once again with no notes or clarification of any kind attached to it.

Lenny looked over at Joe's office, annoyed to see he was still on the same conference call he'd been on for the past hour. He looked like he was close to falling asleep.

He shook his head and returned his attention to the screen, copying over the numbers and changing the math as he did, making sure it all added up.

Just as he finished, Mr. Tarisi turned the corner and walked right up to Joe's office door across the hall. Lenny saw him peek in, but once he realized Joe was busy, he started to leave again.

"Can I help you with something, sir?"

The man didn't look happy, but he didn't seem willing to talk about it either. Lenny was sure he'd ignore him completely and walk away again, but instead, he stepped into Lenny's cubicle and put his hands on his waist, hovering over Lenny like a very large, very angry Thanksgiving Day balloon.

"Joe was supposed to help me with something, but he seems to be preoccupied at the moment."

Lenny looked back across the hall, and saw Joe still on the phone, now with his back to the hallway.

"Yes, sir. He's on that conference call with the managers from the Cleveland and Santa Fe offices. I'm sure he can step off for a couple minutes if you need him though. Want me to knock on his door for you?"

"I know how to knock on a fuckin' door, Abrams. But yeah, actually, maybe you can help me instead. Call up the payroll file."

Lenny did as he was asked, and halfway through his clicking, he saw RJ in the reflection of his screen leaning in closer to look at something. Lenny turned his head briefly to look at him, and saw RJ make a face as he pulled back again. He wondered if he'd seen the tarisi.qbw file in his open tabs.

"Now click over to the Donna Wendt file. Open that up."

Normally, Lenny didn't look too closely at people's individual files, because he really didn't want to know how much more everyone at the firm made than him, and worried the files were tracked anyway to see who had last opened them.

Though he had almost total access, Lenny lived in constant fear that Mr. Tarisi, Joe, or even the U.S. government might be watching him. It was the kind of built-in paranoia he chose to live with as a kind of homeland security for his brain.

The file opened up, and Lenny tried not to look at it too closely. He wondered why Mr. Tarisi needed him to open it anyway, as he must have had access to all the same files too.

Donna Wendt was one of Mr. Tarisi's executive assistants though, so it was certainly possible that she was capable of monitoring which files Mr. Tarisi himself had opened up. If so, he may have simply wanted to check on something about her without her knowing.

As Lenny leaned back from the screen, trying to focus instead on anything else on his desk, including the time, which he still monitored closely, Mr. Tarisi had seen what he needed to see, and he leaned back now too, already thinking about it.

"Do me a favor. Take a screenshot of that, and then email it to me at this address."

He scribbled an e-mail address on a sticky note, and held it out for him.

Once again, Lenny did as he was asked while Mr. Tarisi watched him. When he was done, Mr. Tarisi told him to delete the sent email and then remove the deleted email from his trash. Lenny did that as well. Then he pointed to the screenshot still sitting on Lenny's desktop.

"Okay, now delete that, and then permanently delete it from your trash."

"Okay, sure. Annnd done."

"Excellent. Thanks, Abes."

Abes?

RJ walked away, and Lenny noticed Joe still hadn't turned around by his desk. As he went back to his work though, he couldn't help but smile with some pride, realizing Mr. Tarisi had just trusted him with what seemed like very sensitive information.

Whatever secret it was Mr. Tarisi was trying to keep, Lenny knew he would stay silent. He'd kept bigger secrets than this in the past, and being on the boss's side could only be a good thing. If nothing else, it meant Mr. Tarisi probably wasn't planning on firing him anytime soon.

Around 2:55, Joe finally got off the conference call and opened his door again. He made a hand gesture to his head like he was shooting himself, and Lenny smiled.

"I had to take a dump so bad for the past half hour."

Lenny laughed as Joe started walking away, but then he leaned out of his cubicle and called out after him.

"Oh, Joe, I gotta get going now for that doctor's appointment. I'll see you tomorrow."

"Okay, no problem," Joe called, the bathroom door closing behind him. "Have fun!"

You have no idea.

All the way home, Lenny couldn't stop thinking about Jenn. He checked himself in the mirror at least three times, and even reached for the cologne he kept in his glove compartment, spritzing himself twice on his neck and once on each wrist.

Then about ten minutes away from home, the existential crisis of his brain revved up again for what must have been the fifth time that day.

He thought of what Caroline or the girls would think or possibly do to him if they ever found out. He thought about divorce, and Sam, and how much Olivia hated him for putting her through all that. And he thought about shame, and exile, and ridicule. No one would ever speak to him again if they found out he'd done this, if he betrayed his family's trust, especially with one of Erika's closest friends.

Who would care that Jenn had led him into temptation? Flirted first? Touched him first? No one. She'd be labeled the victim, and Lenny forever the oppressor, especially because of her age.

Why is she still 17, anyway, he thought. *She just graduated high school. Why the fuck couldn't she at least be 18?*

Legal meant nothing, though. Legal was the law, what told the state she was no longer a child, but none of that would matter to Caroline or Erika. To them, he would simply be seen as a predator, a dirty old man who took advantage of a poor, defenseless young teenage girl.

One cute girl with nice tits was hardly worth all that, he decided, and by the time he made the last turn onto his street, Lenny had made up his mind to end this right away. He'd make her cry if he had to, just to get her back out of the house and out of his life forever.

As he pulled into the driveway, he saw she was already there, parked and waiting for him to arrive. Lenny got out of his car fairly quickly, making a beeline for the house, not wanting her out there any longer than necessary. He threw the rental car key on the table by the stairs, then paced back and forth until she joined him inside a moment later.

Jenn appeared in the doorway, and Lenny's jaw dropped open instinctively as she closed the door behind her and locked it. She wore skintight denim jeans and a too-small tank top that stopped just short of her belly button. Her nipples pushed the shirt out from the top, and she already smelled like sex. And youth. And...*strawberries?*

He watched her slack jawed as she walked up very close to him until her tits pushed into his chest, and her waist cuddled up close to his crotch beneath his gut.

"Listen, Jenn," he started, but she leaned in and kissed him. He was very quickly lost in her lips and tongue, a universe unto themselves, and a moment later, her right hand began massaging his dick.

"No, I don't think we should do this," he whispered in between kissing her, but neither of them stopped, and before Lenny knew it, he was leading her up the stairs to his bed, his brain and all common sense be damned.

As he closed the bedroom door behind them, they moved as one body toward the bed, where she fell down onto his bedspread with him on top of her. She grunted a little beneath him, and he shot up again quickly.

"Did I hurt you?"

"No," she said with a quick smile. "I like it."

She reached up and pulled him back down on top of her, and they soon began kissing again.

A minute later, Lenny felt Jenn's legs wrap around him, and with another quick tumble, he had her on top of him. She pulled her T-shirt off and undid her bra, and there they were at last: the finest, roundest, tightest tits Lenny had ever seen in his whole damn life.

Jenn knew how much he wanted them, so she ducked down and gave him the taste he'd been craving for well over three years since he'd first gotten to know her—*and them.*

For the next few minutes, all he did was squeeze and lick them, feeding on her breasts like a baby yearning for his mother's milk. Lenny, truly a tit man if there ever was one, was flying high above the earth and sky through tit paradise.

Before long though, Jenn made it clear she wanted more. As he kept sucking on her tits, she was already undoing his belt and zipper, and taking out his dick for a lick of her own. She'd given three guys at school blowjobs, and each one loved it, so she knew Lenny would too.

Moving down, she sucked him slowly at first, watching as his legs quivered with ecstasy, but then, out of nowhere about a minute in, she began sucking him really, really fast. *Too* fast.

Two horrible things happened then, each in very quick succession. Lenny came without warning all over Jenn's face, and then both of them heard the front door close downstairs.

"Fuuuck!" Lenny whisper-screamed, leaping to his feet and zipping his pants up so quickly, an aneurism threatened to shatter him from within.

"I'm *so* sorry," he panted, barely watching as Jenn scrambled over to the tissue box on Caroline's dresser.

He could tell she was pissed, but the cum in her hair was the least of his problems. Whoever came home early would have seen two cars in the driveway, whether or not they knew whose cars they were. Erika would know Jenn's car for sure, but would Peaches or Caroline?

Lenny put his ear up to the bedroom door and listened carefully, hearing only a faint noise from somewhere downstairs. Looking at Jenn, he apologized again in a whisper.

She told him it was okay, and seemed only mildly annoyed by it all, rather than afraid of getting caught. And why would she be, Lenny realized with dawning horror. Jenn had nothing to lose other than Erika's friendship, and now that they were finished with high school, maybe that didn't even matter to her.

This was always *his* gamble, *his* life to destroy and not hers, and he never felt more foolish.

He was about to open the door, but then heard footsteps coming up the stairs. He strained to listen, to guess who it might be, and cursed himself for never installing a lock on his bedroom door, not that it would have helped him too much then anyway.

Caroline had always said a lock was a bad idea, that they needed the girls to be able to get into their room at any time. Neither of them had ever considered wanting to keep the other one out.

He considered the possibilities. If it was Caroline or Erika coming up the stairs, he was a dead man. If it was Peaches though, he might just get away with this. Peaches was loopy and unpredictable. It was anyone's guess what she might say or do, but at least with her, he still had a fighting chance to avoid disaster.

The footsteps walked past, and a moment later, Lenny heard a bedroom door close at the end of the hallway. It was either Erika or Peaches. But wouldn't Erika have recognized Jenn's car?

More distant noises then, and a moment later, the stereo was on. He opened the door slowly, and peeked out into the hallway toward the music. It was Peaches. Her door was shut and the new-age music playing was definitely her style. He waved to Jenn to follow him, and they both ran down the stairs toward the front door as quickly as they could.

"Jenn, I'm so sorry. I thought this would work, but we shouldn't have tried this. It's too risky here."

She smiled at him like she wasn't done with him yet, then leaned in and kissed him firmly on the lips.

He watched as she walked out the front door to her car, and his eyes moved in slow motion to *the third car* parked behind his in the driveway. It was a car he'd seen before, but he couldn't remember whose it was. Peaches didn't drive yet, but if *she* had come home, then maybe it was—

As Lenny turned around and closed the door, he saw him standing there watching from the entrance to the kitchen. Roger.

Oh my God. How long has he been standing there? What did he see?

"Hi," Lenny barely managed to say, guilt written in big, bold letters all over his face.

"Hi," Roger said.

Lenny's hair was a mess, his button-down shirt was half outside his pants, and a young girl who Roger knew to be one of Erika's friends had just come down the stairs with him before kissing him on the lips and sneaking out.

"Roger," he helped him.

"Right," Lenny said. "Roger. Hi. *Umm*...so listen. Did you happen to—"

"I won't tell anyone," he said.

Lenny didn't know what to say. He put his hands to his face and rubbed his cheeks up to his hairline, feeling sure he was going balder by the second.

"It's just that I don't think—" Lenny started again.

"Seriously. Don't worry about it," Roger said.

They both heard Peaches open her bedroom door again, and a moment later, she was running down the stairs.

"Hi Daddy. Okay, I got it," she said to Roger, who followed her back out to his car.

"Bye Mr. Abrams," Roger said.

The door shut again, and Lenny offered a whispered *'bye'* to the closed door.

For the next minute, he just stood there looking shocked, like someone had shot at him with a silver bullet of truth and just barely grazed his face.

Had he really come that close to completely destroying his life? A life now hanging in the balance, safe—for the moment—in the hands of some kid he barely knew?

He walked back up the stairs and turned the lights on in his bedroom, then quickly evened out the bedspread and pillows. He didn't see any of the dirty tissues Jenn had used anywhere, not even in their little waste paper basket, so he searched left and right to make sure she hadn't stuck them somewhere Caroline would find later on.

Once he was sure everything looked okay in the bedroom, he went into their upstairs bathroom to check himself out in the mirror. No hickeys, no lipstick, no evidence whatsoever. Still, he needed to shower, just in case. If he'd learned one thing from being married to Caroline for 18 and a half years, it was that women had a much keener sense of smell. If Jenn had left any scent whatsoever on him, he needed to scrub it off right away.

Letting out a long, deep sigh, Lenny sensed he'd just gotten away with something incredible, even if there was still a witness out there in the world. And he needed to tell Sam. This wasn't the kind of secret he could hold onto by himself, and Sam was the perfect person to talk to about it.

Chapter 19

Haley got home from work around 5:30 that evening, and went straight to her computer to call up the photos from the wedding. She had to finish the job she'd been hired for, to edit some shots, delete the blurry ones and repeats, then send Stephanie the rest of the pictures, as well as post some to her website.

If photography was her dream job, she wouldn't get anywhere with it if she didn't post her success stories online, especially something as prominent as a collection of recent wedding photos.

After only five minutes, her phone chimed with a new message, a short text from Peaches telling her to check her email. Groaning, Haley opened the browser on her computer and signed into her email, spotting the new message from Peaches near the top.

I started writing this in a text, but it got too long lol. Roger and I are gonna explore the tree house later. My mom has a meeting and my dad said he has to go out too. So as soon as he's gone, sometime soon I think, Roger and I are gonna go do it. Oh and Erika's home now too, but I don't know if she'll be here later. Should I tell her? I don't know if I should? Also, I don't know if you heard, but Grandpa's in the hospital again. Grandma said he's fine, but his knee was getting bad again and his doctor ordered him to get bed rest, only Grandma didn't want to deal with him at the house, so she just brought him over there lol. I hope he has a TV in his room like last time. That was funny putting on Sesame Street and then leaving. I'll text you when my dad goes out.

Haley shook her head. She was nervous about the whole tree house thing, but felt like maybe she *should* go, just in case there *was* something bad up there. She'd be happy to see Roger at least, but was desperate to get through more of the photo editing work.

She clicked reply, then re-read the message from Peaches before typing.

Okay, I'll come over when you tell me to. Don't tell Erika, but if she's there when I come over, then whatever. It's not a big deal. Hadn't heard about Grandpa, that sucks. Will ask my mom if she heard.

Haley clicked send, then went back to her photos before realizing she should text Peaches too. She groaned again, then sent a short text that just said, "replied by email, text me back whenever, don't email".

Once she had all her folders and software opened, and the first picture up on the screen, Haley decided she should also make sure her mom knew about her grandfather. She went downstairs to look for her, but saw her out the back door smoking a cigarette and talking on the phone, so figured she must have been talking to her grandmother already.

Running back up the stairs, she checked her phone to make sure Peaches hadn't replied, then went right back to the pictures.

Almost two hours passed without any distractions, and Haley was thrilled to have gotten as far as she had, but as Mr. Tarisi's face started showing up more and more in the reception photos, Haley couldn't help but look more closely to see where he went. It grossed her out to be tracking the whereabouts of the man in all the shots, but she was terrified she might catch him doing something crazy, like slipping something into Mr. Caraway's drink.

Somewhere halfway through a thought like this, she leaned back and put her hair in a ponytail, realizing how insane her evening was, investigating not one but two separate deaths, neither of which may have even been a murder.

Sitting with her back up tight against her chair as she stared at Mr. Tarisi's face on the screen, she wondered how her uncle even worked with the guy every day. He'd been such a jerk to her that night at the wedding, and nothing about him seemed normal.

Her phone rang out just then, and made her jump. *Peaches.*

"Hello?"

"Hey, my dad just went out. Can you come over now?"

"Yeah, okay. I'll be right over. Don't do anything until I get there though."

"Okay."

"Okay, bye."

"Bye."

When she got down the stairs, she looked around for her mother, but didn't see her anywhere. *Maybe she went out?* As she opened the front door though, Olivia was just coming back from somewhere in her car.

"Where are *you* going?" Olivia asked Haley.

"Just out with friends."

Olivia looked confused.

"You have friends?"

"Yes," Haley lied, still heading toward her car.

Olivia was halfway to the front door and Haley about to get into her car when she remembered to ask about Alan.

"Oh, how's Grandpa?"

"Huh? How the hell should I know?"

"What? Mom, he's in the hospital again for his knee. Peaches told me. I thought you knew. Weren't you just there?"

"No. Jesus."

Olivia went in and closed the door without saying anything else, so Haley drove away.

When she got to her uncle's house, she was surprised to see no cars in the driveway. She rang the doorbell twice, knocked for a bit, and then rang it a third time until Peaches finally answered the door with a big smile.

"Where were you? I was standing out here waiting for like five minutes. And where's Roger?"

"Oh, he can't make it. He had to work tonight. I forgot."

"Oh, okay," she said, trying to sound as casual as possible, and not at all disappointed. "Whatever."

They walked in together toward the back of the house. It was still light outside, but the sun was beginning to set behind the neighbor's house to the left, so Peaches had already gotten two flashlights out for them to use too, as well as the ladder from the basement.

"Wow, look at you. All prepared."

Peaches beamed with pride at first, but then stopped in her tracks. Haley watched as her face quickly changed into a truly horrified grimace.

"Oh my God, Haley. The ladder was behind the stairs? And when I went to get it to bring it to the bottom of the basement stairs before my dad left? A humongous spider jumped out at me, and I screamed so loud."

Haley shuddered.

"So what did your dad say? Like, did he ask you why you were down there?"

"No! He didn't even hear me scream from upstairs in his bedroom. That spider could have killed me and eaten my whole body, and he wouldn't have even known."

Haley laughed.

"Well, as long as you didn't bring any spiders up with the ladder, I'm sure we'll be fine."

Peaches eyed the ladder again suspiciously.

"I checked it, but if you see another one, let me know."

Haley was sad she wouldn't get to see Roger again, but happy their investigation would be quick, so she could get back to her photos at home. If nothing else, Roger being there would have meant she would have spent more time talking to him and flirting anyway. Instead, they could go to the tree house, check it out, and then she could head back home again right away afterward.

##

Over at Sam's new house on the lake, Lenny paced the floor between Sam and the sliding door facing out to the deck, still looking for the right way to tell him.

"Look, you and I have always been good friends, especially since you married Livi, maybe less so back in school. But we can talk honestly about stuff, right?"

Sam watched the side door of the house now and then, nodding his head. When Lenny texted that he was heading over, he'd said okay, but remembered too late that Caroline said she needed to talk to him too, and that Monday after work would work best for her. He texted her to say Lenny was on his way over, but she still hadn't responded.

Well, he decided, *if nothing else, she'll see Lenny's car when she gets here, and know enough to back away from the house.*

As he looked out the sliding glass door behind Lenny, he was grateful to see there was less and less light outside for Lenny to identify any car that might drive up.

"Yeah, of course we can talk honestly, Len. You know that. What's on your mind, buddy?"

"Well, the thing is— I guess I— Well, I sort of had an affair."

Sam was shocked speechless. Lenny was the last person in the whole world he'd have ever guessed would cheat on someone, let alone Caroline, and the one time Sam and Caroline had actually talked about Lenny while in bed, she'd said how badly she felt about that. He was too good for her, she said, and she was too bad for him.

"What?!" Sam managed, still processing it.

"Yeah, yeah, I know. It's crazy, Sam, but there's this girl, this very, very young but very beautiful girl, a friend of Erika's, and she came on to me, like *hard*, and it took everything in my power to resist her. She has these totally perfect tits too, tits like you've never seen before.

"One night last week, late at night, I was driving her home, and she put her hand on my leg. I don't know how, but I managed to resist her. But then on Saturday at Erika's party, she was there again, just staring at me. The next thing I knew, I was telling her to come by today before everyone got home. I left work early, got home, and five minutes later, I'd shot my load all over her face."

"Holy shit," Sam said.

"I know. I know. I don't know what to do."

"No, I mean, why the hell did you cum so fast?"

"Jesus, Sam, I dunno, I haven't had a blowjob in years. Caroline hasn't given me one since well before Erika started high school, and then—and then, get this, Peaches came home."

"Oh God," Sam said, stifling a nervous smile.

"She walked past my closed bedroom door on her way to her room, and didn't seem to notice that Jenn's fucking car was right there in our driveway, or even think to ask me whose car it was, but Peaches I could handle, you know? She's a sweet kid and just loopy enough to lie to without it being an issue, but then I see this friend of hers in my hallway downstairs a minute later, her friend Roger? And this kid totally saw Jenn and me come down the stairs as she snuck out. Like, he totally saw it all, game over."

"Oh my God. So what happened?"

"He swore he'd keep it a secret. He seemed totally cool about it. I wasn't sure at first, but I gotta say, he did seem cool."

"Wow. Even so though, that's not good."

Sam had leaned forward as Lenny spoke, and his face went from happy to shocked to scared to relaxed one after the other. He couldn't believe it, but was happy to hear it too, because if anything bad went down between Caroline and Lenny, it was a relief knowing neither one of them was perfect, and both were keeping big secrets from the other.

"Oh! And then get this," Lenny went on. "Just now, on my way here? A fucking porcupine came out of nowhere, and crossed the street right in front of my car over by the Sugar House. I swerved quickly to keep from hitting it, but I'm so glad I did, because I'm driving a fucking rental today. My car's in the shop over in Rutland for an inspection. I can't imagine what they'd charge me to clean porcupine guts off their car."

Lenny laughed, but Sam's mouth dropped open unnaturally.

"Wait, you're not driving your own car?"

"No. And come to think of it, that may have helped me with Peaches. Maybe she saw two strange cars in the driveway, and didn't even think about it. Who knows. That kid is funny."

Just then, they both heard a car door close outside, and Sam panicked. Caroline wouldn't know Lenny was there.

"You expecting someone?" Lenny asked, already walking over toward the door.

"No, wait!"

"What?"

"Dude, it's nothing. It's a secret," Sam stumbled. He could see the strange look on Lenny's face. "Look, it's for your birthday. You weren't supposed to know about it."

"My birthday's not till October."

Fuck.

"Yeah, yeah, I know," Sam tried. "Just trust me. Go upstairs and stay quiet, okay? And don't look outside at all."

Lenny looked surprised, but not angry, and though part of him still expected shenanigans of some sort, he mostly seemed amused by whatever this was.

He went up the stairs toward the second-floor kitchen and dining room, and diligently stayed away from the windows so he wouldn't see anything.

Sam got to the door quickly, opening it with a finger to his mouth before Caroline had a chance to say anything. He closed the door behind him, watching as she approached him from across the lawn with a curious look on her face.

##

Back at Lenny's house, Peaches and Haley had set the ladder up against the tree, and Peaches began climbing up with a flashlight as Haley held the ladder. Haley didn't think Peaches would find anything inside, but she also worried some kind of animal living in there might jump out at her.

"Watch out that nothing's alive up there, Peaches."

With each step Peaches took up the ladder, her anticipation seemed to increase, and Haley bit her bottom lip nervously as well.

"Imagine if we see a severed arm? Or like, a blanket soaked in blood, or even just some cool diary or something?"

"Ew. No, Peaches. I'm sure there won't be anything like that."

By the time Peaches got high enough on the ladder to peer inside the tree house, Haley's stomach was growling, half from hunger and half from a new fear that there might actually be something up there. And what if they *did* find something? What would they do then?

She saw Peaches look inside a bit, then climb one more rung up the ladder so she could go inside. Haley watched carefully as Peaches turned on her flashlight and started looking around.

A split second later, a hand reached out from the darkness, and grabbed Peaches tightly by the wrist. She screamed out, and Haley turned and ran away with a shriek, only stopping close to the house once she heard insane laughter coming from behind her.

Both Peaches and Roger were in hysterics as they watched Haley turn around to face them, still panting with shock.

She was furious at them both, but couldn't help but smile now too, shaking her head as she walked back to the tree, relieved it was only a trick. She was also glad in another way, because Roger's position up there meant they hadn't already found anything terrible inside the tree house.

"Oh my God, I'm so sorry," Roger said, still laughing, "but when Peaches suggested we do this, there was no way I was missing the chance."

Peaches climbed down the ladder carefully, then gave Haley a big hug to apologize.

"You looked *SO* scared!" she said.

Haley just kept shaking her head, beat red with embarrassment.

"You guys, that was really mean, but I gotta give it to you. Very well done. And Peaches, I owe you an apology."

"Why?"

"Because I totally left you up there in the hands of what I thought was some kind of a murderer or a zombie or something!"

Roger and Peaches both laughed, then Haley pulled the ladder away, acting like she was going to leave Roger stuck up there as punishment for the trick.

"Noooo," he said with a big smile. "Please don't."

Haley smiled and replaced the ladder, then climbed up herself to take a look inside. Peaches was happy to hold it for her this time.

"So I guess you didn't find anything, then?" Haley asked them.

"Nah, it's empty," Roger said. "Just some old pillows and a bunch of empty beer cans."

Haley climbed inside as Roger made room for her, extending his legs out on either side of hers. There wasn't enough room for Peaches too, but she didn't look like she wanted to climb back up there anyway.

In the darkness of the small space, only a flashlight's worth of projected light to go by, Roger and Haley exchanged a glance they both understood. Haley thought about how she could compliment him without sounding weird, and he was thinking the same, only he was more concerned Peaches might be offended. Even though Peaches was five years younger than him, Roger didn't want her to be mad that he liked her cousin.

"Wait," Haley said, her smile fading quickly as she pointed to the wall behind Roger. "What's that over there?"

He turned and bumped his head as he did, but then he saw it too. Someone had written something on the wood wall inside.

##

As Caroline approached, Sam waved his left hand out by his waist with his right index finger still against his mouth, looking up nervously at the second-floor windows as he did.

After Phyllis's stern warning though, all Caroline wanted to do was end things with Sam once and for all, and not play games anymore, especially if he had someone over. The text about Lenny still hadn't gone through.

She was glad when she saw the other car in Sam's driveway though, because she knew it meant he wouldn't start getting physical with her. She'd be able to just let him down easy, and leave him be without making a scene.

"Sam, no," she whispered. "I can't keep doing this."

"No," he said, "you don't understand."

"No, Sam. *You* don't understand."

"Lenny's here," he said finally, putting his hands in his pockets and glancing once again back up at the house.

"What? Oh my God."

She ducked down instinctively away from the windows.

"I sent you a text to let you know not to come over. He doesn't know it's you who stopped by just now. I told him I'd ordered something for him for his birthday, so he's upstairs staying away from the windows."

"What? His birthday isn't till the end of *October,* dumbass." She was completely bent over now and trying to hide. "This is crazy. He can't see me here. I said I was with a client tonight."

"Then I guess you should *go,*" he said more firmly, eager to get rid of her.

"Yeah, but listen, we gotta talk soon, okay?"

"Okay. Fine. Whatever. Just not now."

He watched her stalk back over to her car and drive away, and noticed her looking strangely at Lenny's rental car as she did. He hoped she'd be smart enough not to mention it until Lenny brought it up.

Walking back inside, Sam called Lenny to come back down again, and when he did, he saw he had a strange look on his face.

"You're a really sweet guy, Sam. Thank you. I'm excited to see what you got me now too, but I've gotta get going. I want to make sure I'm home before Caroline gets in. Thanks again for listening to me, buddy. I really appreciate it."

"Sure thing, Len. Anytime, man. I'll talk to you soon."

Sam exhaled loudly once Lenny was gone, relieved to have gotten away with the lie, nervous about whatever Caroline wanted to talk to him about, and annoyed he'd now have to find Lenny an extra nice gift for his birthday, still several months away.

##

At the foot of the tree house, Peaches and Roger peered down at the bright screen of Haley's phone as she showed them the inscription, trying to make out what it said. She'd snapped three photos of it, but it was too hard to read, even by flashlight up in the tree house. As Peaches rotated the phone on an angle, they were finally able to see it.

"KAYAK," Roger read out loud.

"No, that's a 2," Haley said, showing him the picture again. It says KAY2K."

"Oh my God," Peaches said. "It's a secret message. Maybe she was trying to warn someone!"

"What? No," Haley said, shaking her head quickly. "KA is just her initials, and Y2K is short for the year 2000. It's not like a code or anything. Kerry Ann was 16 and hanging out with my dad a lot. She must have just carved it in at some point before she died."

"Right," Roger said, "but at least now you know the tree house *was* connected somehow."

Peaches and Haley exchanged a nervous look.

"Eh," Haley acknowledged. "*Maybe.*"

"Holy moly, Haley," Peaches said. "This is a really big deal."

"No, it isn't. Listen to me. This doesn't mean anything. My dad was seeing her, I guess, and they may have snuck into the tree house at some point. He and Uncle Lenny built the thing, so it makes sense that he brought her there. He was like 26 or 27, so maybe it was the only private place they had one night, I don't know. None of this proves anything though, and it definitely doesn't explain why we've always been told to stay away from the stupid thing. Anyway, this is all creeping me out now. Can we please go?"

Haley started off toward the house, so Roger and Peaches just looked at each other quickly before following. Roger grabbed the ladder, and Peaches picked up both flashlights and ran after them.

Once they put the ladder away in the basement, Haley said goodbye to both of them and left abruptly. Roger was already running late to the pizzeria, so he took off as well.

On her way into her bedroom, Peaches paused and heard the front door. Erika was home, and it sounded like her mother was coming in right after her. She listened for a moment, but once they started arguing, she went into her room and closed the door behind her, shutting the noise out quickly with her stereo.

##

By the time Lenny pulled into the driveway a few minutes later, he was lost in a daydream. The hookup with Jenn wasn't something he'd ever forget, despite how disastrous it turned out, but what was festering much more now, ever so anxiously on the edges of his already frayed brain, was the crazy lie Sam had just told him.

Perhaps it was because of his own new secrets and lies, but Lenny was absolutely sure that whomever had stopped by Sam's house earlier had nothing to do with him getting a surprise gift for his unremarkable 44th birthday still four months away.

Sam was hiding something. Or someone. And after Lenny had just shared his big secret with Sam, he was beyond pissed that Sam was keeping a brand new one from him.

Chapter 20

"Mom, I'm eighteen. I can go wherever I want. You don't need to know about every last thing I do."

Caroline rolled her eyes, but kept walking toward the kitchen.

"But if you could spot me like twenty bucks, that'd be so cool."

"Are you *kidding me?* Are you fucking kidding me, Erika?!"

"Whoa."

"You expect your father and me to just let you waste your life away on beer and pot, not even apply to colleges, and just keep hitting us up for money all the time? No way! I am *so* sick of your childish behavior, young lady, and eighteen or not, high school graduate or not, you are still *my* child living under *my* roof. Is that clear?! Do you understand me?!"

Erika hadn't been yelled at in such a long time, so she wasn't prepared for the diatribe, and as her father wasn't home yet to play good cop, she quickly realized she was stuck. There was no eye-batting sad face to offer Daddy this time, only as much calm as she could muster in response.

"Okay Mom, look. I know what you're saying, but I promise you, I *am* looking for a job, and Lexi's cousin Brittany is quitting her job at Old Navy, so I can easily get that one when she's done."

Caroline looked down and shook her head, unsure where to begin. She was pissed at Lenny for ruining her meet-up with Sam, pissed at Phyllis for catching her in the first place, and now pissed at Erika for a whole litany of new things.

As she looked up again, Erika saw right away that Caroline was far from finished with her tirade, and she literally stepped backward from her mother with dawning fear once she saw the bright red threatening to burst forth from inside her cheeks.

"First of all, you don't just *get* a job at Old Navy because someone else leaves. You have to *apply* for it like everyone else. You know how many high school graduates there are out there looking for jobs right now? You think some guy is just gonna smile at you with a clipboard and say, 'Oh, you're friends with Brittany's cousin? Perfect! Come on in! You can start right away!' It doesn't *work like that,* Erika!

"You had this big plan about going upstate for community college, but nothing seems to have come from that, and you were out way too late again on Saturday night, by the way. I got up to use the bathroom at 3:30, and you still weren't home from that party in Manchester. And holy hell, you absolutely *reek* of marijuana right now. What the hell is *happening* to you? Go upstairs. Shower and change your clothes before you do anything else."

Erika started for the stairs, but Caroline stopped her right away.

"Wait a minute. What the hell are you even doing here? The concert was supposed to start at 8 up in Burlington. Those tickets cost your dad and me a lot of money."

They stared at each other for a while, and Caroline watched as Erika seemed ready to tell her another lie.

"Don't even *think* about lying to me, young lady. Why aren't you at the concert tonight?"

Erika had opened her mouth, prepared to tell her the concert was postponed, but realized she'd soon find out that wasn't true.

"Well, we were actually able to sell the tickets on Craigslist for a lot more than asking price. Some dude in Rutland bought them from us."

Caroline's face, already teetering on the edge of destruction, finally exploded. Though no blood or flesh splattered out across the walls of the house, it was not for any lack of effort.

"Why *the hell* did you need *another* twenty dollars then?!"

"I dunno. I guess I really don't. I just thought you'd forget about the concert, that asking for money would throw you off."

She looked at her mother then with a kind of curious stare, unsure if she'd played it well by being so honest.

"Go upstairs *right now,* and shower that shit off you before I pull you outside and hose you down myself!"

Now Erika was the one rolling her eyes, and as she made a quick move toward the stairs, Caroline ran after her, shouting at her some more.

"I treat people for drug and alcohol addiction, Erika! I don't want my own daughter spending my money on that shit!"

Erika was up the stairs in two seconds flat, grateful just to be out of Caroline's sight, and once her bedroom door slammed in the distance, Caroline went back to the kitchen. She pulled out a joint from her own pocketbook then, ready to light up in the backyard, and was just about to walk out the sliding door when Lenny came in at the front of the house.

This is it, Lenny thought. *She beat me home from visiting with her client, and will ask me where I've been.* He still hadn't come up with a good lie. As he put his rental car key down on the table though, he remembered it all. The porcupine, the inspection, and the rental. He'd just use that, he decided, and simply change the time of day, saying he took care of it after work.

This is it, Caroline thought. *He was at Sam's, but I can't say I knew that, because then my game will be up.* As she watched him make his way toward the kitchen, she thought of an update she could use about Mrs. Tate. A story came to her of something she once heard about another client, a woman so high when she was arrested, she tried to hide her drugs in a fish tank.

As it turned out though, neither of their stories were necessary. Lenny had something else he wanted to talk about first, so all lies would have to wait. He looked at her with a smile as he approached, not noticing the joint in her closed hand, then leaned in to kiss her on the cheek.

Turning around again, he never felt more guilty in his life. *Jenn I bathed in kisses, but Caroline gets only a peck on the cheek? What the hell have I become?*

He opened the fridge and grabbed a beer, then made his way to the other side of the room by the couch. As he sat down, he twisted the cap off and took a long sip before making eye contact with Caroline, who was waiting for him to speak.

She could tell in his face that something was wrong. *Did Sam tell him? Why is he looking at me like that?*

"So I think Sam is keeping something from me?" Lenny said with a strange lilt in his voice, not making eye contact as he said it.

Oh God.

"I stopped over to his new house on the lake just now, and while we were talking, we heard this car pull up."

Oh my God.

"Lenny—"

"So I'm pretty sure he's hiding something from me, Caroline, and I'm sorry to say it, but I think it's got something to do with—"

"Lenny, look."

"—Kerry Ann Jefferson."

Huh?

"What?"

"I think there's a chance, and I hate to admit it, but there's a chance he really *did* have something to do with that poor girl's death. Someone knocked on the door while I was there, and Sam started to sweat. He never sweats. He even made up this stupid lie about how he was planning a surprise birthday gift for me.

"I bought it for all of ten seconds, but really, it was just about the dumbest lie I've ever heard. I've never felt like that before, Car. I actually felt *unsafe* around the guy for the first time since I've known him. I thought he might even do something to me. No one knew I was over there, ya know? It really unnerved me."

Caroline was relieved *and* alarmed by this strange new turn.

"Lenny, that's crazy. In fact, that's beyond crazy. Sam would never hurt you. Your mind is playing tricks on you now. Stop this."

She pocketed the joint carefully and was over on the couch sitting next to him a moment later.

"I mean it, honey. You've got to trust me on this," she said, her mind thinking fast. "In fact, Sam told me about a surprise birthday gift he was planning for you. He's not lying."

Lenny's face changed quickly.

"What?"

He seemed to consider this for a while, and Caroline took the chance to calm herself down while his head was turned away.

"Oh wow," he finally said. "Wow, I guess—I guess I just built it up in my head so fast, especially on the drive back here, that I didn't even give myself the chance to believe he'd never do that. Wow, I feel terrible for even thinking that about him now."

Even as he spoke the words though, Lenny's mind quietly drifted to a much, *much* darker place than before.

Caroline was covering for Sam. He was sure of it. She was lying to his face, and he couldn't call her out on it until he knew more.

"Don't worry about it," Caroline said, shrugging it off. "I've had my own bad thoughts about Sam too in the past, but they're silly. The police didn't find anything. He's innocent."

"Yeah," Lenny said, leaning forward with a fake laugh. "Yeah, you're right, you're right, I'm sorry. God, can you imagine? How could I have ever thought badly of him? He's never done anything to hurt me, and I know he never would. The guy's a saint, and he's my best friend for crying out loud."

He took another sip of his beer as Caroline cringed. She and Sam had done so much to hurt Lenny for so long. It had to stop before things got out of control.

"Oh, uh, did you hear about my dad?" Lenny asked, eager to get off the subject as quickly as possible.

"No? What?"

"My mom called me earlier," he said, again to the room more than to Caroline as his mind kept racing. "She took him over to the hospital today. They're keeping him overnight for his knee, and then doing another small surgery tomorrow. May be a couple of days again like last time."

"Oh, geez."

"She said he's fine, not to visit, but you know how pissy he'll be if we don't. He doesn't have a phone yet though."

"Oh, okay. Maybe we can stop over tomorrow then after work."

"Yeah. Yeah, that sounds good."

"I guess Olivia knows?"

"Ummmm—probably? Not really worried about her though. My dad'll eventually call her if my mom hasn't already."

186

They sat together for the next few minutes, neither of them saying anything. An invisible wall of lies had grown ten feet higher between them, but somehow, as long as they didn't acknowledge it, they each felt safe within their secrets.

##

At her computer a half mile away, Haley went through the wedding photos as fast as she could, all while looking for any shots of Mr. Caraway and Mr. Tarisi together in the same picture. It only happened two or three times during the reception, but each time they were both smiling, or drinking, or dancing with other guests. But then she saw the next photo, and her mouth dropped open.

The picture was so shocking in fact, she found herself just staring at the screen for a while. She clicked forward to see if there were more shots of the moment, disappointed to see none.

Just to the left side of the picture, a cute shot of the groom lifting the bride as they danced, with other guests cheering them on, she saw the two men locked in what looked like a wrestling match out in the lobby. Mr. Tarisi was clutching Mr. Caraway's suit jacket, looming over him like he was going to bite his head off, with Mr. Caraway looking genuinely frightened in return.

Though it was no smoking gun, it was more than enough to unnerve Haley, and she wondered if she should speak to Stephanie about it after all. She was torn. If she said something, she risked upsetting her for no reason, and possibly even angering her too.

As she sat there worrying about what to do, Haley finally decided to at least tell Lenny, since Mr. Tarisi was his boss. Maybe he'd have a better idea of how to proceed. If he told her to calm down about it and just let it go, then that's exactly what she'd do.

She reached over and picked up her phone and called their house, hoping he would pick up.

##

"I'll get it," Caroline said, standing up. She walked over to the phone in the kitchen.

"Hello?"

"Oh hey, Aunt Caroline. It's Haley."

"Hi Haley," Caroline said, turning to look at Lenny. "Everything okay?"

"Oh, yeah, everything's fine. I was just hoping I could stop by there quick and show Uncle Lenny something. Is he home?"

"Yeah, sure. We're all here. Come by anytime."

"Okay, great. Be right over."

##

Haley ended the call, then clicked print on the photo. Though she didn't have nice photo paper to print on, the 8x11 shot was enough to show him the picture, and to see what he thought of it.

On her way out the door, Olivia stopped her, muting the TV.

"Mom, I gotta go to Uncle Lenny's quick. I'll be right back."

"What? Why?"

"Um, nothing. Just a question about his boss and this picture of him with Mr. Caraway. I'm worried something's going on."

"Yeah, that doesn't look good," Olivia admitted, grabbing the paper and then handing it back to her. "Listen, I spoke to Grandma. Grandpa's gonna have another surgery done on the knee tomorrow morning. The doctor said his insert may need some massaging, whatever the hell that means."

"Okay," Haley said, not sure what to say. Her mother looked more concerned than usual, but Haley didn't want to push it.

"Yeah," Olivia said. "So anyway, tell Uncle Lenny for me. I forgot to call him. In case Grandma didn't call over there yet."

"Okay."

##

Inside Lenny's kitchen a few minutes later, Erika had appeared downstairs again to look for food, so Caroline took the opportunity to tell Lenny, in front of Erika, 'what our daughter has been up to'.

Somewhere in the middle of a new lecture from Lenny on driving while high or drunk, the doorbell rang, and Erika was grateful for an excuse to walk away from them both to answer it. He didn't stop talking the whole time, so Erika just rolled her eyes at Haley as she came in and listened to the tail end of it.

"My parents would have *killed me,* Erika," Caroline said.

"Mine too," Lenny added. "You can't keep taking advantage of how nice we are to you. You're gonna get yourself killed one of these days, and if we don't even know where you are, we'll never find you, either."

"You get this kind of thing at your house too?" Erika asked.

"No," Haley shrugged, "but I've never smoked pot, and I really don't drink too much either."

"See?!" Caroline said.

"Sorry," Haley said with a half smile, and watched as Caroline followed Erika toward the front door and then up the stairs.

"C'mon in," Lenny said. "What'd you want to show me?"

She handed him the picture and watched as he examined it. Before she got there, Haley wasn't sure what her Uncle Lenny would think of it, but by the way he was looking at it now, something else was affecting him instead.

"Haley, what was this man doing at the wedding?"

She looked at who he was pointing to with alarm.

"That's Mr. Caraway, the father of the bride. He's the guy who died the night of the wedding."

"Oh my God. He's dead?"

Lenny looked shocked.

"Yes. Uncle Lenny, you knew him?"

"Yeah, I knew him. We all knew him. Sweet guy too. He used to come into the office all the time. Mr. Tarisi just called him JC, but I didn't know his name." He shook his head as the truth of it all came crashing down on him. "So you're saying Tarisi's nephew married JC's daughter?"

"Yeah. Uncle Lenny, JC—*Mr. Caraway*—he was a really sweet guy. Do you have any idea why they looked like they were fighting here? I only ask because I'm worried your boss may have done something to him at the wedding. His daughter said he fell, but—"

Haley watched with alarm as Lenny handed her back the photo and held his hands out. He was already filled with a mix of dread and confusion about Sam and Caroline, so this was all too much for him to handle.

"No. Now listen to me," he said. "Don't do this. Don't try to turn this into something it isn't. I only met this JC guy a few times, and yeah, he seemed nice, and yes, my boss is a total asshole, but none of that means he killed the guy. We can't just go around throwing accusations around like this, Haley. I mean it. People deserve the presumption of innocence."

He'd said it to himself as much as to Haley. Sam just couldn't be guilty. He just couldn't be.

"I'm sorry. You're totally right. I just wanted to see what you thought. That's all. I'm sorry."

She started to turn away from him, quickly flustered by his temper, when Lenny stopped her with a hand on her arm.

"Hey, wait. Look, don't worry about it. I didn't mean to raise my voice. I'm sorry about that. It's just—we've gotta be smart about all this. Your picture doesn't prove anything more than that the two of them got into an argument. That's all. You need more if you're gonna make an accusation like that. That's all I'm saying. You can't assume the worst."

He took another look at the picture again, still in Haley's hands.

"He was a nice guy though, JC. I'm sorry to hear he died. But none of this means Tarisi is a murderer. We can't use our family's BS past to think the worst about everyone else, you know?"

"You're right. I'm sorry I even thought this. It was stupid."

"No, it's fine. I get it. I totally get it. I mean, Tarisi *is* a dick."

They shared a smile as Haley relaxed again and started for the door. As she went to open it though, she remembered to ask—

"Oh, did you hear about Grandpa?"

190

"Yeah, Grandma called me earlier, thank you. Don't worry. Grandpa's made of steel and iron."

Haley nodded.

"Literally, I think," he added with a smirk.

"Okay. Good night, Uncle Lenny."

"Good night, kid," he said.

As he shut the door behind her, Lenny couldn't help but wonder if any of it *was* true. Sam. Caroline. Mr. Tarisi. The secrets, the money trail at work, the sudden, unexplained death. Were things really as fucked up as he and Haley were beginning to think they were?

He needed another cold beer, he was sure of that. Once he pulled it from the fridge and closed the door again, he noticed a picture of Erika and her friends hanging above the ice cube dispenser, a photo taken their freshmen year.

Jenn was on the far right side, her legs turned in with her knees bent and her tits sticking out proudly. He loved the picture, and if he was honest with himself, he'd always thought she looked really cute, even when she was only thirteen. He never craved her back then the way he did now, but she and her beautiful tits were always there, eye level on the fridge, smiling at him just the same.

Upstairs, Lenny heard Peaches, Erika, and Caroline arguing about something stupid in the bathroom—*shampoo?*—and he thought again about his hot but abbreviated hookup with Jenn just hours earlier. It still embarrassed him to think of his early ejaculation, but he was grateful she seemed cool about it anyway.

Whether or not he ever heard from her again was still up in the air, and he certainly wasn't about to go through Erika's phone for her number anyway, although the thought *had* occurred to him

No, best to just leave it alone now, he decided. *Caroline would never cheat on me, and none of them would ever speak to me again if they found out about what happened. Jenn's father would kill me anyway.*

##

Upstairs, Caroline walked away from Peaches and Erika as they continued arguing over the shampoo, and she laid down on her bed and closed her eyes. She still hadn't talked with Sam, but it could wait for another day.

She turned on her side then and fixed her pillow, grabbing something stuck underneath it. *Used tissues? What the?*

Caroline made a face at the door, thinking Lenny must have blown his nose before he made the bed that morning, and shoved them in without thinking. She tossed them in the garbage, then laid back down and closed her eyes, lost once again in dark thoughts of the past.

Chapter 21

Phyllis looked up at the clock for the fourth time in as many minutes. Alan's surgery should have been finished an hour ago, and she still hadn't heard anything. She was growing visibly upset and couldn't sit still.

A Catholic priest stopped by just then out of nowhere, and he asked Phyllis if she wanted to talk.

"I'm Jewish," she lied, as if that was the only answer to his question worth sharing anyway.

"I understand. I can call the rabbi if you'd like."

"No thank you, Reverend. I'm not even a practicing—look, I'm fine, thank you. I'm good, okay?"

He smiled and nodded, despite her snapping like a frightened dog, then went on his way. Priests had unnerved Phyllis ever since parochial school back in Brooklyn, and though neither she nor Alan were religious in the least anymore, it wasn't religion that shook her anyway, but something else. Priests, deacons, rabbis: as far as she was concerned, they were a different breed of human, the kind of creatures she didn't want comingling in her personal space.

Phyllis tried taking deep breaths, but she was never so unnerved in her entire life. Alan had gotten the same procedure done on his other knee not three years earlier, and they were in and out in two hours. More than three hours had now passed, and she still hadn't heard anything from the doctor.

Finally, after she couldn't stand it any longer, she got up and walked over to the nurse's station. Both of the young women sitting there said they still hadn't heard anything, so this time she asked them to go and check.

"I'm sorry, Ma'am," one of them said, an eager but clearly fake smile plastered across her face, "but we have to file reports and watch the monitors for patient activity. We're not supposed to leave our desks."

"Honey, I was a nurse for over 40 years. Don't bullshit me. You have one guy in a room over there playing Tetris on his phone, and another woman down the hall recovering from appendicitis. One of you little princesses can afford to get up off your goddamn asses and check on my husband for me. He should have been out of surgery an hour ago."

The nurse looked both surprised and afraid, then stood up and walked away through the closed double doors behind her. The other nurse avoided making eye contact now, so Phyllis stared her down for a few seconds more before returning to the hallway, and eventually her seat.

Seven *very* long minutes passed, and Phyllis was growing more and more agitated. This wasn't at all normal, and she was sure something had gone horribly wrong.

The double doors opened down the hall, and she watched as the nurse peeked out first and the doctor appeared right behind her a moment later, looking both ways. Once he saw Phyllis, he came over with a neutral grin, and she stood up right away, trying desperately to read his face.

"Mrs. Abrams, your husband is fine. The procedure took longer than expected, but we're all done now, and he's resting comfortably. Overall, we're happy with—"

"What happened?" she demanded, sure as she'd ever been that he wasn't telling her something.

"What?"

"Something happened. This procedure was simple. You just did the same goddamn thing on him not three years ago, and it took only 65 minutes that time. I want to know why you didn't come out here until now. What... went... wrong?"

The doctor just stared at her at first, but then his face changed completely and he nodded, knowing he'd have to tell her.

"Well, we did have some unexpected complications along the way," he said calmly. "We gave your husband what we're sure was the right amount of anesthetic, but as we were still getting his knee prepped, he very briefly flat-lined on us."

"Oh my God."

"No, it's okay, really. It was very short, only a few seconds."

"How *many* seconds, doctor?"

He didn't seem to want to say, so she pressed him again.

"How many?!"

"Well," he said, pausing to rub a new line of perspiration from his forehead, "it was thirty-seven seconds."

"Oh my *God*."

"We couldn't get him back right away, but we're confident he'll be fine. We have him on oxygen still, but he's breathing fine on his own, so—"

"I want to see him right now."

"Of course," he said, glancing briefly behind him before turning to her again. "C'mon. I'll bring you back, and we'll have him out into his own room shortly too."

Fifteen minutes later, Olivia's phone rang at the bank, and Mish barely heard her yell, *"I'm leaving!"* before she was out the door.

Thirty seconds after that, Lenny's phone rang at *his* desk, and Joe only heard *"see you when I,"* as Lenny whirred out the door toward the stairs. He called Caroline on his way to the car, and asked her to call the girls before she headed over as well. Erika said she'd get Haley.

Forty-four minutes later, Haley, Peaches, and Erika arrived at Alan's room at Rutland Regional Medical Center, where they were greeted right away with hugs and waves from Olivia, Caroline, Lenny, and Phyllis. Behind them in his bed, Alan grinned appreciatively beneath an oxygen mask, and Phyllis launched into her now well-rehearsed line to the girls about what happened.

"His heart stopped for 37 seconds, but there are no signs of brain damage, so they think he'll be okay."

"I haven't had to do any trigo*nomery* yet though," Alan muttered with a slur from behind her. "Anyfing's thill poffible."

His three granddaughters all moved in close then, and each one kissed him on the cheek in turn. He smiled at them a bit, but they were quickly noticing the same thing everyone else had when they first came in. Alan looked ancient, weary, pale, and weak.

Somewhere in between all the commotion, Alan's doctor appeared in the doorway. He asked everyone to step outside, so he could see how Alan was doing. They shuffled out obediently, although Phyllis kept her head high and didn't make eye contact with the man, making sure she was the last one to leave the room and shut the door behind her.

"Mom, what did he tell you?" Olivia asked, still unclear how her father's heart had stopped beating.

Everyone looked at Phyllis, who explained as best she could remember from Doctor Clarkson's analysis.

"He said your father flat-lined, that his heart stopped. He indicated the anesthetic should have been perfect, and shouldn't have affected it anyway, but they hadn't really begun operating yet when this happened.

"When I pushed him on the issue, he said they weren't sure if they should do the surgery on his knee at first, but they all decided that since he needed it done to help him get over the pain, they should avoid putting him under anesthesia a second time.

"They went ahead with the surgery, which they completed fairly quickly, and then they waited to see how his numbers were looking before telling me what had happened. He was already awake by the time I got into the operating room."

"I don't understand," Lenny said. "So he died and they brought him back, but instead of making sure he was okay, they played around with his knee for a while first?"

"His knee has been *killing him,* Leonard," Phyllis said, biting back quickly. "He needed this correction or he would have been in *agony,* you don't understand! And he didn't die. He just flat-lined. They got him back very quickly, and as you can see, he's fine now."

No one else dared question her, so the hallway fell silent. Another few minutes passed, and when Alan's door finally opened up again, the doctor held out his hand to stop them all from going back in.

"I think it's best if you visit him one at a time. Don't make him work too hard to find you all or keep track of who's saying what.

196

He needs to just rest now as much as possible. He's on a lot of painkillers and a sedative for his knee anyway."

"What about his heart?" Phyllis asked, challenging him.

"His heart is fine, Mrs. Abrams. If you don't have a cardiologist, I can get you one through the—"

"He has a cardiologist," Phyllis interrupted him. "Doctor Zilish. Are you saying we should speak to him?"

"It might be a good idea, yes. I'll call him too. I don't know why his heart briefly stopped like that, but I can assure you he's fine. He's responding very well to all our tests so far, and I'm confident his knee will be feeling much better now too."

"Thank you," Phyllis said, brushing past him to go back in.

"Hey Ma," Lenny said. "Why don't we let the girls go in first. They just got here, and haven't had time with Dad like we have."

Phyllis looked back and forth between them all with a nod.

"Okay. Who wants to go in first?"

Haley and Erika exchanged a look like they were trying to decide between them, so Peaches stepped forward as if she'd already been chosen. Phyllis watched her pass, then flashed the others a look.

Peaches and Alan had never been particularly close in the past, but Peaches never seemed to realize that. She closed the door behind her, and approached her grandfather cautiously, careful not to make any quick movements. His eyes were open, but he was just looking up at the ceiling when she came in, his mouth squishing open and closed now and then like he was chewing on the air.

As she approached the bed, Alan finally took note of her, and held open his right hand closest to her. Peaches put her hand in his, and smiled down at him.

"I heard your knee is all better now," she said, watching as his gaze returned to the ceiling. "And your doctor said you're doing well with the other stuff, so you should be okay."

Peaches looked away, unsure what else to even say to him. She was caught off guard when he spoke next, his eyes searching hers.

"I've never been particularly nice to you, Jessica," he said, closing his hand around hers a bit more.

She smiled to hear him call her by her name. Even her teachers all called her Peaches. If she thought about it, her grandfather was probably the last one to call her Jessica too, and that was at least four years ago.

"I can be a real grouch sometimes," Alan went on, staring at her intently, "and you deserve a much nicer Grandpa than I've been."

Perhaps it was his apology, or the way he looked at her from his bed, but Peaches was surprised to feel tears welling up in her eyes. She loved her grandfather, grouchy or not, but he'd never expressed this level of kindness to her before, and so she didn't know what to say.

"I'm going to be better now, though. You'll see. I'll change."

His words were soft, the painkillers still doing a number on him, but Peaches sensed he meant it all just the same, that this wasn't simply a medicinal delusion.

There wasn't anything empty about the eyes she saw looking back at her, which made her smile, but her enthusiasm was soon drowned out by his firm grip on her hand.

"I need to rest now, Jessica. Tell your grandmother to come back in if you can. We'll talk more later."

She nodded as she felt his hand loosen, and then left the room quietly, only looking back after she reached the door.

Outside, she told her grandmother to go in, then joined Haley, Erika, and Lenny on a row of seats across the hall. Further down from them all, Olivia and Caroline sat next to each other too, neither one talking. Caroline looked at her intently though, and finally decided to speak.

"You know, Livi. Your dad is gonna be fine. If he wasn't, his doctor wouldn't be so relaxed right now. Besides, your mom would already be on the phone with her lawyer if she thought the doctor did something bad to him. She'd be screaming bloody murder actually, even if she had to hold the pillow over your father's head until he really was dead."

Olivia turned to look at her, shocked to see a big smile on Caroline's face as she started howling with laughter. She couldn't believe it, and had never heard anything so strange come out of Caroline's mouth before, nor seen her laugh so hard. It made her start laughing quietly now too, and before long, the others were smiling and looking their way down the hall, wondering what had set them off.

Olivia looked away again, but as she did, Caroline leaned in and whispered in her ear.

"I'm really fucking high right now, Livi. I'm kinda worried the floor might be trying to eat me."

"Oh my God," Olivia said, seeing her with new eyes all of a sudden, and wondering how she'd even driven herself over to the hospital this way.

Before anyone noticed, Olivia reached over and took Caroline's hand, and together they wandered down the hall in the other direction. Erika made a face at them like they were being weird, then turned in her seat toward Lenny.

"Daddy, can Jenn and Isobel sleep over this weekend?"

Now it was Lenny's turn to act like the floor was trying to eat him. He crossed his legs and shook his head at the ground for a while before responding.

"No. No, honey, I don't think—I don't think that's a good idea this weekend. With your grandpa in here, you know? It's not a good time now, okay? Maybe next week, alright? Not this week."

Erika seemed content with this, then stood up and announced she wanted to find the vending machines. About twenty feet away though, she stopped in her tracks and walked back to ask Lenny for some money.

He handed her a five-dollar bill, then leaned back in his chair and put his head against the wall.

"Daddy," Peaches asked him, "when was the last time you and Mommy called me Jessica?"

Lenny looked at her sideways, making a face as he thought about it.

"I don't know. Maybe, what, three or four years ago? We had to on some health forms for high school, I remember that, but like, to your face? I'm really not sure." He scratched his cheek as he thought about it. "No, I really don't know, honey. Not recently, I'm sure of that. Why?"

"No reason. Just wondering."

He turned in his seat to face her though, worried she was trying to suggest something.

"You *like* being called Peaches, don't you?"

"Yeah," she said with a big smile, then leaned in and rested her head on Lenny's shoulder. He smiled and put his arm around her.

Inside Alan's room, Phyllis was slumped in the chair by Alan's bed, unsure why he was doing this to her. The surgery, the heart, and now the nonsense he was spewing. It was all *'quite too much'* for her, she'd announced, and he *'should certainly know better'*.

"Why don't we at *leassstalk* to Sam about it, *Phylsss*?" Alan said, his words slurring even more now as the pain meds kicked in further. "We should talk t'im. We should. *Itudbeniiice.*"

"No, I really don't think we should, Alan. You're in no place to be making these kinds of decisions anyway, and I'm certainly not going to ring him up and broach that of all topics right now either. It's the past. It's over. Keep it buried along with that girl."

She noticed him looking at her sideways like a dog hoping for another biscuit, perhaps even ready to argue.

"No," she insisted. "I mean it, Alan. It's done. No more talking. Just go to sleep. You need to rest your body and your heart, and for God's sake, rest what's left of your brain. Please."

"But Physs, I need to tellm I know. I know what really happen."

"Go to sleep, Alan. I am done having this conversation with you now."

Alan looked up at her one last time, his eyelids growing very heavy, and within another minute, he was fast asleep.

Chapter 22

Olivia texted Haley to come grab her car key, then waited impatiently, tapping her fingers on the top of the steering wheel. Caroline had finally stopped insisting she was okay enough to drive, and as Olivia looked over at her now, she saw her happily riding the high, a smile back on her face as she seemed to be thinking of something very funny.

Haley came by a minute later and looked in at them both, Caroline waving to her from the passenger side, with Olivia behind the wheel of Caroline's Subaru.

"What happened?" Haley asked.

"Don't worry about it," Olivia said, passing Haley the key to her car. "I parked around back. The trunk might be open too. It's been popping up like a boner lately."

It took Caroline a few seconds to get the line, but when she did, she started laughing hysterically, and Haley smiled at her.

"Oh my God, is she high?"

"No, sweetie. She's just tired," Olivia said, though she knew there was no point trying to hide Caroline's behavior.

"Haley!" Caroline called out, suddenly gripped with excitement. "I'm taking Erika to Boston to see some schools next month. Julie 8th. You should come."

Haley looked back at Olivia briefly with a smile.

"Do you mean *July* 8th, Aunt Caroline?"

"No?" Caroline said, looking confused. "She's not coming."

"Okay," Olivia announced. "Time to go. Haley, do me a favor. Don't tell anyone about, you know, any of this. I'll bring her home and make sure she's okay. I'll see you at the house later. Go back to work if you can. Mish won't miss me, but I'm sure Doctor Finny's going crazy without you."

Haley nodded and left for the back of the hospital toward her mother's car. She'd only been away from her desk for less than two hours by the time she got back, but knew her mother was right. Doctor Finny was probably losing his shit already.

She sped back to Ludlow as fast as she could, then parked out front and practically ran in, breathless.

"Sorry!" she yelled. "I'm back now."

To her surprise, Doctor Finny walked calmly out of his office with a magazine in his hands, shaking his head.

"It's fine. It's been quiet. Mrs. Edden canceled, and I haven't had anyone come in. No calls, either." He turned the page of the magazine, before deciding he was done with it, and dropping it down in the waiting area. "How's your grandfather?"

"Oh, wow. That's great—I mean, not great, but you know. And um, he's fine, I guess. They were really worried because his heart apparently stopped for a while there, but he's resting fine now. I only saw him for a minute until the doctor kicked us out, and then Peaches and my grandmother went in briefly, but my mom needed me to bring her car back to— What's wrong?" she asked suddenly, stopping when she saw the look of concern on his face.

"How long was his heart stopped for?" he asked.

"Oh," she said, thinking. "Thirty-seven seconds, I think it was?"

"Oh, okay," Doctor Finny said. "That isn't too bad then, especially if he's okay now. I'm glad to hear they were able to bring him back, though."

"Yeah," Haley said, her mind trailing quickly. She sat down at the desk and made sure no e-mails had come in as Doctor Finny just stood and looked out at the street.

"What do you mean by *back*, Doctor?" she finally asked him, the thought still gnawing at her. "Back from where?"

The doctor made a funny sort of a face at first, his Protestant background crossing his mind as a smile soon crossed his face.

"Well, back from the dead. He didn't die, I don't mean to say that, but at his age, his heart stopping is just, well, that's usually it. I'm happy to hear they got him back relatively quickly, though."

"Yeah," was all Haley managed, unsure what to think or say.

She wasn't at all religious, none of her family members were, mostly owing to what she perceived as her grandparents' atheism. None of them were brought up going to any kind of temple or church, and even though they all knew Peaches was into some weird stuff over at the Chaos Casbah, Peaches rarely went to any church services either.

For Haley, death was simply something that happened to your body when you died. You ended. You were gone. It was the lack of *anything at all* that Kerry Ann Jefferson and Mr. Caraway now existed in, and the place—or absence of a place—that everyone else would go to as well.

If Doctor Finny had touched a nerve, he hadn't intended to, and he wasn't about to push the issue with Haley any further. In fact, his mind was now solely focused on the small pack of bicycles speeding past the office down Main Street.

While there was virtually no time of year when you wouldn't see at least *some* bicycles—even in the worst winters, there were days with dry roads when locals would venture out for a ride—the arrival of summer meant many more tourists would be coming through soon.

It also meant, he was quite aware, that some of them would get injured, and would come into that very office and ask him for help. With the hospital in Rutland so far off, many would need immediate care from Doctor Finny, and perhaps an ambulance only later on.

He really didn't mean to look at otherwise healthy people as potential victims, but sometimes he couldn't help himself. Business was slow, and maybe one of them would fall off their bicycles right outside his office, and look to him for help.

"Any one of them could fall and break something," he said out loud, forgetting himself for a moment, and Haley, who'd been scrolling through her social media feed, suddenly looked up at him, unsure why he was still looking out the window.

"What?" she asked, snapping him out of it.

"Oh, nothing. First day of summer," he said with a smile, turning around again. "I'll be in my office."

Over at Lenny and Caroline's house, Olivia watched as Caroline collapsed on the couch and closed her eyes.

"I'm good, Livi, honestly. Thank you for driving me back here though. That was very sweet of you."

"No problem," Olivia said, her gaze quickly tracking outside to the tree house.

Something out there looked different all of a sudden, she couldn't tell what, and it unnerved her. Perhaps it was the way the sun's rays painted themselves across the side of the structure, or maybe it was the grass at the base of the tree, or something else, she wasn't sure what, but something was definitely off.

She looked down at Caroline again. Her eyes were closed and she was breathing deeply, so Olivia stepped a little closer to the door then, thinking for the first time in seventeen years of approaching it.

Don't, something told her. *Just leave it be.*

And yet it was right there, so close, so open and inviting, waiting for her to speak to it like some kind of living, breathing being with secrets to reveal. She slid open the door quietly, if only just to close the distance between herself and the tree house by another few feet, and the warm summer breeze blew in on a wave.

They loved hanging around that damn thing, she remembered, Sam and Lenny, and Haley too, though Haley wouldn't remember that now. They'd built the tree house as much for themselves as for Erika and Haley, grown men with little boy brains flush with glee as they finally put up the ladder and rope when they were done. It was a goddamn miracle the structure had lasted this long though, such as it was.

Couldn't have been more than a year after it was up before they stopped using it for good anyway. Olivia had half a mind to come over and take it down in those first few weeks. Caroline was the one who took the ladder and rope off late one night after Lenny and the girls were already asleep, and Olivia always hated her for it.

May as well have wrapped it up in police tape, she thought. Leaving it up without the ladder was a promise of constant pain.

Caroline's snoring stirred Olivia back just then, and she realized for the first time that she and the tree house could be all alone at last. But did she want that? Did she want to prayerfully approach it now, mournfully even, to either greet it hello or wish it goodbye once and for all?

She took a quiet step outside, careful not to wake Caroline, and perhaps with the hopes of not waking the sleeping tree house either. Too many memories. Too much pain. Too much of the unresolved still trapped inside.

As she walked toward it slowly, Olivia marveled at little birds flying in and out of the entrance and the tiny window, fearless occupants clueless to what happened there so long ago.

Footstep by footstep, it grew closer, and taller, and taller, until she finally got so close, she realized she wouldn't even be able to look into it because of the height. Why did they build the entrance so high up anyway?

To keep people out, the answer came in the wind. *To keep unwanted visitors from ever seeing inside.*

It really was *their* tree house, Sam and Lenny's, right from the start. They were both in their twenties at the time, still not ready to grow up. And Sam never had, not even after everything that happened that year.

It was the closest Olivia had been to it now since before that girl was found, and Olivia was sure if she went to look for it, the girl's body would still be up there in the field outside the village, still fresh and wet from the rain like she was when they found her.

She reached up to grab the entrance, to at least *try* to grab a small piece of it, to feel the inside, but just as she got a hand on the tree bark below the structure, she heard the door slide further open back at the house.

Olivia twisted her body around, pulling her hand back down like it was on fire, and soon locked eyes with Caroline.

As they stared at each other, a new breeze blew past Olivia first, and pushed Caroline's bangs up just a moment later. There was a dark truth in the space between them, and they both knew it, but neither was ready, even now, to pull it from the air.

Instead, Caroline just smiled sadly at her, and turned sideways, inviting Olivia back inside.

"Want some coffee?" Caroline asked.

Olivia came back to the deck before she answered.

"Sure," she said, not looking at her now as she went inside. "And I think you could probably use some too."

Caroline slid the door closed again, smiling on her way into the kitchen for the coffee.

"The high's mostly gone now. Fun while it lasted though."

Olivia sat down where Caroline had been lying earlier, and watched her as she made the coffee. There was always something about Caroline she despised, if she was being totally honest with herself, but there was another part of her she found forever alluring. How else but alluring can you describe someone with a family like hers?

She'd married Lenny four years after Olivia and Sam got married, and from the moment Caroline came into their family, Olivia knew things would change.

Phyllis was forever their taskmaster growing up, but Olivia could see from the start that Caroline would keep Lenny in line. He needed that, after all, someone to both love him *and* guide him, hold his hand and tell him the monsters under his bed weren't really there. And while some very real monsters showed up in all their lives soon enough, Caroline had clearly succeeded in growing their family and household into something special.

After Sam left town, Olivia couldn't help but marvel at how their little family grew and prospered, all while she and Haley sat back watching it all with a hard blend of jealousy and resentment.

"We have white, pink, blue, yellow, and green," Caroline said, turning and showing Olivia her bowl of sugar packets.

Of course she has so many choices, Olivia thought. *How does one woman get so perfect? But more importantly, why the hell would she want to?*

"I'll take just plain white, thanks. Two. And a little cream."

Caroline went to work stirring in the sugar and cream for Olivia, then laughed to herself as she thought of something extra dark. Olivia noticed, and asked her where it came from.

"Maybe it's still the pot," Caroline said, biting her lip, "but I just had the craziest thought about putting twelve Splenda packets in a cup of coffee for your mother sometime."

Olivia smiled awkwardly, watching as Caroline handed her the coffee and sat down beside her with her own.

"My mother can't have Splenda. It gives her terrible heart palpitations. Twelve could kill her."

"Yeah," Caroline said with a big smile. "I know."

Olivia couldn't help but laugh. *There it is,* she thought. *This* was the side of Caroline she always liked, the side she could understand.

They sat beside each other and sipped their coffee, staring across at the dining room with mutual disinterest, their minds roaming elsewhere far beyond. It took a strong wind outside to bring their thoughts back to the tree house, as they listened together to the wailing cries of wood rubbing against wood.

"Ever think of just destroying the damn thing?" Olivia asked.

Caroline looked confused, unsure what she meant, but Olivia's stare made her hesitate.

"Don't even *pretend* you don't know what I'm talking about," Olivia said. "That goddamn beast in your backyard that we should have taken down years ago. We should have burnt the whole goddamn tree to the ground, then buried the ashes along with—"

She stopped short, but didn't need to finish anyway.

Caroline smiled briefly and looked away, back to the pile of mail on her dining room table, to the slightly frayed carpet behind the chair, the part she kept meaning to vacuum clean, and finally to the television above the fireplace to her left. She looked anywhere but into Olivia's eyes, thinking carefully about what she could possibly say to appease her.

"Lenny once asked me if we should take it down, probably because you or your mom had gotten to him, but I dunno. I'm not sure it's necessary. Part of me feels like taking it down would be like giving up. Like if we dismantled it once and for all, we'd be dismantling all the good times along with it."

She finally allowed herself a glance back at Olivia, who she saw was watching her intently, an expressionless look on her face. Judgment? Maybe. But maybe not. She wasn't sure.

Olivia turned away from her then, and took another long sip of her coffee. Then she stood up and walked over to the sliding glass door to look out. Caroline slid sideways in her seat to watch her, still unsure what she was thinking.

Finally, Olivia opened her mouth to speak as she leaned against the wall to look at her.

"I think that's an admirable *gesture*," she said, as Caroline watched and waited for more. "It's an admirable gesture, but very—" She paused, thinking of the right words to share the right way. "A very *kind* gesture too? But I also think it's bullshit."

"What? How is it bullshit?" Caroline asked, feigning innocence.

"No. Never mind," Olivia said, waving her hand and sitting down again.

Caroline made a show of putting her coffee mug down, then turned to face her squarely.

"No, Livi, tell me. Why do you think it's bullshit? What aren't you saying here? I want to know. Really."

She wasn't angry, but if the two of them were going to cut through all the bullshit, she wanted to just do it already and get it over with.

"Okay, you really wanna know?" Olivia asked, putting her own mug down too.

"Yes," Caroline said. "Just tell me."

"Well the truth is, Car, I'm pretty sure you and my ex-husband had something secret going on that I never knew about. You wanna tell me what you think about that?"

Caroline could sense herself getting heated, but felt as if there was nothing else she could do now but tell the truth. Maybe it was the pot that had her so relaxed, or just the need to break free once and for all from this particular secret, but without overthinking it, she leaned in close and said it right into Olivia's ear.

"Yes, Livi, it's all true. Sam was *fucking me* while you and him were still together, and he's been fucking me twice a week since he came back. Are you happy now? Does that turn you on maybe a little too?"

Olivia recoiled, and moved over a bit on the couch.

"Are you fucking insane?"

Caroline shook her head and looked away. Throwing the cards out on the table was probably the stupidest move she could've made, but she was glad to have done it anyway.

"You know what? I'm sorry, Livi. I really am. I'm sorry for cheating on your brother. For helping Sam cheat on you. For lying. For all of it. But I'm a mess, alright? I'm a fucking mess. So as long as my whole life is falling apart around me, I might as well let it all happen now."

"Whoa," Olivia said, holding her hands out. "Just stop it, okay? This is unfuckinbelievable. You saying you fucked Sam, *and still do,* I'm neither shocked *nor* angry at, but don't try to pull me into your drama too."

They looked at each other carefully. Caroline sized her up, wondering if maybe she was wrong about Olivia, but deciding again right away that she wasn't, while Olivia just looked shell-shocked, and unsure what else to say.

Caroline stood up suddenly and made fists with both hands, wringing her arms out in front of her several times with a deep, decades-old groan.

"You know something, Livi? Your family is fucked up, but I fit right in, okay? I shouldn't have said what I did, but you know what? Fuck it. I don't fucking care anymore. I'd prefer you not tell Lenny, because despite my past with Sam—and it is in the past now, I assure you—I love your brother very much, I love my kids very much too, and I just want my fucking family to stay sane and happy, okay?"

Olivia looked away. This wasn't the kind of conversation she ever thought they'd be having.

She took a deep breath and considered it all, watching as Caroline finally collapsed with her head in her hands in the couch on the opposite side of the room. She watched her there for a long while, and soon realized she had only two options: watch her crash and burn, or save her somehow, and help her find some semblance of peace. And because she'd already had way too much of the former, she knew what she had to do.

She stood up in place, pausing only long enough to think it out for a few more seconds, then walked over to Caroline and looked down at her.

"Stand up," Olivia said.

"What?"

"I said stand up, goddamn it."

Caroline stood up and looked at her. Neither one of them was sure about any of this now, but Caroline sensed Olivia wasn't angry with her. She seemed to be composing herself at first, but then leaned in quickly and hugged Caroline tightly.

It was the first time in years they had hugged like that, and as they each rested their heads on the other one's shoulder, feeling the healing warmth of the very long overdue embrace, the pain all melted away.

After about twenty seconds, Olivia rubbed her hands on Caroline's back, and Caroline squeezed her a little tighter before they both let go.

"Thank you," Caroline said, watching as Olivia nodded and turned away.

As Olivia sat back down again and grabbed her coffee from the table, she looked over at Caroline and grinned briefly before nodding again.

"You're right though, Car," she said.

"Right about what?"

"This family *is* fucked up, and you really *do* fit right in with the rest of us."

They both let out a huge laugh at this, and Caroline's nerves eased even more as their giggles continued.

"And you may be right about that goddamn tree house too, you know. No matter what you and Sam ever did behind my back, or what may have ever happened in the damn thing, we shouldn't tear it down. It's a reminder of a time when we were all on the same page, and if that was only for one year, one summer, or hell, even just one week, we should keep it up to remember it, the time when things didn't completely suck for this family."

She downed the rest of her coffee, then stood up again and grabbed her purse to head out.

"Okay, enough of this crap. I'm driving your car back to the bank. I'll stop by with it after work, and one of you guys can bring me home after. I'll see you then."

"Bye," Caroline called after her.

Once she heard the car start up and leave, Caroline walked over to the sliding glass door and looked out at it once more: the place where it happened.

Her memory of that night was still hers alone, but she wondered now how much longer her secrets had left to live.

Chapter 23

Seventeen Years Earlier

"Sam! Where is the ketchup?!" Olivia yelled from downstairs.

Sam froze in place in their second-floor bedroom, ready once more to scream at Olivia for her stupid questions, but recalling Lenny's reminder—*'for Haley's sake'*—to keep things calm.

"Isn't it on the door by the half and half?!" he yelled back, as leveled as he could muster from so far away.

Silence. He listened carefully to the little clink the glass ketchup jar made on the shelf followed by the refrigerator door closing. No thank you followed. No apology would either.

He put on his sneakers, then grabbed his keys and wallet from their dresser. Checking his hair again in the mirror, he turned the corner tightly and barreled down the stairs.

"Daddy, how do you spell accept?" Haley asked from inside the living room.

"Uh, is that a trick question?"

"What?"

"Hey," Olivia stopped him, once she realized he was all dressed to leave the house already, far too early. "Where are you going?"

"Gotta meet Lenny quick. Be back in a few."

Just three minutes later, he arrived at Lenny's house. He slapped the top of the steering wheel repeatedly, checked himself in the mirror one last time, then made his way to their front door.

After ringing the doorbell several times, Sam still wasn't hearing anything inside, so he started knocking loudly until she answered.

"Your doorbell goes out way too much. Just replace it. It's gotta be faulty wiring or something."

Sam squeezed past Caroline as she let him in.

"Sorry, I gotta put a sign up. There's no way I'll hear anyone knocking once the music is on." She watched him walk away from her with a smile. "Hey, wait a second," she said, noticing he was empty handed. "What the hell? I thought you were bringing beer?"

"I'm not here yet. Just stopped by to drop off my house key. We're taking Haley to Hartford tomorrow, then staying overnight with my mom in White Plains."

"Yeah, Lenny mentioned. You could have brought the key over later though, right?"

He stopped and looked at her with a stupid grin.

"I hadn't thought of that."

"Sometimes I'm surprised you even know how to drive, Sam."

He nodded with a smile, and she watched him carefully.

"Look, I gotta shower. Leave the key in the kitchen." She started up the stairs. "If my catering helper shows up, just show them into the kitchen. I don't know who Connie's sending. And make sure the front door's unlocked on your way out."

She ran upstairs as Sam made his way into the kitchen, throwing the key down on the counter like he was shooting a basket. He spotted the new tree house through the door, and instinctively made his way out to check on it.

He pulled on the ladder first to make sure it was holding on tight, then climbed up most of the way to look inside.

"Nice fucking job, Newhaus," he said, impressed with his work.

He reached in and pulled out a few stray leaves and a stick, then climbed down, pausing briefly on his way back to the house to admire it one more time.

Inside, he opened the fridge and looked around. Behind some of Caroline's nutty health food crap, he spied a few bottles of beer.

"Score," he said, popping the cap off quickly and taking a swig.

As he drank, a knock came at the front door, but Sam just kept drinking, his eyes darting forward to the piece of door he could see, and then to the kitchen ceiling, wondering if Caroline had heard it.

He made his way toward the front, listening carefully, annoyed to hear the shower already running. The person knocked again. He cursed under his breath, then walked over and opened the door, pleasantly surprised right away to be greeted by an extremely attractive young girl in a ponytail holding three large trays of food.

"Mr. Abrams? Hi. I'm from Connie's Catering."

Sam smiled at her, sizing her up.

"Well, I'm not an Abrams, I'm a Newhaus, but yeah, the lady of the house said you might be coming over. You can go do your thing in the kitchen. She said to make yourself at home."

"Okay, cool," she said, moving past him as he watched her ass sway away from him.

There was no turning away from an ass like hers, he decided, nor a way to let such a pretty little face leave his sight before he'd at least enjoyed it a few minutes longer. He closed the door quietly and listened for the shower, grateful to hear it still going.

"I know Connie," he said once he was back in the living room near the kitchen. "We went to school together. She was nice."

"Yeah, she's cool."

"How long have you been working with her over there?"

"Umm, only the past few months on and off. My dad said I needed to start working somewhere."

"Your dad's a smart man."

She smiled but said nothing, setting out the food and getting a lay of the land. Sam watched her with admiration, appreciating how she opened the refrigerator and the oven, getting an idea of what she had to work with. She skirted past him quickly to the car to retrieve more things, and on her way back in, Sam finally thought to ask her if she needed any help.

"Oh no, I'm fine. Thank you, sir."

Sam shook his head and grunted, halfway through another guzzle, and wagged his finger at her with a new smile.

"No, no, no. *Sam.* Not sir."

"Okay," she giggled. "Sorry. Sam."

She bent over to lift a box of utensils from her bag on the floor, and he took another chance to appreciate her ass and legs.

"And what did you say your name was?"

She looked up confused, like she was doing a math equation.

"I don't think I did. I'm Kerry Ann. Nice to meet you."

214

Chapter 24

"Your blood work is all good, so as long as the tests from this morning come back okay, I don't see why you need to stay another night. You should be home for dinner later, if not a late lunch."

Alan smiled and nodded at the doctor as he left, then locked eyes with Phyllis, who he saw was smirking at him.

"What?" he asked.

"He's assuming I'll make you dinner tonight. I'm not even up for cocktails, let alone dinner, and that's really saying something."

Alan looked away, back to the ceiling. She didn't understand. She didn't even *want* to understand what had happened to him. And for his part, he couldn't blame her. If the same thing had happened to her, how differently would he have reacted? If anything, he'd have been worse. He'd have laughed her away, or scheduled her an appointment with a psychiatrist.

Phyllis sat down and smiled, putting their conversation from the day before far out of her head. It wasn't worth rehashing, she told herself. Once his meds wore off, or he was finished taking whatever pain-relief pills he'd been given this time, he'd change his tune right back again, she was sure.

Silly visions and nonsense were the stuff of medical dysfunction anyway, and at best, proof his medicine was kicking in.

"I was thinking we might ask Livi and Haley over for pizza though," she said. "And I'll have them get it for us, of course. Just mushroom on yours, and maybe a salad. Let's not take chances."

She paused and thought for a moment.

"Did I tell you what Nancy told me about her grandson? He's the one with the nose piercing, remember? She said he wants to start a *band* now. Can you believe it? He's living off her good graces as it is.

"She's already giving her daughter money every month to help pay for the exorbitant little monster, so you'd think the kid would at least pull his weight. And he's not going to help himself any by playing that heavy metal garbage in her basement."

Alan just blinked without responding, as if he was at home on the couch watching a football game or the golf channel, so Phyllis went on.

"I'll tell you what. If we ever laid out that kind of money for one of the girls, I'd make sure they understood the ramifications. There would be *consequences* to their squandering.

"Did you know Erika had the nerve to ask me for money when she was here yesterday? I didn't even look in my purse. I told her I was tapped out, and she should ask her mother or get a job. 'Ask around in town,' I told her. 'Try one of the restaurants or maybe The Book Nook.' 'I'm trying' she says to me with this silly little smile like she's actually out there looking. Bullshit artist, that one. Livi and Lenny were never like that. We forced them to take jobs while they were still in grade school. Sure, it was easier then, paperboy jobs and whatnot, but they learned to pull their own weight early. None of this begging shit, I'll tell you that."

It wasn't that Alan couldn't hear Phyllis. He'd just chosen not to listen. His mind was a million miles away from any desire to talk about this kind of crap. More than a million, if he had to guess. He looked up at Phyllis though, pleading with her to stop. Surely she'd see he wasn't enjoying this. Why couldn't she just call Nancy Hensley and chat with her? The answer came right away. Nancy would interrupt. Alan was just conscious enough to listen to every word, and just silent enough not to argue. He was the perfect conversation partner.

Before he knew it, she had met his glance, and something there told him she understood he wasn't enjoying her banter. She smiled at him briefly, and then continued.

This time, she launched into more about Alan. She may not have more time like this with his mouth covered up by the oxygen. *Carpe diem,* she thought with a grin.

"You know something, Alan. I often wonder what our lives would be like if you and I had never met. I suppose I would have finally accepted Michael Lisante's invitations to dinner. He was always very fond of me, you know. Not as pushy as you were

216

though, which I suppose is what made the difference. He was an excellent thoracic surgeon too. Best in Brooklyn, probably the whole damn city. Certainly had the best bedside manner. I mean with the patients, not with me. I never slept with him, of course. We did *something* together, that's for sure. Just honest workplace flirting though, most of the time. Of course, he's long dead now, so I would have been a widow for quite a while."

She looked out the window and then down at Alan again.

"And you. Where would you have been without me?"

He didn't even look at her when she said this, so she answered for him.

"I'll tell you where you'd be. You would have kept that damn business running for years after you should have, and you'd probably be dead by now too. No one to stop you from overexerting yourself. I'm sure you would have always dreamed about life up here in the mountains, but you'd have never made the move. No, you'd have worked till you were in your late 60s, and died by 70. I'm sure of it."

Alan looked at her again, wondering if she was just joking, trying to get a rise out of him, but no, she really was this sure of herself. She noted his stare now and smiled.

"I know. You disagree. But I'll tell you what, darling."

She leaned in then like she was going to surprise him with a moment of tenderness. Her eyes looked much gentler now, kinder and loving.

"Your business would have done a hell of a lot better with you at the helm rather than that idiot Bob Gillen."

She leaned back wistfully, like she and Alan had just enjoyed a very special moment together, completely unaware of how much she had missed the target, and Alan soon closed his eyes, hoping she'd think he was asleep. She eyed him for just a few seconds, but didn't pause long, not allowing him to escape so easily.

"Bob Gillen was the worst man you could have sold that business to. He was an idiot from the first day we met him, and just because he had the financial wherewithal to grow your business in the short term, you should have known what he was doing to fuck it all up in the end. And his wife. Ugh. That woman disgusted me, what with all the fat coming off her? What did that woman eat, a dozen doughnuts a day? You know she once told me about a restaurant she and Bob liked to frequent. Some place in Chinktown with too many foreign words in its name. And she started rattling off all the items on the menu like she ordered every goddamn one of them each time they went out. I wanted to just slap her."

She grew quiet then, and Alan wondered if she was finally going to leave him be now at last, but the silence only lasted another thirty seconds.

"I *should* have slapped her. That would have shown her, right? If I literally slapped some sense into her, and told her what I thought about her belly fat once and for all?"

Alan winced, still with his eyes closed, and Phyllis finally relented. She stood up and walked over to the hallway, unsure why, or what to do with herself. She looked down the hall toward the young nurses, neither of them making eye contact with her, and decided she needed to be as far away from all of them for a while as she could. The building was large enough to explore, and explore it she would.

The clacking her shoes made as she walked away from them all was the best noise they'd heard all day.

Inside his room, Alan opened his eyes and carefully reached up to remove the oxygen mask. He enjoyed it, but knew it was just an extra attachment between him and the world.

He wanted to stand up and do something, to look around, maybe go outside, but he could tell his body wasn't close to being ready for that yet. Soon, though. The drugs were beginning to wear off, he knew that much, but the experience? The truth? That would never go away.

Chapter 25

A week passed without much to speak of, but the following Friday, Lenny invited the whole family over for dinner. Olivia balked, said she'd pass, and Erika was out somewhere with Chris—*whose existence she still hadn't mentioned to anyone*—but everyone else came.

They expected pizza or something else light and casual, but Lenny and Caroline surprised Alan, Phyllis, Haley, and Peaches with a home-cooked meal of lasagna with garlic bread. Caroline prepared a healthier pasta salad for Alan too, but he enjoyed a fair bit of the lasagna and garlic bread just the same.

By the time they were finished eating, Lenny couldn't help but ask Alan once again how he was doing—*for the third time that evening*—because there was definitely something distinctly strange about him that night.

"Dad, really, I'm sorry to push you on this, but what's going on? You're much quieter than usual, and you're barely keeping up with any of the conversation tonight. Is there something we should be worried about?"

Phyllis wiped her mouth with her napkin, and glanced at Alan briefly before clearing her throat and looking down. It was very unlike her to not speak for her husband, or to at least say something silly at a moment like this. Though Lenny and the girls hadn't noticed, Phyllis was definitely acting just as strange as Alan, if only in a decidedly different way.

Alan smiled warmly at Lenny, and kept his eyes on him for a long time before he responded. When he finally did, he spoke very slowly, as if thinking out each and every word.

"I suppose I owe you all an explanation, although I regret Olivia isn't here for this too. Then again, perhaps that's for the best."

Phyllis was now eyeing Alan suspiciously with her mouth half open, ready to pounce quickly if he said anything too incendiary.

"When I woke up from the operation on my knee, everything was, well, it was a blur. I could barely make out the doctor's coat, let alone his face, and I couldn't remember where I was. I heard his voice, first directed at a nurse, I gathered, and then at me once he realized I was awake. He sounded confident, but fake somehow, like he was simply rehearsing his lines, reciting something he'd read in a book."

Phyllis looked concerned, and Caroline couldn't help but notice the way she put an arm up on the table as she faced him head on.

"But when I started waking up a bit more, I realized he was just saying all the things you'd have expected him to. Telling me about my vitals and my knee, how the operation went, and what had happened. He also told me about the *incident* with which you're all no doubt aware of by now, with my heart stopping."

He paused and took a moment to look at each of them carefully, cautiously, thinking, it seemed, of how best to explain what it was he had to say next.

"Now I've gotta say, this part amused me, just as much now as it did then, because as he was telling me what happened, I knew I could stop him at any point and share with him what I already knew. And then, quickly realizing I might soon lose my chance to surprise him, I told him."

"You told him what?" Lenny asked.

"I told him my heart had stopped, that the machine went off for God knows how long beeping away in that awfully *interminable* tone, and that he and the two attending assistants went to work bringing me back."

"Holy shit," Caroline muttered, and Phyllis eyed her with confusion, unsure why she'd said that.

"Your doctor told us all this, Alan," Phyllis said. "What the hell are you going on about as if it's anything new?"

Lenny and Caroline exchanged a look, realizing what Alan was saying to them, and then Lenny glanced at Peaches and Haley too. They seemed as dumbfounded as Phyllis was, though perhaps, he guessed, more aware of the impending truth.

"Dad," Lenny asked, "you were somehow *conscious* when your heart stopped? You were aware enough or awake enough to realize it was all happening?"

220

"Not only was I aware, Leonard," he said with a sly smile. "I was floating up at the top of the goddamn room, at the ceiling, watching as it all happened."

Peaches slammed her hand down hard on the table then, her fingers flipping bread crusts off her plate in a whirlwind of crumbs.

"Shut *up*," she said, clearly as amazed as she was impressed.

Alan smiled at her, and the two seemed to be sharing a moment, but Phyllis had already heard enough.

"We should go," she announced, quickly standing up. "You should be home resting, not spewing this kind of bullshit."

Alan's face changed immediately. He didn't even look at Phyllis, or anyone else, and before anyone could argue, he stood up as well.

"Wait," Lenny said. "You can't just drop a bomb like that, and then leave. You've gotta tell us more."

Alan shook his head, neither angry nor upset, just resigned to his wife's order for them to leave right away. She hadn't phrased it in the form of a command, but he knew exactly what she wanted, and that was to leave there as soon as humanly possible.

"I'll be in the car," she announced.

She didn't kiss anyone goodbye, either, just grabbed her purse and windbreaker, and made a beeline for the door before anyone could stop her. They watched it all in shock, and no one knew what to say or do about the sudden shift in atmospheric pressure.

"Dad," Lenny said. "C'mon now. Just sit down and tell us, please. We want to hear."

"Yes, please Grandpa?" Peaches begged. "I totally need to hear every last detail. All of it. This is incredible."

"No. I'm sorry," he said softly. "Not tonight. Your mother is right, Leonard. I should go home and rest."

He began walking toward the door very slowly with his cane.

"But this is insane," Lenny said, standing up now and following after him. "You're just gonna let her do this, just silence you like this? Force you to stop telling us about this absolutely, *insanely* incredible moment in your life? Dad, please don't go. Dad? Dad!"

221

Alan opened and shut the door, leaving with a brief wave, and once he was gone, Lenny just stared at the closed door in front of him, listening as Phyllis started her car outside, and a moment later as a car door closed and they pulled away.

Lenny walked back into the dining room and looked at them all with amazement.

"Okay. Pardon my language," he said, "but what the fuck just happened here?"

Caroline smiled at him and stood up, then walked over and rubbed his back. Haley and Peaches watched the two of them for a moment, but no one said anything. Finally, Caroline cleared her throat and spoke.

"I think what happened is, your mother heard your father saying something her brain couldn't comprehend, something that confused her in a way, so she left. Your father *does* need his rest, so I suppose he didn't want to upset her."

Lenny eyed her sideways like he knew she was bullshitting.

"Okay," she relented. "*Or* your mother is a giant bitch, and your father just got bitch *slapped* into silence."

She looked at Haley and Peaches with a frown then.

"Sorry, girls."

Peaches smiled, but Haley just looked confused.

"I've never seen them act like that before," Haley said. "Are you sure they're alright?"

Lenny, still exasperated by the whole thing, and annoyed at both of them, shook his head and shrugged.

"I dunno," he said. "I guess so." He looked toward the front door again. "I'll tell you what, though. We need to hear the rest of that story. I think there's a lot more he isn't telling us."

"Duh," Peaches said. "If he met Jesus, Daddy, I wanna know what he looked like. I bet he's blacker than we think."

Caroline and Lenny exchanged a look, every eyebrow up, but neither of them chose to respond.

Once Phyllis pulled into the driveway, the two of them got out and walked in. They'd made the nine-minute drive in complete silence, but as soon as the front door had closed behind Alan, Phyllis let loose.

"What the *fuck* was that all about? Huh? Some kind of bullshit hysteria? What do you think you're doing, spewing this nonsense? Floating above the goddamn room? Are you high? What the hell, Alan? What are you trying to do to me? I'm on the verge of a nervous breakdown as it is worrying about you and your knee, not to mention terrified you'll incriminate yourself in a goddamn murder investigation!"

He walked into the living room, resting his cane on the side of the couch, and removed his jacket, tossing it down on the seat beside him. Though the TV remote stared back up at him, he didn't reach for it.

"Do you really think you should be saying that kind of crap to our grandchildren? Scaring them like that? And what about me? Did you even stop to think for a second about *my* feelings? Do you even *care* what I think about all this?"

She finally paused long enough for him to respond, and respond he realized he would have to.

"I was simply telling you all what happened to me. The others seemed to be interested. I thought you might be too. I *thought*—"

"No. You didn't think *at all*. You certainly didn't think about me or any of my feelings. You flat-lined, Alan. That's it. Nothing more. Your heart briefly stopped, and then the doctor got it going again. That's all. I *am* beginning to think you have some residual brain damage, though. You're acting sick in the head right now, that's for damn sure."

Again, Alan just remained silent, staring off at the wall above their television, at the photographs of his father and mother hanging there in large frames. There was no point in arguing with Phyllis about this. She wouldn't allow any version of the truth to exist between them unless she approved it beforehand. He was sure some part of her resented him for not telling her any of it in private before they got there too.

If there was one thing she hated more than gossip used against her, it was truth used against her. Rather than allow this particular truth to exist at all, she simply wished it stuffed in a box and thrown to the curb before it could escape any further.

"You really are something else lately, Alan. You really are. I'm not amused, I'll tell you that. This bullshit has got to stop. I won't have it. I will not have it. Do you hear me?"

Alan didn't respond. He just stared forward quietly, waiting for her to run out of steam. He'd long since grown weary of her speaking to him like this, but had learned over time to let her yell whenever it suited her. Refusing to respond was far less dangerous than any argument might have been, and his silence was a gift he gave them both.

Phyllis shook her head at him, then went up to bed without further comment. She knew she'd won for the time being, and that was all that mattered now.

Once he heard her go upstairs, he slipped his loafers off and laid down, soon pulling the afghan draped above the back of the couch over his body. He needed his bed, but for at least an hour, the couch would do just fine.

##

Haley went home, and Peaches returned to her room as Lenny and Caroline cleaned up the mess from dinner. They didn't talk about anything at first, as the evening had ended so much more abruptly and strangely than either of them could have predicted.

It seemed their odd, crazy lives over the past few weeks were destined to only grow odder and crazier. Phyllis and Alan were the backbone of the family too, so if their solid foundation was coming apart, what else might happen to them all?

Lenny threw the last of the newly rinsed soda cans in their recycling bucket, then turned and faced Caroline with a smirk.

"So," he said. "What do you think? What do you *really* think?"

She smiled at him as she finished wiping the counter, and shook her head at first, still thinking it over.

"Well, I think he probably had some kind of a brief but real near-death experience, or at least an out-of-body experience of some sort. It's not completely unheard of. Lots of people have had that kind of thing. Even a few of my clients over the years."

"Yeah, but what do you think about that?"

"I think it's pretty cool. I don't really understand the phenomenon or how it works, but I think it's very interesting. Your mom, though—"

"My mom," Lenny said, still annoyed at her. "She's insane."

"Well, no, not necessarily. Maybe she's just scared, and rather than expressing her fear and confusion in a normal, calm, healthy way, we witnessed her doing what she does when she gets frightened. She runs away. Hearing that kind of thing may have genuinely scared her, and your father may have recognized that. Maybe he heard something in her voice, and saw something in her reaction that he'd seen before, and rather than fight her, he just followed her out. I'm sure they've already discussed it in the car or at home, and come to a peaceful understanding."

"You think so?"

Caroline thought about it again for a moment and then nodded.

"Yeah, I do. I think once they're alone, their dynamic is much different. I think she's calmer and more docile."

Lenny laughed. He'd never once heard his mother referred to as docile, yet he appreciated Caroline's wise advice nonetheless.

Phyllis was hard enough to deal with in person with other people around. He hoped Caroline was right that she was much calmer when it was just her and Alan. He couldn't bear to imagine his dad putting up with her by himself.

"Listen," Caroline said, breaking his train of thought. "How early do you wanna leave for Boston next week?"

Lenny was well prepared for the question, and had an answer ready, but immediately feigned ignorance.

"What? That's next weekend?"

"Yes, I told you we needed to help her look at schools. I already got the room for Saturday night. We'll see what her options are down there, even if it's just something small or a two-year program. Probably too late for anything big now anyway, but it doesn't hurt to check around in person.

"Peaches seemed interested too. I might have asked Haley at some point, but I can't remember now. I didn't get tickets, but maybe we can still do a show or something while we're there? Or just a movie? Any thoughts?"

Lenny's mind immediately went to Jenn.

And her body.

And her tits.

Caroline and the girls away in Boston meant only one thing to Lenny: his chance to return to the soft place of delicious joy between Jenn's left and right breasts. But he'd forgotten already that he'd need an excuse not to go to Boston, one that must arrive now very quickly.

"Well, that does sound great, but I really need to work next weekend. There's been some weird stuff going on lately with the payroll file and my boss. I was thinking of investigating it over the weekend when no one's around to look over my shoulder."

"Why can't you do that this weekend?"

Good question. Think fast.

"Well, Mr. Tarisi is away next weekend, so that Saturday or Sunday would work out perfectly."

I'm getting good at this.

"Oh, okay. Well that sucks."

"Yeah. Sorry. Would have been great to do Boston again, but didn't realize you were doing that next weekend. So you're thinking of seeing a show too, or just some sightseeing?"

"Well, *college* sightseeing, not like city sightseeing, but no, I'm not gonna look into shows if you're not coming. Erika's a pain in the ass with that stuff anyway. Okay, whatever. I'll figure it out."

Lenny couldn't tell if Caroline bought his story at all, but he guessed she had. He analyzed the back of her head for a moment, trying to decide.

Despite the insane urges of his dick, Lenny was still conflicted. If anything had put him over the edge though, it was Caroline herself. The lies from both Sam *and* her about the imaginary birthday gift Sam was planning really unsettled him. Everything felt different now, and their new dynamic was every bit as frightening as it was exhilarating.

Caroline was upstairs before he knew it, and Lenny was suddenly all alone, more alone than just the empty kitchen made him feel.

Sam, his go-to about Jenn, was clearly lying to him about something big, but he wondered if it wouldn't be better to at least stay close to him anyway. He grabbed his phone and pulled up Sam's contact card, deciding whether or not to call.

Dropping it to the counter again, he stared at it for a while. Then he went to the fridge, grabbed a bottle of beer, and opened it up, all while watching his phone from a safe distance, like it was Sam himself.

Finally, after another minute of drinking and staring, he approached it again slowly and picked it up, pressing the call button with a hard push before overthinking it any further.

With a glance toward the stairs at the front of the house, Lenny walked over to the sliding door to the deck and nudged it open with his elbow. As the phone rang a third time, he began to wonder if this wasn't just a waste of time anyway. Maybe Sam was avoiding him now.

Sitting down on a lounge chair, Lenny put the bottle down on the ground and coughed into his other hand, deciding what he'd say on the voicemail, but as the phone rang for the fourth time, Sam finally picked up.

"Hey Len, sorry about that. Was just peeing. Heard the phone, but couldn't shake it out fast enough."

"No worries, man, no worries."

"So what's up?"

"Well—to be honest," Lenny said, looking back at the closed sliding door and then upstairs to make sure none of the windows were open, "I wanted to bend your ear again about this girl Jenn."

"Oh, the chick with the big tits?"

"Yeahhhh, that's the one," Lenny said, laughing darkly, as if there was some *other* girl he'd been messing around with too. "It's just, I have an opportunity to see her again next weekend. Have her here at the house when no one's home? And I'm kinda feeling more than just a little bit conflicted. It's like my brain is screaming no, but my dick is screaming yes, and even though my brain is a hell of a lot bigger than my dick, my dick seems much louder right now, ya know?"

"Mm-hm. I know, I know."

Lenny listened, hoping Sam would say more, but when he didn't, he spelled it out further.

"So what do you think? What should I do? I was kinda hoping you could give me some advice."

He listened again, waiting for Sam, but once again, he was met only with silence.

"Hello? Still there?"

A sigh now, and then Sam cleared his throat.

"Yeah, Len, sorry. I'm here, it's just, I don't know if you should even be asking me advice on this sorta thing. You're such a good guy, and my track record with women is a little less than stellar, you know? I just—I just think maybe I shouldn't say anything about this, you know?"

It was Lenny's turn to retreat into radio silence, but he grunted anyway just the same, and shook his head, looking out toward the tree house. If Sam *was* guilty of killing Kerry Ann, he'd once again shown Lenny some soul, and confused him even further.

"Yeah," Lenny responded after a while. "Yeah, I know, it's okay. I'm just—" He shook his head again. "I'm just really lost at the moment, to be honest with you. My conscience is a lot cloudier than usual, and I figured you might—"

"I might what, Len? Tell you how easy it is to go down the path of evil? To just nudge you forward into sin and sex?"

"Jesus. No, man. God. Sam, I'm sorry, that's not what I meant. I just thought that—you know what, never mind. Sorry to have bothered you."

Lenny ended the call abruptly, pissed at Sam for the attitude, and pissed at himself for not having the balls to figure things out on his own to begin with. He turned off his phone for the night too, if only so as to avoid Sam on the off chance he called or texted back, then picked up his beer again and stood up.

A light rain began to fall, but despite his mood and the weather, Lenny walked out toward the tree house.

He was forever glad he'd slept through whatever happened there so many years ago, but knew he would never forget his part in the whole thing either. Fifteen hours after Kerry Ann was found dead, Lenny had put two and two together before anyone else, and although he was still aloof to the hows and whos, he'd made up his mind then and there to make himself an accomplice nonetheless.

Of all the secrets he'd kept in his life, that was the one he was sure he would end up taking with him to the grave. By summer's end, though, Lenny would lose much more than just that secret.

Chapter 26

Hey, it's Erika. Friday was fun.

She re-read the text for the fifth time, both frustrated and annoyed that he still hadn't responded.

It had already been a week since their first official date, and no boy had ever kept her waiting so long, but Chris had also made it abundantly clear in a host of ways that he was definitely *not* like most boys.

It was ridiculous she had to message him first at all though, she thought. Didn't he know how these things worked? He should have sent her a *sup* two or three days later, then waited a few hours for her to respond. Why was he making this so hard?

"Erika," Caroline said, gripping the steering wheel even tighter. "Why do you have to stare at your phone so much? Are Peaches and I really such horrible company?"

"What?" Erika asked, missing the reason for her tone. "I was just looking around online. It's not a big deal."

Peaches smiled at Caroline from the back seat, and Erika put her phone down in the center console.

"Fine. What did you want to talk about?" Erika asked, annoyed much more at Chris than at either of them.

"Well, we're doing this trip for you. What colleges do you want to visit this weekend? What kinds of things do you want to major in? What appeals to you the most? That could help us narrow down which schools we should be looking at. And remember, even if you don't enroll this fall in any of the bigger ones, and just do community college, you should at least get your application in for the spring semester as soon as possible."

Erika stared out the windshield, trying to come up with an answer. The truth was, she had no idea what to do with her life, and being an adult frightened her more than anything else ever had.

Being a student and hanging out with friends was fine, but going away to a school where she didn't know anyone? It all seemed too daunting, and she regretted agreeing to this adventure to begin with.

"I really don't know, Mom. I'm sorry."

Caroline stole a glance at her as she drove, trying to read her face as much as possible.

"Well, what *part* don't you know?"

Erika shook her head, unsure what to say, or how to answer.

"I mean, do you not know what kinds of subjects interest you, or do you not know what schools we're visiting? I asked you to come up with a short list this week so we'd know where to go. Did you not even do that?"

"No," she snapped, as if Caroline had pushed her too hard, but after a few more seconds, she added a quick, "sorry" as well, hoping to keep her mother calm.

Caroline let out a loud sigh and shook her head as she slapped the top of the steering wheel repeatedly.

She *wanted* to scream. She wanted to scream quite loudly, in fact, and even turn the car around with a string of curses at the very next exit. She managed to seize control of her emotions though, and instead told Erika exactly *why* she was upset to hear this.

"Honey, I'm disappointed, and I'll tell you why. Two things, really. First of all, because I reserved a very expensive hotel room for us tonight. A Saturday night hotel rental in a city like Boston does not come cheap. Driving three hours each way does not come cheap either. Food in Boston doesn't come cheap. Gas doesn't come cheap. None of this is easy, Erika.

"And second, you don't need to map out the entire next ten years of your life, but if you can't even guestimate what the hell you want to do with the next six to twelve *months* of your life, you're a lot less prepared than I thought you were. Life will not just arrive for you on a silver platter. You need to figure this thing out on your own now, and your sister and I were prepared to help you begin doing that this weekend."

Erika remained silent, unwilling to fight, and unable to express her thoughts very clearly at all. She knew she was no match for her mother's intellect, and didn't know what she could say to appease her anyway. From the back seat, Peaches finally leaned forward, hoping to save her.

"Erika, what do you want in life? Like, forget school and work and all that. What makes you happiest?"

Caroline looked both surprised and confused by the questions, and wondered how Erika would react to them.

"I dunno. I guess I like music a lot."

"Okay," Peaches went on. "Good. So do you have any interest in writing music? Or maybe playing an instrument?"

"No," she said, and Caroline bit down hard on her bottom lip.

"Okay, but what about music do you like?" Peaches asked. "Maybe we can find some part of the music business you could take classes in."

Erika thought about it for a little while, and then smiled.

"Well, I really like listening to music. Maybe they have jobs for people to like, listen to new songs, and rate them or whatever?"

She looked at Caroline optimistically now, suddenly excited by the possibility of a whole new life where people would pay her to listen to songs all day.

Caroline took one look at her, then changed lanes right away, almost side-swiping a car as she got off at the nearest exit.

She pulled the car into the parking lot of a Dunkin Donuts, grabbed the keys, and got out, slamming the door behind her. Peaches and Erika watched her every move, worried she was about to scream.

"Mommy's face is getting really red," Peaches observed from the backseat.

Caroline stared in at Erika through the windshield, then marched back over and opened the driver's side door again.

"You can't...*fucking*...do that, Erika!" she yelled, and Peaches thought for a moment she saw actual smoke coming from her mother's ears, but it could have also been the exhaust from a passing car.

Then, for the second time in only thirty seconds, Caroline slammed the car door again, and this time went inside to get herself some coffee.

"Oh my God," Erika said, turning around anxiously. "Peaches, what do I do?"

"I dunno. I guess maybe you should try to learn an instrument or something?"

"No, I mean right now. Mom is totally flipping out, and we're not even in Boston yet. This is a nightmare."

"Oh, that. Well, you should probably go in and talk to her. Maybe that's what she wants you to do."

"But what do I say? 'Sorry I'm such an idiot and a total disappointment?' Or something else?"

Peaches made a face at her.

"Erika, don't say that. You're not a disappointment. Mom just likes things organized, and you're throwing her off by being so wishy washy about all this. All you gotta do is tell her something—*anything*—and she'll lock onto it and forget about everything else. She's like a—I dunno—like a—" She paused, trying to think of the right analogy. "She's like a pit bull for information. Like, if you don't throw her some hard facts, she won't let go till you do."

Erika's eyes glazed over a bit, but she nodded and turned around again.

"I know what you mean, yeah."

"I think you should go inside and talk to her now before she comes back out and turns the car around. I really wanna go to Boston this weekend."

"Yeah. Alright," she said, undoing her seat belt.

Inside on line, Caroline was doing all she could to remain calm and think it all out, so it took her by surprise to see Erika walk in a moment later and walk right up to her.

"Mom, I'm sorry, okay? I'll figure this out eventually. I just need more time to think, and maybe—"

"No, Erika. You've got a lot of nerve lying to me about this trip. You said you had it planned out, but you clearly did no legwork at all. You know how long it's gonna take us to research this on our phones? I didn't bring my laptop either. This is ridiculous. Besides, you should have at least—"

Caroline stopped mid-sentence and looked past Erika in total shock at the woman quickly approaching them.

"Mrs. Tate?"

"Oh my gosh, Caroline! Wow, it's so good to see you again. It's been years."

Erika made a face as the woman leaned in and hugged Caroline.

"Well, maybe not *years,* Mrs. Tate. You know, maybe a week or so," Caroline tried to cover.

"A week? Oh, no. I don't think so, dear. I've been living in Florida for three years now. This is my first trip back up here since the move. We were just in Boston, and now we're on our way up to New Hampshire to spend a week with my sister and her family. Listen, are you gonna be around, though? I would love to chat with you again. My mother and I are getting along so much better these days. Florida really has been good for us. In fact, she's already out there waiting for me in the car, so I have to run, but I'll call your office this week, okay?"

"Okay, yeah. Sounds good," Caroline managed. "Bye."

"Bye now, honey."

When Caroline looked at Erika again, she knew she'd been caught. Erika's face and eyes said it all, and though she knew nothing more than just this one significant lie, she was at least sure now that her mother had been lying to her father and them about where she'd been going recently.

"What can I get for you?" the cashier asked, rescuing Caroline, if only briefly, from the intense death stare Erika now had on her.

"Uh, just a medium coffee please, two sugars and cream."

"And a dozen chocolate donuts," Erika added, still looking at her mother, but more seriously now. "And two Nesquiks. And this travel mug," she said, grabbing one from a nearby display.

Caroline looked like she would say something until Erika's eyes challenged her, so she finally relented, taking out her money to pay for it all.

They had come to an impasse, and there was no reason to fight her on this. Better to cooperate for the moment, and be grateful it hadn't all happened at a Starbucks instead.

Once she paid and got the food and drinks, Caroline made a quick beeline for the door, but Erika stopped her.

"Wait," Erika said, sensing—*quite accurately*—that she still had the upper hand with her mother.

Caroline paused, staring at the door, but then turned around at her a moment later, her eyebrows raised.

"Yes?"

"Mrs. Tate has been living in Florida, even though you have *claimed* on multiple occasions recently that you've driven over to New Hampshire to see her. At the same time, I don't know what the hell I'm doing with my life, and I won't have a really good idea by the end of this weekend either."

Caroline narrowed her eyes at her, unsure what she was saying.

"So let's just leave each other alone a bit, is all I mean. For now, at least. Deal?"

"Sure," Caroline said, nodding to herself and turning around again to walk out. "Deal."

And for the first time in her life, Erika understood the sweet pleasure of the pure power of blackmail.

Chapter 27

Seventeen years earlier

"You are such a fucking loser," Sam said, eyeing Lenny's polyester polo shirt with disdain. "What the fuck, Len? You can't dress like that. People will think you're in your 40s or something."

"Caroline doesn't mind," Lenny said. "So what does it matter?"

"Just because your wife 'doesn't mind' doesn't mean it's cool for you to wear such a thoroughly uncool piece of fabric over and around that big hairy belly of yours."

"Hey, I may have a belly, and it may be hairy, but it is not that big. I only weigh 210."

"Yeah, but you're only 5'4."

"I am *not* 5'4. I'm 5'7 and a half. Leave me alone."

The two leaned back in unison with their beers, once again watching the rest of the party. Sam caught a glance of Kerry Ann clearing plates, and followed her every movement before looking away, back at Lenny.

"You think that hot piece of ass in the apron thinks your shirt is cool too?"

Lenny looked over at her, and then back to Sam with his mouth wide open.

"You have *got* to be kidding me."

"What?"

"You're referring to that *child* who's helping Caroline out in the kitchen today?"

"Oh please, she's not a child. She's a beautiful young woman."

"No. She's a 16-year-old girl. Maybe even 15."

"17."

"No."

"Yes. She told me she was 17."

"What? Why were you asking her how old she was?"

"Well—"

"No, never mind. I don't want to know. It doesn't matter if she's 17 or 16. Either way, she's just a kid."

Sam just shook his head and looked away like he was crazy, while Lenny stared him down for a while with a nervous smile.

##

"What do those two talk about when they're by themselves?" Caroline asked Olivia as she lit her cigarette.

Olivia took a puff and blew it away.

"Probably just boring crap like sex and money."

Caroline looked at her sideways.

"Since when do sex and money qualify as boring crap?"

Olivia offered her a sly smile.

"Interesting as those topics may be, there are many more exciting conversations those two idiots are missing out on. Haley honey, slow down! Jesus, she's gonna run right into the tree."

"Nah," Caroline said. "Haley's smart. It's Erika we gotta worry about. Look at her over there. She's trying to eat rocks again."

Caroline ran off to pick Erika up, staring Lenny down on her way there.

"No, it's okay. I'll get her!" she yelled at him.

"Get who?" he called back.

"Erika! She's got a half a pound of pebbles in her mouth, and you said you'd keep an eye on her!"

They all watched as she got Erika to spit out the rocks as she cleaned her off. Olivia just laughed to herself.

"When are you gonna quit smoking?" Phyllis asked, making Olivia jump.

"Jesus, Mom. Don't sneak up on me like that."

"You know what else is gonna sneak up on you? Lung cancer."

"Thanks, Mom."

"I mean it. Throw those emphysema sticks away now while you can. They're adding tar and who knows what else to your lungs as we speak."

"Feathers?"

"What?"

"Nothing. Just leave me alone."

"Fine, you smoke up like a chimney, and Dad and I will raise your daughter for you."

"I've got a husband, you know."

Phyllis looked over at Sam and smiled.

"Yes you do. Such a sweetheart. But when you're choking to death on your last day on Earth, he won't know what to do, and your father and I will have to raise Haley on our own."

"Wow. I really appreciate how well you've thought this all out, Mom. You're incredible."

"I do what I have to, darling."

Caroline rejoined them, sighing as she looked back at Erika who was playing with another little girl now, and glad Lenny was finally keeping a closer eye on them both.

"You look like you need a drink, Caroline," Olivia said to her. "Come to think of it, why *aren't* you drinking yet?"

"Don't tell us you're pregnant again already," Phyllis added, half joking, but the look on Caroline's face just then said it all, and Phyllis and Olivia quickly exchanged a look of shock.

"Seriously?!" Olivia asked. "What the fuck, Car. When the hell were you gonna tell me?"

"I don't know," she said, shrugging. "Soon."

"Does Leonard know?" Phyllis asked.

"Yes. Of course he knows. I'm already at 21 weeks."

"Holy shit!" Olivia said, far too loudly. She looked Caroline over, annoyed she hadn't seen anything sooner."

"See, and I just assumed you were having trouble losing all the weight you gained from Erika," Phyllis added.

"Thank you, Phyllis," Caroline said with a tone, but Phyllis assumed she actually meant it.

"Oh, you're welcome, dear. So when are you due? I'll tell Alan."

"October 2nd."

"Is it a boy? Tell me it's a boy. The man is driving me crazy as it is with all this legacy nonsense. It's gotta be a boy, right?"

"Sorry. Another girl."

"Fuck," Phyllis said, quickly walking away with her head down.

"Really charming woman, your mom is," Caroline said, and Olivia nodded, blowing the smoke away from Caroline more than she had before. She quickly realized it was all too much though, so she put her cigarette out.

"Goddamnit!" Alan yelled from across the yard.

"Oh. I think my father *heard the good news*," Olivia said in a singsong, sarcastic voice.

##

"I'm gonna get another," Sam said to Lenny. "You want one?"

"Yeah, sure."

Sam made a beeline for the back door, but Olivia stopped him halfway, reaching out and grabbing him by the tail of his shirt.

"What's up?"

"Caroline's pregnant again."

"Whaaat?! Congratulations, Car."

He leaned in and kissed her on the cheek.

"Lenny didn't tell you?" Olivia asked.

"No. Bastard."

"I told him to wait," Caroline said, nodding at nothing in particular. "Figured I might start telling people today anyway. Getting harder to hide the bump now."

Sam laughed, then continued inside to the kitchen, happy to see Kerry Ann cleaning dishes by herself. Something about her was different though, and her face was all scrunched up as if she'd just seen a rat.

"You know," he said, startling her from her work. "I don't wanna sound like I care or nothin', but my buddy out there said you're only 16. You told me you were 17."

She smiled at him nervously and turned the water off, grabbing the towel to dry her hands. Then she turned around to face him head on, glancing both ways as if to check that they were all alone.

"I'm sorry. I didn't want you thinking I was too young."

"No, no. You're not too young at all. I'm just too old."

He smiled and walked to the fridge for two more beers.

"You're not too old. I like older guys. You actually remind me of a hot teacher at my school."

Sam sized her up again, wondering if she'd just invited him to be even more forward than he'd already been with her. He glanced outside to see where Olivia and the others were, then thought out his next move.

"And have you and your teacher ever fooled around?" he asked, much quieter now than before.

"What? No way," she said, unable to contain her laughter. "That would be crazy. Like, insane."

Sam grinned with a quick nod and turned to leave, having received a clear answer to his only real question.

She sensed his mood change though, and stopped him before he got too far away.

"But I mean, if he wasn't my teacher, maybe. I dunno."

Sam popped the cap off his beer and took a long sip. Looking outside again, he decided to hedge his bets and play things safe for the moment.

"Hey, do me a favor," he said, putting both beers down and grabbing the pen and notepad sticking to the side of the fridge.

He scribbled down his number, then tore off the sheet and handed it to her, quickly replacing the pen and paper magnets back on the fridge.

"Call me sometime. That's my private number at work. If I don't pick up, just leave me a message. I might have some projects coming up I could uh, you know, use some help with."

Kerry Ann was sure he was bullshitting, but she took the paper and nodded just the same.

"Okay, sure."

Sam leaned in suddenly and kissed her on the cheek for two seconds longer than necessary, taking a moment to smell her hair as he pulled away. He grabbed the beers again as he smiled at her one more time and left, passing Caroline on the deck as she made her way inside. The two exchanged an awkward glance, but didn't talk.

"Hey, all the dishes done?" she asked Kerry Ann.

"Um, almost. Sorry. I just have like, maybe three more, and then some spoons."

"No, no, no, don't worry. You've already done so much. Thank you, hon, seriously."

She handed Kerry Ann a $50 tip.

"Oh, man. Thank you, Mrs. Abrams."

"No, thank you. Really. I couldn't have done any of this without you. And thank Connie for me again too. She's always come through for me."

"Sure, will do."

Caroline showed Kerry Ann out and waved goodbye, then surveyed the kitchen, happy to see almost everything was cleaned up, and the garbage all out in the pails already too.

She couldn't help but wonder if Sam had been flirting with the girl, and hoped the big tip would at least make up for some of the disgusting things he may have said to her.

As she turned to leave again, something caught her eye. The pad she kept on the side of the fridge had a heavy scribble on the top page from whatever someone had written on the previous piece of paper.

She couldn't make out the phone number, but the 'Sam' with a smiley face was all too clear. She looked outside for him and then back at the closed front door. Ripping off the top two blank pages with the indent, she crumpled them up quickly, and then went back to her guests.

Chapter 28

Lenny searched each of the kitchen drawers for her number, but kept coming up empty. If he was going to go through with this, he was almost out of time. He moved over to the living room next, hoping to find it in one of the two small end-table drawers on either side of the couch.

Caroline and the girls had already been gone for well over an hour, but it was past noon now, and if Jenn was even in town at all, he'd need to set something up quickly for later that day. There was no telling how early they'd return from Boston on Sunday morning.

He was just about to give up when the house phone rang in the kitchen. He looked at it strangely, wondering if he could be so lucky as to get a call from Jenn looking for Erika. Only a handful of people had the house number, but Jenn and her parents were certainly among them.

"Hello?"

"Hey," Olivia said, and Lenny made a face.

"Oh. Hi Livi," he said, and Olivia could sense his disappointment. "What's up?"

"Nothing. I just haven't heard from Mom and Dad all week. Been trying to call them up, but no one's answering over there. Have you spoken to either of them the past few days?"

"No, I guess I haven't, not since last week's little scene."

Lenny smiled and then listened, hoping she'd already heard the story so he wouldn't have to repeat it.

"Yeah, Haley told me something about that. Weird. Was hoping to get Dad alone to see what he had to say, but I guess it can wait. Okay, well, I'll try them again later. Maybe they just stepped out for the afternoon. Things good over there with you guys?"

"Yeah, pretty quiet. Caroline took the girls to Boston so Erika could check out schools. They're coming back tomorrow."

"Oh fun," she said, though she didn't really sound amused in the least. "Don't get into any trouble then while they're away. We all know you're a wild and crazy guy when no one's looking."

She laughed out loud then, offering a quick "see ya" as she hung up.

Lenny hung the phone up and noted the caller ID. As he returned to his search, he suddenly looked up and back over at the phone with a mix of mad shock and joy. *Jenn's cell should be on the recent call list. Erika calls her from the landline all the time.*

He rushed over and began scrolling through the list, finding it almost immediately. Once he did, he was all ready to call her when he realized he should have a cover in case anyone else picked up. Putting the phone down again, he walked into the living room and began pacing this way and that across the house, toward the dining room and back into the kitchen.

Finally, once he had a general idea of what he was going to say, he did the next best thing he could think of. He thought of two *more* lies, just in case the first one didn't work. Then he pressed the call button quickly, before he had a chance to back out, and waited, but not for long.

On just the second ring, Jenn picked up, and unless he was wrong—*though he didn't think he was*—something in her voice told him right away that she was actually expecting his call.

"Hey," he said, hoping he wouldn't have to identify himself.

She shuffled a bit on the other end with a long pause.

"Hi Daddy," she whispered into the phone, and Lenny immediately grew more nervous.

"I wasn't sure if you'd know it was me," he said.

"Well, I knew it was your house phone calling, and I knew Erika went to Boston this morning with your wife and Peaches, so I was pretty sure it'd be you. What took you so long though? Erika checked in at some Dunkin Donuts in Massachusetts an hour ago."

Lenny smiled with some relief, forgetting he could check on their whereabouts often thanks to Erika's incessant need to check in everywhere she went.

"So I was thinking—" he started.

"Can I come over now?" she asked. "Pretty please?"

Lenny had to catch his breath before he could respond, he was so excited by it all.

"Yeah," he said softly, more confidently. "I think that'd work for me."

"Okay," she said. "Just give me a little while. I'll be over as soon as I can. Okay, Daddy?"

Lenny smiled, and nodded.

"Yeah. Yeah, that would be great."

"Okay, cool. I'll see you soon. Bye."

"Bye."

He clicked the end-call button, then stared at the phone with a stupid grin on his face. He hadn't felt this way in a very long time, he realized, and he missed it.

The more he looked at her name there on the phone though, the more his joy turned into sheer panic. *Her name is on the phone.* A dialed call from his house to her private cell phone when no one but he was home. Proof he'd set something up, in fact, while no one else was there to catch him.

He lunged forward immediately, yanking the phone cord from the wall as the screen went blank on the box, but not on the cordless phone itself, which still proudly displayed the most recent call made at the top of the list.

Grabbing the phone like it was an enemy, he turned it over quickly to remove the batteries, shaking them in his hand for a moment like he was playing craps. Then he replaced them again to see what would happen.

The screen was blank for a moment as the light returned, but then the name and number blinked back on as if through some awful built-in memory bank created for the sole purpose of mocking him and all his foolish intentions.

With one hard yank, Lenny ripped the entire beast from the wall again, dropping it to the ground this time as if by accident, but all it did was land clumsily to the tile kitchen floor with a soft thud, not even suffering as much as a single scratch.

244

He shook his head, ready to scold the creature for doing this to him, then decided he had only one choice left. He threw the entire machine in the garbage can, then removed the bag from beneath the cabinet so he could destroy the evidence later.

Looking at the time on their microwave further away, he tried to figure out how long it'd been since they'd ended their call, and how long it would take her to get over there from her house in Saturday afternoon traffic.

Not long, the answer came fast. Just enough time to pee, look himself over in the mirror, and call up his Facebook to be sure Erika hadn't checked in to someplace *closer* all of a sudden.

About twenty minutes later, Lenny paced the dining room floor nervously, his eyes repeatedly scanning the front driveway for any activity whatsoever, or evidence of anyone even driving past. In his mind, he thought about who else had a key to the front door, reminding himself that except for Olivia, no one but he, Caroline, and the girls did, and Olivia had just called earlier. She wouldn't surprise him with a visit anyway.

Finally, after another six minutes passed by, he saw Jenn's car pull into the driveway and back out again, opting to park it on the street instead. It made him smile to see she had learned something from their last encounter, and he started to feel more relaxed about the meeting to follow.

"Hello," he said once she arrived, opening the door widely to greet her. "You look cute. But of course, you always look cute." *Okay, shmuck.*

"Hi Daddy," she cooed, putting her purse down on the end table and cozying up to him as soon as he shut the door.

They kissed, very briefly, and then he took her by the hand into the kitchen. She grabbed her purse to move it again as he did.

"Before we go any further," he said, "I'd really appreciate it if you stopped calling me Daddy."

"Oh no, I'm sorry."

"No, it's okay, it's okay. It's just, I guess it's hot to an extent, but because I have two daughters, there's also something really super creepy about it too, unsettling even."

"Okay, no problem. So what should I call you then? Lenny?"

"No. I was thinking just 'Mr. Abrams', if you don't mind. It's what you always called me as long as I've known you, and still has that forbidden love kinda twist to it." *Shut the fuck up.* "Well, not love, but you know."

"Hot. I like that. So what do you wanna do, Mr. Abrams?"

Lenny looked her over, thinking through all the many, *many* things he wanted to do with her, and all the silly ways he could possibly answer that question too.

"Well, why don't we just start with a drink. Up for a beer?"

"Yeah, definitely," she said, watching as he retrieved two bottles from the fridge and uncapped them both.

They clinked their bottles together and each took a sip, and then Jenn walked over and sat down on the couch, leaning her head back and snuggling into the cushions. Lenny smiled and followed her lead, sitting down next to her, though giving them enough space to sit and talk as well.

His conscience still pulsed in the far reaches of his brain for some form of recognition, but like a headache that's mostly gone once the aspirin kicks in, it wasn't really troubling him much at all.

If Jenn was eager for fun, she wasn't showing it, although he sensed she was a lot more confident than he was, and not at all concerned about rushing things this time either. With the house free, they had all the time in the world, yet Lenny still felt he shouldn't delay the inevitable too long.

She took a long swig on her beer as she locked eyes with him again, and then smiled as she swallowed and put her bottle down. She seemed so much older all of a sudden, wiser and more experienced than ever before too. Was it just that he'd never seen her alone like this with his heartbeat so calm? Or was there something else?

"Can I ask you something, Mr. Abrams?"

"Of course, Jenn. What is it?"

She flashed him a Cheshire grin, looking away briefly toward the kitchen.

"Did you know we've been stealing beers out of your fridge for the past two years?"

Lenny laughed midway through a gulp of beer, nearly spitting it out all over himself. Jenn's smile widened, and Lenny nodded with clear guilt all over his face.

"Yeah, I kinda figured," he said, "but I also kept track of how much was in there too, and never kept too much in stock just for that reason. I didn't want you guys getting too drunk on my watch. I get the impression you've been able to buy some through someone else though?"

"Yeah, my brother came through a bunch of times, but he's got a *diwi* now, and just lost his license. One of the guys at the 7-Eleven in Rutland sometimes lets Isobel buy with her fake ID, but he can be a weirdo. Like, he's this old guy flirting with her and making it like he'll only let her buy beer if she goes out with him."

Lenny's face changed quickly as his guilty conscience restarted itself. He was just as much a creep as the guy at the 7-Eleven, more so even.

"I can't believe I'm such an idiot," he said, pushing back away from her. "God, I am such a complete and utter fucking dumbass."

He stood up and walked away toward the kitchen as Jenn looked on in shock. She waited for him to say more, but he just leaned on the kitchen island with his back to her for a long while.

"What happened?" she asked. "Did I say something wrong?"

Lenny shook his head and stared up at the ceiling for a few more seconds, unsure how to even respond. When he turned around again, his face wore deep pain.

"Look, Jenn. I'm obviously not such a great guy here. I'm just as much a creep as this 7-Eleven dude, and you shouldn't waste your time with an old guy like me anyway. I'm cheating on my wife, and I'm just—I'm a mess. You can obviously do much better than me too. I think you should go."

Jenn didn't know what to say. She looked at her phone and then at the wall, unsure how to proceed. Though Lenny hadn't yelled at her or blamed her specifically, he was clearly depressed, and she didn't want to upset him any more than he already was.

As she looked over at him, she could tell he was more confused and conflicted than anything else. She stood up and looked at her phone one more time, and then decided to just tell him.

"What if I told you your wife was cheating on you too? Would that make a difference?"

Lenny looked at her like she was crazy, and as he shook his head at her with a dark smile, she could tell he didn't believe her.

"Caroline is *not* cheating on me," he said defiantly. "Like, no chance. Zero. Zilch. She may keep secrets from me occasionally, I can't deny that, but trust me, she'd never do that to me, not in a million years."

He watched as Jenn looked at her phone, eyebrows up, and shook her head. Lenny looked at her suspiciously, and approached slowly as Jenn held her hand out.

"Look for yourself, but take a deep breath first, and definitely don't freak out, okay?"

He grabbed her phone with more curiosity than anything else. *What could Jenn possibly have on her phone that could implicate Caroline in such a thing?* He read through the text string quickly.

My mom is totally having an affair
What?! How do you know?
I just caught her in a massive lie...she's been telling my dad and us about this client of hers in NH, but we just fucking saw the woman in Massachusetts, and she said she's been living in Florida for three years now! My mom's face was insanely guilty!
Wow! Holy shit!
I know!
So what are you gonna do?
I'm totally holding this over her now...like, she's riding my ass for school shit but riding some coworker's dick secretly too? Fuck that!

Whoa...so her coworker?
No clue, just saying
Yeah

Lenny handed her the phone back and walked away, once again to rest against the island in the kitchen. His eyes wide open with a mix of horror and betrayal, Lenny was suddenly overcome with insane jealousy, completely disregarding his own affair with Jenn. *How could she do this to me?*

Jenn, grabbing her beer again and making her way into the kitchen, sensed his anger, and was annoyed by the double standard he seemed to be ignoring. Was he completely delusional or just plain dumb?

"Can I ask you a question?" she said once she was across from him, finally blocking his intense stare-down of the kitchen cabinets. "Why is it okay for *you* to fuck around with me without *her* knowing, but the moment you hear of even just the possibility of her doing the same thing, you flip out? Don't you see how fucked up that is?"

Lenny *did* see how fucked up it was, but he also knew his opinion of Caroline, always greater than his opinion of himself, had just come crashing down like a flaming plane wreck.

He shook his head, not at anything Jenn had said, but only at what she didn't seem to understand. Her much shorter list of life experiences had not yet provided her the kind of smackdown Lenny's life had, and she was lucky to still have so much of her innocence completely intact.

"God, you're such a hypocrite," she said, putting her beer down.

She grabbed her purse then and started for the door.

"No, wait. Jenn, please."

She didn't stop, so Lenny screamed out after her.

"I'm a fucking pathetic piece of shit, and I know it, okay?! Is that what you want me to say?!"

Jenn turned around and stared at him again, unsure what to think. Lenny sighed and shook his head as he looked down.

"I know I'm an idiot, okay? I know I'm a disgusting, infuriating, foul piece of sludge. This has nothing to do with that. I'm not being a hypocrite, alright? I'm being a husband. A partner. Caring what my wife does is part of my job. It's normal."

She approached him again cautiously and looked up at him.

"I don't understand."

"No, I don't expect you to. Look, it's okay. And I don't mean that condescendingly either, by the way. It's just—Caroline and I have been through a lot of crazy shit together. Like, a lot. Like two miscarriages, a breast cancer scare, and my brother-in-law's murder trial kinda crazy. And through it all, we've always been really, really tight. I know her, or, I thought I did, but I honestly never saw this coming. Fuck. I don't even know if it's true yet, but—"

He trailed off, and Jenn just waited, searching his eyes.

"But I know it is. She's been keeping something from me, and an affair, well, that's just great. I'm not so much surprised or pissed as I am sad."

Jenn put her purse down on the counter and cuddled up beside him, leaning her head and breasts on Lenny's body, not, it seemed, to tease him into sex, but simply as a genuine sign of affection. He appreciated it too, both emotionally and sexually.

Finally relaxing a bit, he put his arms around her into a much-needed embrace, appreciating her warmth as much as her smell. He wondered how girls even managed to put so much time into themselves. If he'd ever been annoyed at his own wife and daughters for spending too much time in the bathroom, he was only appreciative now of whatever time Jenn had invested to look and smell this way.

"What the hell has my life become?" he groaned, not expecting an answer. "I always thought Caroline and I had it so good too. I mean, sure we had our dark points. Who doesn't? But this? Her cheating on me, maybe for months? How did this happen? What did I do?"

Once again, all Jenn could think of was the two of them, and the mutual desire she knew they both still had to be naked and having fun, rather than clothed and bitching and moaning about life. She shook her head into his armpit then and leaned away.

"You know what would make you feel better?" she asked, watching as Lenny smiled at her. "My 18-year-old lips wrapped around your cock."

Of all the magic words he could have heard just then, Lenny had to admit, those were some pretty damn good ones.

"You're 18 now?"

She nodded.

"And you really want that? To suck me off? This isn't just about—I don't know—pity?"

She looked confused at first, and then smiled.

"God, you make it sound like you're an ogre. You're sexy, Mr. Abrams, and you don't have to agree for me to think so."

He balked, unsure what else to say. He was more confused than ever. And that's when she took off her T-shirt, undid her bra, and knelt down on the kitchen floor, quickly unzipping his fly.

After their last encounter, Lenny was able to control himself much more this time, but he also stopped her soon enough too, taking her hands in his, and leading her up to his bedroom.

Chapter 29

The next morning, Lenny awoke naturally a little after nine, smiling as he thought of the day and night before, more so once he saw the small note Jenn left for him on an old receipt.

Until next time. XXOO

Jenn's handwriting was circular and graceful, elegant even, although Lenny couldn't help but imagine her Os were her breasts, and wished she'd added nipples on them too.

He allowed his arm to drop back down with the piece of paper slipping away onto the sheets, and as his eyes fell on his phone sitting precariously on the corner of his bedside table, still in the place he'd tossed it the night before, he remembered his short but painfully strained text conversation with Caroline.

There? Girls and I are calling it a night soon.
Lenny? Still up?
Okay, good night. See you tomorrow.
Okay then
What?
Nothing, good night
Night

He let out a long sigh and stood up, grabbing his phone and the note from Jenn as he did. Once he peed and threw some water on his face, he went downstairs and put on a pot of coffee. Then he reached into the drawer in front of the now-missing downstairs phone, and pulled out a lighter. He held Jenn's note over the sink and burned it, washing the ashes down the drain as he did.

Turning around and looking at the living room furniture for a while, he reminded himself where they'd been the night before.

Though they enjoyed some amazing sex upstairs, they'd later hung out in the living room and watched TV until Jenn decided she wanted to go for a second round. The couch, coffee table, and recliner all took turns hosting Lenny's body as Jenn rode his dick from every possible angle.

Lenny was sure he'd cleaned up everything enough after the fact, but he took another minute to check again as the coffee pot gurgled its last. He was surprised at first at how stiff he felt, but the more he surveyed the scene of the crime, the more he recalled the various positions and quick movements that had led him to attain the collateral damage.

By the time he had some coffee and thought things through some more, he realized he'd have to drive over to Rutland anyway for a new phone, and decided he may as well stop by the office while he was at it. There was probably some snooping worth doing there after all.

##

Caroline had just passed the sign welcoming them back to Vermont when her cell phone rang, and as she instinctively reached for it to answer, Peaches undid her seat belt and lunged forward from the backseat.

"No, Mommy!"

She quickly switched on the Bluetooth connection for Caroline, then answered the call on the car's console. Caroline grimaced as she saw Phyllis's name flash on the screen.

"Hello, Phyllis," she said louder than she had to. "You're on the speaker phone *with me and the girls.* We're driving home from Boston right now."

Caroline could handle some tension with Erika, but Phyllis mentioning more than that accidentally was not an option.

She listened for a moment then, worried Phyllis hadn't heard her, when she finally responded.

"Okay," Phyllis said, uncharacteristically quiet. "Okay, that's fine, but when you can, call me back so we can talk."

Caroline had never heard her so despondent, and was worried something had happened.

"Hi Grandma!" Peaches chimed in from the back, missing all sense of the tone, and Erika reluctantly added her own quick hello as well.

"Hello, girls."

"Phyllis," Caroline said. "Is everything okay? Do you want me to pull over right now and call you back?"

"No, no, no," the response came quickly, more forcefully this time. "Just call me when you're home, okay? And tell Leonard to call me too. I haven't been able to get a hold of him."

Caroline bristled at this, but didn't push. *Where is Lenny? Why didn't he pick up? Did something happen?*

"Okay, I will. I'll talk to you la—"

Phyllis hung up before she could finish, and Caroline was left wondering what the hell she'd missed back home. Just 24 hours away, and everything suddenly felt different.

##

Lenny grabbed his phone, shoved it into his jeans pocket, and got out of the car. He'd been busy making coffee when Phyllis called the house line earlier, but since the only working phone was upstairs in the bedroom, he never heard it.

She tried reaching him on his cell phone while he drove to Rutland, but Lenny still hadn't turned up the volume since he woke up, and hadn't noticed the screen light up on the passenger seat as he drove to work.

He was relieved but not surprised to see no other cars in the parking lot at work on a Sunday, opting to park on the side street himself anyway, but once he got upstairs to his desk on the second floor, he decided to take a casual walk over to the executive wing just to be sure.

Dropping his phone and keys off first, still not noticing the light of a new voicemail flashing at the top of his phone, he made the short walk over to the other side of the building.

Only about sixty employees filled the floor on the busiest of days, but they were spread out on either side of a large glass conference room often used by other companies in the building. Executives, HR staff, and their secretaries all filled larger offices and cubes on their side of the building, but except for the rare document drop-off, Lenny rarely went over there anyway. They did have a much nicer men's room on that side though, so Lenny made use of it occasionally.

Reaching the corner on the opposite side of the conference room, Lenny could survey much of the area fairly easily. With just a quick glance, he was sure no one was there, but as he turned to walk back again, something else caught his eye, a picture of JC— *John Caraway*—he'd never noticed before. He looked around him to be safe, then walked into the large cube a bit to look more closely.

To his surprise, it wasn't just JC in the photo, but an old picture of him, RJ Tarisi, and Donna Wendt. Lenny stood up straight then and looked at the fancy nameplate on the wall by her desk. Sure enough, this was Donna's cube. Feeling suddenly uneasy, Lenny backed away as fast as he could, soon returning to his own much smaller cube on the other side of the building.

He sat down and scratched his chin absentmindedly for a moment, thinking it all out. *It's nothing,* he told himself, *just a coincidence,* paranoia getting the better of him once again. Donna and Mr. Tarisi both knew JC socially, and JC was dead, but that didn't mean anything. Neither did RJ's sudden interest in Donna's personnel file.

##

As they walked in the front door, Erika's phone chimed with a new message. From him. *Finally!*

Hey...how's it going?

Erika smiled, excited to respond, then froze, realizing she shouldn't reply right away. But what if he had a read receipt on his end? He'd know she'd read it. *Shit.*

Sighing, she ran up to her bedroom, shut the door behind her, and plopped down on her bed to start typing.

Hey, good to hear from you...was starting to think you forgot about me

Impossible, he replied a minute later, and Erika blushed.

So what's up? she typed, trying to sound casual, but guessing that ship had already sailed.

Three exceedingly long minutes passed then with nothing at all, and Erika was quickly growing frustrated. She couldn't handle this kind of a conversation, and hated it when people didn't reply to her right away.

Just as she began typing *Hello?*, he responded.

Phone broke...hard 2 type...can I call?

She shot up in bed, taking in a huge new breath and biting her lip before responding.

Yeah, sure...call me, she typed, then stared at her phone with her mouth open, waiting for it to light up. She fixed her hair too, absentmindedly.

After about thirty more seconds, the phone finally lit up with the incoming call.

"Hey, sorry. I dropped my phone on a concrete sidewalk a few days ago, and I haven't gotten a new one yet. Wanna make sure I get the right one. I really hate this shit."

"Oh, okay, that sucks." She shook her head, suddenly more grateful than ever for the magical device in her hand. "I wouldn't be able to go that long without a new phone though."

"Well, I really don't text much, which is the hardest part, so I still have use of the phone, but the cracked screen is awful. I keep feeling like tiny shards are crawling into my ear, slicing my brain up while I'm sleeping."

Erika laughed, and Chris was glad for it. He wasn't able to make most girls laugh. Usually they just pretended to, or simply groaned under their breath at his silly comments, but he could tell Erika was genuinely amused.

"So listen," he said. "Last Friday was hot. Your bowling sucked. But your mouth—okay, so your mouth sucked too, but in a really good way."

She laughed again, much louder, and Chris stifled one too. He'd actually planned that line out, and was relieved to hear she liked it.

"Wanna grab a meal or something?" he asked her. "I'm free tonight if so, or we can do it later in the week if that's better."

"Uh, yeah," she said. "Tonight works. Rutland okay? That's like halfway for you, right?"

"Not quite, but yeah, that works fine. How about Applebee's at 6? I'd rather get to bed early tonight, because I have a phone interview for school tomorrow morning."

"Perfect, cool. So I guess I'll see you then," she said.

"See you then. Bye."

"Bye."

Erika ended the call and tossed her phone on the comforter, then dropped her head back as well. She still needed to tell Chris the truth about her family, but what could she possibly say? That her uncle may have, at one point in time, attacked and murdered his aunt?

Worst of all, she couldn't even tell anyone about him. Her family would order her to politely decline his offers and stop seeing him, while Isobel and Jenn would probably egg her on just to see how it went. She wasn't sure either of those approaches were right, but knew no matter what she did, Chris deserved the truth.

##

A text arrived from Caroline just as Lenny went to check his phone and turn his volume up, that she and the girls were home from Massachusetts. He stared at it for a while, thinking he might just ignore it, but then decided he ought to at least send a quick message back.

Okay, good...welcome home...at work

He'd left her a note to say where he was, but now he wondered if she didn't believe him.

Was this their new normal? Not just lies but expecting lies too? It made him think of his car parked out on the side street. *If she drives over here to look for me, she'll think I'm lying. Whatever.*

He put the phone down and stared at his recycle bin contents. It seemed as if Donna Wendt's file was gone for good, and there was no way to ever get it back.

He leaned back in his chair as he thought it through. The personnel file was gone, but he still had access to payroll, as well as the entirety of the World Wide Web. Maybe there was still a way to figure out what was going on after all.

If he was being completely honest about it, Lenny hoped he *wouldn't* uncover anything incriminating about John Caraway's death, but if there *was* some kind of funny business going on related to Mr. Tarisi, this was at least his chance to dig in deeper.

Calling up the most recent month's payroll accounts first, Lenny scrolled through, searching for her name. Though RJ was paid through a separate process, Donna Wendt's records would be in there for sure. After just a few seconds of scrolling, he found her name near the very bottom, and clicked the link to call up her payment schedule.

##

On the other side of the building, RJ Tarisi walked into his office, having just climbed the two flights of stairs on his side of the building. He dropped his keys on his desk, then carried a tall cup of coffee mixed with Jack Daniels around to his seat.

##

As Lenny read through the details of Donna's file, he found nothing out of the ordinary. She was paid well, far better than him, but that came as no surprise considering her age and job title.

Donna had been there much longer than Lenny, and at 58, she was also the most beautiful older woman Lenny knew. Maybe that was why Mr. Tarisi hired her to begin with. He wouldn't have been surprised to find out there was something else between them too, either past or present.

He opened up Facebook in a private window, logging in as Rusty, his dead dog. Joe taught him the trick a few years back, said it was a great way to check out new hires without them realizing it.

He searched for Donna Wendt and found her almost right away. Unfortunately, it seemed she shared very little on her page, at least publicly with anyone other than friends. He scrolled through anyway, looking for anything about her that might stand out, and especially anything linking her with Mr. Tarisi.

##

Across the building, RJ Tarisi downed more of his *coffee*, then scrolled through Twitter before clicking over to a website filled with Chinese lettering and young girls in various stages of undress.

Stars and smiley faces covered their breasts and other body parts, with call-to-action bursts all over the page.

He grinned and clicked through, looking briefly out into the hallway to make sure no one else was there. The large, tinted windows behind his desk overlooked a patch of trees, so no one could see in that way. It was one of the main reasons he'd chosen that exact office location to begin with.

##

Lenny scrolled through Facebook posts going back six years, but found nothing, not even a single photo of her and Mr. Tarisi together. He was just about to stop when he saw a pic she was tagged in that looked like it was taken at a barbecue. It was a blog post, he saw, and when he clicked through, the photo was at the top of the page.

259

He right-clicked the image to view it larger, pleased to see he could magnify it a bit more too. As he scanned the screen, he was surprised to see Donna sitting right next to John Caraway at a picnic table. No Tarisi in the image at all.

Looking back at the blog post, he saw it was titled "Webster Family Reunion", and as he read through the blog, he found a caption for the photo in the second paragraph that listed all those sitting around the table. John Caraway was mentioned by his full name, but instead of Donna Wendt next to him, *her* name was listed instead as Donna Caraway.

Just then, Lenny's cell phone rang, and he jumped a bit in his seat. *Sam Cell* the caller ID read.

"Hey man, what's up?"

##

As the two began talking, RJ Tarisi pushed back from his desk, eyes wide open. He'd heard a cell phone ring once in the distance, and someone pick up and begin talking, but he didn't know who it was or where it was coming from.

Out in the hallway, he listened carefully, realizing it was coming from the other side of the floor past the conference room.

##

"Yeah, I can come by in a few if you'd like. Just over at work right now. Nothing big though, right? Just a couple old couches?"

"Yeah, two couches, a coffee table, and an old bookshelf," Sam's voice came through loudly from the phone as he spoke. "I can probably do the coffee table and bookshelf by myself if I had to, but could definitely use your help with the couches."

"Okay. Don't push yourself, man. We're not kids anymore."

"Alright, thanks Len. I appreciate it. What the hell are you doing at work on a Sunday though?"

"Well, I actually came by to—"

Out of nowhere, Mr. Tarisi's head appeared above the outside wall of Lenny's cube, and Lenny practically jumped from his seat, dropping the phone on his keyboard and accidentally—*miraculously*—minimizing the picture of John Caraway and Donna Wendt on his screen.

"What the fuck are you doing here, Abrams?"

Sam listened on the other end as Lenny started speaking to someone there at the office. He couldn't hear much, but knew Lenny had been surprised by whomever it was.

"Oh my God, Mr. Tarisi. You scared the hell outta me. I'm sorry, sir. I was just making sure the June payroll was all correct. I drove past the building this morning, and remembered to check on something Joe mentioned to me on Friday."

RJ Tarisi sized him and his desktop up briefly, saw nothing amiss, and then nodded at him.

"Alright. Good man, Abes. Thanks."

He left again, and after listening for a moment to make sure Mr. Tarisi was still walking back to his desk, Lenny stood up carefully, both to retrieve his phone and to make sure Mr. Tarisi was long gone.

Catching his breath, Lenny got back on with Sam as he started closing all his programs before shutting down his computer.

"Hey, sorry about that," he said in what sounded to Sam like a panicked whisper, his voice shaking noticeably.

"You okay, man? I heard a kind of crashing noise and then another person's voice on your end."

"Yeah," Lenny said. "That was my boss, the guy I was looking into here to begin with. Scared me half to death. I'll tell you about it when I see you. Be over there soon."

Turning off his monitor and pocketing his phone, Lenny allowed himself a long sigh of relief before he got up. He couldn't believe his luck, but made a mental note to stop pushing it so often.

Chapter 30

Caroline sat in the living room flipping through channels, hoping to find a good sitcom to cozy up to after the long drive home.

She had enough drama in her life already, and despite her finally calling things off with Sam over a strained text conversation from Boston, she sensed the distance between her and Lenny had only grown further, something they both swore they'd never allow to happen.

Somewhere in what she thought might be the middle of her search, aiming her sights on a much higher channel, Caroline landed on a rerun of an old Golden Girls episode, and realized it was the perfect distraction. Three older women whose husbands were long dead living with a fourth older woman whose ex-husband was nothing like Lenny anyway, save for the hairline, would make for an ideal time-filler.

She didn't laugh at the first few jokes she heard, and barely smiled at the ones that followed after, but the show was quickly doing the trick, helping her slip away into another time and place, far, far away.

Halfway through a new episode, she heard the girls coming down the stairs together, gratefully not fighting with each other either. The trip to Boston had helped them all, she realized, even if Erika still had the upper hand for the moment.

Peaches went straight for the fridge, and Erika seemed ready to do the same, but Caroline locked eyes with her first, a guilty smile appearing in the air between them.

"Come over here," Caroline said to her then, muting the TV. "I wanna talk to you."

Peaches grabbed a yogurt from the fridge and a spoon from the drawer as Erika walked over and sat down beside her mother on the couch.

Caroline reached out with both arms and pulled Erika in for a tight hug then too, completely surprising her.

"You know I love you two very much, right?"

Erika tried to read her face, then watched as Peaches arrived, sitting on the other side of Caroline and offering her a similar funny look.

"Yeah, of course we do," Erika said. "Why? What's wrong?"

"Nothing. Nothing's wrong. I just wanted to take this moment to tell you both how much I love you."

Peaches smiled but said nothing. She just spooned her yogurt out dose by dose, resting her head on Caroline's lap as she tucked her legs up on the couch, forever her baby.

"Does this have anything to do with our conversation yesterday?" Erika asked suspiciously, saying nothing to incriminate her in front of Peaches.

"No," Caroline said quickly. "Well, maybe a little," she added with a smile. "No, but really, I just feel like we've all been so busy lately, we haven't spent enough time together as a family. Not as much as we should, at least. Boston was fun, but without your dad, it was a little weird too."

Peaches started giggling, and Caroline and Erika realized she was laughing at something on the screen. Even with the TV muted, without any dialogue or laughter to follow, the outfits two of the Golden Girls wore amused Peaches enough to keep giggling nonstop now, and soon Caroline and Erika were laughing as well.

Erika reached forward to unmute the TV, and for the next nine minutes, the three of them enjoyed the rest of the show together.

Once it ended, Erika stood up to go to the kitchen, and as she did, she finally thought to ask.

"Hey Mom, where *is* Dad?"

Caroline didn't look at her at first, just flipped through channels again, but when she did, her voice sounded harder somehow.

"He was at work, and now he's over at your uncle's house helping him move furniture out to the dumpster."

Silence snuck back in then as Erika retrieved a bottle of Diet Coke from the fridge, and Caroline finally landed on a documentary about Egypt. Once again, all three began watching quietly together for several minutes.

When the commercials came back on, Peaches stood up and stretched, her empty cup of yogurt in one hand and her spoon in the other. She took a few steps toward the kitchen, but then stopped, turning back around to face Caroline and Erika.

"Mommy? Did you ever call Grandma back?"

##

Sam and Lenny were halfway up the driveway, a large, very heavy couch between them, when Lenny's phone started ringing.

"I'll call them back," he said to Sam, halfway through their conversation. "But if Caraway is her maiden name, then she's gotta be his cousin at least, right? If not his sister? I don't know how this all plays together, though."

The two grunted their way up the steepest part of the driveway, a sharp incline going from the lake up to the road, and by the time they got to the top, they barely made it a few feet further before they dropped the couch and collapsed down on either side of it, completely out of breath.

A minute or so passed as they just sat there on the old piece of furniture, neither one ready to speak yet. Once they did have a chance to relax a bit more, it was Sam who spoke first.

"Lemme ask you something, Len. Let's say you find out this woman and your boss have something going on, even some financial bullshit with the company. What the hell does any of that have to do with this Caraway guy? Why would she want her own brother dead, or her cousin or whatever? For that matter, why would your boss?"

"Well, I don't know yet, but—"

"No, hang on here. Just hear me out. *A,* what the hell does any of this have to do with *you?* Like, why get all up in their shit and risk your job over it, and *B,* why even suspect foul play to begin with? Why the hell can't anyone just die in this state without everyone in the whole fucking world trying to pin it on someone?"

Lenny, who'd been looking at him intently, quickly turned away. He knew Sam wasn't just talking about John Caraway anymore, and Lenny wasn't sure he even wanted to discuss this with him any further.

There was a comfort in not knowing any more than he needed to regarding Sam and his history, and for seventeen years, Lenny was grateful to have safely avoided the better part of it.

"You're right," he said, hoping Sam wouldn't push him. "I'll drop it. It's silly, and I shouldn't risk losing my job over something like this anyway."

He stood up, brushed himself off, and started for the house.

"One more piece?" he called back to Sam.

"Yeah, just one more," Sam said thoughtfully, his mind returning to the past. "Just the coffee table." He stood up and started heading back as well. "I tried it myself, but it's too heavy."

Inside the house, Lenny pulled out his phone and saw both Phyllis and Caroline had called, and he had a text waiting now too.

Call me ASAP!!!, Caroline had written.

"Jesus. What the hell?"

Sam saw the concern on Lenny's face as he dialed Caroline's cell, and looked at him for an answer.

"I don't know," he told Sam. "Something's up."

The phone rang once in Lenny's ear before Caroline picked up.

"Hey. I just saw your—what? Oh my God. When? Well does she know where he went? Jesus. No, I'm still here with Sam, but I'll meet you over there in a few minutes. Yeah. Okay, bye."

"What's going on?" Sam asked.

"My dad took off somewhere. He waited for my mom to go to the bathroom, then left. She says it has to do with his heart stopping, that his brain's not right. I gotta head over there."

"I'll go with you," Sam said.

"No, man. Livi will be there. Don't worry about it."

"Yeah, but maybe I can help you find him."

"Look, if we have any leads, I promise I'll let you know. Just keep an eye out for his car in the mean time. Apparently he took

265

off in the Lincoln a couple hours ago. Maybe we'll do a Silver Alert or something in case he's driving on 91. I'll keep you posted."

##

Lenny pulled into his parents' driveway a little while later, and saw Caroline and Olivia were already there. When he walked in, he looked across the open-floor-plan house where the two of them were chatting with Phyllis while standing together in the living room. Phyllis was busy telling them what she knew, but as soon as she saw Lenny, she stopped mid-sentence and rushed over to meet him with a huge hug.

He flashed Caroline and Olivia a nervous glance, realizing Phyllis wouldn't show such affection unless she was truly scared.

"Thank God you're here," she said, leading him by the hand into the living room with the others. "So here's what I know. He's been acting very strange lately, ever since the operation. You two heard him going on about the damn ceiling," she said, pointing to Lenny and Caroline, who now stood beside each other.

"The what?" Olivia asked, confused. "The ceiling?"

"Your dad saw them operating on him from above," Caroline told her. "He had an out-of-body experience."

"Oh, right. That thing."

"It's all such nonsense," Phyllis said. "Fantasies of a twisted, oxygen-deprived brain—*a very small brain at that, I assure you*—and nothing more."

Lenny and Olivia shook their heads at each other like they didn't want to get into it, but Caroline reached forward, resting her hand gently on Phyllis's arm. Phyllis clearly didn't like it though, and pulled herself free again quickly.

"Phyllis, why didn't you just tell me he was missing when we spoke earlier on my way back from Boston? We could have all started looking for him hours ago."

Phyllis cocked her head sideways at her, annoyed she'd dared correct her at all, much less in front of her children.

"I called you as soon as I found his note, Caroline. I was *upset.* I'm so *sorry* I wasn't able to conjure a more thorough response for you, dear. If I have offended you in *any* way though, *please* accept my sincere apologies."

Her angry sarcasm lit a new flame under Caroline, but before she could respond, Olivia stepped forward.

"Hang on. You called Caroline before me?"

"No, of course not," Phyllis said, walking away from all of them toward the kitchen. "I called Leonard first, and when he didn't pick up his goddamn phone, I called Caroline, hoping he was with her. Then, once I realized I'd just have to wait for him to get back to me, I called you."

She'd said it all very logically, as if calling Olivia should have been understood to be a last resort.

"Don't," Lenny said, locking eyes with Olivia, moving past her to follow Phyllis into the kitchen.

"Mom," he said. "Where's Dad's note? Does it give us any clue whatsoever as to where he might have gone?"

Olivia and Caroline, now equally annoyed at Phyllis, just watched from a distance as Lenny followed her to the front of the house, where she'd left Alan's note by some papers and books she had piled there.

She handed Lenny what looked like a small piece of notepad paper, then returned to the kitchen by herself.

"What does it say?" Olivia asked, her arms crossed nervously, watching over Caroline's shoulder as Lenny read it.

He finished reading, then looked over at them in a daze as he shook his head. Then he looked back up at the top of the note, and read it out loud as he walked toward them.

Phyllis, I'm leaving for a while. Probably just a week or two, maybe more. Need to think things out for myself, preferably far away from your incessant nagging. You really have a problem, you know that? I took cash out yesterday, so I'm good for a while. I won't do anything crazy, at least not without talking to you first. Don't worry. See you soon. Love, Alan.

Olivia let out a loud sigh of relief, and Caroline, who'd been trying to contain herself halfway through, finally allowed a laugh to escape. She couldn't see it with her back turned away from her, but Phyllis's eyes narrowed at Caroline as she sipped from a fresh glass of red wine.

"Alright," Lenny said, walking back into the kitchen. "At least he seems to know what he's doing. Do you know how much cash he took out?"

Phyllis just shrugged, and was about to answer him when Olivia interrupted.

"Looks like two grand," she said, reading her phone. "I'm on his account for protection."

"*His* account?!" Phyllis asked, slamming her glass down so hard on the counter it broke, sending red wine and ice cubes spilling everywhere. She stepped away from it quickly as the others gasped, maintaining direct eye contact with Olivia as she moved. "Why *the hell* does your father have his own account, and how did I not know about this?"

Lenny and Caroline rushed in to clean up the mess, and to make sure Phyllis's hand was okay too.

"Mom, relax," Olivia said. "It's just a small savings account he set up years ago with five grand he had on the side. He gave me access in case Haley needed anything. We've never touched it, and it's been gaining interest anyway."

Caroline stopped what she was doing and stood up straight.

"Well that was awfully nice of him," Caroline said, but something in her tone told them she was hinting at much more. She made eye contact with each one there as she walked over to look at Olivia's phone. "Sixty-three hundred bucks for *one* of his three granddaughters. How sweet of him."

"Oh, get *over* yourself, Car," Olivia snapped. "Please. I'm raising Haley on my own, and at the time he set this thing up, my hours were cut at the bank. Don't go making this into more than it is."

"I'm not, Livi. I'm just pointing out—"

"Shut it, Caroline," Phyllis said, stunning her to momentary silence. "Alan may not have had a hush money account set up for your daughters, but what would they do with it if they had one? Spend it on liquor and drugs? Breakfast meetings out with that black boy?"

"Oh my God, what the fuck is wrong with you?" Caroline hissed back, but Lenny jumped between them, hoping to calm things down.

"Alright everyone, just cut it out, okay? And Mom, Caroline was simply asking a very reasonable question. There's no need to be so cruel to my daughters and their friends like that."

"I was not—" she tried to interrupt.

"No!" he yelled. "Cut it out. I'm serious. I'm not gonna let you speak to my wife that way, or say such awful things about my children. I'm not at all shocked that Dad took off like this either, you know. You're ridiculous, you know that? You're insane, and totally out of line."

Phyllis looked at him in stunned silence, and for a brief moment, Lenny thought he had gone too far. Olivia and Caroline looked on nervously too.

In the silence of the extending moment, Phyllis seemed to be composing herself, while Lenny still braced for impact just in case. She hadn't smacked him since he was a teenager, but every bit then as now, he most certainly earned one, pushed for it even in his careless yelling when his anger got the best of him.

Phyllis was not in the mood for such retribution though, and instead, they all watched as she turned her back and opened her see-through kitchen cabinet door to retrieve a new wine glass. She carried it to the refrigerator, added two new ice cubes, then poured herself another glass of red wine.

As she took a sip, still not looking at any of them, she shook her head to herself.

When she finally did look up at them to speak, her voice was soft and tender. Too soft, though. *Dangerously* soft. Softer than any of them could ever remember her speaking before.

"I'm going to lie down now. Goodbye."

They watched as she moved past them like a ghost toward the stairs, her nightgown floating around her gracefully as she took each small step along the way up to her bedroom.

Once they heard the distant sound of a door shutting upstairs, they felt safe to look at each other again, but none of them were sure what to say.

Caroline let out a quiet sigh. She brought the kitchen towel she'd been holding back into the kitchen, draping it over the shiny brass hook near the sink. She was about to speak, but Olivia, who was watching her carefully, wouldn't allow her the honor.

"I'll stay here for a while and make sure Mom is okay," she said to Lenny. "I don't want to leave her alone until I'm sure she's alright. Maybe I can find something here that'll help us figure out where Dad went. You and Caroline go home, and if I hear anything, I'll let you know."

Lenny nodded, locking eyes with Caroline, and they both nodded their agreement to Olivia.

He leaned in then and kissed his sister on the cheek as Caroline followed him out the front door. The two women barely glanced at each other one last time.

Once they were gone and she heard their cars start out in the driveway, Olivia immediately set about on her first important task of the afternoon: making herself a large glass of something thoroughly alcoholic.

If she was destined to be trapped in her parents' house for a while longer, all alone with her mother, she sure as hell wasn't going to stay sober.

Chapter 31

Seventeen years earlier

"My parents think I'm at a concert in Albany," Kerry Ann said, her face a strange mix of excitement and apprehension.

She'd never been inside a motel room before, but wasn't sure she should tell Sam that yet. Eying the strange yellow overhead light suspiciously, her first impression was that the room smelled awful, as if the entire town used it to smoke cigarettes together.

The bed looked large and comfortable enough, but she found her way to a chair by a table instead, hoping they would just talk a bit first anyway. She didn't even take off her coat.

"You want anything to drink?" Sam offered. "I bought us some beer, and I have some vodka here too."

"Um, yeah. I guess so. Whatever."

"Cool. Why don't we have the vodka first then, and we can always have the beer after. Liquor then beer, in the clear."

He flashed her a strange smile, hoping he was teaching her something new, educating the youth of tomorrow in the ways of the world, but she'd already heard the rhyme several times before, so it didn't really register.

"I got some ice from the machine down the way there, and I brought some cups over from my place."

She watched as he went to work, taking note of his tight jeans and cutoff tee shirt. It was a hot look for him, she thought, even if this whole meetup still unnerved her.

Kerry Ann had never even been to New Hampshire, as close as it was, let alone seen the inside of a motel room, but this one was twice as dingy as she imagined it. Agreeing to meet Sam here had sounded exciting at the outset, but she was already quite scared.

With only one bed in the room, she would have to sleep with him that night if she stayed, whether or not they even did much, and though she felt safe enough with him at the moment, the whole setup still felt strange.

"Here you go," he said, handing her a cup of cheap vodka on ice. "Cheers." He tapped her cup with his and downed two gulps.

Kerry Ann took a small sip, quickly wincing at the taste. The flavor was gross, but if nothing else, she knew it'd help her relax.

Sam smiled awkwardly, not wanting to call attention to the taste himself. He knew it wasn't the best either, but as he'd forgotten to buy more, it was the only one he could easily slip away from the house without Olivia noticing.

"You look really pretty," he added softly, hoping to relax her some more. "You wanna take that coat off though? Kinda warm in here, isn't it?"

Kerry Ann nodded and began removing it. For the first time since she'd been there, she wondered whether he had turned up the heat on purpose to get her naked faster. The two times they'd met before, he'd seemed a perfect gentleman, but now in this little room with a bolt on the door, she felt extremely uneasy.

Her coat off, she was surprised to watch him take it from her, along with her purse, and drape them both over a chair on the other side of the room. The *back* side of the room. *Far from the door.*

Sam smiled again, then sat down across from her on the bed, his long legs easily touching the floor, even from his place atop the high mattress.

As they each took a few more sips of their vodka, Kerry Ann told herself to relax. Sam hadn't done anything wrong, and there was no reason to read into every last thing he said and did anyway.

"I brought condoms," he announced, like it was the next thing to naturally say, as if they were already on the subject anyway.

They hadn't even discussed sex, just him getting the room so they could hang out together in private, and though she expected to at least suck him off, sex was never a part of the equation.

She knew her face was making that clear to him now too, as they'd never spoken of this before. There was no way he could mistake her reaction after he said this.

"But we don't have to do *that* right away," he stammered, almost nervously. *Almost* nervously. Fakely, she thought. "We'll just build up to it."

"Yeah, I don't know if I want to do that," she said, making eye contact with him only briefly.

She thought of the pepper spray tucked in her new purse. Tucked in her new purse now hanging on the back of a chair on the far side of the room. Twenty feet from the door.

Be cool, be cool. Just stay calm.

"But we'll see," she added with a quick smile, locking eyes with him now for a little bit longer. *Stay on his side.*

Sam nodded with a grin, and took a moment to examine the bed again. He liked that there were four pillows. Some rooms only had two.

Taking another big swig from his cup, he remembered something Kerry Ann had told him the last time he saw her.

"Oh, hey. How did that thing go with your brother?"

She relaxed a bit at the question. He was asking about something important, something she wasn't sure he even remembered, and she appreciated it.

"Oh, well, he chickened out, actually," she laughed, despite her discomfort. "I totally knew he would." She relaxed a little more. "I told him if he didn't just do it when the topic came up, he would totally bail later. So yeah, missed his chance, I guess."

Sam nodded and smiled.

"He'll be fine," he said. "World's changing fast. He's just gotta do it when he's ready."

Something about the way he said this changed something in Kerry Ann, and her fears seemed to start lifting. Or *maybe,* she wondered, *maybe it was just something in the drink.*

Either way, she was definitely more relaxed now, and as she crossed her legs in front of her, her ankle bracelet caught her eye, and she wondered whether Sam had noticed it too. She'd worn it specifically for him because he'd mentioned that being one of his turn-ons. She was about to ask him too, when—

"Your uh—your ankle bracelet is um—well, it's very nice," he said, breathing heavily as he looked at it, and then at her, and then at the wall. "God, *I'm* nervous now, and I never get nervous."

Kerry Ann looked at him with new eyes, and decided he *must* be telling her the truth. She was sure the other stuff was a bit much, but this for sure was the real him, the guy she'd fallen for.

She stood up then and walked over to sit next to him on the bed, her feet dangling well off the floor.

Sam watched her as she moved, admiring her skirt, her legs, and her ankle bracelet. As he felt the cup of vodka in his hand rocking back and forth while she got comfortable, he locked eyes with her at last.

She smiled softly, eyeing his lips as she leaned in closer, waiting for Sam to kiss her first. When he did, it was slow and passionate, confident and wet.

He led the dance, but he didn't push her at all. He didn't even touch her until she put her hand on his leg, but even then, he just held her hand in his, rubbing the tops of her fingers.

By the time they stopped kissing, some six or seven minutes later, she felt as if everything would be okay. Nothing to worry about at all. Sam was a perfect gentleman, and he would never do a thing to harm her.

Chapter 32

Erika sat across from Chris at Applebee's, hoping he wouldn't ask any questions about her family, or at the very least, that she could fudge her way through any answers until she was ready to say more.

Mercifully, all he wanted to talk about was himself at first, and while she'd normally be annoyed at such a maneuver, tonight she was practically giddy with relief.

"So yeah, I saw a few of the schools I was accepted into, but I'm locked into BU now, which I'm happy about."

"Oh my God," she said. "I was just there this weekend. My mom drove me down to look at it. It's a really cool campus."

"Wow, so are you thinking of going there too?"

Erika stammered for a moment, surprised by the question, and then looked down in shame as she thought out her response.

How could she tell him she hadn't even applied yet, and was pretty sure she wouldn't be accepted to such a great school anyway? Worst of all, the community college she'd *planned* to attend already closed their enrollment for the fall, and she still hadn't told her mother.

"Well, maybe next year," she said, "but I decided to do community college first, so I'll be in Vermont a little while longer."

Chris nodded with a polite smile, and Erika couldn't tell whether it was pity or genuine understanding that crept behind it. A long, awkward pause followed as they looked at their menus, but they were soon saved by the waiter returning with their drinks.

"Okay, here you go. Have you decided what to order?"

Chris motioned for Erika to go first.

"Um, yeah, I'll have the Caesar salad with grilled chicken? And can I have a little creamy Italian on the side too?"

"Okay, sure. And you?"

"I'll do the cheeseburger, well done, no bacon, and sweet potato fries instead of regular."

"Okay, sounds good. I'll put that right in for you."

Once he was gone, the two exchanged another awkward smile, and Chris noticed she looked very nervous all of a sudden.

"Is everything okay?"

Although she didn't *want* to talk about her family too much, she realized there was no way she'd be able to avoid telling him about her grandfather now. She flashed a fake smile and shook her head.

"I dunno, it's weird. I have a family thing—" she started, thinking of how to explain. "It's just, my grandpa had an operation recently, and he's been a little out of it since then, and now he's gone. Like, he disappeared today, and my grandma doesn't seem to know where he went. It's just a little strange."

"Whoa, yeah. That's wild. Do they suspect foul play, or—"

"No, no, nothing like that. He apparently left a note or whatever, but my grandma's worried, and my dad seems confused about it too. It's all really crazy though, because he's this old, powerful figure in my family, but with the surgery and all, he shouldn't be out on his own."

"Yikes, yeah," Chris said, taking a sip of his soda, unsure what to say. "We could have postponed this if you wanted."

Erika shook her head.

"No, I wanted to see you again. It's okay. So," she said, remembering her plan to keep him talking about himself, "what else should I know about you? I feel like we barely know each other still."

Chris began speaking, but Erika was already chastising herself for saying 'each other', as that meant he'd be expected to ask her a bunch of questions too once he finished.

"Boston will be fun, but I'm already missing home and my friends. Well, friends more than home. Things have been weird lately. Last week my dad's partner got into it with my grandma again. I think I told you they have some history? Anyway, it just drives me nuts, because—"

What am I even doing here? I should have stayed away from him as soon as I found out who his family was. Who cares if his lips are perfect and his body is amazing and he's a totally sweet, funny, awesome guy? If he finds out who I really am, he'll want nothing to do with me anyway.

"My uncle says I shouldn't argue with facts. Says we should all be together as one unit on this, and not—"

Great, and he's already talking about his family. I'm screwed. I am so completely screwed. He'll probably make a scene here in the frickin' restaurant too. I'm fucked. There's no way out of this now except to lie and take off before he figures it out. Maybe something to do with Grandpa. Throw a twenty down on the table and apologize quickly, then head for the car before he can stop me.

"They think I'm being stupid, of course. They say the guy is totally guilty, and I'm naive to think otherwise."

Wait, what?

"But I dunno. Maybe it's like with your grandfather. Maybe people are flipping out for no reason, you know?"

Erika was just staring at him without nodding or speaking, and Chris had finally noticed. He felt bad for even bringing it up in conversation, and seemed to be cursing himself under his breath.

"God, I'm so sorry. You're worried about your grandfather's safety, and I'm rattling on about my dead aunt and my fucked-up family. Jesus. What the hell is wrong with me? I really am sorry. Never mind."

She blinked for a moment in shock, realizing things might not be as bad as she thought, and held her hand out toward his side of the table with her gaze fixed momentarily on the bottom of her glass of iced tea.

"Wait," she said, looking up at him now. "Say that again? I kinda flaked out for a second there."

"No, never mind," he said, once again shaking his head. "It was dumb of me to bring it up with everything going on with your grandfather. Seriously, don't worry about it."

"No, *seriously*," she said, touching his hand now. "I want to know. I do. Please tell me what you were saying."

Chris looked across at her, appreciating a different side of her he hadn't noticed before, a genuinely tender, caring person. He was glad to have met her and hooked up with her, but until this moment, he still wasn't sure if she was *'a woman of substance'*, as his grandmother often urged him to find.

But maybe Erika *was* more than she seemed. Maybe she really was the kind of girl he could date seriously, and not just have fun with for a while.

"Okay, well, I was only saying, this thing with my aunt is really awful, because it's like, not only is she dead, but they all act like she's still dying out there somewhere right now. Like, let it go, people, you know? But my grandma says I should read up on the case before I jump down their throats, because he really did kill her, no matter what he says."

"But you don't think so?"

"No way," he said. "The case was dismissed, and that loser left town anyway, so who cares? It's over. Just move on with your fuckin' lives already, you know?"

Erika leaned back quickly when he said it, and immediately felt herself go pale. If there was one thing she hated more than anything else, it was this. Seriousness. Real-life, honest-to-God serious talk about things well beyond her understanding.

It was like she knew her brain could only handle so much of it, and she'd long since reached her designated tipping point. There was no way she would manage this well.

"What's wrong?" he asked.

"He's back," she heard herself say, her heart a noisy drumbeat in her head. Yet she plowed forward before she could stop herself. "He left Ludlow years ago, but he came back again last month."

Chris knew who she meant, but asked her anyway. *Slowly.*

"Who...is...back?"

"Sam Newhaus. The *loser* your family says killed your aunt."

She shook her head, still looking away. She couldn't manage eye contact now, and Chris could tell she was upset. Even so, her knowledge of the case mattered more, and he had to ask her how she knew.

"How do you know the name of the guy who killed my aunt?"

Erika's eyes darted back and forth between people and things across the restaurant, looking anywhere but at him.

A dark cloud of dread absorbed her from top to bottom, as if she herself had killed the girl, revealed at last as the murderer, just for keeping this terrible truth from him for as long as she had, even though they barely knew each other.

"Erika? It's okay. Just tell me. How do you know the guy's name? And how do you know he's back?"

There was no way out. She hated that this truth between them was so terrible, despite it having so little to do with either of them.

As she finally turned her head back to the table, she took another long moment before she was able to look up at him again, and into his eyes.

"Because he's my uncle. Sam Newhaus is my uncle."

##

Roger closed his car door and waved at Haley, who was waiting for him by the entrance to the catering hall.

"Hey, what's up?" he asked, looking concerned.

"Hey, thanks for coming. It's nothing big. I just didn't want to do this alone, so I was hoping you could keep me company. I thought about asking my uncle, but I think he'd rather stay out of it. I hope I didn't take you away from work or anything, though?"

"No, no, not at all. I'm not on tonight. I was just gonna be home playing video games anyway, so I'm glad you texted me," he said with a smile, ready to walk in ahead of her.

"Okay, wait," she stopped him. "So here's the thing. I know I told you I just had to pick some things up, but it's actually something else completely different. Since we hit a dead end on the whole Kerry Ann Jefferson thing, I wanted to at least investigate this other situation as much as I can before I let it go."

"Haley," Roger said, shaking his head. "Please don't tell me your dad was accused of more than one murder."

She laughed out loud as he smiled.

"No! Stop it! No murders. Well, not this one at least, and I don't even know if it *is* a murder, or if I'm just freaking out over nothing. But it's not related to him anyway. It's just another weird situation I need to investigate, and I didn't want to do it by myself."

"Okay, no problem. So what is it?"

"Well, basically? I got hired to take pictures for a wedding by this really sweet guy a few weeks back, the father of the bride, but the night of the wedding, he collapsed in the men's room, and he died a little while later on the way to the hospital."

"Whoa," Roger said. "Okay?"

"And just for my own peace of mind, I begged Meredith, the catering manager here, to let me come over and check out the video feed outside the men's room that night, just in case there was anything weird."

"Why do you even think there's something suspicious going on? Just because of all the shit with your dad?"

Haley smiled and looked down with a nod. Her uncle had warned her against the exact same thing, but she still couldn't shake the possibility there was more here.

"Look, maybe I *am* just being paranoid, but that's why I want to at least look at the footage and see for myself. Once I see everything is normal, I'll be happy to let it go."

Roger nodded.

"Okay. I get that. So what about me? What's my job?"

"I dunno, I just thought you could come with me so I didn't have to be alone. Hope you don't mind?"

"No, no, not at all. That's easy. Let's do it."

They walked in together and immediately admired the beauty of the place. Even with no events going on, and not many lights on either, the building offered a special kind of elegance worth appreciating. Meredith was nowhere to be seen, but looking at her cell phone, Haley saw they were still eight minutes early, so maybe she wasn't even there yet herself.

She walked in a bit further, taking a moment to briefly scan the large room used for Stephanie's wedding reception that night, and as she turned around again she noticed the men's room door opposite the bar in the lobby. *The scene of the crime,* she thought.

"Heyyy," Meredith called out, rounding a corner from the other side of the long hallway. "You're early. That's good. And good to see you again."

"Hey, you too. Thank you so much for letting me come over."

"So when's the next party we'll see you at? Or are you working for Time Magazine already?"

Haley blushed as Meredith shook Roger's hand and introduced herself, and then offered Haley a hug hello.

"No, no Time Magazine yet," Haley said. "Just freelancing, hoping for the next gig."

"Well, that's life, honey, what can I tell ya," she said quickly, already leading them away from the banquet room toward a hallway around the corner. "So I still think you're a lunatic for wanting to go through that footage, but it's easy enough for me to cue it up for you just the same. The office is right over here," she said, leading the way. "As soon as you're done, just text me. There are two or three other people here tonight, but I'll let them know you guys were okayed by me to be in here. Please text me right away when you're done though, okay? I have to keep the doors locked, so I'll show you out again afterwards, alright?"

"Alright, thank you so much, Meredith. I really appreciate this."

"No problem. Hope you don't find nothin' on there. But if you see any of my staff doing anything wrong, I sure as hell want to know about it!"

Once they were all set up with the footage loaded, Haley and Roger watched the screen carefully until they reached the approximate time when Mr. Caraway was found in the bathroom.

"That's me leaving with my tripod and camera bag," Haley pointed out to Roger. "I think they found him within a half hour or so after that, because the reception was over then, and a lot of people had left already by the time it happened."

She fast-forwarded a little more, and then pressed play to watch the footage in real time, quickly getting excited when she saw Mr.

Caraway shake the hand of someone who was leaving before he ducked into the bathroom by himself. To her great relief, no one else seemed to have entered before or after him for a while.

"So I guess it was just a heart attack or whatever," Roger said, and Haley nodded without saying anything.

She turned her head and looked at him shyly, feeling ashamed.

"I'm really sorry to have dragged you over here for this. Ugh. This was so stupid. Of course it was a heart attack. I don't know why I always do this, either. I guess I thought that—"

"Whoa. Rewind that," Roger said, leaning in quickly, and pointing her back to the screen.

"What? Why?"

"I totally saw someone duck into the men's room, but I don't think it was a guy."

##

Chris looked like he'd just been given a horrible diagnosis from a doctor—*only weeks left to live*—and he instinctively turned his head away from her with not just shock, but growing dread as well.

What are the odds? he thought, especially since he'd met her down in Manchester only weeks earlier, and would soon be off to college in Boston.

Before he could even process it all, Erika grabbed her purse and started to leave, quickly sliding out from the booth.

"I should go. I'm sorry," she said, speaking softly. "I really am. I figured it out the night I met you, but I just really liked you, and I thought that, I dunno, maybe if we avoided the topic for a while, we could still have a good time? But I was stupid. I'll leave you alone. I'm sorry."

She turned around and started walking away toward the door.

"No! Stop! Don't go!" he yelled out, much more forcefully than he'd intended, quieting everyone else sitting nearby. "Sit down, please. Let's just—let's just think this out first."

Erika glanced nervously at the other diners around them, and saw they were all watching them both carefully now.

She didn't want to be there anymore, not with this between them, especially since she had such little knowledge about what *this* really was. But standing there as people stared couldn't last much longer either.

"Please," he said again, much softer than before, and she finally locked eyes with him. "Please don't leave. Let's just talk, okay?"

She decided to at least sit back down for a moment, if only to give him a chance to say whatever he wanted. Sitting down on the edge of the seat, she was still prepared to leave at any moment.

"So what if he's your uncle?" he whispered, thinking it out. "He's not here right now, right? Neither is my aunt. It's just you and me. We should at least be able to talk about this."

Despite his control of the situation, Chris was clearly just as frazzled as she was by the awful fact laying dead between them on the table.

Two teenagers, neither of whom were out of diapers yet when Kerry Ann was killed, sat across from each other now no longer as a boy and a girl out on a date, but as two equally unwilling representatives of their feuding families.

For a long while, they just stared off at nothing in particular in shocked silence, Erika still thinking she should leave, as the laughter of others wrapped around them like an unpleasant bubble of insanity.

Chris composed his thoughts much slower than usual for the next minute or so, deciding what he should say, hoping to speak the exact right thing if at all possible, when the waiter suddenly appeared again, chipper and clueless to the strange darkness between them.

"Hey, I am *so sorry,*" he said, the artificiality oozing from his lips, "but I totally forgot to write it down. How did you want your burger cooked?"

Chris gazed up at him with confusion at first, and Erika took the opportunity to watch him while she could, one last chance to see his eyes, and imagine kissing him again.

"Well done," he whispered, much more seriously than the waiter expected, and he finally noticed the tension at the table. He eyed them both nervously, then nodded quickly and walked away.

"Chris," Erika said, saving him for the moment. "I really don't know too much about what happened. My parents never talk about it. And I've only seen my uncle once since he moved back anyway. I barely know him."

"No," he said, eyeing her gravely, and her fear returned as she saw his eyes, and the way he looked at her.

"I'm so sorry."

"No," he said again, more firmly this time. "No, Erika. This is ridiculous. I don't know my aunt either. None of this is *your* fault. You didn't do anything. Your uncle, he—"

Chris broke off again, and Erika just watched as he put it all together, as the words came quicker.

"He may not have even *done* this. He was charged, but they didn't prove anything, other than the thing with the underwear, and that he may have moved her body."

Erika listened carefully, hearing things no one in her family had ever told her before.

"The case against him was dismissed. They didn't have enough evidence to prove foul play, and that's that. My dad told me all about this before he moved to Colorado, and I've looked it up online myself on multiple occasions when I was fighting with my grandma. Your uncle—I guess he was dating her or whatever? He said he was innocent, and the reason he's still free is because they didn't have enough proof he had done it."

"So you don't think he did?" she asked.

"I don't know. Maybe? But it doesn't matter. My point is, this has nothing to do with you or me. It's just something that happened between our families a long time ago. We should still be able to see each other without this getting in the way."

Erika looked down at her purse, which she still held tightly between her hands, and after a while, she finally nodded and looked back up at him.

"I dunno," she said. "This all feels wrong now."

"Erika, just think about it. Did you or I ever kill each other?"

She smiled at the question.

"No, but—"

"Did you or I ever kill each other's relatives?"

"No, but—"

"Then that's all there is to this. Is it weird that something so crazy happened when we were little? Yeah. Is it a wicked, fucked up situation from top to bottom? Fuck yeah, it is. But that doesn't mean we can't still see each other."

She nodded, looking away.

"I mean it, Erika. Fuck them all," he said, leaning forward to keep her looking at him. "All of them. They may have fucked up their lives years ago, and my aunt—*may she rest in peace*—might have gotten herself into some kind of stupid situation too for all I know, but none of that means you and I aren't allowed to be happy."

"You're right," she said. "I mean, of course you're right, but I also think it'd be better if you don't tell your family about me. Like, at all. It would just be asking for trouble. And if you're going away to college in a couple of months anyway, I might not even see you again after the summer ends."

Chris felt the sting of her words, but he knew she was right. A new romance at this point was terrible timing to say the least.

"Next month," he said, looking down.

"What?"

"Next month," he repeated, looking at her again. "I only have six more weeks before I move into the dorm in late August."

"Oh. Right," she said, nodding quickly, her eyes once again darting away from him.

"Listen, Erika. Can we just relax for a little while, and have a nice night, and not even talk about our families anymore? I'm sure there's a lot we can talk about other than our fucked up family situation anyway."

Erika smiled. It was exactly what she'd wanted from the start.

"Totally," she said, relaxing a bit more and putting her purse back down. "That would be nice."

##

"Are you sure you don't know who she is?" Meredith asked, standing behind them and leaning forward to see the screen.

"No," Haley said. "I *have* seen her face, though. I know her from somewhere. I just can't for the life of me remember where."

"Well, she must have been a wedding guest then," Meredith said. "Look at her dress. We only had one wedding here that night. It should be easy to cross-check the guest list and figure it out."

Haley looked doubtful though, so the two of them waited for her to respond.

"What is it?" Roger finally asked.

She looked up at him and shrugged.

"Look, I'm a hundred percent sure that woman wasn't at the reception. I photographed absolutely everyone, as in *every single person*. It was my first time shooting this kinda thing, so with a hundred guests, I made sure everyone made it into the pictures. But that lady? With that dress? No way was she one of them."

From the angle of the camera, all they could see was a single side glimpse of the woman's face going into the men's room, then leaving just twenty seconds later with her head down, but as Haley stared at the screen, she was more determined than ever to find out who she was.

Chapter 33

The nine members of the Stir Call Circle were all gathered for their monthly meet-up, Roger included, and Gloria had just finished calling in the directions. A pleasant mist of sage filled the room as they all got comfortable again on their yoga mats and chairs.

"This month," Gloria announced, "we'll journey a bit in the second half. For now though, I thought we could just go around the room, and share with one another what we're wrestling with most in our hearts right now. You don't have to share anything if you don't want to, and certainly don't share anything too personal if you wish to keep it to yourself, but please do mention anything you'd like, trusting in the safety of this sacred space we've created here. Jane, would you like to begin?"

"Sure," Jane said, holding her hands out in front of her as she composed her thoughts. "Well, my son yelled at me again this morning, nothing new there, only this time, he got right up in my face like he might hit me. He didn't, thank God, and he apologized later on as he always does, but I'm starting to worry he may need to go back into the live-in program. Some of you may remember I used to bring him to a place in Hartford that my cousin works at. Anyway, there's that, she said," as if this wasn't enough, "and then there's my daughter Stacey, who just broke her arm last week in her gymnastics class."

The group let out a small groan as Jane smiled and nodded, looking much more tired than normal, many realized.

"Yeah, so that was a whole thing. Not just the hospital and the crying, but with her teacher too, who Stacey blames for her accident. Says she made her do something she couldn't do, and she should have known better. I want to take Stacey's side, but the teacher is such a sweet girl, and I find it impossible to believe she forced Stacey to do this particular maneuver."

"Did she fall?" Gloria asked. "Is that what happened?"

"Yeah," Jane said. "She was doing a cartwheel on the beam, and lost her balance. Landed on her arm."

Again, everyone groaned, but this time wincing more, as if they had all just experienced the fall themselves.

"So that's my life right now," Jane said, offering them all a smile. "*I'm* doing okay, but never a dull moment with my kids."

"Thank you for sharing," Corinne said from across the room.

"Marty, how about you," Gloria asked, moving clockwise in the circle. "How are things in Marty's life?"

"Well, no broken bones or anything. My mom is doing better these days. She was in and out of the hospital for a while, but she's been home and healthy now for the past three weeks, so we're grateful for that. My wife and I are thinking of adopting a puppy, but we'll need to make sure the puppy gets along just as well with my mom as with Karen and me, so we may need to do a trial period first once we pick one out, just to see how the dog does in our house with the bed set up and all. And Karen just got a promotion at work too, so we're very happy about that right now."

"Oh, very nice," Gloria said.

"Yeah, things are generally good. I gotta say though, I feel like I need more than just this monthly gathering in my life. Karen and I were talking, and despite the situation with my mom, we may be going back to church soon. We miss the community we had at our old church, and though we're still at odds with the pastor running things there right now, there's just too much we loved and lost when we stopped attending services. Still not sure, but we're leaning toward going back."

"He didn't ask you guys to leave though, right? The pastor?" Ellen asked.

"Well, the pastor is a *she,* but no, not at all. We just weren't ready for some of the changes they made when she came in, but we think we'd like to give it another shot now, see how things go for a while, you know?"

"Yes, of course," Gloria said, looking at the others briefly, then back at him. "Some endings are not stop buttons at all. Just pause buttons. And you may be surprised by what shows up when you press play again."

"I totally agree," he said. "I'm open to whatever. Anyway, that's where things are for me right now. Thanks for listening."

Gloria turned to Roger and Peaches next, who sat together across from her against the wall.

"Roger, I'm so glad you came back. It's good to see you here again. If you don't want to share, you don't have to, but if there *is* anything you'd like to talk about, we're all ears."

He smiled and nodded, locking eyes with Peaches briefly, who seemed to already know what he was going to say.

"I'm actually glad you suggested the sharing thing this time, because I have a situation at home I wanted to mention."

He paused and allowed his eyes to slowly reach Gloria's before his head dropped down to face the carpet in front of him.

"My mother's boyfriend has been a real asshole lately, more than usual. He knows I've got no choice but to put up with his shit, and my mom lets him get away with it all too, because he's helped us out so much financially the past two years."

"What kind of work does he do?" Gloria asked, intrigued as to how much Roger and his mother were actually getting from this relationship if it was also hurting them both so much.

"I don't really know. I've never seen his office, but my mom says he has a really good job, and because her take-home pay isn't that great at the restaurant, she says his help has really made a big difference for us. We live in a nice house and all that."

"What does he do to you, Roger?" Gloria asked. "Does he hurt you or your mother physically?"

"No, no, nothin' like that. He's just a dick. Like, he'll call me names and treat me like shit, and I mean, he sometimes does that to my mom, but not usually. Usually it's just me. My mom knows, but she doesn't wanna do anything about it. I think she figures things are going okay, so she tells me to stay away from him. I live with the guy though, so it's not easy to avoid him. Sometimes we're both just there, face to face, and things get heated quick."

"Is your mom's boyfriend white?" Peaches asked, and he nodded, but Gloria pushed forward, unsure why she'd asked that.

"Are you sure he hasn't physically abused your mom at all?"

Roger seemed to think about it for a moment, but then shook his head.

"I really don't think so. I mean, she's pretty good, you know? Like, happy? She just tries to make the best of the situation, and does seem to like the guy. His house is really nice too, a lot better than the place we used to rent out." He looked at Peaches briefly as he continued. "And he's not racist to me either, so don't think that. He calls me names and stuff, but he's never made me feel like it's racist. Just him showing off his power over me or whatever."

Silence followed, and the group looked at each other, unsure what to say. Finally, after about 15 seconds had passed, Ellen cleared her throat to get their attention.

"My husband used to hit me, when we first met," she said, and very quickly everyone turned to look at her.

Ellen's eyes were locked on Roger's.

"Before we were married. I made him get help. I made myself get help too. But no one ever knew. I never told anyone, except some friends in the support group I attended, and now you. I only mention it because your mom could be hiding something, Roger. I hope she isn't, and she may swear she isn't, but she might still not be telling you everything."

He nodded and looked away again, composing his thoughts as the others let him.

"I don't think he hurts her that way," he finally said. "Just verbally, but I know that's abuse too. I'll keep an eye out though."

Gloria gave him a few seconds more, to make sure he was finished, then thanked him for sharing. The others whispered their thank yous as well, and Gloria reminded him he could talk to her or anyone else there in the circle anytime in complete confidence if he wished. He nodded with a friendly smile.

"Okay, and Peaches?" Gloria asked. "What has life brought you? What would you like to share with us this evening?"

"Well, three things," she said. "I guess the biggest one to let you know about, though—and this is a secret, so don't tell anyone—is that my grandpa ran away from home last weekend."

They all let out a laugh of shock, unsure what she meant. As far as everyone knew, because none but Roger had ever met Alan, he was an older man. Running away from home didn't sound like the right phrase at all.

"He left a note for my grandma, said he needed some time away to think or whatever, and he's been gone for five days now. But he didn't do it out of the blue, either. Like, three weeks ago? He had an operation on his knee? And while they were fixing him, his heart stopped beating."

Peaches grew more and more excited, even to the point of smiling, as she continued.

"The week after that, he told us after dinner one night that he floated above his body during the operation."

"Oh my Lord," Krystal said from the far corner of the room.

"Very cool," Dennis added with a smile.

"So wait," Roger said, suddenly very intrigued. "He like, *saw himself* from above while they were bringing him back to life?"

Peaches smiled and nodded.

"What else did he say? What happened?"

"Well, my grandma got really upset when he started to tell us, and then they left pretty fast. I don't know if she didn't believe him or if she just didn't like hearing about it, but there was something really different about him when I saw him right after his operation, and then again at my house the next week. He just seemed much nicer, like, I'm not sure how to put it."

"So do you think it was a near-death experience?" Gloria asked, leaning forward with her hand to her head and her elbow on her knee. "Or maybe just a hallucination?"

"It was totally a near-death experience," Peaches said, still very excited to be telling them about it. "I looked it up. A lot of people have reported these kinds of things happening, and they can tell the doctors and nurses what was said in the room, which scientists say is impossible.

"Some people say that maybe their hearing is still working, and the brain imagines itself outside of the body as a kind of stress relief thing? But other people say no, that they actually saw things happening in the room too, things they couldn't have seen with their eyes closed and under sedention."

"I think you mean *sedation*," Corinne offered.

"Oh, right. Yeah, that. But he didn't tell us more, and now he's gone, so we don't know what to think."

"I heard somewhere once," Marty interjected, "that there's a very high divorce rate for people who have had an NDE, a near-death experience. Apparently, it can really change a person, affect them deeply, and totally mess up the dynamic they had with their spouse before it happened."

Peaches nodded thoughtfully, thinking she may have read that along the way too.

"Wow, Peaches," Gloria said. "That is quite something. So no one knows where he went?"

She shook her head no.

"My dad says he's probably at a hotel close by somewhere, but they called a bunch of places, and still haven't found him yet."

Gloria shook her head with a smile.

"How about that," she said, unsure what else to say, but then her voice changed as she remembered how Peaches started. "Wait. Didn't you say there were three things you wanted to say?"

"Oh, right. Well, two of the things were my grandpa. The running away part and the flying above his body. But I also wanted to tell you that my cousin and I are trying to solve the murder of the girl who died seventeen years ago, the one who everyone thinks my uncle killed."

Roger looked around after Peaches said this, noting the strange looks on everyone's faces. Gloria seemed to be eying Corinne, and she was the one who spoke first.

"Peaches," Corinne said, "maybe you should let that go. If the professionals never found anything seventeen years back, why get involved in it all now? Maybe it's best for you guys to just leave things as they are."

"Especially if your uncle *was* involved somehow," Marty added. "Maybe he didn't kill her, but there's always a chance you'll find out something else that will only upset things in your family."

Peaches looked like she was about to respond, but Ellen jumped in first.

"I totally disagree with them, Peaches," she said. "I mean, please don't do anything foolish or dangerous, but if someone really did hurt that poor girl, they ought to pay for it, whether they're your uncle or not. I don't believe in the death penalty anymore, but if a murderer is out there enjoying his life and freedom because he never got caught, you and your cousin should absolutely feel free to investigate it."

"Don't you think the authorities should handle it themselves, though?" Gloria asked her.

"Well sure, the authorities can get involved with an actual arrest, but why shouldn't Peaches and her cousin poke around a little if it's safe for them to do so?"

"Peaches," Krystal asked, "is your cousin who's helping you your Uncle Sam's *daughter,* by any chance?"

"Yep," Peaches said, a big smile on her face as she nodded.

Krystal and Ellen looked at each other now, an unspoken thought between them, and Ellen responded.

"Peaches, if she's your cousin, I'm guessing she's trying to prove his innocence then. I imagine you might be too?"

"Oh, totally," Peaches said, another big smile on her face.

"Yeah, but my point is, what will you do if you find out your uncle was actually involved? That he did in fact kill the girl?"

The smile on her face disappeared quickly, and Peaches looked down, thinking it out as the others all watched and waited. It seemed she hadn't even thought of that possibility, or what she would do.

"It isn't very easy telling on a family member," Gloria offered, "especially when something awful like murder is involved."

Peaches nodded, still not looking up, but a moment later, she seemed to have gotten the answer she wanted, and looked around as she told them.

"I would tell the police. If he really did that, he's probably living with the guilt anyway, and he would need to answer for it. I know it wouldn't be easy, but I also wouldn't be able to keep that secret if I found out."

As the group sat there in silence for a while, every single one of them began thinking through the exact same question: would *they* have the courage to report their own family member for something so serious?

It was a question none of them had ever considered before. None, that is, except Peaches, who had already been wrestling with a concern about more than just her Uncle Sam. Because of what she'd seen in the basement weeks earlier, and still not told anyone about, her greater fear was that one or both of her parents was involved in the murder somehow too.

Chapter 34

Roger kept pressing the channel-up button until he eventually came back to channel 2, annoyed he'd found nothing on TV once again. Even with their expensive cable package, he couldn't find anything halfway decent, and he wondered how humans had ever survived before cable.

He kicked off his sneakers and readjusted on the couch, happy to at least be alone for a while. That's when he heard the back door open up much too fast—his mother always wiggled it gently until it released—and he knew it meant the asshole was home.

Mercifully, RJ managed to spend an extra four minutes between the kitchen and bathroom before he wandered into the sunken den with his beer. He eyed Roger briefly before nestling into his La-Z-Boy recliner. Whether he was pissed or not before he got home—*one never knew*—Roger could tell right away that he was annoyed by the channel surfing.

"Just put something on," he finally said, his first words to Roger of the evening, and, Roger realized a moment later, the first in several days.

"I'm trying to," Roger said, as level and calm as possible.

More channel surfing, up, up, and up, before RJ retracted the footrest, marched over, and grabbed the remote out of Roger's hand. He instinctively turned on A&E, where *Duck Dynasty* was on.

"See? It's *not that hard, retard.*"

Roger shook his head a bit into the cushion. There was no way he'd lie there and watch those stupid old men say obnoxious things, funny or not. He stood up a minute later and poised himself ready to leave, but before he could, RJ stopped him.

"Hey. You should stay here and watch this show. Maybe you'd actually learn something."

"No thanks," Roger said, walking toward the kitchen.

"Hey! Stop! You sit your ass down and watch this."

"Are you kidding me? No. You can't make me watch it."

RJ stood up and ran over quicker than he ever had before, and Roger immediately smelled the liquor on his breath, something he must have had before coming home. He'd vastly underestimated RJ's mood.

"Listen to me. You sit your black ass down on that couch, little boy, or you're gonna be turning black *and blue* tonight."

He'd used the line before, so Roger simply smirked, figuring he was once again just being a jerk, but a second later, RJ slammed his fist hard into Roger's face, almost knocking him down.

"What the hell, man?"

"You do as I tell you in this house, *boy!*"

Roger was in pain, and though he knew he was half RJ's size and skinny as hell, he wanted to do something—anything—to punish the man for the violent attack. RJ, now blocking Roger's exit, was fully in command though, and Roger knew his choices were few and far between.

He held his face in pain, staring RJ down a while longer before he turned around and retreated to the couch.

If his mother was home, she wouldn't have been able to stop RJ from hitting him, or calming any of his other behavior, but she would've at least made sure Roger was allowed to leave the room.

He collapsed back in his place on the couch, and turned away from both RJ and the TV, resting his face, still stinging with pain, into the brown leather couch. He'd have to wait a few minutes now, and time his escape with RJ's mood. He wouldn't keep him there forever. He just wanted to show Roger who was boss, and Roger would have to let him.

On the TV, one of the Duck men said something funny, and RJ howled much too loudly. A minute later, the same man explained what a certain tool would help him do, and RJ turned to look at Roger.

"Hey pussy, listen up. This show is teaching you something."

Roger didn't move, so RJ just shook his head and took another drink. He was very quickly near the end of his beer, and wanted another, but didn't want to get up. Eyeing Roger again, he smiled.

"I'll make you a deal, fuckface. Go get me another beer, and you can pussy up to your bedroom or somewhere else out of my hair."

For the first time in minutes, Roger turned over to look at him, and as he caught RJ's gaze, they both knew he wanted to say, 'you have no hair', but instead, he stood up for the kitchen.

"Hey, boy. How 'bout you take the empty too?"

Roger spun back around to grab the beer bottle, and RJ farted loudly as he did.

Would be a nice time to have some poison, Roger thought, heading into the kitchen and shaking his head, eager to get away from him.

He rinsed out the bottle and put it in the recycling pail, then went for the fridge. By the time he got there, he'd forgotten what brand RJ was drinking, as three possibilities stared him in the face.

"Fuck."

He walked back to the recycling bin and looked down, grateful to see RJ's bottle on top of some water bottles. Knowing which one to grab, he went back and got it, screwing off the cap just as he reached RJ, who flashed him a fake face of gratitude, wiping the top of the bottle thoroughly before he put it to his mouth.

Roger once again turned to leave, but RJ grunted loudly as he swallowed his beer.

"And take those goddamn sneakers out of here with you."

Roger ran in and grabbed them before RJ could corner him again, then went up to his bedroom and locked the door, making a note to replace it with a much stronger lock as soon as possible.

Placing his sneakers down carefully beside his four other pairs, he climbed in bed and grabbed his phone, calling up his secret Facebook account and furiously typing out a new status message.

Fuckhead racist step-dud punched me in the face just now. If he wasn't ten times my size, I'd have thrown down with him right there, but then he kept me prisoner in our den till I watched his stupid Dick Dynasty show (aka old white racist homophobic assholes shooting ducks for the pleasure of other white racist homophobic assholes). Goddamn, I want that man dead! He nearly broke my fucking nose.

He posted the message, then got up to look in the mirror to make sure he didn't have a scar. It was a little red, but didn't look too bad. He sized himself up, chin raised high, pleased enough with what he saw.

Getting back in bed, he took his shorts and tee shirt off, turned on some music in his room, then eventually cued up some porn on his phone with his headphones on. Jerking off would help relax him, he decided.

Once he found a video he liked, he got hard and came quickly. Cleaning up just a few minutes after he started, he finally took off his headphones.

In the distance downstairs, he heard RJ and his mother yelling at each other. He lowered his music to listen then, while still cleaning himself off.

"Just don't fuckin' hit him. Okay?"

RJ must have told her what had happened, rare for him but pleasing to Roger nonetheless. She usually acted as if Roger exaggerated RJ's bad behavior. It was RJ's house and his rules, so she could only do so much if she wasn't gonna leave him.

Not married, they'd come close a couple times, and Roger always wondered why she stayed with him at all. They weren't poor, but RJ's house *was* very nice. Even so, his mother never seemed to care much about that. He figured she was too tired from her job and life to change anything.

As he sat there thinking it out, he was surprised to hear a knock on the door, stirring him alert.

"Honey, can I come in?"

He looked down at the wad of soiled tissues in his hand and shook his head with a sigh.

"Yeah. Just a minute."

He threw them in the trash, ran his hands under his bathroom sink, dried off, and then pulled on his shorts and leaned in close to the door.

"It's just you though, right?" he asked in a whisper.

"Yes." she said. "Just me."

Roger unlocked the door and let her in, then relocked the door behind them both. She looked annoyed at the maneuver, but tonight more than usual, she understood a little better.

"Where did he hit you?" she asked, seeing the red on his face and holding his head in her hands.

"It's fine. Don't worry."

She *should have said,* 'No, it's *not* fine. It's horrible. I'm furious with him, and I'm so sorry he did this to you.' Instead, her face shuffled through emotions quickly until she arrived at a strange kind of smile from God knows where.

"Okay, good. Good boy. So how was work?"

He looked confused, wondering why she always did this. How was she able to skip over entire passages of pain with a single leap? He decided it must be how she survived at all, how she managed to stay sane in such a crazy situation.

"It was fine," he said. Busier than usual, 'cause I worked the early evening shift, then went to the circle with Peaches."

"Oh *goooood,* she said, offering him an even bigger smile now. "So good tips then?"

"They were alright."

Roger was sure people would tip him more if he was white, but the money wasn't bad overall. Some people even seemed to give him more *because* he was black, as if they were trying to prove they weren't racist.

"Good. Good. Good," she repeated in a weird way. "Good."

As he looked at her with a brand new wave of annoyance, she took her cue and quickly kissed him good night, then left before any real conversation could take place.

Roger stared at the wall beside the door for a moment and shook his head, then locked the door behind her and undressed for a shower.

Chapter 35

Seventeen years earlier

"You know what? Lemme just run into the bathroom for a second. I'll be right back."

She got up quickly, grabbing her purse on the way to the bathroom, and locked herself in, relieved Sam hadn't stopped her on the way.

She moved back and forth in the small room like she was looking for something, and Sam just stared at the dark carpet while he waited, wondering with each passing minute why she was taking so long.

Kerry Ann had mentioned being nervous, but after seven long minutes, he was ready to put his shirt and shorts back on.

As if reading his mind, Kerry Ann opened the door just then, and looked at him with a sheepish grin, dressed now only in a bright red bra and matching panties.

"Well damn," he said, turning around on the bed.

"I'm sorry I took so long. I just bought these last week, and I hadn't taken the tags off yet. I was also making sure they fitted me okay. Do you like them?"

He stood up and walked around the bed, slowly sizing her up from just a few feet away.

"Yes, I do. Very much."

Kerry Ann blushed. She'd only ever been with two guys before, one her age, and one older, but she still hadn't lost her virginity.

Sam had promised he wasn't interested in pushing her in any way, but as he admired her body now, he was definitely looking forward to running his tongue up and down—*and inside*—any part of her she'd let him taste.

"I've never been in a motel room before," she confessed, breaking from his stare and trying to relax. "It's a little nicer than I thought it'd be, I guess, but still pretty small."

Sam smiled and looked around the room. He'd used the place before, and planned to many times again. Situated not far from the Vermont/New Hampshire border, it was the furthest place he could find to sneak away from Olivia without anyone in town catching him in the act. No one from Ludlow worked over this way either, as far as he knew.

"It's alright," he said. "Serves its purpose. Just gotta be careful because of your age is all."

"I thought you said 16 was okay?"

"It is, but these places, motels and whatever, require you to be a little older. They never check, but that's why I asked you to wait till I got the room. It's fine though, don't worry."

She looked concerned, especially by his use of the phrase 'never check', which seemed to indicate he brought a lot of young girls there. She smiled quickly despite her feelings, then nodded, her arms still crossed awkwardly in front of her.

"You really look amazing," he said, eyeing her up and down, and then pulling her arms softly away from her so he could see her body better.

She looked down shyly, spotting his hard cock beneath his boxer briefs.

"So no sex," she announced. "Just, like, other stuff."

"I know, it's cool," he said. "Why don't you come over here by the bed though, so we can get more comfortable?"

He walked her over, and she sat down next to him, but Sam was beginning to feel uneasy about her anxiety, especially considering how little she looked, how much shorter she was than him. He'd cheated on Olivia four times since they'd been married, but never with anyone so young. When *he* was Kerry Ann's age, he hadn't done much more than kissing and heavy petting.

Almost 27, Sam was no old man, but he was still significantly older than Kerry Ann. Worst of all, her apprehension was contagious, and he began to worry he might even break her somehow if he touched her too hard.

"So what do you want to do?" she asked, not looking at him now, even after he turned to face her.

Jesus. She's scared of me.

He turned away again and sighed, then decided to at least get comfortable. He got into bed and propped two pillows up behind him, his legs flat behind her. Kerry Ann watched him move, but couldn't understand his face. *Why is he looking at me like that?*

"Is something wrong?" she asked.

"No, not at all. I just—" He paused, thinking of the right words. "I just don't want to push you into doing anything, you know? I'm a horny bastard, no doubt about it, but I'm not a *total* asshole, so if you don't feel comfortable with me, neither of us are gonna enjoy this too much."

Her face changed almost instantly. She smiled and looked much more relaxed all of a sudden, and within just a few seconds, she had climbed on top of him. Practically purring once she felt his hard cock beneath her pussy, she really wanted to suck him off.

She leaned her head down first, waiting until he kissed her. Her lips were soft and small. Too small, he decided, as she'd not yet learned the fine art of kissing. He could teach her, he was sure he could, but whether or not to *tell her* she wasn't doing it right was still the question.

She leaned back after a couple more minutes, and again enjoyed the feel of his hard cock below her, rubbing herself back and forth on it for their mutual pleasure.

"You like that, baby?" she asked, reciting a phrase from an online porn video she'd watched that morning to prepare.

"Mm-hm," he said.

Kerry Ann smiled and took off her bra, and Sam took a moment to admire her tits for a while before feeling them. She cooed at his touch, whether sincere or not he didn't care, and a moment later, he had as much of her left breast in his mouth as he could, tonguing it while his hand reached down and rubbed her pussy through her panties.

302

A knock on the door then, and they both jumped up right away in bed.

"This room is taken!" Sam yelled.

"Oh, sorry. I'm looking for Monica," a man's voice said.

"Do I sound like a fucking Monica to you?!" he barked back, angry at the surprise visitor.

"Sorry dude," he said, and Sam could see the guy's shadow move away beyond the closed curtains.

"Fucking idiot," Sam said.

He turned around and saw Kerry Ann sitting on the other side of the bed now, her back to him.

"It's okay," he said. "He's gone."

She nodded without turning around, then grabbed her bra and went for the bathroom. Sam heard her lock the door right away.

"Jesus," he whispered to himself, shaking his head. "Are you okay in there?" he called in, pissed she'd disappeared once again.

"Yeah," she answered right away. "But I should go. I don't think motels are for me."

Fuck!

He shook his head at her, even though she couldn't see him, then looked back at the door to the room with disgust, pissed the stranger had fucked this up for him.

Inside the bathroom, he could already hear her getting dressed.

"Listen, I paid for the room. I have it till 4. Just c'mon out and hang with me for a while."

Silence. More shuffling as before, but this time much quicker.

He put his hands through his hair as he waited. A minute later, Kerry Ann opened the bathroom door and moved right away toward the front of the motel room. Seeing Sam's face on her way there, she paused briefly by the door to apologize, unlocking it as she spoke.

"Look, I'm sorry. You seem sweet. I just don't want to be here anymore. I don't feel comfortable."

She went for the knob.

"Wait. Just wait, okay? At least let me get my clothes on to drive you back to Ludlow."

"I have a friend waiting for me outside. She said she'd hang out for a while in case I needed her."

Sam's face changed right away, and his temper shot up. She was treating him like some sort of criminal.

"You *told her* about me?"

"No," she said, shaking her head. "Well, I mean, yeah, but not your name or anything. Look, I'll talk to you soon."

She was outside with the door shut behind her before he even had a chance to reply.

He listened to her footsteps running away, and once he felt sure she was gone, he slammed his fist down hard on the bed.

"Never again. Never fucking again," he muttered. "No little girl is gonna fuck up my day like that. Little fucking bitch. No fucking way am I letting her do that to me again."

Two blocks away, Kerry Ann's friend Patty looked up nervously behind the wheel as Kerry Ann jogged toward the car.

"What happened? Are you okay? Did he hurt you?"

"No, everything's fine. I'll tell you after. Just go. Drive. Now!"

Patty shook her head and pulled away quickly, and Kerry Ann eyed the motel nervously one last time as they drove off back toward Ludlow.

Chapter 36

Doctor Finny's office was packed all day Tuesday, much more crowded than Haley had ever seen it before. He'd even brought out extra folding chairs from the closet in the back before she got in that morning, and was there at the door to greet her as well.

She was sure, in fact, that he must have been waiting patiently near the window watching out for her. Maybe even keeping an eye out for her car, just so he'd know when she was about to park and grab her coffee down the block.

"A busy office is a happy office," he'd said only seconds after greeting her with a quick good morning. "And a busy waiting room always makes people feel safer, that the staff of doctors on call will give them the very best treatment possible."

She'd opted to simply nod and smile when he said this, deciding any reminder that he was the only doctor on staff was pointless and rude, at least enough to put him in a bad mood.

The entire day was filled with patients though. Patients in, patients out, and even patients on the phone. What brought this on, she wondered, and why had so many new people started coming in on the very same day? Had another doctor's office closed nearby?

Haley tried several times throughout the day to ask Dr. Finny, but he was always too busy. Finally around 5:30, just after the last patient paid his copay and left, Haley breathed a huge sigh of relief.

"Wow," she said, watching as Dr. Finny approached her eagerly with a huge smile. "What happened today? Where did all those people even come from? You don't seem surprised by it."

"I put an advertisement in the *Rutland Herald*. It ran yesterday for the first time."

"One ad brought in that many people?" she asked in shock.

He walked over to the chairs in the waiting room and found the newest edition of the *Herald* folded in half beneath the other magazines he kept there. He sat down and paged through it until he found it, then stood up to show her, beaming with pride as she read it out loud.

"Want to die tomorrow? No? Then get a checkup today!"

It was followed by his name, phone number, and picture, plus a small blurb welcoming walk-ins and all insurance plans. Haley couldn't help but smirk as she read it.

"I didn't guarantee they wouldn't still die today, but I guess it worked well just the same. People who hadn't been to a doctor in years came in for a checkup. I'm guessing many of them made appointments to come back in six months too as I suggested?"

Haley nodded, quickly calling up their schedule for January and February.

"Yeah, we're already looking busy for January, even though that's usually your slowest month. And I have appointments lined up for you for the next three weeks too."

Dr. Finny, normally quite calm, could barely contain his excitement, and as he shook his fist in the air, barely waist high, Haley couldn't help but laugh at him.

At home an hour later, she pulled up the last of her photo project for Stephanie's wedding. She needed to give them one last run-through, making sure to crop and color correct anything that still needed her attention, but also now to check for that woman's face anywhere too.

If there was anything in those pictures that proved someone had done something bad to Mr. Caraway, so far she'd missed it, but maybe if the mysterious woman was in the photos somewhere, she could piece together where she was and when, and figure out who the hell she was.

After just a few minutes though, Haley was once again positive the woman was not at the church *or* the reception, at least not as an invited guest. Not a single picture showed her there, so the security camera at the catering hall remained her only lead.

Frustrated and annoyed, Haley closed out the folder of pictures and opened up her Facebook. Without thinking, she found herself calling up Sam's page, which he'd barely updated in months.

Curiosity got the better of her then, and she began scrolling through his feed just to make sure she didn't see anything incendiary or incriminating.

After a few minutes of mindless scrolling, she went back to the top to check out his friends list, something she'd done only once before at least two years earlier. This time she stopped when she saw Sam's ex-girlfriend's page, and was alarmed to see no updates at all since December.

Jumping over to Instagram next, she called up the woman's account on there, and was once again shocked to see that she hadn't updated it since the middle of December, some seven months earlier. *What the hell? How could she just completely disappear from social media?*

A sudden knock on the door made her jump in her seat. Her mother never knocked; she'd just turn the knob to enter on her own, or yell for Haley to unlock it and let her in.

"Yes?"

"Hey, it's Peaches."

"Peaches? What are you—"

She went over and unlocked the door, letting Peaches in and then relocking the door quickly. She ran over and turned her radio on right away too, so her mother couldn't listen in.

"What's up? How'd you get over here?"

"I walked. It's nice out."

"Oh. Okay. Cool. Hey, listen, as long as you're here, check this out. I was just looking at my dad's Facebook, and then I went over to his ex-girlfriend's?"

"Uh-huh?"

"And there are like, *no* new posts from her on either her Facebook or her Instagram since last December. Isn't that weird? Like, I was never friends with her or anything, but I would still look now and then, just to see if she had posted any pictures of my dad? And she updated her feed really often before December too."

"Was she old?" Peaches asked. "Maybe she died."

Haley just looked at her for a moment, wondering if she was dumb or really that aloof, deciding quickly on the latter.

"No, she wasn't old, Peaches. She was younger than my dad. I'm serious. This is freaking me out now. How could she just totally disappear?"

"Well, she may be taking a social media break, but I agree, seven months with nothing is a really long time. What's her full name?"

Peaches pulled out her phone, ready to look her up.

Haley pointed to her computer screen, and Peaches noted it before typing away quickly on her phone.

"She lived in Las Vegas," Haley told her, "and then moved back up to Ogden, Utah where she was from. At least that's what my dad said."

Peaches kicked off her sneakers and leapt up onto Haley's bed, making herself comfortable with the pillows.

For the next two minutes, Haley just watched as Peaches made all sorts of faces as she typed and scrolled away through her phone. She bit her bottom lip and stuck her tongue out too, and seemed to be hitting dead ends along the way as she searched the internet for Sam's ex-girlfriend.

Haley looked through the wedding photos some more as she waited for her to finish.

"Okay," Peaches finally announced. "I found two people your dad is following on Instagram who *might* be her, but both accounts are private. One is a picture of a cat, and the name is different, but it could be a fake name or whatever, and the profile on the other one shows a 1-800 number, and the woman in the picture looks like a slut."

Haley sat down on the side of the bed and grabbed the phone from Peaches to look. A cat and a hooker were hardly the leads she was hoping for, especially since her father's ex-girlfriend was a Mormon and allergic to cats. She'd certainly never approve of sex workers, let alone be one herself.

"Ugh. Peaches, this is crazy. How could she just disappear? Doesn't that worry you? She and my dad supposedly break up and he moves back here after all these years, but now she's nowhere to be found?"

"Why don't you just ask him? Uncle Sam wouldn't mind you bringing her up, right? And if he acts weird, you'll know he might be hiding something from you."

Haley nodded. Thinking such awful things about her father was starting to give her a stomachache, and she regretted even getting this far.

They sat there in silence as Peaches already started playing a game on her phone. *Another dead end.* Haley went back to her computer, clicking forward through a few more images, her heart already out of it.

"Ooh, are those the pictures from the wedding? Haley, they look amazing. Can I see?"

Haley scrolled through them slowly as Peaches came over to ooh and ahh from behind her.

"How come there are none of you?" Peaches asked, and this time, instead of getting annoyed, Haley just smiled.

"Well, because I wasn't hired to take selfies, silly. They paid me to take pictures of the wedding and reception. See this one here? This guy was in my way like two seconds before I took the shot. He looked over his shoulder, saw me there with my camera, then dodged sideways. That's why he has that funny look on his face.

"And that woman in the back? That's Meredith, the catering manager. She helped me out so much that day. Everyone at the reception loved her. She went around yelling at the waiters to get drink orders in, so people wouldn't have to wait on line at the bar in the lobby."

"Sounds like fun," Peaches said, smiling at all the happy people she saw in the photos. "And that cake looks amazing."

Haley laughed, remembering the cake as much as the events of the night itself. What had started with mounting stress at the church had calmed to a mostly enjoyable afternoon, and despite the small check RJ Tarisi gave her at the wake, it was still a good amount of money.

She thought about creating an ad like Dr. Finny had, something small but powerful to attract more business, but then she remembered the problem she'd run into with something like that. For the first time in her life, Haley realized her last name was a proven liability, a serious detriment to her hopes for notoriety, at least in that part of Vermont.

"I would have stolen the cake," Peaches announced confidently, and Haley smiled at her. "You should have said you wanted to take a few pictures of it outside, and then hidden it in your trunk."

Haley laughed now, but her face quickly shifted into shock.

"Or maybe just eaten the whole thing quick, so there'd be no evidence," Peaches said as she laughed, stopping once she saw Haley's face. "Oh my God, what's wrong? What is it?"

"The trunk," Haley said. "Holy shit, the trunk."

Peaches looked scared now.

"Okay? What about it?"

Haley didn't answer right away, just blinked a lot of times and stood up.

"Peaches, I totally forgot I took a few pictures of the church with my smaller point-and-shoot camera before the wedding that day. There might be something on there that can help me find this woman."

"Your dad's girlfriend?"

"What? No."

Haley caught Peaches up on her trip to the catering hall and the woman she spotted on the camera, then ran out into the hall and down the stairs as fast as she could, grabbing her car keys as she opened the front door.

"Hey," Olivia called from the couch. "I think Peaches came by before looking for—" but Haley never heard the rest of it.

She popped her trunk and searched around before she found it, then closed the trunk and ran back in, holding the small camera in her hands like it was a long-forgotten treasure, a precious heirloom representing all that was wise and good in the world.

Breathless with her bedroom door once again closed and locked behind her, Haley raised the point-and-shoot camera triumphantly toward Peaches.

"*Oookay,*" Peaches offered with a smile, still not understanding.

"Peaches, this could be the missing piece to everything! I have to look at these pictures right away!"

"Okay, cool," Peaches said, already returning to her phone. It chimed with what sounded like two new texts, and Haley wondered if it was Roger.

"Who was that?" Haley asked, still plugging the memory card into her computer and trying to sound nonchalant.

She waited impatiently as Peaches texted the person back without responding. At least 30 seconds passed before Peaches finally looked up absent-mindedly and stared at Haley, trying to remember her question.

"Oh, that was Erika. She wants to borrow my iPad for a camping trip. I told her she could borrow it as long as she wanted, and she seemed really happy, but I don't think she knows it stopped working a few months ago. I'm not gonna tell her. I still think the 1-800 slut account is your dad's girlfriend, by the way. Did you look at it yet?"

"What? No way. My dad would never—"

But Haley went back to the profile anyway, the seed of doubt diffusing through her brain. The account was private, and the woman's profile picture taken from a distance, but Haley was sure it couldn't be Kim. Even so—*just in case*—she requested to follow.

Opening the folder containing the point-and-shoot pictures, Haley was annoyed to see there were only five photos. She'd hoped she'd taken many more that morning. She selected all the files and clicked them open, and a second later, five new windows opened up on her screen.

Staring back and forth at each photo, she didn't see anything unusual, and no glimpses of the mysterious woman.

"Damn. I was really hoping this would—*oh my God!*"

Peaches sat up straight in Haley's bed, dropping her phone and looking concerned.

"What is it?" she asked, but Haley didn't answer.

Peaches got up and walked over to the screen, watching as Haley zoomed in on three of the pictures in succession, her face still stuck in stunned silence.

"Haley, who is that?" she asked, leaning in.

Haley finally looked at her with a deep sigh before returning to the screen and pointing.

"That guy there? That's your dad's boss, RJ Tarisi. He's the groom's uncle. And the woman in the car? I don't know who she is yet, but she's definitely the same woman who snuck into the men's bathroom at the catering hall that night, the place where Mr. Caraway was found dead a few minutes later."

"She looks familiar," Peaches said, and Haley spun around in her chair.

"What?! You know her?!"

"No, but I think I must've seen her in town or something. Maybe at The Hatchery."

"Peaches, I need to find out who this is. I think she and your dad's boss may have murdered Mr. Caraway."

Chapter 37

Seventeen Years Earlier

The school bell rang at the end of the last class, and Kerry Ann packed her notebook away as she and her friends got up to leave.

It had been at least a month since she'd seen Sam at the motel, and she was finally starting to feel more relaxed about the whole thing, if not completely at ease yet about Sam himself. The new school year helped distract her from everything that happened that summer too.

Once the girls reached the parking lot, Kerry Ann was quickly shocked to see Sam standing out there waiting for her. Her friends looked back and forth between the two of them nervously, but Sam just stood by his truck with a goofy smile on his face and a shopping bag clutched in both hands.

"God, not this guy again," Patty said.

"Shh. Don't let him hear you," Kerry Ann said. "Stay here. I'll be right back."

They watched suspiciously as she walked over to meet him.

"I'm sorry to bug you," he said. "Hey, that's a really pretty outfit. I just felt really bad about what happened, and I wanted to make it up to you."

"No, you don't have to. It's okay."

He handed her the bag anyway and smiled.

"Look, it's the least I can do. I could tell you got spooked by that asshole who knocked on the door, and I thought a lot about it, and at your age, well, that must have really unnerved you. Anyway. Take it. Please."

"What is it?" she asked, finally looking inside the bag past the tissue paper covering the gift. "Oh my God. What? Is this a cell phone?" She took the box out and looked it over. "Holy shit. This is a new one too."

"Yeah. That's the newest one Nokia they had. The guy I got it from says it's much better than the old ones. It's got an extra large

2.4-inch screen, a calculator, and a stopwatch built in there too. I'll take care of the billing for you too. Your parents might get weird with that kinda thing, so don't tell 'em it's from me."

"Oh my God. This must have cost you—"

"An entire paycheck?" he asked with a laugh. "Yeah, but it's alright. I felt really bad about what happened, and I thought you'd like this."

"Yeah, but this is *really* expensive."

"Hey, you're worth every penny. And listen, my number is in the bag. You know, just in case you lost it since last time? I'd love to see you again too, so call me when you get that set up, okay?"

Kerry Ann blushed and nodded, then watched as Sam got in his truck and pulled away, waving at her as he did.

Chapter 38

On Saturday the 29th of July, the entire family except for Sam—*who most didn't consider part of the family anyway*—arrived at Alan and Phyllis's house to convene a new plan regarding Alan.

"It's been *three weeks* since he disappeared, and I'm worried sick," Phyllis announced. "This has gone on far too long. We need to do more."

They all sat around her large living room looking much more concerned than they previously were, mostly due to the hysterical behavior of their matriarch.

If Lenny and Olivia had first written off their father's disappearance as a strange, maybe even humorous distraction, the three long weeks coupled with Phyllis's escalating emotional instability had made them that much more uncomfortable.

"The police have done nothing, the state has done nothing, and winter is approaching quickly."

Lenny felt a big laugh come up unexpectedly at her words.

"Mom, c'mon now," Olivia tried to interrupt, but Phyllis plowed on.

"No. I mean it. August starts next week, and the first snow last year was in November. If we wait too long, God knows what could happen to him."

Caroline rolled her eyes at Lenny, but he just shook his head in response, his smile fading fast. Phyllis wasn't making any sense, and though they all knew it, it was also becoming abundantly clear they *did* need to do more to find Alan, if for no other reason than to keep Phyllis from drowning herself in merlot.

The girls all looked worried, but Lenny guessed Haley was more concerned about her grandmother than a freak August heat wave giving her grandfather frostbite in some posh hotel room somewhere.

"They refuse to issue a silver alert because he left of his own volition, and because he took all his medicine with him, but how long will that supply last him, I wonder? When will he run out of his pills and die?"

"Okay, stop it," Lenny said, cutting her short much more forcefully than he'd intended. "You need to just calm down already. This is getting silly. Dad was on two pills for the pain in his knee, which the doctor assured us should be much better now anyway, and beyond that, all he was taking was some over-the-counter stuff for arthritis, and a low dose aspirin. The man is not suffering with dementia or any number of other serious diseases, it's only July 29th for crying out loud, and we all need to think this out clearly and calmly if we're gonna find him."

Phyllis, at first angry at Lenny for interrupting her, slowly relaxed as he spoke, then made her way over to the kitchen to refill her wine glass by the time he had finished.

"What about the Vermont missing people page on Facebook?" Erika asked. "Didn't we get anything from that?"

"That goddamn page sends out twelve fucking alerts every day!" Phyllis shouted back, rejoining them and swallowing the last of a cookie she'd shoved in her mouth. "Some damn kid goes out playing videogames with his friends, and the family reports him missing. It's nonsense! They only shared your grandfather's picture twice, and Nancy Hensley's son says only a hundred people shared it beyond your parents and aunt. No foul play suspected?! Are you fucking kidding me?!"

Erika looked frightened.

"I'm sorry, dear," Phyllis added, rubbing Erika's shoulder briefly, though far too hard, as she found her seat again. "It's just impossible to get any goddamn help from anyone, and I'm running out of choices!"

"What hotels have we called so far, Mom?" Olivia asked, watching as Erika rubbed her now-sore shoulder. "Where's the list? Maybe we should call a few more."

They watched as Phyllis drank her wine quietly, shaking her head. Exchanging another look, Caroline and Lenny were both ready to ask Livi's question again, but Phyllis had a coughing fit then, and pointed over toward the back of the kitchen.

"The list is back there by the toaster. We've called them all. Every one of them within fifty square miles. Every ski resort, hotel, Air B&B, and shitty motel between Amherst and Montreal."

She made a point of looking at Caroline after she said this, as if to say, 'yes, even that one'. Even under such extreme stress, Phyllis was glad to lord something over her.

"Okay, let's just think this out," Olivia said, taking charge and pulling up the calendar on her phone. "He left on Sunday the 9th, and today is the 29th, so that's—" She paused as she did the math. "21 nights at a hotel room. With a senior discount, we'll just say $2100, not including food, which would be, what? Another $20 a day easy?" she asked, looking around.

Lenny pulled out his phone now too, and he did the math for them all on his calculator.

"That's another $420, so you're looking at $2500, which is half the cash we think he had with him. That means he *could, in theory,* be gone for another three weeks, but—"

He paused, holding out his hand as Phyllis started looking worried again.

"He'll want to buy aspirin and other crap too, so maybe only two more weeks. At most."

"Have you tried calling Benjie?" Caroline asked Phyllis, who shot back a death stare in return.

"Yes," Lenny said, answering for his mother. "She called Uncle Benjie and everyone else down in New York right away."

Something in the glare Caroline offered back at him told Lenny she was feeling the strain of their relationship every bit as much as he was.

"Okay," Olivia said, once again ready to run the meeting. "Haley, Erika, and Peaches, I need you to go on a little social media blitz. Post your grandfather's picture on all the local Facebook pages and groups you can find. Okemo, Killington, the Ludlow Fire Department, Lake Rescue, Lake Pauline, the Green Mountain

Sugar House, all of them. Ask people to share the picture along with his details and how long he's been gone. Actually, Haley? You're good with that spelling and grammar crap. Can you write something like that up and then share it with the girls to send out?"

"There's a recent picture of your grandfather in a small frame on the front wall near the stairs," Phyllis offered, pointing over at it, and Olivia smiled at Lenny first and then at her.

"We have some pictures from Erika's graduation party that Haley took, Mom. Already digitized and everything."

"Okay, good."

"Lenny, Caroline, maybe you could think of some places Dad likes to go to in the area, favorite restaurants and antique stores, and stop in with his picture, see if anyone's seen him recently?"

"Great idea, Livi," Lenny said.

"And I'll go through the list of hotels with Mom, make sure we haven't missed any, and call a bunch of them back. I don't know if he's still in Vermont, but we'll try them anyway. Oh, and Haley, can you also make a surprise visit to your father? I'd like you to make sure he's not harboring Grandpa over there. Because if he is, I'll want to know, just so I can get Grandpa to a safe distance before I blow up the house."

Everyone laughed at this, even Haley.

"Mom," Olivia added, "I promise you we'll find him soon, if he doesn't just show up on his own first."

"Thank you," Phyllis said. "Thank you, all. Alan is a strong man, and I know he can take care of himself, but it's been three weeks now, and I'll just rest much easier if I know where he is. I don't even need to know *where* he is, as long as you find him and make sure he's alright."

A minute or two passed then as the girls typed away on their phones, and Lenny and Caroline stepped away to talk.

"Listen," Lenny said to her softly, so no one else could hear. "Something's going on with you and me, and we should probably talk about it. Not here, though. Maybe at home later on?"

Caroline was surprised to feel tears in her eyes as she nodded, looking away.

"Okay," she said with a sniffle.

"There's some crap at work too, a thing with Tarisi and his secretary. I'll tell you about it later."

He returned to the living room right away, not wanting to get into it any further, and Caroline went off to the bathroom to blow her nose.

"I'd just like to say," Phyllis called out to the room. She tried to stand up, but fell back down again right away. "I love my family very much. Every thingle one of you. And when Alan ith back, we thould all have a big party here to thelebrate."

The girls barely glanced up from their phones with nervous smiles, but Lenny and Olivia looked at each other with alarm.

"The latht three weeths have been very, very thrange for me to thay the leatht," she continued, suddenly standing up straight and shaking her head, "but when you really look at thith all carefully, I mean really, really carefully. Really genuinely, clearly, and clairvoyantly, you can thee how muth family meanth to you. To everyone, and to everything. Everywhere. You can thee how important it ith to thay cloth to one anotha."

"Okay, Mom," Lenny said with a nervous laugh. "Maybe you should lay off the wine for a few hours."

"Oh no, I'm fine, I'm fine."

"Well, how 'bout something to eat, Mom," Olivia tried. "Want me to make you something here, or you can come back to my house for a while?"

"No, no, no. I ate already. I juth had a cookie."

"Ooh, where are the cookies?" Peaches asked, sitting up and scanning the kitchen from her seat on the couch.

"Your motha hath thum there in her purth, dear," Phyllis said, her head drooping unnaturally as she pointed over toward the kitchen island.

They all looked and saw Caroline's purse propped wide open beside the bottle of red wine.

Peaches stood up and walked over to get one, and Olivia gasped loudly in a near shriek.

"Oh my God," she said.

"What is it?" Lenny asked.

"Peaches!" Olivia yelled, jumping up quickly and chasing after her. "Stay *away* from that purse!"

"Why?" she asked, looking back sadly as Olivia barely beat her to the kitchen to grab the purse.

Olivia closed the Ziploc bag sticking out from the top, and pushed it down a bit out of view. Looking up at Lenny, he suddenly realized what had happened. His eyes grew wide as he reached over and gently took the glass of wine from his mother's hand, and put it down softly on the coffee table.

"Hey, Mom? Why don't we go for a little walk?" he said, taking her by the hand.

"Where are we going?" Phyllis asked as they began walking, already staring back longingly at her glass of wine.

"Just upstairs to lie down."

As everyone watched them, the phone suddenly rang out, and everyone froze before Olivia sprinted over to pick it up.

"Hello? Oh, hi Mrs. Hensley. No, she's—she's not available right now. No, nothing yet. Yeah. Okay. Oh, that's very sweet of you. You shouldn't have. Yeah, maybe just bring them by tomorrow though, okay? Not today. Okay, great. Thank you so much. Bye now."

She hung up the kitchen phone and turned back to them all.

"Mrs. Hensley made lasagna. For all of us, it sounds like. I told her tomorrow would be better."

Caroline appeared just then and stopped in her tracks as she watched Olivia clap her hands together and welcome her back. She didn't seem to understand what was happening until Livi waved to her, holding up the Ziploc bag from Caroline's purse.

"My mom *loved* your cookies," she said sarcastically, a twisted smile crossing her face as she watched the look of supreme horror arrive on Caroline's.

At this point, everyone but Phyllis and Peaches understood what had happened, and Lenny just grinned back at them as he led his mother up the stairs. Haley watched them go up with a quiet groan, annoyed she lost her chance to tell him about the new pictures and the mystery woman. She joined Erika and Peaches in the kitchen, where the two of them were trying to look into Caroline's purse, but Olivia kept it away from them all.

"Wait, are those mine?" Erika asked, and Caroline swooped in and took back her bag from Olivia.

"No, they are not *yours*. I took them from a client last week, someone like you who shouldn't have had them anyway, and I'll take any from you *too* if you have some. These things are dangerous if you don't know who made them."

"Caroline," Olivia said, much more seriously than before, "please tell me my mother will be okay."

"Yes, I think so," Caroline whispered, looking guilty. "Looks like she only ate one, and—" She paused, looking away. "These aren't too strong."

Erika and Haley laughed, although Caroline and Olivia barely snickered, trying to remain serious in the presence of the kids.

"Girls, you go home now," Olivia said, shooing them out of the kitchen. "And get on all that social media stuff. Haley, you'll send them the copy?"

Haley nodded, and the three of them left together.

"I should go too," Caroline said, closing her purse and turning around quickly for the door.

"When are you gonna tell Lenny?" Olivia called after her.

Caroline stopped and looked back at her confused.

"Tell him about what?" she asked.

"About that pregnancy stick in your purse."

Chapter 39

Later that night, Haley fidgeted this way and that on the couch in her living room, biting her nails, tapping her feet, and flipping through TV channels much faster than she could see what was on.

She'd already resigned herself to not watching anything at all, but flashing through the choices relaxed her a bit anyway, and gave her something to do as she waited for the doorbell to ring.

I need this, she told herself, and the plan she'd hatched may have been her last hope for sanity anyway. Either that or some unconscious proof she'd gone insane after all.

A car door stirred her up from the couch, and she pressed the off button four times before the television finally went dark. Taking a deep breath, she stood in place and waited for the doorbell. When it finally rang, she walked over as slowly as she could, then opened it up.

"Hello," Roger said, offering her a big smile.

He held the box of pizza out as Haley invited him in.

"I'm not hungry, actually," she said, blushing and taking the box inside to put it on the kitchen counter. "I just wanted to see you. So um, you know, I didn't want to make it weird by asking you out, so I drove past the pizzeria earlier and looked out for your car from down the street to make sure you were working tonight. And then I timed the delivery for what I figured would probably be the very end of your shift."

"Wow," he said, processing all the information she'd just dumped on him. "Okay."

Roger's eyes scanned the empty wall to his right, still computing everything she'd told him. Haley couldn't tell if he was impressed or thoroughly freaked out, already concerned she'd achieved the latter.

"I'm sorry," she said. "I know this is weird. I just felt strange asking Peaches to set something up, and I thought maybe this would be easier. For me, at least. My mom's staying with my grandma tonight, so it seemed like a good chance for us to just

322

hang out and talk. I mean, if you want to. Or if not, I understand. Whatever. Oh, and here's the money for the pizza."

Roger pocketed the cash and shook his head with a smile as he thought out his words, finally looking at her intensely.

"No one's ever done this before," he said.

"I'm sorry. I'm a total weirdo. I shouldn't have been so crazy about all this. It's just, I thought that maybe—"

"No, it's cool. I'm happy," he said, smiling. "I meant no one's ever gone through this much trouble for me before. It's really cool, actually. Crazy, yeah, but also really cool."

She blushed again and nodded, then pointed the way into the living room where they sat down next to each other on the love seat. It'd been over a year since Haley had gone out on a real date, and at least five months for Roger as well, though neither of them knew that.

To Roger, Haley was a hot girl with a super sweet personality, the perfect mix as far as he was concerned. He found it both intense and alluring that she'd surprised him like this too. And to Haley, Roger was a sexy, funny guy with a mysterious air about him she really found attractive. His depth begged her for at least a round-trip voyage.

"I don't know what to say," he said with a laugh, breaking the awkward silence, and Haley laughed and nodded as well.

"Well," she said, "tell me about yourself. How's life? How'd you end up here? I know you didn't go to my school, but you seem to live nearby, right? Or am I just completely forgetting seeing you at Green Mountain?"

"No, you're right. I went to high school in Stamford. In Connecticut. Grew up there. Kept my nose down and stayed out of other people's business. After my mom and dad got divorced a few years ago, we moved up to Northampton, Massachusetts, then Brattleboro, and now here. Right now we're living at my mom's boyfriend's house up in Stockbridge. The only reason I work in Ludlow is 'cause of Peaches. She's really cool. Weird as fuck sometimes, but super cool."

"I still can't believe I thought you two were dating. I'm sorry about that."

"No, I understand. I mean, she's funny and cute, but not my type anyway, besides the age difference."

"Oh? What's your type?" Haley asked, feeling bold.

"I guess it depends. Someone sweet and pretty. I dunno."

"Cool," she said, barely smiling as she looked away, scared to ask the next question on her mind, whether or not she fit into that type for him. As great as their connection seemed to be, she still wasn't sure.

"I actually really wanna kiss you right now," he said, and she turned back immediately, a shocked smile on her face.

"What? Really?" she asked, as if he was only joking.

"Really," he said. "May I?"

Haley nodded, and they each leaned in, soon locked in a deeply romantic kiss. It was everything she had hoped for, having built it up in her head more and more over the past eight weeks since the day they'd first met at Dr. Finny's office.

His tongue met hers with an eager explosion of saliva and passion, and his hands held her head and neck gently as they moved back and forth against the cushioned couch.

She let her body fall into the couch as he began taking control, scared to touch more of her than he should, but wanting to enjoy every inch of her with his hands and tongue just the same.

Finally, after several minutes of this, she pulled away, her lips aching with the pain of leaving his, and she stared into his eyes.

"Wanna go upstairs?"

Now it was his turn to nod wordlessly, still breathless from their kiss. She took his hand and led him around the couches and toward the stairs. With each step they took together, Roger marveled at his luck. With each new stair they climbed, Haley marveled at her joy.

##

Over at her house a few miles away, Phyllis appeared at the bottom of the stairs looking thoroughly confused and completely exhausted. Olivia was on the couch staring at her phone, the muted TV sending out flashes of jarring light all around the otherwise dark downstairs area.

"What time is it?" Phyllis asked, and Olivia finally looked up and saw her standing there like an apparition.

Phyllis's face looked gaunt and ancient, and between her ivory silk nightgown and the pulsing light around her, she really did seem like some sort of an angel. *From Hell,* Olivia thought, smiling darkly as she looked at her phone again.

"Quarter after 11," she said.

Phyllis raised her eyebrows as high as she could, as if willing her eyelids into better vision, then took the final two steps into the open space, ready to join the living once more.

She shuffled toward the kitchen in her soft, pink slippers, pausing just long enough to eye the glass of red wine in the living room, not far from where Olivia was sprawled out like some sort of a wild animal.

"Are you drinking my wine?" Phyllis asked.

Olivia glanced at the glass and then back to her phone.

"Nope. That's yours from before. You feeling better?"

Phyllis shrugged, as if that was an acceptable enough answer for the time being, and then found her way over to the refrigerator.

Surveying her choices at first, she soon opted for the orange juice, and after pouring herself a very large glassful, she returned the container to the fridge before opening the freezer. A bottle of Ketel One appeared in her hand a few seconds later, and she poured as much of it into her glass as she could before returning it to its side on the door of the freezer.

Olivia watched this all from the corner of her eye as she hid behind her phone, then let out a quiet sigh once she saw her mother making her way toward the living room.

"How did it get so late?" Phyllis asked.

Olivia sat up, resting her phone on the cushion beside her.

"You ate one of Caroline's pot cookies with what we think must have been at least three or four glasses of red wine, so you conked out for a while. Lenny said you fell asleep pretty quickly though once he brought you up to your room."

"You're telling me I was high? And I didn't even enjoy it?"

Olivia shrugged with a nod.

"Well that's just pathetic," she said, taking a sip of her cocktail.

"You were definitely acting weird, Mom. Weirder than normal I mean, and Len said you were speaking in tongues by the time he left you alone up—what the hell is that thing on your nightgown?"

Olivia squinted to see the large stain going down the side, but Phyllis just took another sip and brushed her off.

"It's nothing. I vomited earlier."

Olivia stood up right away and headed into the kitchen. Phyllis listened without watching her as Olivia made her way first to the paper towels and then to the sink. She didn't want her making a fuss, but appreciated it just the same, mostly wondering what had happened after she left. Had the others called the hotels already? Was that *her* job?

"Livi, darling. Oh, thank you, dear," she said, leaning her shoulders and screwdriver back a bit so Olivia could attend to her gown. "Did we already make all the phone calls? Was that our job or your brother's?"

Olivia finished the cleanup and returned to the kitchen to dispose of the dirty paper. Only when she was finished washing her hands and reclaimed her spot on the couch opposite her mother did she reply.

"I called most of the hotels in the area a second time, and called the hospitals too. He hasn't shown up anywhere yet, at least as far as anyone can tell me. Haley saw Sam. He was pissed we thought he might be harboring Dad without telling us, but he let Haley look inside anyway. Nancy Hensley called again around 8. Asked if you'd seen General Hospital on Friday, then asked about Dad. Said she's praying for his safe return soon. The girls got busy on their social media assignment as far as I can tell, and Lenny and Caroline are still driving around, last I heard.

"We're doing everything we can, Mom. Dad's probably got his feet up in some Air B&B place watching ESPN right now. He's got a takeout steak and cheese hero on a dirty paper plate to his left, and a scotch on the rocks in a glass on his right. Come to think of it, we should put his picture up in the liquor stores too. That'll speed up the search."

Phyllis smiled slyly and took another sip of her drink, hoping Olivia was right. She was glad he hadn't done anything crazy yet, or spoken to the police, but there was no telling what he might do now after his experience in the hospital. Her only hope remained that he'd come home long enough for her to talk some sense into him once and for all.

##

Roger and Haley sat up next to each other in her bed, Haley hugging most of the sheets tight against her body. Breathless and still smiling, neither of them knew what to say.

"I hope that was alright?" she finally asked him, and Roger nodded vigorously right away.

"Yeah, totally. That was great. Really great. I liked it. I mean I loved it, like, a lot."

"I'm sorry we didn't do more. I'd just prefer to get to know you better first. Not that I don't want to do, you know, *more* with you."

Roger, tired but fully satisfied, had no complaints at all.

"No, it was great," he said again.

His eyes darted back and forth at different places in her bedroom as he tried to think of what else he should say to her.

"I don't know if this'll sound weird at all," he finally said, "but like, *thank you?* I mean like, for doing all that?"

Haley blushed, meeting his eyes briefly.

"It's okay, I liked it. I mean, I liked doing it, although I also liked *it*," she said, pointing down at his crotch.

"Your first black dick?" he asked her, and she couldn't tell if he was joking or really asking.

"Uh, yeah?"

"Cool," he said with a nod and a smile. "And yours was my first uh, you know."

"Oh. Okay. Cool."

Her stomach growled just then, and she thought about the pizza still waiting patiently down in the kitchen.

Would eating pizza together after what we did be normal? Would asking him if he wants to eat freak him out? God, I don't want to freak him out if I suggest that. Shit. Maybe I'll just mention something dumb about getting a slice after he leaves.

"I kinda wanna go have some pizza now," he said, and Haley smiled at him.

"Okay," she said, as if agreeing to an idea she hadn't even thought of. "That sounds good. Yeah, let's go have some."

They each climbed out of bed on opposite sides, soon looking around awkwardly for their clothes. Haley found his underwear on her side, and he retrieved her bra and skinny jeans from his side.

They exchanged a smile as they dressed, and Haley took the chance to peek at his body one more time before she turned around and slipped on her jeans. Roger was likewise happy to steal another glance at her ass as she did, feeling grateful he'd finally been able to grab it with both hands. *Some dreams do come true.*

She'd squeaked when he first touched her ass, but only, she swore, because his hands were colder than she thought they'd be.

Roger smiled as he thought of it all, and over on her side of the bed, Haley was doing everything she could not to jump and shout out with joy. Or leap into Roger's arms and start making out with him again. Or begin sucking him again. Or asking him to put his tongue on her breasts again. Still, she decided, food first either way.

##

"Darling, have you spoken to Sam yet?"

328

Olivia looked up from her phone with twisted shock.

"Have I *spoken* to Sam? Have I *spoken* to him? Why would you even ask me that? Are you still high?"

"I most certainly am not. I'm simply wondering if the two of you have chatted lately. He *is* your ex-husband after all, and the father of your only child. It would not be unheard of for a woman to use the gift of speech to express various thoughts and feelings she might have in a manner conducive to finding some degree of peace with the man."

Olivia stared at her mother for another long moment, then went back to her phone. Arguing with her about this was pointless, and probably what she was looking for anyway, a bona fide fight.

No. She wouldn't give her mother the satisfaction.

"I have friends with adult sons, you know," Phyllis went on. "Nice men too from what I gather. My friend Alice has three adult sons who all live nearby. They were at her 70th birthday celebration in February."

She watched Olivia carefully, waiting for some sort of a response, and when none came, she continued.

"There are also dating rooms on all the computers. Places you can access with a user name and password to find eligible bachelors nearby who'd be willing to meet you in a supermarket or a fast food place for a beer or something."

Now Olivia couldn't *help* but respond. She put her phone down with a big, dramatic flair, and sat up in her seat on the couch to face Phyllis.

"Mom. When in your whole *life* have you ever seen two people meet in a supermarket for a beer to get to know each other?"

She paused, allowing Phyllis to think it out, but as she was about to respond, Olivia continued.

"Never. The answer is never. You have never in your whole life seen two people drinking beer inside a supermarket. Probably never in a fast food place either, but at least that makes more sense. More to the point though, why do you even *ask* me these stupid questions about Sam? Or my dating life? What good do you expect could possibly come from these insane little moments?"

Phyllis seemed taken aback at first, but she composed herself and took another long sip of her vodka and orange juice before responding.

"Well, I suppose I was just curious if you even liked men at all," she said, and she only glanced at her daughter briefly after she'd said it before looking away again.

Olivia stared her mother down until she finally met her eyes.

"Am I a lesbian? Is that what you're asking me, Mom?"

"Yes," Phyllis said defiantly. "It is."

Olivia shook her head with a sigh.

"No, Mom. No. I am not a lesbian. I like men. I *hate* them, but I like them."

A smile crept across Phyllis's face as she looked away again. Downing the last of her drink far too quickly, she got up and went to the kitchen to make herself another.

##

"Okay, I'm done," Roger said. "I can't fit another bite."

"See?" Haley said, still chewing. "This is really good stuff you guys sell."

"I know, I know. I guess it's just 'cause I work there and never have time to eat, although one of the guys in the kitchen knows how much I like pasta, so he's always making bowls for me in my down time."

Haley smiled, making a note to make him pasta sometime soon.

She was relieved to have had such a perfect first date with him, even if she *did* have to arrange it all so strangely to begin with. Having the house to herself was the rarest of rare gifts though, as Olivia had virtually no social life whatsoever, so there was no way Haley *wasn't* going to take advantage of the empty house.

"So I'm glad this worked out," she said, and Roger looked at her kinda funny, unsure what she meant.

"You mean tricking me into coming over here for this, or like, us in general?"

Her face turned bright red and she looked away from him, feeling guilty as sin.

"I'm sorry," she said in barely a whisper. "I shouldn't have done this to you, you're right."

Roger stood up suddenly then, and Haley watched as he walked over and took her hands in his, leaning in close as he spoke to her.

"I am *extremely* happy you did this, Haley. I was trying for weeks to figure out how to even ask you out on a date, and now not only did we hang out together—*like alone, finally*—but we got to fool around too? *And* pizza? Like, whaaaat? This was perfect."

He kissed her softly on the lips, and their tongues entwined again, just as before. It took everything he had not to carry her inside to the couch, or back to her room, but since they'd already had such a perfect date, he didn't want to mess anything up.

She was everything Roger wanted and more, a beautiful girl with a brain as sexy as her body, and he knew he'd do whatever he could to keep her.

As their lips parted slowly, mouths still wide open, they reluctantly retreated from each other at last, sex still firing on all cylinders in the air between them.

Next time, each thought. *Next time will be even better.*

Haley walked him to the door and opened it for him. He leaned in again and they kissed each other passionately for another minute before standing apart to smile at each other in the doorway.

Just then, a car door shut on the street nearby, and they both looked out toward the noise. Footsteps then, very slow and deliberate. And as the person finally appeared in the light, it took everything in Haley not to scream out when she saw the gun.

"Oh my God!"

"Holy shit," Roger said from beside her.

"Grandpa?!"

Chapter 40

Caroline arrived back home about half an hour after Lenny, and once she realized Erika was out and Peaches was already asleep upstairs in her room, she knew the time had finally come for her talk with Lenny.

She made her way to the living room quietly.

"Got a minute?" she asked, surprising him while he was reading a book. He hadn't even heard her come home.

"Hey. Yeah," he said, sounding exhausted. "What's up?"

He put his bookmark in place, then laid the book down on the table beside the couch.

"I think you and I should talk now, like you said. I feel like there's this giant wall growing between us, and it's not gonna help either one of us to let this keep stretching on forever. Erika's out, and Peaches is upstairs, so as long as we've got the time and privacy, I figure now is as good a time as any to talk."

He watched her as she walked in and sat down across from him in a chair near the entrance to the dining room. She looked worried, sick even, and Lenny didn't want to prolong her pain any more than necessary.

"There's something I need to tell you," she said.

"You're cheating on me with Sam."

Caroline's mouth dropped open in shock as her whole body slumped in the chair. She couldn't believe he already knew.

"How?" she managed to ask, completely breathless. "How did you know that?"

"I had a weird feeling a long while back, but I let it go. Then, well, between the way you and him have been acting lately, it all just—I don't know—it all just made sense. And then Erika—"

"She told you?"

"No, not at all," he said, looking away, "but she did tell Jenn, and then Jenn told me."

"Jenn? But how would Jenn have told you?"

"Because I've been cheating on you too," he said. "With Jenn," he added a moment later, as if to clarify the obvious.

Caroline leaned forward and put her head in her hands, staring down at the floor between her feet.

"Lenny, she's only 18."

"And Sam is my best friend, my sister's ex-husband, and your niece's father," he said, raising his voice a bit more than he'd planned to.

Caroline knew there was no point going back and forth with him over this, so she just leaned back in her chair before standing up and walking into the kitchen. She paced back and forth there for a while as Lenny watched her.

"I love you very much," he said, surprising them both.

He didn't know how she'd react, but he needed it said anyway.

"I love you too," she said. "Very much."

As they gazed into each other's eyes, they each believed everything would turn out okay somehow, that they'd get through this, because even if they couldn't yet forgive themselves, they'd at least need to start by forgiving each other.

Caroline was relieved Lenny already knew, and she was glad he seemed to be taking it so well. She guessed his own affair might be having the same effect on her truth as *her* affair had on his. But what would this mean?

"Look," he began, as she walked back into the living room and sat down again, but Caroline waved him off.

"No. Wait. Just—just hold on a minute, Lenny, okay?"

"Okay?"

"I just want to say that if you're willing to work through this, I would very much like us to do so. Sam was an easy fuck for me and nothing more. I care about him as a friend, and as my brother-in-law, but he's not you, Len. He's never been you. He's not the man I fell in love with."

Lenny smiled and nodded, tears in his eyes.

"I feel the same way," he said, pausing to look away and think it out for a moment. "The Jenn thing—it was only about the sex."

She looked at him then with a huge smile as she shook her head. She couldn't help herself. She *had* to say it.

"No shit?" she asked, clearly mocking him. "That's all she was to you? It was only about the sex?"

The two of them both burst out laughing then, despite everything, and the moment was as glorious as it was healing.

##

Phyllis rubbed her temples, staring down at her third screwdriver of the evening, which now collected quite a bit of condensation above the coaster.

It was almost midnight, and she wasn't feeling tired at all. She cursed herself for napping so long, and cursed Caroline for leaving her damn pot cookies out so carelessly to begin with.

"I'm going to bed," she announced, if only to herself, and Olivia, sitting alone on a stool by the kitchen island, turned around to look at her.

"Are you gonna be able to sleep okay?" she asked.

"I'll be fine. I'll take a Trazodone and be out like a light."

"Mom, wait. What about the liquor? Should you be taking something like that if you've been drinking?"

"Ordinarily, no, but I've built up a tolerance. I'm an expert now, my dear. Don't you worry."

She retreated up the stairs a minute later with a tall glass of water, and Olivia prepared to make herself comfortable in the downstairs guest room as well. She'd already put her purse in there, along with the bag of pretzel sticks she'd snatched from her mother's pantry. All she needed now was one more cigarette, and she'd call it a night.

Grabbing her pack and lighter, Olivia made her way to the mudroom in the back of the house and unlatched the heavy lock they kept on the door. The large portal to fresher air resisted a bit at first, clearly wishing Olivia would just leave it alone already, but it finally gave way on her third pull. She decided against shutting it all the way once she was outside, lest the old nuisance refuse her reentry later on.

Lighting up, she inhaled and breathed out as she pocketed her lighter, feeling the stress blow away from her like smoke in the cool night air. The crickets were loud, much louder than usual she thought, and her parents' yard was darker than she'd remembered it ever being in the past too. *Wasn't there a light back here?*

She eyed the large garage suspiciously, realizing the light above the door had to be awoken by some sort of movement, and the crickets weren't helping her any with that. Grabbing her phone, she called up her most recent text thread, still waiting for a reply.

Olivia couldn't help but smile, despite the awful situation building around them. Even so, going over there now was the wrong move, and she didn't want to wake their neighbors with the car anyway.

Taking another drag and then holding onto the cigarette tightly between her lips, Olivia clicked into the message and began to type.

Just can't. Maybe tomorrow night if my daughter isn't busy sniffing around too much into other people's business.

She smiled and switched on her phone's flashlight, walking out a few feet toward the garage to make the light go on. She waved her hand out and around a bit, but nothing happened, so she walked closer to the motion sensor, still trying to jar it awake.

By the time she was right underneath it, she realized the thing must not be working, and she gave up, ready to go back toward the house, but that's when she spotted it in the beam of the flashlight.

Inside the garage behind their long-retired lawnmower on a dirty old shelf: Olivia's yellow raincoat, a distant relic she thought long gone, neatly folded there below a pile of old newspapers.

##

On their living room couch a half-mile away, Caroline leaned her head on Lenny's shoulder, and stared blankly at the table in front of them.

"Any leads yet on your dad?"

"No," Lenny said. "I gave up for the night. Livi and my mom are still calling hotels, last I heard. If I had to guess, he didn't go too far though. His knee's better after the surgery, but he hasn't been driving all that much lately. I'd honestly rather just leave him alone now, let him have the peace and quiet away he seems to want for himself."

"Well, what about his phone? Can't they just ping the location or something?"

"I checked that out, but he barely uses it since we got it for him. Turned off the location thing right away too. Said he didn't want to let the FBI know where he was every second of the day."

Caroline smiled, and nestled in more comfortably on the couch. They hadn't discussed their affairs any more, but for now, that was for the best. The demons of their past and future could come knocking again some other day, but for at least this moment, she celebrated the calm.

##

"Are you two alone?" Alan asked, still pointing the gun at them as he limped up the driveway with his cane.

"Yes," Roger said, a terrible fear in his voice. "Sir, I promise you though, I didn't do anything to hurt her. I would never hurt her at all, sir. Please. We were only—"

"I saw you. You were kissing my granddaughter."

"Yes sir, yes, but I promise you, it isn't what you think. Me and your granddaughter—Haley—see, she ordered a pizza, and I—"

"Stop talking," Alan said, getting very close to them now, and still holding the gun out in their direction.

He sized the two of them up for a moment, then looked past them both into the house.

"Your mother's not here, right?" he asked Haley.

Haley shook her head.

"No," she managed to whisper.

"Okay, good. Listen, young man," Alan said, looking behind him briefly toward the street. "That kiss I just interrupted. It didn't look like anything all that bad to me. Don't worry about it."

He shoved the gun back into his coat pocket, surprising them both, then walked right up to them with a soft smile.

"We haven't been properly introduced," he said, offering Roger his hand to shake. "Alan Abrams. Nice to meet you."

"Yes sir, Mr. Abrams. Roger, sir. Nice to meet you. If you don't mind me asking though, weren't you missing?"

"Missing? I dunno. Maybe to some. Not to me. I always knew exactly where I was. Hello, sweetheart," he added, leaning in and kissing Haley on the cheek with a hug. "I'm sorry if I startled you two just now, but I thought I might see someone else over here."

"Grandpa, where have you been? We've been looking all over for you. Grandma's really worried."

He smiled and nodded, looking away, and then up at the stars.

"She'll be alright," he laughed to himself. "And anyhow, you couldn't have been looking *all* over, because you would've found me by now. I think instead, you were simply looking *some* over, and nothing more."

He smiled again, much wider now, and enjoyed the confused faces they offered him in response.

"Hey listen, Roger. Do me a favor? Don't tell anyone you saw me here tonight? I'm trying to finish something up, and I'd really appreciate it if I could stay *missing* for another 12 hours or so."

"Um, okay?" he said, unsure how to respond.

If Haley's grandfather was back, and she'd seen him in her driveway, was he still really missing anyway?

"And leave me alone now with my oldest granddaughter. She and I need to talk about a few things, okay?"

Roger and Haley exchanged a long look and a nod as Roger walked to his car. Alan and Haley waved as he drove off, and then Alan turned to Haley looking concerned again.

"Grandpa, what's going on? We've been really worried."

"Your mom's not home? No one else is inside?"

"No, it's just me. Mom's sleeping over at your house to keep Grandma company."

"What? Whose dumb idea was that? Geez. It'll be a miracle if they're both alive by morning. Alright, let's get inside. I need to tell you something important, and I need you to hear me out."

They walked inside and sat down in the living room, Alan resting his cane up against the end table.

"Grandpa, what's going on?"

Alan seemed to ignore her question, and peered instead over at the kitchen, specifically at the large pizza box he spied there.

"Is that pizza?"

"Grandpa? Yes, it's pizza, but what's going on? Where have you been? We've been really worried."

Alan nodded, then took a moment to compose his thoughts. Haley felt he'd never looked so old before, so tired, like someone who'd been stuck in a nursing home or solitary confinement. His back was bent over much more than usual too, and he hadn't shaved in weeks.

"I want you to call everyone up. Your cousins too. And your dad. *Especially* him. Tomorrow though, not tonight. It's too late now. And tell them to meet over at your uncle's house at noon tomorrow. Tell them I'll be there, and I'll explain everything. No strangers, though. No friends or boyfriends or any of that crap. Family only, okay? That's important. I need to settle a few things once and for all, and I need our family to all be together in one place when I do."

A deep fear came over Haley then, and she worried her grandfather was going to do something horrible with the gun still resting within his right jacket pocket.

"Grandpa, I'm sorry, but I need to know now. Not tomorrow. I need to know you're not gonna do anything crazy with that gun. You're really scaring me here."

Alan surprised her by grabbing the gun from his pocket, and immediately resting it out on the coffee table in front of her.

"It's not a real gun. Look at it. It's just an old cap gun, a toy. I was worried *he* might be over here, is all."

"Who?" Haley asked, but her face told Alan she knew who he meant. She didn't want him to say it though. She didn't want to hear him say the name, or even think it could be true.

"Your dad, Haley. I'm so sorry, but it's all true. Your dad did it. He killed Kerry Ann Jefferson."

##

Inside the garage, Olivia held out her old yellow raincoat with one hand as she sized it up in the light from her cell phone.

Looking around, she found the inside light switch and turned it on, switching off her phone's flashlight and pocketing the phone again quickly.

Why do they still have this thing? Why didn't they ever give it back to me?

She shook her head and returned the coat to its spot on the shelf, grabbing the newspapers and putting them back as well. Only once she turned around to shut the light off did she realize what they were though, and she went back to look at them again.

Every one of the papers was from that time. That year. *That week.* That horrible week seventeen years earlier when all their lives changed forever.

##

"No, you're wrong, Grandpa. My dad may not have been completely innocent back then, but there's no way he killed that girl. I'm sure of it."

She waited for him to respond, but all she heard was the distant cackle of crickets outside. Alan just nodded and turned away from her, already grabbing the top of his cane like he was ready to leave.

He shook his head then and smiled, standing up slowly as he took both himself and his cane around the couches and closer to the front door. Haley watched him move, wondering if he'd even heard a word she'd said, or if he was still somehow convinced of Sam's guilt.

"I'm sorry, honey," he finally offered her. "I shouldn't have told you this tonight. But I'll explain it all tomorrow at your uncle's house. Just make sure everyone is there, the whole family, including your dad. Call them early tomorrow, not tonight. Let them get a good night's rest in without worrying about me."

He turned to leave, but Haley shouted after him.

"Grandpa, wait! Tell me why you think he did it. Tell me why, so I can try to understand."

Alan already had his hand wrapped around the brass handle of the door. His back turned to her, he just shook his head sadly one more time, then cleared his throat before opening the door.

"It's true, Haley. I'm afraid the facts are all stacked against him, and that's that. Too much pain. Too much needless, awful pain. I'll explain everything tomorrow. Have a good night."

"Grandpa, wait! Grandpa!"

She stopped the door from closing, but all she could do was watch as he walked back down the driveway, disappearing once he turned onto the street toward his car.

##

Caroline stared out through her reflection in the glass of the sliding door. Lenny had already returned to his book, and she stared out as the light from their kitchen seemed to cut the tree house in half down the middle. She couldn't take the pain of this any longer. It had to come down, all of it, and soon.

"Hey, Len?"

"Yeah?" he asked, looking up from his book, but he could see right away that something was wrong. "What is it?"

"I need to tell you something," she said, her voice distant and tired, a strange, empty look on her face as she spoke. "I need to tell you what I saw, and what I—what I *did* that night."

"What night?" he asked, though he already knew exactly which night she was referring to.

Caroline turned her head then to look at him, knowing she was about to reveal a secret she never thought she'd ever tell a soul, not even Lenny.

"That night," she said again, her voice breaking free from her mouth as if by some dreadful mistake.

Lenny's throat clammed up, and as he stood up to face her, he wanted to say 'okay', but the word never came. No words would come. Only dead air and a terrible kind of fear.

Caroline looked out at the tree house one more time, and then back at him as she spoke.

"The night Kerry Ann was murdered."

Chapter 41

Seventeen years earlier

Kerry Ann sat anxiously with her hands between her legs, her face the picture of fear and tension. She regretted all of it now, and hoped this nightmare was almost over.

Waiting for him to return from the kitchen, she thought about running away, leaving his house, leaving school, Ludlow, and everything else behind too. Escape to another state far away seemed her only option.

"Here you go," Alan said, handing her an iced tea and sitting down across from her in his favorite old chair.

He crossed his legs and smiled, holding up a Jack and Coke in her direction, then took a long sip before he continued.

"You know your options now, young lady, so I'm sure we can work something out between us. There's no reason for me to call the police."

Kerry Ann nodded, still not ready to make eye contact, still unable to even speak to him. She felt like throwing up, and barely sipped at her iced tea, worried she might be sick at any moment.

"The marijuana possession is bad enough," Alan went on, "but I tend to think they'd go easy on you for that, especially since you're a first-time offender. But stealing cash from your employer? Uh-uh," he said, wagging his finger. "Now that's *surely* a felony, guaranteed to land you in federal prison for a long, long time."

Kerry Ann nodded again without looking at him, too afraid to even acknowledge what was happening. She didn't know that Alan had caught her in the first place because he'd been spying on her outside the school that night. She knew only that she was screwed.

This man knew exactly who she was, of course. He'd recognized her from a family party, the same party he'd caught her trying to steal from Caroline. Grabbing cash from her purse in the kitchen. A theft he'd caught only because he'd been spying on her that day too. All he'd have to do now was call up Connie, and that would be that. Her life would be over.

Alan stood up and downed most of his drink, dropping the glass on the coffee table. He'd followed her that night to the school just as he'd followed her after the party at Lenny's house to find out where she lived. And as he stood behind her now, he knew he finally had her. Even if Sam *had* enjoyed her first.

He put his hand on her right shoulder, squeezing it gently.

"I'm sure we can work this out between us," he said again, making sure she understood. "I'm sure we can resolve this civilly, like *adults*."

He moved his hand down further then across her breast, rubbing it thoughtfully for a while. Kerry Ann froze, scared to move or speak, scared to even breathe.

"It's okay," he said sweetly. "Just relax."

Relaxing was impossible though, so instead she crumbled. A part of her just let go all control, all hope.

"Stand up," he ordered her, and she rose very slowly to face him like an injured animal aching to survive. "Now put the drink down and come closer so I can examine you better."

She did as he instructed, still too frightened to even look him in the eye.

Once she was in place, he put his arms around her in a strange sort of hug, and for a moment, Kerry Ann thought this might be the worst of it, that he'd let her go and keep her secrets, just as she knew she'd be forced to keep this one.

Instead, his hands went down her skirt in the back, and his fingers began to rub her as she tried to wiggle away, desperate for him to stop.

"Keep that up and this is over," he whispered. "Federal prison at your age would be terrible. Just terrible. Stop moving, and this will go *much* better for you. That's a good girl," he said, smiling as her body went completely limp against him.

She began to cry quietly into his shoulder as he continued, and in his growing disgust at her whimpering, he shoved her down hard to the ground and undid his zipper.

"Okay fine, crybaby. Just suck me off and I'll let you go."

Crying even more now, she forced herself up into position, and once she caught her breath long enough to manage it, began sucking him.

It took almost 12 minutes, but he finally came, forcing her to take every drop of it as well.

Once it was over, Alan walked away and returned to his chair, zipping himself up as he grabbed his drink.

"Now get the fuck outta here before my wife comes home."

Kerry Ann scrambled to her feet and ran out toward her car, barely managing to close the front door behind her as she did.

In the ensuing silence, Alan stared at her full glass of iced tea for a while before he stood up and grabbed it. Walking it into the kitchen, he spilled out the contents, then threw the empty glass in the garbage.

Reclaiming his place on the chair, drink once again in hand, he turned on the television and took a long sip.

From the guest room in the rear of the house, a door opened up and Phyllis appeared. She walked into the living room and took a seat on the couch closest to Alan, watching quietly as he flipped through channels.

"Have fun?" she asked.

"Yeah, not bad," he said with a grin, and Phyllis smiled too.

Chapter 42

Early the next morning, Sunday morning, long before anyone inside Lenny's house was awake, the first rays of daylight pierced the empty tree house, as if God himself was shining a mighty flashlight in for clues.

The old shack of wood and nails had only lasted this long because no one ever used it. Enjoying it too much would have surely brought it down, and yet, because it remained forbidden territory for so many years, it was allowed to hold onto its secrets for exactly this long, for exactly this moment in time.

As if by some divine intervention of a thoroughly twisted variety, or perhaps just really bad luck, two of the old boards on the inside of the tree house buckled enough on this early Sunday morning for the tree to finally feel the weight of the awful thing, certain to change the futures of all those forever connected to it.

A chipmunk scurrying past the tree just then may have heard a faint sound: the squeak of the bending wood, the breath of a breath of the tiny bit of dust as it fell loose, or the muffled scream of Kerry Ann Jefferson echoing forth one last time, so many years after her awful demise.

Why had nature bent in the morning breeze with just so much pressure in just such a way on just such a day as this? Had there been some mysterious, mystical push of fate or spirit, or was it simply its time?

The tree house entrance maintained its safe space calmly, like a baby bird peeking out from its mother's nest, waiting for something to happen, even though the something to happen was not due for another four hours.

All around the framework of the tree house, not another hair of evidence existed anymore, save for one small inscription once carved on the inside, and since almost seventeen years had passed since Kerry Ann's body breathed its last, not even that could prove much of anything anyway.

The empty, looming tree house, a silent witness to a torrent of tears and pain, was forever the innocent bystander, yet somehow allowed to coexist with Kerry Ann's fate for all this time.

As a new breeze wrestled through the branches of the old tree, and its remnants tickled whatever blades of grass were not already trampled on nearby, the long forgotten foot traffic between the tree house and the basement steps held their own sorrowful mystery.

It was somewhere there on the grassy path that Kerry Ann had rested after the incident, just feet from where she'd been dragged moments later, and not at all far from the place where she last saw anything at all before her eyes shut forever.

Further along the path and down the basement steps, the little draft of remaining breeze might find its way to the spot where Peaches saw the tarp on which the tiniest spatter of something she was sure was not tomato sauce stared back up at her, as if pleading for help, the help Kerry Ann herself had never received.

High above it all, two flights up and two hours later, Lenny eventually awoke to an awful nightmare, with a gasp loud enough to stir himself but not Caroline from a long night's rest.

He blinked his eyes open as much as possible, and soon found his bathrobe resting on a nearby chair. Grabbing his phone as an afterthought on his way to the bathroom, he took note of the time, realizing it was still too early to get the breakfast going.

Just coffee, he told himself. *Just coffee and email for now.*

Downstairs as he waited for the coffee pot to finish a little while later, he finally looked at his phone and saw he had a text waiting. From Haley.

Call me as soon as you get this. Grandpa's back!

Lenny stared at the text in shock, then stirred to action quickly, calling her up. It rang only once.

"Hi, Uncle Lenny. He came by late last night and promised me not to call everyone until today. I don't know where he is now, but he said he'd meet us all at your house at noon today."

"Okay, did he say why? Did he look alright?"

Haley took a deep breath before she answered. She *wanted* to tell him what Alan had said about her father, and she wanted to tell him what she thought of that too, but instead, she answered his second question first, and dodged the first as much as possible.

"He looked really tired, and older than he has in the past. He was moving much slower with the cane too. He wouldn't tell me much, but he said it has to do with Kerry Ann Jefferson."

Lenny heard the name as if in slow motion, as if it had been spoken out loud only once before in his entire life, with the promise of a bookend second time he'd finally heard now. His face went pale, and he felt sick to his stomach, but Haley's voice stirred him alert.

"Uncle Lenny, I'm really scared. What if he went to the police already? What if we'll have no time to clear this up before he makes some kind of a crazy accusation? I should have kept him here last night. I shouldn't have let him go. I'm so sorry."

"No, no. It's not your fault, kid. Grandpa's just a little unwell, and we all know he's been through a lot lately. Maybe all this time away from everyone made him want to get the whole Kerry Ann business behind us now. It doesn't have to mean more than that."

As he spoke, Lenny realized he was talking to himself even more than to Haley. His paranoia ran deep, and in his breath, he tasted fear.

Alan was nothing more than a gentle, sleeping dog all these years since he retired, but a close call at the hospital could have stirred something insane within him.

"Listen, I'll wake your Aunt Caroline and the girls. What time did you say he's meeting us here?"

"Twelve," she said, her voice aching to even say it.

"Okay. Call me if you hear more. And come over here whenever you want. It'll be okay. We should just be glad he's home safe now."

They ended the call as the coffee machine beeped, and Lenny thought it out for a moment before he went to wake Caroline.

Halfway up the stairs, she met him on her way down with a smile and a quick kiss.

"Thanks for making the coffee," she said, not yet noticing the look on Lenny's face.

She made her way into the kitchen and grabbed a mug, filling it up before she saw Lenny standing in the hallway looking in at her. His body and face sagged unnaturally, and she knew something was terribly wrong.

"Oh my God, what is it?"

"My dad is back, or will be today."

"Oh, thank God," she said, breathing a sigh of relief. "You scared me. I thought something had happened."

She grabbed the sugar and cream and stirred her cup, but just as she turned around again, she realized Lenny was still standing out in the hallway, still crestfallen with news she'd yet to hear.

"Lenny? What's wrong?"

Lenny tilted his head down a bit and shook his head, his eyes darting this way and that as he put it all together.

"You know that thing you told me about last night?" He glanced back toward the stairs to make sure the girls weren't up yet. "The thing in the yard seventeen years ago?"

"Yes?" she asked, not wanting to hear more.

"My dad knows something. He knows who killed Kerry Ann."

##

Olivia turned over in bed and willed open one eye, unsure where she was or how she got there. She couldn't figure out why there was a painting of Paris in her bedroom, nor why the walls were painted so dark.

Once she realized she was still in her parents' guest room, she closed her eyes again, only to open them a few seconds later as she realized the light on her phone was pulsing with a new alert of some kind.

She stretched out her arm toward the phone, but it was just too far away, and since she'd have to actually move to reach it, she decided instead to fall back asleep.

Forty more minutes passed by as she continued to sleep soundly, and when she finally woke up again, her eyes fell onto the flashing phone once more. This time she realized that with her father missing, she should probably check her messages.

She elbowed her way to the phone, aching to reach it with as little movement as possible, and when she finally had it in her hand, she let out a sigh of gratitude, as if delightfully surprised the bed was still beneath her, still there to offer her comfort and repose.

Two new messages, one a text from Haley, and the other a voicemail from ... *Dad!*

Olivia shot up in bed and immediately clicked through to her voicemail, raising the phone to her ear.

"Good morning, Livi. I'm glad I got your voicemail. This'll go much easier for me now. You're going to hear this sooner or later from Haley, but I wanted to say it here first. Sam is guilty. He did it. I didn't want to believe it all this time, but now I know.

"I'll be coming back today, and I'd like everyone to meet me over at Lenny's house at 12. High noon, as it were. Been doing some research in my free time, but also some vital soul searching, and I think it's time we answer for our past transgressions. Sam *and* me. I'm no innocent either, I'm sad to admit. I can't say more here, but I'll explain it all later on at Lenny's."

When the message beeped at the end, Olivia just stared off in the distance for a while, unsure how to manage the waves of emotions crashing down on her. After another minute passed, she finally looked down at her phone again, and called up Haley's message. She read it quickly, and then got up to wake her mother.

##

Haley stared out through her bedroom window, watching as the wind rustled menacingly through the trees. She'd woken up that

349

morning in a hot sweat, having forgotten to turn her bedroom air conditioner on before going to sleep. The heat alone served to remind her it was sure to be a day of painful reckoning for her family, and she suspected big changes would soon follow.

Though her grandfather hadn't said too much about her dad, it was clear he'd uncovered something serious. There seemed to be new information he didn't have before, and she wondered where he'd found it. Most of all, she worried her father might leave again if confronted with the evidence, perhaps even disappear from her life forever.

Her cell phone rang out, and Haley jumped in her bed, almost dropping the device onto the floor. *Peaches.*

"Hey, Peaches. What's up?"

"Hi. I heard about Grandpa. What do you think he's gonna say about the tree house?"

"Jesus, Peaches. Why do you keep thinking this has anything to do with the damn tree house? That thing may have just been some weird side incident that had nothing to do with any of this. Why are you so convinced it has to do with Kerry Ann Jefferson?"

Peaches didn't reply, and Haley was unnerved by her silence.

"Peaches?"

"If I tell you what I know, you're just gonna call me crazy, or mock my shamanic training."

Haley sighed. *Not this again.*

"Look, Peaches. I'm not trying to mock whatever it is you do over at Chaos Casbah, but you've gotta admit, it is pretty out there. Even if you have good news about my dad, it's still really freaky, and I don't think I want to hear about it anymore, okay?"

"Okay. Just do me a favor though?"

"What?"

"Give your dad a chance. Let him explain whatever he has to."

"Of course I will. Jesus, Peaches. He's my dad. Why wouldn't I believe him? But that doesn't mean Grandpa's nuts either. You're the Jesus freak in the family anyway. If Grandpa had a fucking near-death experience, maybe he knows something we don't. Ever think of that?"

Haley ended the call abruptly, and Peaches was left alone, staring at her phone in shock. Haley had never screamed at her like that, or even cursed at her as far as she could remember. *What is happening to everyone?!*

She texted Roger right away.

Hey, u awake? I really need to talk to u...in person...like right away

Only a minute passed before a text response came back. Roger had left his phone on, hoping to hear from Haley, but worried now that something had gone down with Alan after he left.

Okay, I can come by now. Everyone alive and all? No one hurt?

LOL What? Yes...just need your advice about Haley and something we have going on now w/my grandfather

K, be there in 15

Peaches got dressed and made her way downstairs. Lenny had finally started making breakfast, and he offered Peaches a friendly smile when he saw her come in.

He'd woken the girls up earlier to tell them about their grandfather's return. Peaches was still half asleep then, annoyed he'd come in so early, but he saw she was much more alert now.

"Peaches, hon, what do you want to eat? I'm frying bacon, and I'll have some eggs on in a few minutes."

"Whatever," she said, making her way over to Caroline, already on the couch and staring at the television.

"Hi Mommy," she said, but Caroline didn't budge. She just stared at the TV like it was off, even though a commercial was bouncing around quickly on the screen.

"Mommy?" she asked again, and this time Lenny took notice, looking back and forth between the spattering bacon in the pan and Caroline on the couch with some concern.

"Caroline!" he yelled, and she finally turned her head to him with a blank look on her face, but still didn't seem to notice Peaches sitting right next to her.

"Peaches just said good morning to you," he said.

Caroline blinked at him absentmindedly for a moment, and then looked at Peaches.

"Oh, I'm sorry, honey. Good morning."

She smiled warmly at Peaches, but then turned to face the television again. The show was back on, but the TV still muted, and Caroline just watched it as she had before, wearing an empty stare of sadness.

"What's going on?" Peaches asked her. "Is this about Grandpa? Or Uncle Sam?"

Lenny turned around again and looked at the two of them on the couch, Caroline with her gaze set firmly on the television, and Peaches just staring at Caroline.

"Is this about Kerry Ann Jefferson?" Peaches asked now. "Do you know who killed her?"

Caroline sprang to life as soon as she heard the name, sitting up straight in her seat and locking eyes with Peaches briefly and then Lenny, a look of fear bouncing anxiously in the air between them.

Peaches was stunned to see them completely switch gears just a moment later.

Lenny came rushing in with a big smile on his face, crouching down in front of her like she was only five, and Caroline completely turned herself in the couch to face Peaches with a twisted grin on her face as well.

"Of course not, honey," Caroline said. "Everything's gonna be fine. Grandpa's just being Grandpa. You know how he is. And he's getting so old now. He probably just spent so much time away from us, his mind is tired and confused."

"That's right," Lenny added with a laugh. "And after we make him feel at home here, we're gonna bring him back to his house with Grandma, and everything will go back to normal, okay?"

"Okay," Peaches said, deciding to play along. She faked a smile, and they both seemed relieved to see it.

"I think I'll go play in the tree house then," she said, standing up quickly and walking over to the sliding door.

352

"NO!" they both screamed out together, and Peaches stepped back away from them slowly, her eyes wide with a new kind of fear she'd never felt before. Something was wrong, *very* wrong. She'd never seen them look so scared, so unhinged like this, and coupled with Haley's outburst on the phone minutes earlier, she wasn't sure what was happening to her family.

"What is going on with everyone?!" she yelled, still backing away from them toward the front hallway. She wasn't worried they'd hurt her. She just wanted them to see how much they were freaking her out.

Lenny and Caroline glanced at each other then and looked away. Caroline at the TV, which she soon switched off with the remote, and Lenny toward the kitchen, where he saw the bacon was burning in the pan. He rushed over to it and turned the gas off, then put the pan on the back burner to cool.

Erika came down the stairs just then, completely aloof to the situation building around her, and was just about to head into the kitchen when Peaches held out her arm to stop her.

Erika was about to snap at her, but then she saw her parents and the showdown already in progress.

"What's—*going on?*" she asked.

"That's what I'm trying to figure out," Peaches said. "Mommy and Daddy are hiding something from us, and it has to do with Kerry Ann Jefferson's murder, which I think happened inside our tree house."

Erika stared at them all for a moment as Peaches let her arm come down slowly.

"Wait. *You* told me the tree house just wasn't safe enough to play in," she said to Caroline.

"It isn't. That's the only reason."

"Caroline, don't."

Now Lenny and Caroline stared at each other, and Peaches and Erika just watched the two of them with growing dread. Neither wanted to believe that either of their parents could be involved, but something was definitely strange about their behavior now, and it was thoroughly unnerving them both.

As they watched and waited, Caroline looked like she was about to tell them something, but then the front door opened up, and Olivia walked in with Phyllis close behind her.

As her grandmother closed the door behind them, Peaches glimpsed Roger just arriving, out by the very end of the driveway.

"Good morning," Olivia said, practically pushing her way in past Peaches and Erika, soon finding her way past Lenny too, where she picked up a slice of cooked bacon from the pan.

"Let's just get this shit show over with already," Phyllis said, annoyed at everyone, especially at Alan. "Do you have any red wine over here?"

She made her way into the kitchen, and as Peaches, Erika, Lenny, and Caroline all looked at each other one last time, they knew the secrets would stay secret for just a little while longer.

"Roger's here," Peaches announced. "I'll be right back."

Her whole family felt like strangers, people she didn't really know anymore, and it made her both agitated and angry, feelings that only worsened by the time she got outside.

She'd opened the front door expecting to see Roger about to ring the doorbell, but instead, he was still out on the sidewalk beyond the bushes lining their front yard, and he and Haley were locked in what looked to be a very passionate kiss.

Closing the door quietly behind her and walking out, Peaches made her way right up behind them before Haley even saw her standing there. She pulled away quickly from Roger once she did.

"Peaches. Hi. Roger and I were just—"

"Can I speak to Roger alone, please?"

Haley nodded, offering Roger a quick smile as she retreated to the safety of the house.

Peaches shook her head at him, then found her way to the street, where she sat down on the grass behind Roger's car.

"Look, Peaches," he said. "This thing with your cousin just sorta happened last night. We hung out, and one thing led to another and—"

She held out her hand, telling him to stop, and Roger faithfully obeyed, frustrated she'd found out like this, and worried she was angry with him. Or worse, with both of them. Peaches just sat there for a half minute in silence until Roger finally sat down beside her, and when he did, she looked at him with a sad smile.

"I'm having a really bad morning," she said. "It has nothing to do with you, or you and Haley. It's just everyone."

She paused and shook her head again.

"I feel like this whole thing with my grandpa is a huge moment for my family, but I don't want to be here for it. I want to just run away from it all, and stay away from every one of them forever. I know I can't, or I shouldn't, or both, but this is just really scaring me now. I'm worried my parents know more about the Kerry Ann thing than they're telling me, and that they've been covering something up this whole time too."

"You think they had something to do with it?"

"I dunno. I hope not, but— I just don't know anymore, Roger. Something feels really weird all of a sudden."

She turned in place, looking at him with her eyes wide open.

"Wait. You said you were with Haley last night? Did you see my grandpa too?"

Roger nodded, unsure what he should say about that. Should he mention the gun? What did Haley tell her?

"Well, how did he look? Was he okay? Was he acting weird?"

"He was definitely acting very different, that's for sure. He was super friendly to me too, which, I dunno, seemed really wrong for him, like, I wasn't sure if he was faking it or what."

"How do you mean?"

"Well, he just seemed like this scary old white dude when I saw him here at your sister's graduation party. And he and your grandma ordered pizza once after that too, and when I brought it to their house, they both looked scared of me."

"What? How could anyone be scared of you?"

"Old white people are just like that sometimes. It was dark out when they answered the door, and there's this black kid standing there. They're freaked out easily, I don't know what to tell you. I'm used to it, and they're not the only people who give me the evil eye. It happens all the time."

"That's awful," she said, as if learning this life lesson for the very first time.

They sat together in silence for another minute until Roger looked at her sideways and decided he needed to cheer her up. Peaches was the happiest person he'd ever met, and seeing her like this was affecting him much more than he thought it would.

"Look, Peaches. I've got a crazy family too. I hardly ever see my dad anymore, and my mom is dating this total asshole—well, actually, she *was* dating him. She packed up all our stuff last night when I was out with Haley, and we're in a hotel now. She wouldn't tell me what happened."

"Wow, what do you think—"

"It doesn't matter. Look, my point is, I really hate a lot about my life right now, but you know what I do to stay sane?"

"What do you do?"

"I play little mind tricks on myself. I focus on the stuff that doesn't suck, and the people that don't suck. I think of my mom, and how much I love her, and how much I need to protect her in case her crazy ex-boyfriends ever do anything to her. And I think of *you,* and how cool you are, and how you reached out to me when no one else would talk to me at that poetry reading, and how you invited me into the Stir Call Circle, and how you introduced me to your family, and Haley—"

Peaches smiled at him strangely then, and he realized he needed to say more about that.

"Listen, Haley and I have had something between us since the moment we met at that doctor's office. We have chemistry. I'm as surprised as anyone that we're actually together now though, because I sure as hell never expected her to like me as much as I liked her."

"Why not? You're a great guy, and you're really cute."

"See, you say that, and I appreciate it and all, but I totally don't see it. I didn't think I was even worth kissing. The girls I've been with in the past seemed to use me and then dump me pretty quickly, but with Haley, I dunno, it's only been a few hours, but it already feels different this time."

"That's awesome," Peaches said, offering him a really big smile now. "I'm happy for you. For both of you."

"You mean it?"

"I don't lie. Of course I mean it."

At the mention of the word *lie* though, Peaches started thinking of her parents again, and the tree house, and the murder, and her uncle, and her grandfather, and Haley's mean words to her about her spirituality.

Roger watched her face change as her eyes stared out sadly again at the street, and he could tell she'd just retreated back into her family's drama.

"You okay?" he asked.

Peaches didn't answer at first. She only sighed and shook her head. When she turned to face him, she took a moment to look back at the house, where she remembered the look of fear on both her parents' faces. Something crazy was going on with them, and she wondered if maybe running away, even if only for a few weeks like her grandfather had, wasn't still a good option.

"I think my mother did something to her," Peaches said, glancing back briefly toward the house.

"Did something to who? To Haley?"

"No, not Haley," she said, looking sadder than before. "To Kerry Ann Jefferson. I think she was the one who killed her."

Chapter 43

Seventeen years earlier

Kerry Ann leaned up against her car, eyeing the house nervously. It looked completely dark, and she was sure no one was still awake inside, but where was Sam? He said he'd meet her there with a special surprise, but as the thunder rumbled in the distance, he was late again.

As she stood there waiting alone on the dark street, she worried once more that she was making a mistake. Even though Alan hadn't harassed her again after the blowjob, Sam was still a married man, and his generous gifts weren't nearly reason enough to keep seeing him like this.

She thought through her options, and what she might say to him, what lies she might use to stop this once and for all.

A few more minutes passed as she thought about leaving, but when she finally heard a car approaching, she smiled when she saw his face past the steering wheel. He waved as he parked, then got out and kissed her sweetly on the lips.

"Thank you so much for meeting me here," he said. "Come with me."

"I was about to leave. You're later than you said you'd be."

"I'm glad you didn't. Sorry about that. I got held up. This'll be worth the wait though. You'll see."

He took her by the hand, and led her along the side of the house between the fence and a row of bushes, where a small side gate allowed them access to the backyard.

"What are we doing here?" she whispered, scared they'd wake up the people inside.

"Don't worry," he said. "My brother-in-law sleeps like a bear, and his wife has a little baby in there, and another one coming soon. If she wakes up at all, it'll be to quiet a screaming child, but it's pitch dark, so don't even worry about it. Their bedroom faces the front of the house anyway, so it's fine. They won't hear us."

358

He led her closer to the tree house, still cautiously looking up at Lenny's house just to be sure.

"Follow me," he said, climbing up the little wood ladder he'd built for the side of the tree. "I made this thing. Well, me and Lenny," he added, pointing to the house once he was up inside.

Kerry Ann hesitated.

"The ladder's perfectly safe, I promise. Here, look. I brought a little flashlight."

He turned on the flashlight from above her, and Kerry Ann smiled up at him. Glancing back toward the house one more time, she thought she saw something move over by the side gate, then quickly followed him up the ladder, if for no other reason than to escape the unfamiliar darkness of the yard.

Chapter 44

"Just call me when it's over," Roger said. "I'm gonna stay in town in case you guys need me. I don't wanna go back to that hotel yet anyway. I'll probably just hang over at the pizza place, or chill with Ellen for a while at Chaos Casbah. I think she's working today."

"Okay," Peaches said, leaning in to hug him goodbye.

"Good luck in there," he added, and Peaches just nodded.

She walked back inside as Roger got into his car and drove away. At the end of the block as he rounded the corner off their street, he saw Sam turning his pickup truck onto the road. The two eyed each other briefly, then watched as the other got further away in their rear-view mirrors.

Inside the house a minute later, no one was talking. Lenny had finished cooking the bacon, but like everyone else there—*even Peaches*—he'd found his appetite had decreased significantly with every moment closer to Alan's expected arrival.

Lenny looked at them all sitting around his living room in silence, no one speaking to anyone else, and he took the moment in thoughtfully, like he'd be telling someone about it one day. His mind began drifting into the past when the doorbell rang, jarring him alert again.

Eyeing Olivia briefly, he got up and walked to the front door, then opened it up. *Sam.* He showed him in, but neither man spoke a word to each other, not even a hello.

Once he got into the living room, Sam realized the tension was even worse than he expected.

Not knowing the contents of Alan's conversation with Haley, only that Alan was back and looking to meet everyone, he was reluctant to show up at all. This though? This strange cloud of silent uncertainty in the house? It was unlike anything he'd ever seen from any of them before.

"Haley," he said, breaking the silence. "What's this all about? What did Grandpa say?"

Haley looked around at everyone for a moment, and saw they were all watching her very carefully, perhaps even suspiciously.

"He just said he has new information about Kerry Ann Jefferson, and he wants everyone to be here to hear it from him. And he said no one else but the eight of us should be here. Peaches, did—"

"Roger left."

Sam found a seat as far from Olivia as possible, and he nodded at Haley as he did, anxiously rubbing his hands together with a sigh.

"Okay, good," he said after another 20 seconds had passed. "This is good. If your grandpa has new information, then he can tell you once and for all that I'm not guilty."

Phyllis's eyebrows went up as she blinked away a passing thought, but she didn't look at Sam, and said nothing. Sam didn't seem to notice.

"Dad—" Haley said.

"Look, Sam—" Lenny said at the same time, and the two of them exchanged a nervous glance before they both looked away.

"What?" Sam asked, sensing the sudden shift. "What is it?"

Olivia surprised all of them by leaning forward and locking eyes with Sam from across the room. She spoke to him very slowly, but not, Haley felt, with any animosity this time.

"My father says he has *proof* you killed the girl, Sam. He says he knows now for sure that you killed Kerry Ann Jefferson, and he's called us all here to explain how he knows this."

They stared at each other for a very long time, and everyone else in the room took note, not just of their eye contact, but of the words themselves. Was a huge fight about to break out? Was Sam going to storm off and disappear, just as Haley feared he might?

Instead, he only shook his head sadly and looked away again. He couldn't believe it had come to this.

Caroline glanced back into the kitchen to see what time it was, surprised to see their kitchen phone was missing.

"What time is it? And where the hell did the phone go?"

She looked at Erika as she asked this, as she was the most probable suspect she could think of.

Erika shrugged, looking surprised, but Lenny quickly cleared his throat.

"Actually, I got rid of it recently. Long story."

No way I'm telling that one right now.

He pulled out his cell phone and looked at the time.

"It's 11:22," he announced to Caroline, and to anyone else who cared to know.

"So we still have to wait here another 38 minutes for your father to arrive?" Phyllis asked, clearly growing more upset and anxious with each passing minute. "Why *the hell* did we come over here so early, Olivia?"

"Because *you* told me you couldn't take waiting at home any longer, *Mom*."

The silence resumed, and all but Sam sat still. Haley watched him carefully out of the corner of her eye, trying to read his body language, but all she saw from where she sat was Sam's leg shaking.

She wondered again if it could actually be true, just as her grandfather had said. Nothing about her father was the same now. Every part of his body was in motion, even while he sat.

Their eyes finally met as Peaches leaned back, and Sam was sure Haley thought the very worst of him. He was sure she could see through all his little ticks and movement, and had come to her final conclusion.

"Look, Haley," he said, pleading with her, "just give me a chance to explain. That's all I—"

But he wouldn't finish. Just at that moment, the doorbell rang.

No one moved now, not even Sam. For several long seconds, no one seemed to even breathe. There was only silence and fear in the air, a deadly cocktail of dread pulsing within each person's chest in the place fresh air once moved about freely.

Olivia took a deep breath and stood up then as the others all watched her, and she made her way to the front of the house as they listened in carefully. To her footsteps. To the door opening up. A hug then perhaps, and some quiet shuffling as the door closed once again.

"Are you okay?" Olivia asked him, and he must have simply nodded, because no one heard him respond.

Footsteps and more shuffling then, and his cane, which grew louder as they approached the back of the house. Olivia reappeared in the doorway to the kitchen first, and the slow steps of someone walking with a cane followed her in three seconds later. And then there he was, looking more haggard than ever before: Alan Abrams, grandfather extraordinaire.

It unnerved each one of them to see him there at all, even though just a day earlier they were all desperate to find him.

As he took another step closer, he looked like some sort of a stranger or villain, and not even Phyllis stood up to greet him. He'd summoned them all there with promised information about the Kerry Ann Jefferson murder, but no one knew what to say or think about that.

Lenny finally stood up despite it all, and he walked right over and hugged Alan warmly.

"I'm so glad you're home safe," he said. "We were all very worried about you, Dad."

"Thank you, Leonard," Alan said, his voice a bit hoarse, and as he looked around the room, all he could offer them was a sad, quiet smile. All but Sam and Phyllis returned it too, but when he looked at her, at his wife he'd left so suddenly, all he saw was the deep pain written across her face.

Tears streaked down both her cheeks, and Alan rushed—as quickly as his knees would allow him—to her side.

"I'm sorry, dear," he said, falling like a sack of laundry into the seat cushion beside her. "I just couldn't take it any longer. I had to get away from the house, from you, from everyone, just until I could figure everything out."

Phyllis wiped her tears away and took out a tissue from her purse to blow her nose.

"And *did you* figure things out, Alan? Did you find all the answers you were so desperately searching for?"

He nodded after a moment, and took her hands in his, kissing them both in turn.

"I did."

When he turned away from her, he looked at only one other soul there. *Sam.*

Their eyes met, and Sam suddenly felt like a caged animal.

"Why don't we have the girls leave now," Sam said to Alan. "They don't need to be here for any of this, and it'll be easier to just talk this through one on one, don't you think?"

Haley leaned forward and looked at her father straight on.

"No, Dad. We're not going anywhere. We all deserve to hear the truth. We all need to know exactly what happened that night. Grandpa," she said, more softly now, looking across at Alan, "what did you find out?"

Alan's eyes still hadn't left Sam's, and the two seemed to be sizing each other up like feuding dogs, seeing each other for the first time in weeks as they walked on opposite sides of the street.

Chapter 45

Seventeen years earlier

Inside the tree house, Kerry Ann gasped once she saw the tablecloth, potato chips, soda, and red rose Sam had laid out for her in the middle. He lit a candle in the center too, then turned off the flashlight.

He sat on a small bed pillow, and pointed her to another one on the opposite side for her to sit on as well.

"Oh my God," she cooed. "I wasn't expecting to see all this inside a tiny tree house. When did you set this up?"

"About an hour ago. Except for the candle. Then I called you from a payphone in town while I stopped off for gas."

"*That's alright, that's okay, you're gonna pump our gas someday*'," she sang absentmindedly, but Sam just looked at her like she was crazy.

"Huh? What was *that* about?"

"Oh my God, you haven't seen *Bring It On* yet? We should totally go. My brother and I have seen it three times already."

"No, sorry," he said, offering her a shy grin, suddenly feeling the huge age gap between them. "Haven't seen it yet."

"It's okay," she smiled, looking down at the candle between them, "but I'm afraid to ask you now. *Why* did you do all this?"

"Well, because the first time we hooked up, you were scared off by the whole motel business. I know we've found time here and there since, but I wanted to give you something more romantic and real. And because I figured it doesn't get any realer than a tree house picnic under candlelight, well, here we are."

She took off her sweater and got more comfortable, eyeing both Sam and the space between them for any more surprises.

"Okay," she said, nodding at it all. "I gotta say, I'm impressed."

Sam laughed, taking a moment to look back at the house.

"Really?" he asked her.

"Yes, totally. I felt bad about the motel thing, but I would've never in a million years guessed you'd do something as wild as this.

It really is romantic, Sam. Thank you. I've never even been in a tree house before. We should totally carve our names inside here somewhere too."

"Eh. Maybe just initials or something," he said with a smile.

Sam passed her the chips, and Kerry Ann took one and chewed it as they stared across at each other. Then Sam took one as well, and studied it for a moment in his hand.

"You know, we *could* just sit here and eat potato chips for a while, or maybe, if you want, we could do some *other* things?"

"Oh?" she asked, teasingly. "And what *other things* were you thinking of exactly? The space is pretty tight in here, don't you think? Not much room."

"Well, I built this tree house big enough for kids or adults to sit inside easily enough, but I bet we'd be a hell of a lot more comfortable if we were lying down. That sound alright to you?"

She nodded as she took one more potato chip, then reached for the candle between them, blowing it out. With only the moonlight to go by, they found each other's faces in the dark space, and soon began to kiss.

The kissing turned to undressing before long, and within just a few minutes, they had pushed aside all the food and drinks, and were having ravenous sex.

Sam had to shush her several times, but despite the great danger of getting caught, they never did see the little light go on inside the house, and from where they were fucking so far out in the yard, neither did they see *her* staring out at them from behind the curtain of the sliding glass door.

Chapter 46

Alan sat on the far left side of the couch with Phyllis tucked in tightly on the right in the corner, their three granddaughters filling the smaller sofa across the room from them on the other side of the coffee table.

Sam and Olivia flanked either side of the girls, both of them in chairs, while Caroline and Lenny each sat on stools they'd pulled out from the kitchen island.

"I started off heading south," Alan told them. "I had some casino comps stored up at Borgata, so I wound up down in Atlantic City first, where I spent far too much time and money just feeling sorry for myself. I ate alone, I played the machines alone, a little craps and poker here and there too, but after a couple weeks filled with that kind of nonsense, I realized I was only delaying the inevitable. I needed to head back north. And not to Vermont either. Further up.

"It was a ridiculous drive, and I only barely made it past the New Hampshire-Maine border before I fell asleep at the wheel and crashed my car. No, no, don't worry," he said, seeing all their faces. "It was just a little thing, and I got it fixed. I spent the night in Ogunquit, Maine. Gorgeous town, and delicious food. Really nice folks up there too. Phyl and I went there about 30 years ago. Do you remember?"

Phyllis barely acknowledged he was speaking, but didn't nod.

"Anyway, once the car was all fixed up, I drove up some more till I got to where I was heading: Hallowell, Maine, a little south of Augusta. That's where Captain Kipps lives now. He's the fella from Sam's trial, and the Sherriff up there in Hallowell these days. Said being Captain was too much of a desk job up there, but Sherriff suited him just fine, so he took that.

"So he and I got to chatting once I tracked him down having coffee at this little breakfast place up there. Nice place. Told him I was from Vermont, but he didn't seem to care until I told him *what part* of Vermont I was from. 'Oh', he says. 'That's funny. That's

367

where *I'm* from.' I smiled and nodded at first, but after we'd each taken another sip of coffee, I told him I knew that already, that I was actually up there in Maine *because* of him.

"He looked at me kinda funny then, as you might imagine, unsure what to think, but when I told him I was Sam Newhaus's father-in-law, he noticeably pushed back a bit from the table. It amused me to see him backing away from me like I was some sort of a villain myself, so I just laughed at him. Don't think he liked that, though."

"Dad, is this going somewhere?" Olivia interrupted.

Alan nodded and looked down, still composing his thoughts. What he'd say next was sure to surprise them all, so he chose his words carefully.

"Kerry Ann was a sweet girl. She was no angel, but what one of us is? Except for maybe Jessica over there," he added, smiling at Peaches. "But no, Kerry Ann's only fault, her only *real* mistake in this life, was to have ever met any of *our* family."

He paused and looked around at them, but mostly at the adults.

"Our fucked up, disappointing, but ultimately *redeemable* family," he said, punctuating his remarks with a strange mixture of both harsh criticism and gentle love.

"She was a good girl. She was a sweet girl, and a beautiful girl too, and someone who certainly didn't deserve to die at the hands of one of us."

An uncomfortable silence followed next, but then—

"Did you know her too, Grandpa?" Peaches asked.

He went to answer, but Lenny spoke first.

"We all did, honey. She worked for the catering company your mom and I used to hire for big parties. Not that we used them too much before then, and certainly not much after."

He looked over at the others with a sad smile as he spoke.

"We didn't know her too well, of course, but she would come right in here to the kitchen and set up all the food for the parties, and she'd help clean up afterward too."

"Yes, that's all true, of course, Leonard," Alan said, "but I also knew her outside of all that."

"Alan, this is ridiculous," Phyllis interrupted him for the first time. "What good could *possibly* come from any of this now? The girl is dead. Please stop this."

Phyllis's whole demeanor had changed, and she was up quickly on the edge of her seat, looking much more unnerved than before. Alan reached out a hand to her, and she grabbed it tightly with both of her own.

"Please, Alan. Let's just go home."

She stood up, hoping to pull him away too, but Alan wouldn't budge, so she reluctantly sat back down as he shook his head.

"No, I need to make my amends now. I can't live with this guilt anymore. Not one more day. You see everyone, Kerry Ann and I had a, well, a brief affair. If you can call blackmailing her into sex an affair."

He looked into their faces, as each one of them shook their heads or turned away from him completely.

"No, I suppose you can't. You shouldn't. I hurt her. I hurt her both physically and emotionally, and I blackmailed her into keeping quiet about it all too. I had more than enough dirt on that girl to ruin her life, in fact. I know how that must sound to you, and how sick you must think I am—and I *am* sick, or was anyhow, that's for damn sure—but I *also* know that none of this will come as any shock whatsoever to Sam over there."

Sam stared Alan down now like he was ready to attack him, but Alan just smiled back at him calmly. He knew his words had to be said out loud, despite how much it would hurt his family, and any relationship he ever hoped to have with them again.

"Kerry Ann and I only met four times that summer," Alan continued. "Once was here at the house for a party. That was the first time I met her. She wore a catering apron and had her hair up in a ponytail. Kerry Ann thought she had the run of the place, which is why she was so frightened when I caught her taking money from Caroline's purse."

Caroline looked up at the ceiling just then with a deep breath, and Lenny seemed confused.

"You knew about that?" he asked her. "That she tried to steal money from you?"

Caroline confirmed it with a quick nod, but didn't turn back.

"Technically," Alan said, "she *did* steal the money. This happened when you were all going on about Caroline being pregnant again. I couldn't hold it any longer, had to come in here to pee, and that's when I saw her with a fistful of cash above Caroline's purse. She started to panic, so I ordered her to count the money. Then I pulled out my own wallet, shoved just as much if not more back into Caroline's purse so she wouldn't miss it, and told Kerry Ann to pocket the money she'd taken quickly before anyone noticed. Then I went to the bathroom to relieve myself."

He paused and shook his head, leaning back into the couch and getting more comfortable again.

"When I opened the bathroom door a couple minutes later, I could hear Kerry Ann over there talking to Sam." Alan pointed toward the kitchen briefly as he spoke. "He was laying it on real thick too, obviously flirting with her, so I slipped out the front door and came around the back again through the side gate. I blended in for a while, talked bullshit with Caroline's dad, some nonsense about sports no doubt, but all the while I was watching the house. Waiting for Sam to come back out again.

"When he finally did, he had this real shit-eatin' grin on like he'd just busted a nut inside. 'Course I knew he didn't have time for any of that, but what was it Sam? A kiss? A fondle? What?"

Sam's eyes narrowed, having never stopped staring at him, and if the others thought Sam wouldn't even answer the question, they were soon proved wrong.

"I kissed her on the cheek," he said, looking away from Alan for just a moment toward Olivia and then to Haley.

"I could tell Kerry Ann was nervous about something when I walked in, but we just made small talk. Nothing more. She looked up at me with this pouty, perfect mouth of hers, and I couldn't help but kiss her cheek softly before I left. Nothing pushy. It was mutual. I knew she loved it every bit as much as I did."

"That's great, Sam," Alan said, more cheerfully than the moment warranted. "That's really great. And then you seduced her some more that summer, had some more fun at her expense, as well as your family's, and then you took your chance one night in September and you killed her. Isn't that right?"

"No," Sam said, but he looked guilty again. "I didn't kill her."

"You know, Sam," Alan went on. "You keep telling yourself that little story, and maybe one of these days you'll actually believe it. I know for a fact you took her to the tree house that night. I know you had sex with her in there too. And come to think of it, your mistress knew it all too." He paused again for effect, this time looking to the seat beside Lenny. "Didn't you, Caroline?"

All three girls turned their heads toward Caroline now, and they watched her as she smiled strangely, first at the ceiling, and then back at Alan.

"You think you have this all figured out, Alan? You think you're Sherlock fucking Holmes all of a sudden? Just swoop in here and pronounce judgments on the rest of us without really owning up to anything yourself?"

"Mommy—" Peaches started, but Caroline held her hand out toward her as she continued.

"You know what, Alan? I think you ought to explain how exactly you know so much about all this, seeing as you've stayed far away from this case from the very beginning. You never even went to the courtroom as I recall. Why is that?"

"I'm not here to pass any more judgment on you or Sam than I pass on myself as well," Alan said, looking down sadly, silencing Caroline momentarily. "But am I correct in saying that you were or *are* Sam's mistress?"

Chapter 47

Seventeen years earlier

Caroline woke up only an hour after she'd fallen asleep, and she immediately began crying. It was a ritual now, a practice she'd come to expect, and though the tears fell quickly just as they had every morning for the past month, she once again kept every single one of them from Lenny.

The post-partem depression after Erika was born had lasted for months, but this? This was something worse. With a second child on the way, Caroline didn't know how she would survive it all.

Making her way down the stairs in the darkness, she found her path through the front hall toward the kitchen, where she switched on the lights under the cabinets. In her right hand, she clutched the small baby monitor she kept by her bed, so she could hear if Erika woke up.

Exploring the cabinets, she found the bottle of Jack she usually left out for Alan, and soon poured herself a small glass over ice.

One little drink will be fine, she told herself.

The sting of the alcohol hit her hard, and the harsh taste helped jolt her momentarily from her sadness.

It was only then that she heard a small noise from outside, and she went over to the sliding glass door to look out and investigate. She saw nothing at first, but as her eyes slowly adjusted to the darkness of the yard, she finally realized there was movement coming from *inside* the tree house.

An awful fear overtook her suddenly, and she practically ran across the room with her glass of whiskey splashing about to turn off the lights. Once she did, she crept back over to the place by the door, and peered out again past the curtain toward the tree. Much more clearly now, she could see them there at last: two people having sex inside.

It took everything in her power not to drop the glass of liquor as the crippling pain overtook her again, the same helpless pain she'd lived with for eight long months already.

Her body almost collapsed beneath her then as she barely managed to rest the glass on the countertop before making her way to the cold floor in front of the sliding glass door.

Reaching up breathlessly in place, she found the small lock with her fingers. She needed to know. She needed to know for sure if it was him.

Caroline's hand trembled terribly as she finally managed to slide the lock up, to push open the door just an inch or so to listen. Waiting there on the floor in the darkness a moment more, she soon heard their voices whispering in the night air as clear as day. Sam. And *her.*

Chapter 48

"Sam and Kerry Ann," Caroline finished speaking. "I knew it was them. I knew they were in there, in that *place*, and that he was *fucking* her. Hard."

Everyone sat in mesmerized silence, none more so than the three girls sitting closely together on the sofa opposite their grandparents: Haley, Peaches, and Erika.

"I didn't realize your post-partem went on so long," Lenny said, trying to take himself, if not everyone else too, further away from the events surrounding Kerry Ann's murder.

"It didn't," she said softly. "It was something else."

No one else knew, save for Olivia and Sam.

"Well what else was there?" Lenny asked. "Why were you still so sad?"

Caroline couldn't stop the pain swelling up within her. It heaved and groaned inside her body as if using its own broken lungs to breathe. Part of her was still on the floor seventeen years earlier, eight months pregnant with Peaches, gasping for the same forbidden air.

The agony was too much for her to handle anymore. She shook her head back and forth with the memory of it all, and felt sure she'd break down completely if she dared even look Lenny in the face now.

"You should just tell him, Car," Olivia said softly, jarring her alert. "And tell *her.*"

Caroline locked eyes with Olivia, and they stared at each other for a very long time as Caroline tried to compose herself, a teardrop breaking loose as she finally looked away. At nothing. At no one. At anyone but the two of them.

"They deserve to know, Caroline," Olivia went on, much more firmly than before, "and it's gonna come out now anyway, so you may as well."

"Tell me what?" Lenny asked, barely in a whisper.

She shook her head once more and opened her mouth, but when she was finally ready to speak, it was not to him that she looked, but to Peaches.

"Peaches, honey. I'm so sorry to tell you like this."

Her voice caught up in her throat as she allowed the words free passage at last.

"Dad is—Dad is not your father. Your Uncle Sam is."

Peaches turned white, and looked like she'd just been smacked hard across the face. She threw both hands up to her head and bent over quickly, panting with shock as much as with pain, as if all the life and family she'd ever known were just yanked away from her in an instant.

"Oh my God," Erika said, looking at Haley as they each put an arm around Peaches from either side.

For his part, Lenny crumbled. He began hyperventilating, sobbing out tears first that quickly turned to loud screams of deepest anguish, as Peaches echoed every grunt of it herself from across the room.

No one knew what to do. What to say or how, or to whom. The entire room was filled with pain, and not one soul of the nine there was left untouched by the revelation, because of the profound sadness expressed by both Peaches and Lenny in turn.

All the girls could do was try to console Peaches somehow, but Erika and Haley were shell-shocked too. One had just gained a sister, while the other felt like she just lost one.

Caroline was unable to lift her arm towards Lenny, but she knew he wouldn't want her to touch him just then either. She looked at Olivia pleadingly instead, and Olivia stood up and went over to Lenny, wrapping her arms around her little brother with love, rocking back and forth with him through his pain.

It was a secret that had lasted 17 years, a secret truth Sam, Caroline, and Olivia had faithfully kept from everyone else, and often themselves. Not even Alan and Phyllis knew it, although judging by their faces now, and the brief look the two exchanged, it didn't come as much of a shock either.

Looking around the room at all the pain and sadness, and the many years of lying caused by this one sad but simple fact, Haley somehow saw through it all to the good the truth would bring.

Despite all her strange and often troubled interactions with Peaches, especially regarding her wacky brand of spirituality, she suddenly felt much closer to her. Stranger still, she felt closer to Erika as well.

Now *Erika* was the odd one out, and it created a new kind of profound, nurturing love for her younger cousin that she hadn't known before. As Haley rubbed Peaches on the back, she reached across to Erika too, and their eyes locked with a knowing affection.

"I know I should have told you years ago," Caroline cried out, "and I had so many opportunities every year since, but somehow everything just worked out as it was, and I didn't think I needed to upset the balance our family has right now. Peaches, honey, Dad is still your dad. He loves you very much, and he always will. He's loved you like his own, and that's all that should ever matter."

Peaches barely looked up at her, and at Lenny, but she nodded anyway, the tears still coming fast.

"The only reason I'm even telling you this now, in this already awful conversation, is because Sam is a better man than so many of you think he is, better even than I used to think he was. Yes, we had an affair, and yes, we've seen each other again since he's been back. Lenny knows," she said, pausing to look at Phyllis.

"But what you should also know is, Sam supported Peaches every step of the way. So much so that he moved to Vegas to begin with because of a business opportunity there, and with the hopes of supporting both his daughters, and me, and Erika, and Olivia, for all these years. The houses he bought on the lake are in all three girls' names. He's not gonna make a penny on them himself once they're paid off."

"This is insane," Phyllis snapped, sitting up straight in her seat. "Sam hasn't supported Olivia at all! He ran out on his family. That's all he did. Just because he sent his daughter checks in the mail, and this one besides," she said, referencing Peaches without saying her name, "doesn't mean he really cares about you. And he certainly doesn't care about Olivia either, for crying out loud."

"Yes he *DOES*, Mom!" Olivia yelled out at her, and the room fell silent.

Peaches and Lenny both stopped crying, and everyone in the room looked at Olivia now like she was delirious. All but Sam, who just shook his head at the floor with a sad smile.

"What?" Lenny asked. "What are you saying, Livi?"

Olivia leaned back from Lenny, her head in her hands briefly before composing herself and looking around the room.

"Sam and I haven't been the enemies we all make you think we are. It's not that we've had it perfect, either—*God knows we haven't had it perfect, Sam*—but we've somehow made this work. For 23 years, we've made this crazy, fucked up friendship work."

Sam let out a dark laugh then, and Olivia smirked sadly as their eyes met through the sea of pain between them. The new truth had a strange, calming effect on the rest of them, and even Lenny and Peaches seemed much less sad all of a sudden.

"I don't understand," Phyllis said. "What the hell is this? What's happening here?"

"I know it must seem crazy to you all, shocking even," Sam said, "but this really is—"

"No. *You* shut up," Phyllis interrupted him, holding a hand out his way and staring at Olivia. "You're telling me this jackass not only had an affair with your brother's wife, not only had a fucking *child* out of wedlock with her, but he also fucked and murdered a girl, and you're *okay* with that?"

"He didn't murder anyone, Mom," Olivia said, much more seriously now, returning to her seat between Caroline and the girls.

She pulled out her cigarettes and lit one up too, figuring all rules of decorum were temporarily on hold.

Once she'd inhaled and blown some smoke away behind her, away from the others, she relaxed a bit more in her seat, then finally stared down Alan when she spoke next.

"Dad killed Kerry Ann. Didn't you, Dad?"

"What?" Alan asked, taken aback.

"You did it, Dad. It's okay. We know already. Sam and me."

"No," Alan said. "No, it was Sam. Captain Kipps told me everything. Sam's DNA was found on her underwear. You all know *that*. He had sex with her that night, and then he brought her out into that damn field and killed her, leaving her out there for the animals. Kipps said the position of her body made him sure the murder happened there, and not back here."

The way he said it, *not back here,* made the girls retract a bit in their seats. Something *had* happened right there in the yard just feet from where they all sat, and some of the adults in the room seemed to know exactly what it was.

"Look, I had sex with Kerry Ann in the tree house," Sam said, wagging his finger out toward Alan. "That's true. That part is all true. But that was the night *before* Kerry Ann was killed. I didn't even speak to her the next day, except by text."

"That's a lie though, isn't it, Sam?" Caroline said, looking across at him sadly, looking at her former lover like she'd lost all trust in the man for the first time in her life, and feeling gutted she'd never seen through to arriving at this conclusion before, despite everything she knew.

"I saw you there that night, Sam. *Both* nights."

"No. Caroline, no. It was the night before. I didn't—"

"No, Sam. You came back here and you fucked that girl all over again the following night."

Chapter 49

Seventeen years earlier

After the scene she'd witnessed in the tree house the night before, along with the numb darkness of her head and heart, the hollow emptiness she thought she'd never be able to shake off, Caroline couldn't sleep at all the following night.

She spent most of the overnight hours between Erika's crib upstairs and the couch in the living room, where her drinking had begun to get worse, critically dangerous for her future child.

She passed out around midnight, the baby monitor still rising and falling on her tummy with each new breath, but just after one in the morning, she was awoken by a noise from the front of the house, followed shortly after by the familiar squeak of the side gate.

The late-night *wrongness* of the sounds stirred her awake, the baby monitor falling to her side on the seat cushion.

The living room, completely dark save for the time on their VCR, spun around her from the liquor as she sat up in place. Above her head, Caroline spied the narrow window above the living room couch still propped open. Lenny, she remembered, had opened it earlier in the day to push out an invading bumble bee.

She listened intently for any more noises from the yard, but heard nothing. *Was it a dream?*

After a few more minutes, Caroline laid down again, prepared to fall back to sleep. But that's when she heard *her voice* through the open window above the couch.

"Sam?" Kerry Ann spoke into the darkness, just loud enough for Caroline to hear her from inside. "You up there already?"

"Yeah, c'mon up," she heard him say.

Caroline listened carefully for another moment, but heard nothing. Two minutes more passed in silence until finally she heard them fucking, and once again, her whole body began to shake with the sadness.

Despite all they'd been through, all the sex, the sneaking around, and now his baby, he was still doing this to her right there in her own backyard, just feet from her house, two nights in a row no less, and she felt powerless to do anything about it.

Ten minutes more passed as Caroline moaned through her pain, trying to block out all the noises from the tree house, but suddenly a loud shriek and a thump came from outside, and she was certain someone had just fallen from the tree house.

She stood up on the couch to listen through the window, frozen in place against the wall as a terrible fear ran through her bones. Careful to stay hidden inside away from the window, she heard the second person come tumbling down the tree house steps a moment later. Silence then, and then running, and grunting, followed by the squeak of the side gate.

Caroline didn't want to look outside, terrified by what she might see there. If it was Kerry Ann, she worried the girl might see her inside, and start begging her for help. Help she didn't want to give her. And if it was Sam who had fallen, she was scared she'd see him there lying dead.

Tip-toeing to the sliding glass door, Caroline was prepared to peer out, when a sudden bout of extreme nausea hit her all at once, and she barely made it to the downstairs bathroom at the front of the house before vomiting, half on the toilet lid and half inside.

By the time she returned to the back of the house and the sliding glass door a few minutes later, not yet cleaning herself or the bathroom up, she took a deep breath before pulling back the curtain a few inches to peer out.

It was a long while before she could see much of anything, but once her eyes adjusted enough, she saw her there. Kerry Ann. Laid out on the ground at the foot of the tree house. She was flat on her back with a hand to her right leg, panting, it seemed, with pain.

Caroline looked around the yard as much as she could, but couldn't spot Sam anywhere. He must have gone off for help, she decided, not wanting to wake anyone inside.

Chapter 50

"Despite my drinking," Caroline continued, "and everything I knew about Kerry Ann and Sam, I also knew I had to help the girl. I switched open the door lock, and was about to slide the door open when I heard the squeak of the side gate. It took everything in my power not to throw up again right there, this time from fear, but I backed away slowly, over there, to the far side of the kitchen. Through the curtains, I saw Sam had come back again, and was dragging her away as she sobbed."

"That wasn't me, Caroline," Sam said. "You've got to believe me. I saw Kerry Ann the night before, out there in the tree house, just as you said, but not that night. I don't know who that was, but I promise you it wasn't me."

"It was me," Alan said then, reluctantly, as if only to himself, and if anyone looked at him when he said this, it was only out of instinct, as they quickly turned away from him again, no one wanting to hear any more.

He shook his head back and forth before continuing, speaking very slowly as he did, sad to even hear the words leave his lips.

"She and I had an arrangement, you see. She never *had* to have sex with me, but I told her it was either the sex or the money, and she chose the sex. But she hadn't satisfied her end of the bargain. I know how that must sound to all of you, and I agree it's sickening to even imagine myself doing it now, but that's just what the situation was at the time. It's who I was. When I caught up to Kerry Ann in town the week before, when I cornered her looking for more, she called me a disgusting old man, and she taunted me to tell on her, promising to out me too if I did.

"So I started following her every move, more than I already had been. I tracked her here the night before, and I watched it all from the side of the house, on the other side of that damn squeaky gate, as she and Sam had sex up there in the tree house. From there, it was easy enough for me to get her to meet me up there too, I figured, as long as she thought I was Sam.

"Jesus Christ," Haley said, feeling like she might vomit now too.

"I put a note on her windshield the next day. I told her to meet me—*Sam*—out there in the yard at 1:15 that night."

"God, I knew it was *you*," Olivia said, shaking her head at the floor, and crying now as she looked up at Alan.

"I always knew it was you, Dad, or I guessed it was you. I didn't *want* to believe it, you know? But I knew. Deep down, I knew. That's why I kept up this crazy business against Sam all this time, to protect you. I knew Sam was innocent, and they'd never be able to prove anything, but— *Jesus*, Dad. Why did you have to *kill* her? Why didn't you just wake up Caroline and Lenny and call a fucking ambulance or something?"

Alan looked at his daughter in shock, and he shook his head at her again as he spoke.

"No. I didn't kill anyone, Olivia," he said. "I told you I didn't. Kerry Ann fell from the damn tree house and she broke her leg. Well, we *thought* she had broken her leg, anyhow, but the evidence just said she was cut up a bit on her face and hands. Internal bleeding, but no broken bones."

A new, dreadful silence filled the room all of a sudden.

"*We* thought?" Haley asked.

"What?" Alan said, surprised by the question.

"You said 'we', Grandpa. '*We*' thought she had broken her leg. Who is the 'we'? Was it just you in the tree house that night, or was there someone else up there too?"

"Of course it was only me," he said, flustered and looking around at them all, Phyllis last, who was clearly glaring back at him. "It doesn't matter, Phyllis," he said softly. "Sam is to blame. He did something to her that night after you left her there. You were just trying to help her."

He looked back at the others then and sighed, shaking his head.

"Look. I drove home and woke up Phyllis to come and help me, and we drove back over here together. She's a nurse, and I knew she could help out a lot quicker than any emergency crew from the fire department would have anyway. What would they do? Give her the Heimlich maneuver? No. It would have been too dangerous to involve them."

"I don't want any part of this conversation," Phyllis said, grabbing her purse and standing up. "I'm sick to my stomach over all of this, and all of you. All I did was try to help you that night."

"No one's disputing that, darling," Alan said, reaching up and holding her arm. "It was Sam who killed her. You only tried to help her. I saw it."

"What I saw," Caroline said, "was a man who I thought was Sam come into the back yard here and drag Kerry Ann away."

"That was me," Alan said, "but I didn't kill her. Phyllis waited in the car and I came back here to get Kerry Ann. I wanted to bring her to the hospital. My knee was killing me, though. I took a hard fall down the damn stairs of the tree house that night, and my knee has given me trouble ever since. I couldn't lift the girl. I couldn't lift her at all, so I grabbed her arms and dragged her over to the side gate and out to the car."

"So then you just left her out in a field to die?" Erika asked.

"No, of course not," Alan said, growing upset, his eyes darting around at each one there. "I'd never do that! Phyllis dropped me home, because my knee was hurting me so much, and then she brought Kerry Ann over to Sam and Olivia's house. After that, Sam must have brought her out to that field and killed her. Punished her for cheating on him perhaps. Captain Kipps said he was sure she was still alive out there, that she died where they found her. I didn't kill her though, I'm telling you. It wasn't me."

He paused and looked around at them, realizing too late that they were all staring not at him anymore, but at Phyllis, and he didn't know why.

"Look," he said, trying to get their attention. "I didn't want to believe this about Sam either," he went on, "but Phyllis, well she had nothing to do with it. She tried to *help* Kerry Ann."

"You just don't know when to shut up, Alan, do you?" Phyllis asked, sitting back down and looking away from all of them.

"Phyllis, it's fine. Sam did it. You said so yourself. He went out there and killed her to keep his affair quiet, and because he resented Kerry Ann for having sex with *me*. Kids, honestly, we've kept this a secret for years to *protect* you, and the only reason I'm coming clean now is because I can't live with the guilt anymore. I needed to confess my part in all this once and for all, and do whatever I can to make this right."

"Mom," Olivia asked, her voice breaking unnaturally as she spoke. "What did you do?"

"What?" Alan asked. "She didn't do anything, Olivia," he persisted. "Your mother *helped* Kerry Ann, don't you see? She brought her to your house. To Sam. She thought she was helping Kerry Ann, and helping me. And she and I have covered faithfully for Sam all these years because of you and the girls."

"This is all such bullshit," Phyllis said, first locking eyes with Olivia and then looking up at the ceiling as she shook her head. "This is absolute bullshit, every bit of it."

"What...*did you*...do?" Olivia asked again, waiting until Phyllis looked at her again. "Tell me."

"Listen to me, Olivia," Phyllis said. "That little slut wiggled her legs around two of the three men in this family, and I was supposed to do nothing when given the chance? I was supposed to just let her have her way with everyone? Oh hell no. What? Did you want Sam to have a second child out of wedlock? Did you want her and your dad to have a baby too? Sure, that'd be great. That way, she wouldn't only be the slut your husband went to once he was done fucking you and Caroline, but she'd be your goddamn step-mother too."

She paused and shook her head at the wall.

"What kind of a hick-ass name is Kerry Ann anyway? Pick a name already. Kerry or Ann. Jesus Christ."

Chapter 51

Seventeen years earlier

"That's the mountain," Kerry Ann muttered drowsily from the backseat. "My house is the other way." Even through the rain on the windows, she could tell they were going in the wrong direction.

"Don't you worry, honey," Phyllis said, clutching the steering wheel tightly with her black gloves, a calm smile arriving naturally as she stole a glance at Kerry Ann in the rear-view mirror. "I know a little shortcut."

She pulled down a side road that led up the hill not too far from Sam and Olivia's house, then turned her headlights off once she got close to the top. Going along slowly a little while further, she thought out what she needed to do, and in what order.

"How's your head, honey? Still have a headache?"

"Yes," Kerry Ann said, barely able to speak. "I think it might be a concussion. I feel really weird."

"That's just the chloroform. Try not to fight it now. I can give you a little more in a minute."

"What? Wait. What is that? Is that a good thing or a bad thing?"

"It's a very, very good thing," Phyllis said with another smile, and she stopped the car with a glance back at Kerry Ann as she undid her seat belt.

Eyeing Olivia's yellow raincoat on the floor of the backseat, she smiled, glad to have the extra help. She put it on quickly, then got out of the car in the rain and looked around for a moment. Once she was satisfied with the location, she opened the back door of the car and leaned past Kerry Ann to the young girl's purse to look around for her phone.

Grabbing it and closing the door again, she dialed Sam's house number and waited until someone picked up, thrilled when she heard Sam's voice on the other end. Then she waited approximately 15 seconds and hung up again, throwing the phone away onto the grass nearby.

Next she yanked Kerry Ann from the car, amused to see her head hit the ground with a little bounce. She slid the girl forward then through the muddy grass to a spot beneath some overhanging tree branches.

"Now take a deep breath," she told her sweetly. "It's okay, honey. I'm a nurse."

Kerry Ann did as she was told, her mind already clouded by the chloroform, but as soon as she inhaled, Phyllis pinched the girl's nose shut tightly with one hand and began smothering her mouth with all her might with the other.

Kerry Ann's eyes broke open wide with dread as she fought with whatever energy she had left to break free.

"Good bye now, dear. It's time for you to rot in hell, you filthy little cum dumpster."

Phyllis increased the pressure for as long as she needed to while Kerry Ann hoped for air that would never come.

The blur of falling raindrops on her unblinking eyeballs was the last thing she ever saw.

Chapter 52

Stunned to silence, the entire Abrams family stared in horror at Phyllis with an unfamiliar kind of hateful energy they'd never known before. She wasn't just a murderer, they saw, but an unremorseful one besides.

"I gave that girl an out," Phyllis went on, looking at each and every one of them carefully. "I gave her a very simple, very peaceful *exit* from this godforsaken world, and I'll tell you what else. She and her whole family owe *me* a goddamn debt of fucking gratitude for it. If I hadn't put an end to her that night, who knows what would have happened next? You should all be *thanking* me."

She stood up straight then, looking proud.

"Every one of you should be thanking me for this. I cleaned up that mess. I *fixed* the situation, is what I did. Sam and Alan made their mistakes, but I fixed it! You hear me? I fixed it!"

She marched into the kitchen and sought out a bottle of wine that would never appear. Grabbing the large bottle of Jack Daniels tucked in close to the wall instead, she slammed it on the kitchen counter and grabbed a glass from the cabinets. Shoving it under the ice dispenser on the outside of the fridge, much more ice came out than she needed, and the extra cubes toppled across the kitchen floor before she filled her glass with whiskey and downed it in several long gulps.

"And I'll tell you what else," she said, already pouring herself another glass. "If I go down for this, you all will too. Alan knew what he did to that girl. Sam and Livi both *covered* for Alan this whole time too. And Caroline? Well congratulations, you big dumb fuck. You just outed yourself as well. So how about that? How about all five of us go to jail, and leave Lenny to raise the girls on his own? Is that what you want?"

"All six of us," Lenny said, barely audible, and everyone turned to him, even Phyllis from the kitchen. "I'm no innocent either," he added, looking at Erika, Peaches, and Haley. "I'm sorry, girls. I always thought your Uncle Sam might have had something to do with it, but something Livi once said to me made me think about it all differently."

He looked at Olivia with a sad smirk.

"Remember after Sam moved to Vegas, you told me we just needed to keep an eye on dad now?"

She nodded.

"You walked away from me when you said it," Lenny went on, "but man, if you didn't plant a seed of doubt in me *that* day. And— *I dunno*—it's not like I really *wanted* to think about any of this over the years. I certainly didn't want it to be either one of you, but—"

His voice trailed off then. He stood up and walked over to the sliding glass door, and opened it up to look out at the tree house.

"I woke up early that next morning. Caroline was fast asleep in here on the couch, and I'd already gotten Erika out of her crib and into her playpen. I told her not 'to wake Mommy', and she faithfully obeyed. Then I opened the sliding door to let in some fresh air.

"And I spotted it. Right away. Even from back here. Fresh blood splattered across the old ladder."

A new wave of nausea swept through the room at the words, and Peaches slapped a hand to her mouth.

"I didn't know whose it was, of course. Hell, I thought it might have even been Caroline's, but—"

His voice quieted as he seemed to choke on his breath a bit.

"A part of me wondered if it wasn't Sam all along. I knew he'd seen that girl we hired, and I'd kept his secret for him like a good friend, but if something *had* happened out there? In my yard? Well, I just didn't want anyone to know, so I—"

Lenny began to cough just then, and he spun around quickly, barely making it to the garbage can before he threw up.

Erika ran to the bathroom at the front of the house, and she threw up as well.

Only Lenny's coughs and the clink of ice cubes in Phyllis's glass broke the long silence that followed. The water ran in the front bathroom, and a minute later, Erika returned to the kitchen as Lenny continued.

"I wiped the ladder down, and I threw some water down on the grass out there too, because I could tell there was blood spattered here and there on the lawn as well."

He turned and faced them all again.

"I covered it up. No two ways about it. I knew something happened, but instead of leaving it there and maybe calling the police, or even just asking Caroline or Sam, I instinctively got rid of the evidence."

He shook his head and wiped his mouth and face again as he stared outside.

"Should have lit that whole goddamn tree on fire right then and there. Should have torched the whole fucking yard."

"That would have made things even more suspicious," Erika said, now leaning on the wall behind Phyllis with her eyes closed.

Lenny turned to look at her.

"Yeah," he said. "Probably. Yeah."

Olivia was still fuming, carefully eyeing Phyllis when she wasn't looking, in between exchanged looks with Alan, Sam, and Haley.

"I can't believe I get shit for staying out late and smoking pot, and my whole family has been involved with all this," Erika said.

Phyllis snorted with a big laugh then as she took another long sip of her drink, but Erika was quickly jarred alert.

"You don't get to do that," she snapped at her grandmother. "You don't get to kill an innocent girl, and then stand there and laugh at whatever you find funny. This isn't funny. None of this is funny. You're sick, you know that? You're really fucking sick."

"Don't you *dare* speak to me like that, young lady. You don't know what I've been through or why I did the things I did. Especially since you're busy whoring your way through life just like Kerry Ann Jefferson did."

A loud gasp let out from around the room, but Phyllis plowed on quickly.

"Grandpa and I saw you with that football goon in our garage a few weeks ago, you know, and I wouldn't be surprised if you're letting that nigger boy fuck you now too."

At this, Erika lunged at Phyllis with both hands, and everyone was up out of their seats right away. Lenny got there first, as he was still on the other side of the kitchen, but he was quickly joined by Olivia and Caroline, all desperate to pull the two women apart. Erika managed to scratch Phyllis's face hard before they separated.

"Erika, go upstairs," Caroline ordered her. "You can't be doing this kind of thing. We'll take care of this."

Erika ran away, crying on her way up the stairs, and after a moment, Caroline decided to run up after her as well.

"What the fuck is wrong with you?!" Olivia screamed at Phyllis, right up in her face. "How could you do such a thing?!"

"After everything I have done for you, for all of you, *this* is how you talk to me?"

"You're sick, Mom. You're sick in the head and the soul, if you even have a soul. I can't believe you did something like this."

"Yet somehow you were fine with it when it was just your father who had killed the girl? *That* you could forgive? Really?"

"Yes, Mom, because if dad did it, I knew in my heart it was a horrible accident, but you just admitted to us all that you *chose* this. You did it on purpose. You killed Kerry Ann, and you let us all think it was Sam or Dad the whole time. And unlike Dad, you *knew* *this* all along, and you still accused Sam of murder. How fucking sick *are* you?"

Phyllis took her drink and walked away from her, away from all of them, head held high out into the backyard, as Olivia just watched her.

Every vile thing she'd ever thought about her mother over her lifetime came back to her then, and for the first time in her life, even she began contemplating murder. In her head, she saw herself jumping behind Phyllis and beating her over the head with the bottle of Jack Daniels.

Seething, she followed her mother outside. Lenny quickly exchanged a nervous glance with the others, and then he followed them outside too, as Alan, Sam, Peaches, and Haley followed last.

"Now don't do anything crazy here, Livi," Lenny said to her, and Phyllis spun around to face them all.

She threw back the rest of her drink with a mighty thrust of sudden energy, then spun around and hurled the empty glass hard against the tree house, shattering it to pieces.

A smile grew slowly across her face then, and as she turned around to stare them down once more, she began to laugh. A thin stream of blood slipped down her cheek, where a single shard of glass had bounced off the tree and hit her just below the eye.

"You were the murderer, Sam. You. They all hate *me* now, but only because they know the truth. They've hated you for all these years, the whole town and half the valley. And there's no proof I did this at all anyway, so guess what? They're *still* gonna hate you, for as long as you live."

Her face relaxed into a calm smile as she looked away, appreciating the light summer breeze on her skin. Then they watched her with renewed horror as a manic look came over her.

"Hello?" she said in an elegant voice, holding a hand to her ear like it was a telephone. "Yes officer, I thought you should know Sam Newhaus is back in town, and he's been acting *very* suspicious. No, I don't want to give you my name. I just wanted you to know where you could find him for further questioning. Yes. You're *very* welcome, officer. Goodbye."

"You're a monster," Olivia said, as Sam came up beside Olivia to hold her back. "You're a fucking monster!"

"Oh, dear. I know you think that now, but give it some time and you'll see why I did it. You'll come to see I actually saved you a lifetime of heartache."

"You—you *saved* me?" Olivia asked, barely able to even get the words out.

"Yes. That's what mothers are for."

"We need to call the police," Olivia said, turning to Sam. "We need to call them right now, and tell them what she's told us. She needs to pay for this. For all of it."

"Well hang on now," Sam said, looking back at the others. "Wouldn't that implicate everyone else too?"

"That's right, Livi," Phyllis said, smiling. "Listen to Sam, now. He's being very smart about this. I would just have to let the police know the whole story. About your father. About you and Sam, and Leonard, and Caroline. All of you. You don't really want that now, do you?"

"Are you *dead* yet?" Olivia snapped back, and for the first time, Phyllis actually looked scared.

Olivia had never spoken to her this way, not even in the worst of their angriest arguments over the years.

"How dare—"

"Are you fucking dead yet?!" Olivia screamed out. "You don't get to speak anymore, Mom! You don't have *anything* to do with this family anymore. We're *done* with you. You understand that? All of us!"

Phyllis turned her back to her, looking up at the tree house with new tears in her eyes, tears she wasn't willing to show them just yet.

"Everything I did, Olivia, I did for this family. I did it to protect you all, and to keep you from ruin. I gave you and your brother a good life, a far better life up here than you would have ever had back on Long Island, that's for damn sure. Away from all the gangs and the drugs."

As she spoke, she looked at the tree house as if it alone was the source of all her problems, the tawdry, awful place where her son-in-law and husband had each fucked Kerry Ann in secret. The place that girl never should have entered. The place Sam and Lenny never should have built.

Reaching up on her toes, she felt the old wood of the inside, her hand caressing the entrance of the tree house for the very first time. It brought her a strange sense of comfort too, as if she could go back in time, un-build the thing somehow. Stop Alan from even talking to that girl, let alone blackmailing her, or fucking her.

As she felt around with her fingertips, she just barely grazed the end of one of the two old pillows inside, and recoiled quickly, holding her hand to her chest like it'd been burned somehow, burned by the girl whose life she'd ended that fateful night so many years ago.

She turned around to look at them, and once more saw the hatred on their faces, and the pure disappointment of her grandchildren. On the edge of the deck, Caroline and Erika had joined them again, and just behind them in the doorway, she was shocked to see Captain Kipps staring out.

Alan looked back at him once he saw Phyllis's face change, but he just nodded at the man, not too surprised to see him there it seemed. Even so, he held out his hand, asking the man to wait.

"You *brought* him here?" Phyllis asked Alan, incredulous at his betrayal. "How fucking stupid are you, Alan? Did the doctor remove your whole goddamn brain that day too?"

"Look, Phyllis—" he started, but she went on.

"What the hell is wrong with you? What the hell is wrong with all of you? That little slut ruined your lives seventeen years ago, and now you want to let her ruin your lives all over again now? How fucking dumb are you all?"

She paused and looked around at them, each and every one of them looking back at her like she was insane.

"You all think I'm mad because I killed that little bitch, yet I'm the sanest fucking one standing here. *You're* all insane if you think I did something wrong. I gave her the fucking help she deserved. I shut her up once and for all, and she died quickly, okay? Is that what you all want to hear, that she died nice and fast? Well it's true. Within ninety seconds, after her eyes glazed over and her body stopped shaking beneath me, she was gone, alright? Okay? Nice and quick."

Captain Kipps shook his head and pulled out a pair of handcuffs then, moving through them all to arrest her.

"No, no, no. You stay the hell away from me, sir," Phyllis said, her eyes wild with fury.

She watched as he approached her very slowly, weaving his way through her family members as if invisible to them, like a jaguar stalking his prey.

"I mean it," she said, stepping back against the tree. "You come any closer and I'll, I'll—"

She had nothing, and Captain Kipps knew it. He took a few steps closer until he was standing beside Olivia, just six feet away.

"Why don't you just come with me, Ma'am, and we'll sort this all out," he told her.

"No," she said, her voice shaking. "I will *not* go with you. I will not go to jail for this. You all see what's happening here?" she asked, looking around at all of them. "You see what you've done? You see what *your* carelessness has caused?! Everything was *fine* before this. Before *you* did this."

Soon only Alan was caught in her glare, and all he could do was shake his head at her sadly. He couldn't believe she'd come to this.

Captain Kipps took two steps forward again until he heard it.

"No!" Phyllis yelled, holding her hands out to stop him, but she had heard the strange noise too, coming from somewhere just behind her.

A great shifting rumble sounded out just as Phyllis turned around to see it, and the entire structure of the tree house fell apart, as if on cue.

From the very top, a large plank finished the collapse, sliding straight down across the top, and directly at Phyllis's head. She barely noticed it coming at her before it slammed into her skull.

No one moved, and all but Captain Kipps had their hands to their faces, horrified by the scene before them. Phyllis's face was bashed in so much, she was gargling blood, and in the ensuing silence, with only the soft, painful sounds of panting horror from the family as Captain Kipps and Alan rushed forward to help her, a voice came from *inside* the house.

"Hello? Helloooo? Anyone home?" Nancy Hensley called out. "Oh, here you all are," she said, proudly holding a large tray of lasagna with a big smile on her face.

She couldn't see Phyllis, Alan, or Captain Kipps from where she stood, and as no one was ready yet to speak the truth of what they'd just witnessed, all they could do was stare back at the woman, mouths wide open, their faces all frozen in shock.

She smiled at them strangely then, uncertain why they all looked that way, but then she saw the wreckage of the tree house just past their heads.

"Ohhh," she said, letting out a little laugh as she relaxed a bit. "You took the tree house down?"

Chapter 53

Roger, Haley, Peaches, and Alan sat together in DJs for an early dinner. It was already a week since the funeral for Phyllis. Not many other patrons were there yet, and they were still enjoying their warm rolls and salad course when Dr. Finny walked in with his wife. Peaches noticed them come in first, and then Alan, but from where they sat, Haley and Roger had not.

As soon as they were seated, Dr. Finny gave the waitress his drink order, and after she left, he looked over and saw them there.

Peaches smiled at him with a wave, and Dr. Finny smiled and waved back. He said something to his wife then and came over, smiling again a second time to see Roger and Haley sitting across from Alan and Peaches.

"Hello, all. I'm sorry to interrupt. Haley, what has it been— hours? Alan, my sincerest condolences once again," he said, reaching out to shake Alan's hand. "And to you girls as well. How are you all doing?"

"Much better, Jack, thank you," Alan said. "Rough week, but I think we'll all be a lot better now. Thank you for coming to the service. That was very nice of you. Phyllis didn't really suffer at all, so in a strange way, that made it much easier to handle."

He glanced briefly at the others with a knowing smile, one they were all too familiar with now. Each and every one of them agreed their family needed to heal from the past together, and so they hadn't revealed anything else to Captain Kipps, except for the other details Phyllis had revealed to them just before he arrived.

"Good, good," Dr. Finny said, unsure if he should even bring up the amazing cover story he had read in the *Rutland Herald*.

In an incredibly specific and powerfully honest story—as honest as the family let her be—Haley detailed exactly what had happened in her uncle's house and backyard that day, explaining how her grandmother was the murderer all along, and how it felt as if Kerry Ann herself had reached back from the grave for vengeance in the end.

'The massive blow to my grandmother's head wasn't fatal in itself, it turned out, but because of all the drugs and alcohol in her system, she apparently suffered a massive stroke on the spot. The doctors declared her brain dead just two hours later.

'The tree house wood itself, we learned, was only a catalyst, a contributing factor in the larger picture of events. Her substance abuse, only worsened once her guilt came closer to being revealed, is what really killed her in the end.'

Haley had included several beautiful pictures she'd taken of the tree house too, some from weeks before, and several after it had fallen apart.

"Did you read her article?" Peaches asked with a big smile, and Dr. Finny's eyebrows went up quickly.

"Well yes, yes, as a matter of fact I did," he said, looking now at Haley. "I'm sorry I didn't mention anything at the office, Haley, but truth be told, I wasn't really sure what I should or shouldn't say."

"It's okay," Peaches said. "We know how it is. It's just really sad and crazy."

"Yes, Peaches," Dr. Finny said. "That's true. That's a good way of putting it, I suppose, and I'm sure it must be very strange for all of you."

The table grew silent then, and Dr. Finny took his cue.

"Alright, well, I just wanted to give you all my best. If there's anything my wife and I can do for you, please don't hesitate to reach out anytime."

"Thank you, Doctor," Haley said, and the others exchanged awkward smiles as he walked back to his table across the room.

"So," Peaches said, rubbing her hands together. "You all ready for this?"

"Yeah, I'm starving," Roger said.

"No, not *this*, silly. The Stir Call Circle."

Haley made a face, and Peaches noticed the look she gave Alan as well.

"I don't know, Peaches," she said. "Are you sure they'll be okay with us showing up without any notice? Maybe you should just give them a head's up this month, and we'll try to come next month."

397

"No way," Alan said, surprising them with his enthusiasm. "We told Jessica—oh no, I'm sorry, *Peaches*—that we'd attend, and that we will. I for one am looking forward to it, and I'm sure it'll be very enlightening."

"Will you finally tell us more about your near-death experience, Grandpa?" Peaches asked him, suppressing a smile.

"Perhaps," Alan said with a grin. "If you're lucky."

"Will you be paying the $10 donations for us too?" Haley asked him, immediately sipping her iced tea.

Alan let out a big laugh.

"Wow, first dinner for you miscreants, and now a free Shamanism class too? What's next? Ice cream?"

"Yes!" both Roger and Peaches yelled out, and they were all still laughing as their food arrived soon after.

By the time they were done with dinner, and Alan had paid the bill with an extra generous tip, they left the restaurant with a wave to Dr. Finny and his wife on their way out. It was only then, when they were halfway out the door, that Haley realized she *had* to go back inside.

"I'll meet you guys over there," she said strangely, looking very uncomfortable all of a sudden.

"What's wrong?" Roger asked as Alan and Peaches looked on. "Stomach not feeling well?"

"No, I'm fine, I'm fine. It's just—I have to go back in there for a second. I'll meet you guys over there soon."

Haley walked back inside, and Roger looked on with growing concern. As she turned the corner inside the restaurant to the area she'd been sitting in earlier, she locked eyes with Dr. Finny's wife first before she got there. The woman looked back at her concerned, and then quickly got her husband's attention as Haley approached them.

"Haley?" he asked. "What is it? What's wrong?"

He could see the deep consternation written on Haley's face as much as his wife had, and the two exchanged a worried look once Haley got right up close to them. She looked like she'd just seen a ghost, and Dr. Finny was almost ready to check her forehead, she looked so ill.

"Haley, you okay?" Roger asked from behind her, but when he got there and saw her face too, he knew right away why she'd gone back inside.

There was no doubt about it. Dr. Finny's wife was the woman they'd seen go into the men's room at the reception hall.

Haley didn't remember seeing her there at the wedding, but she was more sure of the woman's identity now than she'd ever been of anything else in her entire life.

"It was you," she said to Mrs. Finny. "It was you who did it. I saw you on the video footage at the catering hall."

Mrs. Finny shook her head then, and said she didn't know what she was referring to, but there was something in her voice that sealed it for Haley, and she knew she was lying.

"Oh my God, Jack," she finally said, looking very upset now at her husband, and Dr. Finny's face changed on a dime.

"Haley, why don't you sit down here for a second."

Haley hesitated at first, but finally did once Dr. Finny moved in on the deep booth a bit more to make room for her and Roger.

She watched in silence then as Dr. Finny and his wife looked anxiously at one another, and Mrs. Finny put a hand to her mouth like she was deeply troubled by this unexpected confrontation.

"You killed him?" Haley asked, looking across at her from between Dr. Finny and Roger. "You killed Mr. Caraway?"

"What?" the woman said. "No, Haley, no, of course not. John Caraway was my cousin, and perhaps the sweetest man I ever met. I would never do a thing to hurt him."

"Your cousin? But Dr. Finny, you—you didn't seem to even know him when he came in."

Dr. Finny nodded and shook his head, glancing once again nervously at his wife, and then at Roger, and across the way, making sure no one was listening in.

"JC was a good man, but I'd only met him a few times. He came to me that day in the office for something other than a checkup.

That little performance you witnessed was all for you, I'm afraid, just to keep things on the up and up."

"I don't understand," Haley said, exchanging a look with Roger. "You knew your wife was going to kill him?"

"Please keep your voice down. Donna didn't kill anyone, Haley. Quite the opposite actually. John Caraway was dying. He was gravely ill, and in quite a bit of pain. He was on God knows how many painkillers for his cancer, and no one in the family knew how ill he was."

"But then what did you—"

"He begged me for something he could take to end it all quickly. He wanted to go out on a high note after the wedding."

"Holy shit," Roger said, as Haley let out a gasp.

"I didn't want to give it to him, of course, but he pleaded with me. Told me he was doing everything he could to stay alive till the wedding, to walk his daughter down the aisle, but he was going through hell. I finally relented, and gave him a drug I knew would have fatal consequences when mixed with the medicine he was already taking. Haley, Roger, I cannot stress to you enough how important it is that you keep this quiet. I could go to jail for this."

"Wait," Roger said. "If you gave him that bad stuff, what were *you* doing there?" he asked Mrs. Finny.

"I was furious with my husband when he told me what he'd given John. I understood it, but I didn't want Jack to get in trouble if someone traced the medicine back to him. What if someone found the bottle, and there were fingerprints on it or something? I'd been begging him to give me the bottle back, and when he refused for the last time the morning of the wedding, I asked a friend of his I know from work to do everything he could to get it away from him instead."

"RJ Tarisi," Haley said firmly, and Mrs. Finny nodded.

"I don't know how you know that, but yes. I'm RJ's secretary, and John has an account—*had* an account—with the company."

"Wait," Roger interrupted, his eyes wide with a deranged look of confused fear. "My mom's boyfriend is connected to all this?"

400

Now it was Haley's turn to look confused and scared.

"What? Your mother is dating RJ Tarisi?"

"Yes! She was till last week, at least. They broke up."

Haley took a moment to absorb it all, and it looked like Dr. Finny and his wife were busy doing the same, once again looking around to be sure no one was eavesdropping.

"Roger," Haley said, resting her hand gently on his and rubbing it, "RJ Tarisi is my uncle's boss. He stiffed me on the wedding photos I took, and he's the one I thought killed Mr. Caraway."

"RJ Tarisi is no killer, Haley," Mrs. Finny said. "He's no angel, I'll give you that, and cheap as all hell besides, but a killer? No. He and I spent the whole day of the wedding begging John not to kill himself. He'd thrown out the little vile Jack gave him, so I retrieved it quickly from the trash, then hightailed it out of there before anyone saw me. I didn't think anyone would ever look at the video footage, though."

"But Stephanie—his daughter—she said he died in the ambulance on the way to the hospital."

"They may have *declared* him dead in the ambulance, dear, but trust me, he was gone. I can't tell you how hard it was seeing him there and not crying my eyes out, but I just didn't want anything to happen to Jack. He'd be ruined."

"But if anyone caught you in the bathroom—" Haley started.

"RJ took care of that. He staged a distraction, and phoned me once he was sure no one would see me. I waited in the ladies' rest room, and just had to slip out one door and into the other. RJ spoke to me on the phone the whole time, assuring me it was safe to come out when I did. The only reason I did it at all was because RJ knew his reputation was bad enough for people to think *he'd* done something to poor John."

Haley and Roger exchanged a sad look, and Dr. Finny and his wife could tell she'd built up something entirely different in her mind about John Caraway's death. About RJ Tarisi too.

"Roger," Dr. Finny said. "I imagine if your mother was that close to RJ, you're probably well versed in his—well, his *style*. I confess I've had my own run-ins with the man too, but I must echo Donna's insistence that RJ is on our side, as in, the side of people who cared very much for John Caraway, and didn't want him to leave us that way. None of that means RJ isn't still an incredible asshole at times, but there are many thousands of miles between asshole and killer."

"I'd add too, Haley," Donna said, leaning forward and reaching a hand out, "that just because your family has this very unfortunate past history related to that girl, especially your grandmother, not every death involves malicious intent. Poor John was going through hell in the weeks before the wedding, and he just couldn't take it any longer."

"My Uncle Lenny tried to warn me at one point not to let our family's past get in my head too much. Now I feel like an idiot. So you're Donna Wendt," Haley said, piecing it together from what Lenny had told her.

"Well, no, I'm Donna Finny now," she corrected her with a wry smile. "I haven't been Donna Wendt for years, except at work. Just never bothered to change anything there."

"God, I really feel awful now. Not just about poor Mr. Caraway, but for thinking you and Mr. Tarisi were somehow involved."

"Don't be sorry," Donna said. "We were involved, after all. Just not the way you thought we were. But I trust you don't mind keeping this quiet?"

The waitress arrived then, and asked Dr. Finny and his wife if everything was okay.

"Oh yes, but I'll take a glass of red wine, please, Liz?" Donna said, and the waitress smiled and left again to fetch some.

Donna's request for Haley's silence still sat in the air between them, but before Haley answered, she asked *her* a question first.

"You don't like ice in your red wine, do you?"

"What?" she asked.

"Never mind," Haley said with a smile.

She and Roger slid back out of the booth.

"I'll explain later," she muttered to him.

"Okay, we have to go. Dr. Finny, Mrs. Finny, I'm so sorry to have bothered you, but I'm glad I got this figured out now. I can't tell you how relieved I am to hear all this. I mean, it's so awful about Mr. Caraway, but I'm glad to know it wasn't something *more* awful, and I totally understand what you did. Have a good night."

"No worries, Haley," Donna said. "And Roger?"

"Yeah?"

"You let us know if you need any more help with RJ. I'll be happy to back you up anytime."

They left with smiles and waves, and Haley breathed a huge sigh of relief once they were walking out of the restaurant again.

"I can't believe you had to live with that guy." Haley said. "I'm gonna help you get out of there soon."

"We're already out," Roger told her. "My mom packed our stuff up last week, so now we're just looking for someplace cheap nearby so we can keep our jobs around here."

"Oh, wow. You know, my grandfather said he's thinking of renting out some of the space at his house. You should totally talk to him about it."

"Okay, cool. I will."

He took her hand with a smile as they crossed the street to walk down the block and meet the others at Chaos Casbah.

Chapter 54

Roger and Haley joined Peaches and Alan over at Chaos Casbah down the street, and Peaches introduced Alan and Haley to the circle members who'd already arrived. As they all perused the cool things for sale in the main floor gift shop, some of the circle members asked Peaches privately if Alan was the grandfather who'd recently gone missing. She nodded yes, but hinted they'd have much more to tell the group once they were downstairs.

Only Ellen and Dennis, who lived nearby, already knew what happened in the Abrams family. Both had read the long article Haley wrote, and both attended the service for Phyllis as well.

Downstairs a little while later, Shaman Gloria entered last, as was often the case after her long drive north to Ludlow, and she greeted Alan and Haley warmly when Peaches introduced them.

Once they smudged and set the circle, Peaches was happy to see her grandfather and *new sister* were noticeably more calm and attentive. Something about the smell of burning sage and the peace of the quiet, candlelit space relaxed them much more than either could have predicted, and they were surprised when Gloria singled them both out by name.

Even though fifteen minutes' worth of various activities and conversation had passed since she met the two of them, she remembered each of their names, and knew Peaches had brought them there for something very important.

"Peaches," she said, "why don't you lead us now in what you have planned for tonight."

Peaches stood up and walked to the front next to Gloria, where she looked around at each of them with a soft smile. Taking a deep breath, she closed her eyes and concentrated her energy on the intentions she made known to her spirit guides before the evening began. She breathed deeply and whispered her intentions quietly to herself, though still with some sadness that the other members of her family hadn't come as well.

She'd extended the invitation to everyone else too, but all had offered her different excuses as to why they either could not come or did not want to attend.

Breathing in and out over and over again slowly as she reminded herself what she wanted to have happen, she finally opened her eyes again, surprised to see the rest of her family joining them after all. She smiled as they entered from the stairs toward the back, each in turn removing their shoes and sitting down behind the others.

"Thank you for coming," she said. "This is the rest of my immediate family," Peaches told the room, "and I invited them all here because we need some major healing right now. I know some of them don't believe in this stuff, but that's okay. The rest of us believe more than enough for everyone else."

They all smiled at this, but Peaches quickly continued.

"I don't mean that to sound rude though. It's just, I don't want any of you to feel weird. Roger felt weird when he first started coming, but he's used to it now."

He shrugged, and Haley offered him a quick knee rub.

"My family and I just went through something kinda crazy," Peaches continued, "so I'm really glad they were willing to come here tonight. A lot happened, and I'm not gonna mention everything, but basically, we found out my grandma was the one who killed that girl all those years ago, and then our tree house fell down on top of her and killed her, and my dad's not my dad. My uncle's my dad. But my dad is still my dad too."

The members of the Stir Call Circle, except for Roger and Gloria, all stared back at her with their mouths wide open. Though some were noticeably unnerved when they saw Sam walk in with the others, they were all much more shocked by the truth of it all as Peaches spoke.

"Anyway, I called Gloria yesterday, and we talked for a long time. She said we could do something different tonight if you were all up for it. I know for my family members here tonight, this'll seem really strange, but if you just open yourselves up to what the others are gonna do, I promise you this'll be really great for all of us. Okay, can we do it now?" she asked, turning to Gloria.

"The sooner the better," Gloria said with a warm smile. "Would Peaches and all the other members of her family please sit together in the center of the room in whatever direction you'd like to face? And friends in the Stir Call Circle, could you please form an outer circle with me as best you can?"

For the next minute or so as they all got into place, Gloria collected her drum and smiled warmly at everyone gathered there. Once they were in place, she gave them her own brief introduction of what would happen.

"Here in this circle, this sacred space we have set for ourselves, you should always feel completely safe and secure. If at any time you feel uncomfortable, you are welcome to leave the room, but I do ask you to be quiet and reverent if so. Please make sure your phones are off or on silent, and know this: we will be doing a shamanic healing on your family today, but we cannot do this without your permission, so if you remain here, we will take that to mean you are okay with this."

No one left, but a few of them exchanged nervous looks, which Gloria picked up on right away.

"There is nothing strange or evil about what we'll be doing. No voodoo magic, I promise," she said as they laughed. "To my friends here in the Stir Call Circle, once I begin to drum, I'd like you to keep your hands out in the direction of the family gathered here in this space. You may rest them facing upward on your legs as well if you'd prefer. Journey to your spirit guides and teachers, and ask them to call upon as many helping spirits as possible to join us in bringing healing to this family.

"Members of Peaches' family, I ask you to simply close your eyes and breathe quietly once the drumbeat begins. I understand many of you are not spiritually inclined, but for those who are open to it, invite in any of your family's ancestors, recent or long past, even ancients who you may be related to, to help you all heal from the events your family experienced. Okay, everyone ready?"

406

"Gloria?" Krystal asked.

"Yes?"

"Maybe just tell them briefly about the drum beat and callback."

"Oh, yes. Thank you so much. Okay, so as we do this, I will be beating the drum quickly but quietly somewhere around 200 beats per minute, which will activate the theta waves in your brain. This will calm your brain into a semi-trance like state, allowing your soul to go on a kind of adventure in between sleep and awake. Shamanic journeying is what the Stir Call Circle members will be doing, so just relax and allow the others to send you all their light and love. After about fifteen minutes, I'll break the rhythm of the drumbeat to let you know we're ending. At that point, any of you are welcome to tell us what you may have experienced."

"And if you don't seem to experience anything," Peaches added, "that's okay too."

"Yes," Gloria smiled. "No worries. Okay, everyone ready?"

Once they were all nodding and ready, Gloria began to beat the drum. Watching the clock as she did, she allowed twenty minutes to pass as she and the others all asked their spirit animals, spirit guides, and other helping spirits to send Peaches and her family light and love, healing and blessings.

Each member of the Stir Call Circle went about this differently with their individual spirit guides, and each member of the family, at least at the start, did their best to ask for help and healing too.

At the end of the twenty minutes, Gloria broke up the pattern of the drumbeat, then stopped. She walked over to the doorway and turned up the lights a little too, just so everyone would know it was time to open their eyes and discuss what had happened.

Back in her chair, she took a moment and thought about her own experiences, and when she was ready, she looked around at all of them.

"Why don't we all spread out again first," she suggested, and once they were all ready, she looked up and spoke.

"I'd like to begin, if you don't mind, and then I'd like to hear from others who would like to speak. For my part, I could sense there was still great pain here, in the hearts of many of your family members. Years and years of conflict, untruths, and damaged relationships that need mending. But as soon as I realized this, I was also shown that with time, you will all find the healing you desperately need. Trust in that. Trust in the power of time. Time was already a powerful factor for you all over the past 17 years or so, and I believe it will continue to be a powerful factor going forward. I also must say, I feel like something new is coming soon to your family. I hesitate to say what I saw, but—well, I'll leave it at that," she laughed. "Okay, who would like to go next?"

Lenny held up a hand, and Gloria was happy to see it, nodding for him to say what he wanted.

He cleared his throat at first, and glanced at his family members with tears in his eyes as he began to speak.

"I didn't want to come here tonight, and without outing anyone, I wasn't the only one. Even once I was here, I wasn't expecting much at all. I don't know *what* I was expecting, to be honest with you. Something in the drums and the positioning of everyone though, it—"

His voice trailed off as he sniffled a bit and wiped his eyes.

"I *felt it,* is what I want to say. Like, I felt something happening to me, and not just around me, even though I knew no one was touching me. I'm not sure what I felt yet, but I just wanted to say, well, thanks," he laughed. "Thank you for whatever you did."

Silence followed this as the others quietly reflected on what Lenny had said. Olivia had felt something too, but was surprised to hear Lenny speak at all, especially after what he'd said in the car on their way there, that they were all just wasting their time. But if she was surprised to hear her brother speak, she was even more surprised when Sam spoke up next.

"Hi everyone. I'm Sam. Sam Newhaus. Some of you may know *of* me if you don't know me personally. So uh, I'd just like to say, for the past 17 years, my life has been something of a strange ride at like a carnival or something, but I'll tell you what," he said, looking at Olivia, Haley, and Peaches especially before continuing,

"I wouldn't trade too much of it. I made a lot of mistakes along the way, and I hurt the people I care most about, but I also had to deal with being accused of a murder I knew I never committed, so I hope to God my family knows I was dealing with more than my fair share too."

He locked eyes with Olivia then and reached out a hand her way. They held each other's hands as the others watched, but then he let go slowly and reached an arm around Erika, sitting to his left.

"This young lady right here has had a strange go of it too. Erika woke up one day last week not knowing she was about to lose a family member and gain another, right?"

Erika smiled at both her parents, who were smiling back at her. Only the two of them and Sam knew what he was referring to, as he had accidentally walked in right after she told her father.

"So, apparently," Erika said, first looking at Peaches and then around at the rest of them, "not only did I lose my Grandma," she said, pausing as she got choked up, "but I also found out that I'm pregnant. I took a pregnancy test, but I totally misread it. My mom found it in the garbage, and confronted me about it. I thought at first she was just angry that I had unsafe sex, but instead she was asking me why I didn't tell her.

"I was like, *Wait, what?*' And then she couldn't even stay mad at me because she saw how happy I looked when I found out, and I realized how dumb I was for misreading the thing in the first place. I was on the pill too, so it came as a really big surprise."

The rest of the room, especially the rest of her family, celebrated with Erika immediately when she told them, and Caroline asked Alan if he was ready to be a great-grandfather.

"No!" he said loudly, a big smile on his face. "But I'm so excited anyway! This is crazy. Crazy but amazing."

"This is what I saw," Gloria said. "A baby! I was so worried you didn't know though, so I didn't want to say."

"Actually," Erika said, once the room calmed down again, "crazy is a good word considering who the father is."

They all looked at her with quite a bit of concern now.

"I recently started dating this really sweet guy. His name is Chris, but his first name isn't the problem." No one seemed to understand what she was saying, so she went on. "His last name is Jefferson. He's Kerry Ann Jefferson's nephew."

Various gasps let out around the room, but lots of smiles too.

"Well, that'll be a fun wedding," Peaches said, and everyone began laughing, with not just a few anxious faces mixed in as well.

"No. No wedding yet!" Erika added with a laugh. "We didn't plan for this to happen obviously, but Chris and I have fallen in love so quickly, and we're both really happy about it."

Alan began to sob to himself, and Peaches put an arm around him as the room grew silent once again. He was very quickly a mess of tears and snot, and it made some of the others, especially Olivia and Lenny, begin crying as well.

"Maybe we should take a break," Gloria offered, but Alan waved her off right away, trying his best to compose himself.

"No. No, I'd like to say something. My family members know what part I played in Kerry Ann's death, and though I've spoken to them all individually, I need a kind of public airing here as well, if that's okay with everyone. I did not kill Kerry Ann, but I was a, well, *a greatly contributing factor,* I guess you might say.

"I was mean to the girl. Beyond mean, actually. I was a real asshole. And I've been an asshole my entire life. Racist, homophobic, and—what's the one where you mistrust people who are different than you?"

"Xenophobic," Corinne offered.

"Yeah, quite a bit of that one too," he said. "I was just a hateful son of a bitch, and it's gonna take me a long, long time before I really come to terms with all that. If I'm given enough time at all, that is. And to that point, Peaches," he said, turning to face her, "you're about to get an answer to that question you had for me."

Peaches smiled, and her eyes grew wide with suspense.

"I had an operation on my knee last month," he announced to the room, especially to the members of the Stir Call Circle, "and while they were busy doing whatever it is they needed to do in there, my heart stopped for a little while. Not long as far as time passes here, but for me, well, many, many hours went by."

He paused and wiped a new tear from his eye before continuing, the entire room hanging on his every word.

"Now I know some of you may expect me to say I met Jesus or God or Gandhi or someone else like that, so I'm sorry to disappoint you, but I did meet a couple other people I sure as hell wasn't expecting to see there. You see, I rose up out of my body, and I looked back down at the people operating on my knee. Everything was fine for a while, although they seemed to be moving in slow motion, barely moving at all, really. Then the damn machine started going off, that insane flat line noise we all know so well. I watched as their heads turned very, very slowly toward the monitor, as if looking at it was even necessary. Maybe the machine makes the noise by accident sometimes? I have no idea. But as soon as their heads turned to the machine, I felt myself sucked out of the room as if by a cosmic vacuum.

"A split second later, I was sitting on top of a car out in the middle of God knows where. Farmland, it looked like. As far as the eye could see. Out to my left, a farmer with a strange-looking hat and what looked like a suit vest of some sort yelled out, 'lunch!', and a whole flock of young men in beards and overalls came running in from the field.

"I didn't know what I was seeing, but then a voice came from my right. 'You see that, Allie?' he said. 'Even the hardest working souls need to just relax and have a good time now and then.' It was my father, and he looked exactly the same as he did all those years ago when I was a little boy, so much younger than I knew I must have looked to him. 'Am I dead?', I asked him, and he just smiled at me before he responded. 'Only a little bit,' he answered. 'Just enough for us to have this little chat.'

"He told me he'd been watching my life closely since he passed, and that he was sad to see how far off the path I'd gotten since he died. He spoke to me in words and visuals somehow, flashes of things I'd done to others, and the many ways I'd veered off the

411

roads I was meant to travel. Then he pointed over at the barn those nice young Amish fellas were working on before they went in for lunch. 'You see how much care they put into building that structure? How even everything is, and how clean?'

"I nodded yes, wondering what he might be getting at. 'Well,' he says, 'that kinda thing matters an awful lot when you want to make sure the house won't fall on you, but none of it matters when you're building a life. Life is gonna be reckless and messy no matter how fine-tuned the structure of it is, so you may as well just roll with the punches'.

"I felt like I was shot up into the sky then, into outer space maybe, and it went on like that for an eternity, but the next thing I knew, I was sitting inside a plush living room surrounded by pillows of every shape and color, most of them fuzzy and brightly colored. But this time, I was expecting to see someone else, so I started looking around for them all over. A few minutes passed, and it seemed like I was all alone, so I started to think that maybe I was dead after all.

"But that's when the scenery started to disappear, pillow by pillow, wall by wall, color by color, until it was just the inside of the tree house, and I saw her there like she'd been sitting across from me the whole damn time. As if I hadn't noticed her yet. Kerry Ann.

"I'll tell you the God's honest truth," he said, shaking his head. "For a moment, I thought maybe I was actually in Hell, but without saying anything, she told me I wasn't. She didn't speak, but she smiled, and I knew what words she had for me just the same. 'I only have a moment to talk to you, so listen carefully,' she said.

"I'll never forget what she said next. 'Allow truth to lead the way', she said. 'Lies spin the Earth backwards, but truth moves everyone forward.' She smiled at me warmly then, as if none of my sins against her mattered anymore, and then the light grew much brighter than it was before. Suddenly I was back in my body, and the doctor was calling my name."

All around the room, Alan saw the faces of those he loved as if for the very first time all over again, just as he had after seeing them in the hospital that day. He'd been given a second chance at life, a second chance to right the wrongs he'd made for as long as time would allow him to do so.

"And so you see," he finished, "I knew I had to figure out what really happened that night, why Kerry Ann seemed so comfortable with me, why my dad had visited me too, so that's why I decided to just go away for a while to think things out. Phyllis, well—"

He sighed and shook his head.

"She didn't want to hear what I saw, and neither did she get the same second chance I received. What you all saw that afternoon at the tree house? That's not too far off from how I might have reacted before my surgery, before my near-death experience.

"I would've most likely screamed out, and cursed the whole lot of you, and done everything in my power to keep the whole thing quiet too. Perhaps a tree house may have even fallen on me too."

Olivia laughed then, and it made Alan turn to look at her.

"What?" he asked her.

"Sorry," she said. "I just got a weird *Wizard of Oz* flashback."

Everyone laughed then, and it broke some of the mounting tension in the room. In the hour that followed, several more people discussed their experiences during the journey, and how the Abrams family would need a lot more time to continue processing everything, but all there also agreed that if Erika did end up marrying Chris Jefferson, the two families would need to spend some quality time talking with one another first.

After they closed the Circle, Alan invited everyone, including the members of the Stir Call Circle, back to his house for ice cream. Not a single one of them declined the offer, even those for whom the night had already grown late. And in the hours that passed at Alan's house, each one there spent time talking through what had happened, and what would need to change for them all going forward.

Alan would take better care of himself, walk more often to exercise his knees, and even start seeing Nancy Hensley now and then for breakfast at The Hatchery. More-than-friends would take a little while longer.

Haley would accept an offer from the *Rutland Herald* to be their newest full-time photojournalist, and Roger would happily accept Dr. Finny's offer to take Haley's place at the office, with one small condition: Peaches would work any weekend shifts, so Roger could keep his job at Village Pizza. He was still determined to get his own place, or maybe one with Haley, but he and his mom would move in with Alan that September in the mean time.

Lenny and Caroline would enter couples counseling that fall, as both wanted to fix what was broken in their marriage. They knew they had years' worth of trust issues to work through, but they were determined just the same to find happiness together on the other side of therapy.

Sam and Olivia would remain friends, but to her surprise, Olivia would soon begin dating someone new, ironically a man she met while buying beer at the supermarket. Just letting go of her secret friendship with Sam would end up being a catalyst to great new things in her life, and great new people. She would even give up smoking. And start using coasters.

Erika's baby would be born in early May the next year, and she and Chris would be relieved to see members of both their families surrounding them in the hospital that day.

All of this was the bright future just ahead of them all, but as they laughed and cried and celebrated together at Alan's house that night with the members of the Stir Call Circle, three others celebrated as well.

RJ Tarisi clinked his beer bottle together with Dr. Finny's, and each of them in turn did the same with Donna's glass of red wine, filled to the very top with ice.

tree house done!

acknowledgements:

There comes a time at the tail end of my initial writing process when I realize my story is finally ready to be seen by more than just my two eyes.

As you might guess, this is often a truly nerve-wracking checkpoint on the way to publishing, but it's always quite exciting too. That which only existed for my amusement—*in this case for almost three years of my life*—is suddenly in the hands of other people, some of them complete strangers.

My beta readers vary from book to book, but they are, each and every one of them, invaluable members of my team, and I owe some very special thanks this time around to a few wonderful souls who helped me out by beta reading *tree house down*.

I was very lucky to get two teachers, one author, and a paralegal to beta read this time, and each one helped me out in a host of different ways.

Andy Charles, Rick Tomack, Meredith Linsley Charles, and Jim Daubenheyer, you each helped me out so, so much, and you gave me a ton of great feedback I really needed. *Important* feedback too, questions that forced me to see the book as *you* did, to step out of myself and into the shoes of many different types of readers from many different backgrounds.

You forced me to think things out differently, to express some passages in a more clear and concise manner, and to deliver my beautiful book to all my beautiful readers with the maximum possible impact at each and every turn. Meredith, Jim, Rick, and Andy, thank you all so much for your priceless feedback and fixes. I am forever grateful for your help!

Big props to Rebecca Batchelor who recruited one of the above people to join my team of superhero beta readers, so as always, Becky, thank you for all your help and support! You rock!

Thank you, Shaman John Gilroy, for your willing wisdom and kindness regarding the various Shamanic circle references. I drum and journey with Shaman John every month, and he's forever a source of great joy and insight in my life. I could not have written what I did and *how* I did without his teachings and thoughtful advice. I gave him the pages related to the Shamanic circle in advance, and he helped me nail down a more articulate version of what I'd originally written. Thank you so much, John. I really do appreciate your valuable help!

I'll say much more in the following section about Ludlow, Vermont, but I'm happy to start right here with a huge debt of gratitude to every single resident of Ludlow for doing what you do to attract so many tourists like me through the town and village each and every year. Many thanks to the warm and friendly folks at Chaos Casbah, the staff at DJ's, The Hatchery, and Village Pizza (who I'm sad to say don't really offer pizza delivery), the whole team over at the Green Mountain Sugar House, and the Edden Family on Lake Pauline. The Eddens are a very important part of why I return to Ludlow every summer, and I'm forever grateful to them for my home away from home.

My supreme thanks also go out to the creative community of writers at NaNoWriMo (National Novel Writing Month). I wrote the first 50,000 words of this book through NaNoWriMo in November of 2016, played with it to no end over the following 24 months, and then wrote *another* 50,000 words' worth during NaNoWriMo 2018.

The program is run by some truly awesome people, and the local NaNo community on Long Island is growing and thriving with each passing year thanks to the hard work and dedication of our local leader in Nassau County, Laura Cerrone. A fantastic writer herself, Laura sets up write-ins and meet-ups for Long Island writers all the time, and we're all so very lucky to have her.

Special thanks to the incredible staff at *Newsday* for their help spreading word about *tree house down* and the entire NaNoWriMo program. Field reporter Mary Gregory, photographer Jeff Bachner, and Books and Travel Editor Tom Beer, you helped me out so much with your reporting, and I truly appreciate all your valuable time and interest.

Recognition from such a prestigious publication really helped build the buzz in the months prior to this book's release, so I'm extremely grateful to the above team members at *Newsday* for all their help and support!

Another book means another fabulous cover. My friend and cover artist Teresa Carboni came through once more with a beautiful presentation for *tree house down*. Thank you for being patient with me throughout the process, Teresa, and thanks as always for helping me reach the right results, even when I often try steering you *the wrong way* early on. The finished product is what matters, and it's once again great!

And last but never least, special thanks with so much love to my partner Andy. He has not just proven himself a fantastic beta reader over the years, but forever offers his attention and personal knowledge willingly too.

As a beta reader, Andy lets me know which sentences are clunky and need of repair, but as my best friend and life partner, he also shares with me more thoughtful reflections about which scenes he loves the most, which moments surprised him, and even which character names tickled his fancy (he really loved 'Peaches').

There are so many people to thank even beyond these several I mentioned here, not least of whom are the many good souls who support me constantly online with their likes, comments, and shares. Thank you so much, everyone!

I really do appreciate every single second you spend talking up my books and articles, sharing them, and even just acknowledging their existence with a simple 'like' or 'love'. I couldn't do this without you all, so please help me again this time too!

a love letter to ludlow:

I've been visiting Ludlow, Vermont with my family and friends since the early 1980s. I'm a big fan of the village itself, the restaurants and businesses within, all the beauty of the town and the region, and the warmth of the people who live there.

I'm simply a visitor though, and not a resident. No matter how many times I've driven through the village, spent my money, snapped my photos, or enjoyed my meals, there is simply no changing the fact that I am still very much an outsider. A flatlander at that.

Since I don't *really* know what it's like to live there, all my words in the pages you've just read are mere suggestions of possibilities, random articulations of a creative imagination, and nothing more.

I do *know* Ludlow, though. I know it's a wonderful place to visit, eat in, shop in, and explore. Gorgeous area to walk around too. I have a Shaw's card, a pile of old fishing licenses, and scores of pictures and videos I took before, during, and after Hurricane Irene back in 2011. Along with three family members, I was trapped in my house rental on Lake Pauline that week as the waters of the lake rose almost seven feet higher than normal, all while mudslides and mountain water from above Route 100 threatened to push our house down into the lake.

I watched as emergency crews and volunteers everywhere (Vermont strong!) cleaned up after the storm, and I marveled at the incredible dedication of our property's owner as he and my brother worked through the storm to secure our safety, and the stability of the house. For days after the rain stopped, I walked past crying neighbors, destroyed homes, and overturned trucks as National Guard helicopters flew over, and the Red Cross went into action.

My mind often wanders as well to all the places that are no more: Mr. B's, The Art of the Chicken, Christopher's Sports Bar, and Ralph's Bait Shop to name just a few. Ralph loved to tell customers about the big old bear that crossed the road every night, and how the creature seemed to enjoy *relieving himself* right there in the middle of the highway too.

I don't know what it's like to live in Ludlow, Vermont, but I do know Ludlow as much as any visitor can, and I tried my hardest in this book to honor the town I love as much as I could with the words I have.

My apologies, however, for the bad behavior of my characters. I did not write this family as some atypical representation of Ludlow, Vermont. Not at all, in fact! Instead, I simply chose Ludlow as my setting because I love Ludlow, and I chose my characters and their personalities because I love a good drama. To that point, join me now as we take a deeper look at—*there's really no other way to say it*—this beautiful but truly fucked up family.

the enneagram numbers of the characters:

Before writing a single word of *tree house down,* a crazy thought came to me out of nowhere one day in the summer of 2016: what if I made the family members of my next book different representations of the nine personality types of the Enneagram?

I was excited by the idea, and although I had never read a fictional novel based on the Enneagram before, I was sure the concept was rare. Searches for the Enneagram on Amazon turn up plenty of teaching texts, but there were no novels I could find based on the nine types.

Any-uh-what? Oh, right. The Enneagram is a millennia-old personality chart based on nine unique personality types. It's actually a circle with nine unique points, and each point or personality type is linked in some way with several other personality types. When we're at our best, we exhibit defining attributes of a different number. Likewise, when we're at our most stressed, we're often mistaken for another number's least attractive attributes.

We are, each and every one of us, one of these nine personality types. Alan, Phyllis, Olivia, Lenny, Caroline, Sam, Haley, Erika, and

Peaches each represent one of the nine types, and though I've studied the Enneagram for over 25 years, I'm the first to admit I still don't understand every nuance of every type completely. If I did my job well, however, I hope you *at least saw* the characters as very different from one another.

Since a person can be a healthy, average, or unhealthy version of their Enneagram personality type, some of the people in the Abrams/Newhaus family are either better or less ideal versions of themselves than their number might indicate. Even so, what follows is my interpretation of each character based on the design I implemented from the beginning.

You'll see I've added some other details here about each character, which I kept solely as reference points as I wrote, information you won't necessarily find elsewhere in the book. This end section would go on too long if I listed *all* my notes out, but I thought at least some of you reading this might appreciate a few new details here and there.

Phyllis Perfetti Abrams, born in 1945, is a "1" on the Enneagram. She's the perfectionist, also known as the achiever or the reformer. Her virtue is serenity but her vice is anger, attributes that both helped and hurt her at times in her career as a nurse, first in a hospital and later at a veterans' home. I've known several Enneagram Ones in my life, including my father, and I've learned they can be overly concerned with keeping up appearances, most specifically the appearance of their household, workplace, attire, and family.

While not all Ones are neat freaks, many are, but you'll usually see their personality type come through more loud and clear in their idealism. They often have a rigid worldview of how things *should* be, and Phyllis is no different. She and Alan fell in love in the summer of 1969 when he came in for a routine physical exam at the hospital, and they were married by the fall of 1970, much to the consternation of *her* Italian Catholic family and *his* Orthodox Jewish family. Despite all her sins, Phyllis always acted for the protection and wellbeing of her family, whether or not they understood any of her reasons or motives.

Haley Newhaus, born in 1994, is a "2" on the Enneagram. She's the helper type, the mother. Her virtue is humility but her vice is pride. I don't mind saying that I am a Two, and as such, I used Haley as one of the focal points of the story simply because I know how she thinks and operates better than the others do. Haley's dream is to run her own photography business called New View, a play on her last name.

Though not all Twos are smothering-mother types, or overly involved in the affairs of others, many are, so it was important for me to show Haley fairly and honestly to the best of my ability. An unhealthy Two goes even further than Haley does, though. Manipulating a forced hookup with Roger, parenting her own mom and dad, and meddling in two separate murder investigations is just the tip of the iceberg for an Enneagram Two.

Alan "Allie" Abrams, born in 1942, is a "3" on the Enneagram. He's always on stage, whether or not anyone else cares to realize it, and even when he doesn't consciously choose to be. It's just who he is, as if he can see his words appear in front of him on a prompter, ready for him to read them out like a classic actor on a Shakespearean stage. These people skills served him well when he started his own apparel business in Brooklyn at the age of 25. Though he never cared much about clothes himself, Alan saw an opportunity for big sales in tee shirts in the late 60s and early 70s. He sold the company years later for a pretty penny, but unfortunately just one month before a boom hit in the mid-80s, a fact Phyllis never let him forget.

I painted Alan as a horrible person in some ways, but mostly as a flawed but ultimately redeemable human being, so that by the time he had his operation and near-death experience, you'd be confused by the math regarding his virtues and vices, and what kind of a person he really was going into the final chapters of the book. The Three's virtue is truthfulness, but his vice is deceit. As such, an Enneagram Three often enjoys a casual stroll down the thin tightrope between fact and fiction. Alan is no different, and in some ways, he hides the truth from himself just as much as he hides it from others.

Sam Newhaus, born 1973, is a "4" on the Enneagram. The Four is a romantic, an individualist, and an artist. His virtue is levelheadedness but his vice is envy. Fours love their peace and quiet, but they also value their place in a group or family, and fiercely defend any and all assaults against them, which they see as an attack on their character. Knowing Sam was a Four made it easy for me to sympathize with his overall plight, and keep him off in the shadows a bit more than the others. Though he was clearly "no innocent", he was caught up in a super stressful situation, and I couldn't help but sympathize with him from the very beginning.

Sam knew there was no *real* proof tying him to Kerry Ann's murder, and just enough doubt surrounding his side of the story. He went deep into his emotional well, as many Fours tend to do, and he absorbed all this negative energy directed at him while at the same time redirecting his life's work and purpose to protecting not just Alan, but his entire family too. In Vegas, Sam made a great living designing rock gardens for homes previously surrounded by grass. He saw this work as a kind of art form more than as just a profession, and he plans to do much of the same for the lake houses he bought in Ludlow.

Caroline Hesse Abrams, born 1974, is an Enneagram "5". She's the silent observer personality type, the wise owl. Her virtue is nonattachment, but her vice is greed. While everyone else in the family moves about her in good ways and bad, Caroline just watches them all carefully, making her mind up about what's really going on. She's also guilty as sin in her own ways, so her "Fiveness" was cool to play off of throughout the book.

To that end, I really enjoyed making my "silent observer" *silently observe* the two tree house scenes. Interesting note: she knew for certain that the tree house was connected to the girl's murder, yet she willingly covered for Sam all these years because of her blind lust for him. The two of them actually met and hooked up for the *first* time after a church picnic when Sam—inebriated and high—was 17, and Caroline was 16, but he didn't seem to remember her the next time they met, so Caroline never told him.

Lenny Abrams, born 1973, is an Enneagram "6". He's the fearful, stability-craving personality type who steps up with courage when necessary to protect the people he loves. Lenny's trysts with Jenn throw everything he knows in turmoil though, and that combined with his stress at work makes for one hell of an unstable summer for him. The only reason Lenny dared clean up the blood not already washed away by the rain the night before was to protect his wife and family, who he loves more than life itself.

The Six's virtue is courage but his vice is fear, so it's a constant battle for Sixes between opposing forces, each with their talons wrapped tightly around one or the other shoulder, like an angel and devil vying in turn for their captor's attention. Even so, it took great courage for Lenny to clean up the blood that next day, and courage once again to admit he did so in the final scene with the whole family gathered.

Erika Abrams, born 1999, is an Enneagram "7". The Seven's virtue is sobriety—sober thinking as much as sober living, but her vice is gluttony. The seven is sometimes referred to as the party animal, but they're better understood as the party planner, the fun, happy-go-lucky friend or family member whose bubbly personality keeps things light. Going deep is so often the Seven's greatest fear, because that means an end to the party. While Erika loves having fun with her friends, we see her begin to change after she meets Chris, whose personality calms and soothes her.

It was very important for me to keep Erika front and center in the story, because I felt her slipping away too often near the start. It's why I gave her Chris, in fact, and why their story arc is so pivotal to the book. Erika and Sam were each on the outside looking in for so long, but because the mysteriousness surrounding Sam served my plot well, it was Erika who needed her own storyline. It makes me very happy to know how important her baby will be for the future of her family's story going forward.

Olivia Abrams, born 1971, is an Enneagram "8", the natural-born leader type. When I first began writing *tree house down*, I mistakenly thought Caroline and Olivia were both Fives, and none of the family members were Eights. I soon realized, however, that Olivia was actually an Eight caught up in unhealthy Five behavior. Because the Enneagram is fluid, each number is simply a starting point for a larger dance. An Eight at their unhealthiest is an uncaring couch potato (a worst-case scenario for Fives like Caroline), but at their best, Eights take on the best attributes of the Two, becoming extremely caring and willing to help.

As an Enneagram Eight, Olivia's virtue is other-centeredness but her vice is self-centeredness. Just as she moves to the best parts of Haley's personality type when she's at her personal best, she also moves to the most unhealthy parts of Caroline's personality type when she's at her most stressed. Caroline drunk or high on the couch is not too dissimilar then to Olivia at the start of the book, flicking ashes on the cushions and leaving her glass on the table without a coaster.

And finally, Peaches Abrams, born in October of 2000, just a few weeks after Kerry Ann Jefferson was killed, is an Enneagram "9". This young lady was so much fun for me to write, but I also did my very best to keep her weird sensibilities in check just the same. Despite all her funny moments, Peaches is a truly sound, thoughtful, caring young woman with so much to offer the world. I almost killed her off too, but in the end, I just couldn't bring myself to do that. (You're welcome, Peaches.)

As an Enneagram Nine, her virtue is action but her vice is sloth. At her best, she's engaging and fun to be with, an active peacemaker for her family members and friends, happiest when everyone else is happy too. At her most stressed, however, Peaches retreats from the crowd, into her music or her phone, and slumps into the fearfulness of the Six. Peaches was originally named Jessica after Caroline's Aunt Jessica who was killed on 9/11, but when I decided to make Peaches 16 going on 17 in the book, the math just didn't work out for a story set in 2017. I suppose Caroline's Aunt

Jessica must have met some other sad ending early on for Caroline to have chosen that particular name for her second-born child. For now, I'll have to leave it a mystery.

I encourage you to learn more about the Enneagram when you can. There's a wealth of free information available online, and many books and CDs available besides. And if you enjoyed this book, you might even like rereading it now that you know which person is which number on the Enneagram. Understanding a character's personality type unlocks so much more about their motivations and desires. It also helps explain why certain characters might fall in love with other personality types, constantly fight with another personality type, or perhaps even murder them.

While I'm still uncertain about the other characters in the book, in case you're curious, here's my current thinking. Roger is a 1, Doctor Finny is a 6, Mrs. Finny is a 5, RJ is an 8, Roger's mom is a 2, Nancy Hensley is a 6 or a 7, Jenn is a 7, and Chris is a 4. And as for poor Kerry Ann? I think she was probably a 7 like Erika. Or maybe? Maybe I'm just wrong about all of them.

an apology to doctors and nurses everywhere:

Some of the characters in this book are very poor representations of those in the health profession. I hold nurses and doctors in the highest regard, and I sincerely apologize here and now for disparaging them through the sometimes terrible words and actions of Phyllis Abrams and Doctor and Mrs. Finny.

planning a murder:

Although Kerry Ann Jefferson and John Caraway are not—*by far*—the first characters I've ever killed off, this novel does represent my very first foray into the murder mystery genre.

I'd previously written a lot of religious fiction, and *Outside In* was my first coming out story, set in a monastery no less, but for this project, my intentions were clear from the start. I wanted to write a mainstream novel filled with heterosexual characters that steered clear of religion as much as possible. In other words, I wanted to get out of my comfort zone, as well as prove I could do something completely different.

Yeah, I ended up inserting a fair bit of spirituality into this book anyway, but I kept it broad and generic, and except for Peaches, the family members involved are virtually all atheists. Though the surname Abrams is Jewish, the last truly Jewish member of their family was Alan's father.

While I've enjoyed adding suspense, mystery, and oodles of subtle misdirection to my previous books, this is the first time I've written an entire novel around the question, 'who did it'?

This isn't my favorite genre by a long shot, but I certainly watched my fair share of *Columbo, Miss Marple,* and *Murder, She Wrote* with my father growing up. In recent years too, I've enjoyed marathon-watching episodes of *Midsomer Murders* with my father-in-law down in North Carolina. Watching a murder investigation get resolved can be really fun, but as I've learned through writing *tree house down*, it's a hell of a lot trickier than I ever thought it would be.

I decided very early on in the first draft that because suspense and misdirection come much easier for me, I'd rely heavily on both, rather than on some crazy, complicated, clue-filled puzzle my readers had to work their way through from the beginning.

Maybe you guessed who the killer was from the start, or somewhere halfway through. Perhaps you guessed wrong, and I succeeded in surprising you. Or maybe, just maybe, you're still sure *someone else* did it, all my words be damned. Good! If the story worked you into a frenzy of any kind, I succeeded in doing my job.

I spent almost three years on this book because I believed it had the power to move my audience the way it was constantly moving me as I wrote it. I cried along with Peaches and Lenny when Caroline told them Sam was her real father, and with every tear I shed, I knew many of my readers would be crying too. I growled and I laughed and I cringed and I hissed throughout the book, and with each new emotion, I hoped and prayed you would experience all the same feelings as well.

I've gotta say though, planning a murder? It's unnerving! In a way, I was only helped by not needing to write the actual scene of the crime until the very end of the book. That way, as I and later the reader moved closer and closer to the answer, the question becomes that much more enticing, and the answer that much more satisfying, regardless of the color and substance of the moment.

Phyllis killed Kerry Ann in what investigators would call a crime of passion. She barely planned out how she'd do it, which in my mind tells me she was already experienced in the technique necessary. This begs the question: has she killed before? Has this nurse disgraced her profession and behaved similarly in the past? Or is she simply seizing the moment, covering her tracks well and trusting in the young girl's inability to fight back once the chloroform had further debilitated her?

These are all questions I cannot answer, or rather questions I choose not to answer. I leave those to you, just as I leave you to decide for yourself how evil or not others in the story really are. How much do you hate or sympathize with the motivations and actions of Lenny, Alan, Caroline, or Sam? How much do you want a tree house to come crashing down on any of them too? More questions, and none with any easy answers to offer.

I'll simply leave you with these few final thoughts, colored with what you now know about the Enneagram. Be careful whom you hate, for the object of your hatred may look an awful lot like your most awful self. Be careful whom you loudly champion as the best of the best, because what you see as best, may make others stress. And most of all, beware of anyone who drinks red wine on ice, because that's just psychotic.

Books by
Sean Patrick Brennan:

Tree House Down – 2019

The Angel's Guide to Taking Human Form – 2018

Outside In – 2016

Finishing Forty – 2015

The Knowing – 2015

The Papal Visitor – 2014

The Uniter – 2013

Available in paperback and Kindle through Amazon, in paperback through Barnes & Noble online, and sold through many other online bookstores worldwide. Please consider using your Amazon and Barnes & Noble gift cards to support self-published authors and artists of every kind.

* * *

PLEASE LIKE
my author page over on Facebook at:
www.facebook.com/planetinbetween

The page is a wealth of information about past, present, and future books, so I'd love you to join the wonderful online community we have there! I promise I don't post too often!

YOUR REVIEWS
on Amazon and Goodreads help me out SO MUCH, as do all your public posts and shares about my books. Without a marketing team, I NEED all the reviews I can get! Thank you for whatever kind words you can share online—maybe right now?—especially on Amazon, that will help introduce new readers to my books!

Made in the USA
San Bernardino, CA
05 September 2019